The Other Alcott

Elise Hooper

WM
WILLIAM MORROW
An Imprint of HarperCollins*Publishers*

PUBLISHERS
— Since 1817 —

P.S.™ is a trademark of HarperCollins Publishers.

HarperCollins books may be purchased for educational, business, or sales promotional use. For information, please e-mail the Special Markets Department at SPsales@harpercollins.com.

FIRST EDITION

Designed by Diahann Sturge

Library of Congress Cataloging-in-Publication Data has been applied for.

ISBN 978-0-06-264533-3

17 18 19 20 21   RS/LSC   10 9 8 7 6 5 4 3 2

Fantastic praise for *The Other Alcott*

"An atmospheric and engaging read, *The Other Alcott* widens the Alcott family spotlight to position the charismatic, artistic May as a rightful equal to famed Louisa. Hooper skillfully draws the reader into the complicated, competitive dynamic between two sisters determined to master their work and love each other."

—Joy Callaway, author of *The Fifth Avenue Artists Society* and *Secret Sisters*

"In *The Other Alcott*, Elise Hooper has crafted a sweeping and deeply personal tale of a young woman's struggle to emerge out of her famous sister's shadow and define herself as an artist and an independent adventurer. You will never look at *Little Women* or the Alcott family the same way again."

—Laurie Lico Albanese, author of *Stolen Beauty*

"With its globe-trotting, sibling rivalry, old-fashioned courtship, art-world intrigue, and one very difficult choice, Elise Hooper's thoroughly modern debut gives a fresh take on one of literature's most beloved families. To read this book is to understand why the women behind *Little Women* continue to cast a long shadow on our imaginations and dreams. Hooper is a writer to watch!"

—Elisabeth Egan, author of *A Window Opens*

"Elise Hooper's debut novel, *The Other Alcott*, is a delightful, moving book about the strength of women, the impetus of creativity, and the indelible bond between sisters. If you loved *Little Women* (or even if you didn't), this engaging take on the real-life relationship between the Alcott sisters will fascinate and inspire. More than ever, we need books like this—in celebration of a woman overlooked by history, one whose story helps shed light on our own contemporary search for love, identity, and meaning."

—Tara Conklin, *New York Times* bestselling author of *The House Girl*

For Dave

May 26, 1878
Meudon, France

Louisa,

Here I sit in my studio, writing another letter to you that I will not mail. Instead it shall live in this journal. I know, I'm sure the vision of me scribbling away in a journal gives you a good chuckle, but it's a gift from Ernest. He looked so pleased when I opened it, I couldn't bring myself to confess how I despise such self-confessionals. The whole practice takes me back to those dreadful family meetings—all of us huddled around the dining room table with journals gripped in our hands, prepared to reflect on the day's triumphs and trials and discuss paths to self-improvement—those dreary evenings left a mark on me.

Yet now you have figured it all out. Yes, I've seen you digging back into your dog-eared diaries and rewriting old accounts of our lives into rosier, more harmonious versions of the truth. Did you think your secret editing sessions escaped my notice? I daresay your revisions are quite ingenious, but it makes me wonder, how will you go back and rewrite the story of us?

Do you regret your treatment of me? Your disapproval

of my actions pains me, but I refuse to apologize. Though our estrangement weighs upon me, I cannot forgive your demands. Still, I long to turn back the clock and mend the rift between us, though now that I think on it, if I could go back in time, when would I go back to? When was our relationship ever simple?

I almost missed your gift, tucked as it was behind Anna's recent letter. Is it intended as a taunt? A peace offering? An apology? I've hidden it until your intentions become clear.

Yours,
May

Part 1

October 1868–June 1869

Concord, Massachusetts

Chapter 1

May spent the morning in high feather preparing for the party, dusting and scrubbing the parlor as though elbow grease alone could solve everything. The persistent ticking of the small clock on the china shelf reminded her there was no time for dawdling, so she darted to the kitchen to start a batch of molasses candy and stood over the black cast-iron stove, stirring the boiling syrup around and around in foamy circles. Lost in the luxurious smell of melted butter, she was startled when Louisa burst into the kitchen, slamming the door open into the already-crumbling plaster wall.

"They're here. The reviews are here." Her older sister clutched a thin, brown-papered package out in front of her. Mother, their sister Anna, and Anna's two young sons trailed behind Louisa like the tail on a kite.

May's heart quickened, and she clapped her hands in anticipation. "Let's all move into the parlor to hear the exciting news," she said, thinking of her time spent sprucing up the front rooms. "Boys, please run and fetch your grandfather from the barn."

But no one budged as Louisa ripped into the envelope.

"Heavens, you're a savage," Anna murmured.

Louisa's hand trembled as she pulled out a light green piece of paper embossed with the bank's seal and *two hundred dollars* written in a flowing script, an amount enough to render the group speechless. Her earlier novel, *Moods*, had fetched a first check of a mere twenty-five dollars. The beginnings of a smile perked at the corners of Louisa's mouth as she laid the payment down on the kitchen table. Paper crackled as she dug back into the package and withdrew a handful of newspaper clippings. May held her breath, scarcely containing her pride. She believed the illustrations she'd produced for her sister's book to be her finest pictures yet.

Louisa read aloud from the article: "According to *The Nation*, 'Little Women* will undoubtedly be this season's novel that every American girl will want to read.'" The nephews broke into cheers while Mother and Anna clapped. May joined in with the applause, but she watched her sister scan the rest of the newspaper column. Louisa frowned for a moment before tucking the clipping under the bank check. She sifted through more pages, quoting passages full of praise, as she slid a few more of the clippings out of sight. Had anyone else noticed Louisa's sleight of hand?

"Auntie May, the candy . . . it's burning!" Johnny said.

May whirled around to see black smoke puffing up off the molasses. She grabbed a dish towel to cover her hand, yanked the pan off the stove top, and tumbled through the kitchen door into the backyard. Once outside, she dropped the smoldering mess on the gravel path and stared at the charred remains. A moment later, Louisa appeared in the doorway. "Are you burned?"

"No . . . I just forgot about the stove." May smoothed down her disheveled blond hair with her hands. Nothing was going as planned. "What about the celebration? The parlor's ready."

Louisa took a step outside and handed May the newspaper columns from the folds of her skirt.

"You need to see these, but don't take them too hard. After all, I've gotten so many rejections over the years, you'd think I'd have thrown myself off the roof long ago."

May looked down at the papers and silently read a review from *The Nation*: "May Alcott's poorly executed illustrations in *Little Women* betray her lack of anatomical knowledge and indifference to the subtle beauty of the female figure." A shrill buzzing rang in her ears as she registered the meaning of the words.

She flipped to the next column from *The Youth's Companion* and read: "May Alcott's figures lack realistic proportions and look stiff." Another clipping from *Publishers' Circular* claimed: "May Alcott's illustrations detract from the agreeable little story of *Little Women*." Shame burned her face all the way to her hairline, and black speckles edged her vision as if she viewed the hazy words reflected on an old, tarnished mirror.

She looked up to find Louisa studying her.

May swallowed past the thickness of her throat. "Did you think my drawings were as bad as they say?"

"No, of course not. Now don't get yourself into a pucker." She smoothed the gray silk of her dress. "I know it must be a bit of a shock since everything always seems to go your way, but you'll recover. Somehow I always do."

"But you receive a letter in the mail from an editor saying no. Your work isn't mocked in print for all the world to see."

"Don't get ahead of yourself. The whole world isn't reading these reviews. And don't expect me to apologize for my success. I've received my fair share of negative reviews before." Scowling, Louisa glanced away and reached out to flick some chipping bits of dark brown paint off the side of the house. "Isn't your new beau, Mr. Bishop, coming out from Boston for a visit today?"

What did he have to do with any of this, May thought, resisting the urge to snap at her sister. "No, tomorrow."

"Well, then you'll probably have forgotten all about this by tomorrow evening. You're good about always finding enjoyments, while all I do is sit around and write. You're lucky, you're always full of good spirit, you don't take yourself so seriously."

Did a satisfied smile flash across Louisa's face? Of course May took her art seriously, but she refused to complain about the trials of hard work. Was it so wrong to have a little amusement here and there? Louisa often complained about her younger sister's unending stream of luck, but did she not see how hard May had been working for the last twenty-eight years of her life to make good fortune happen? She glared at her older sister, but then Louisa's limp dark hair, parted plainly in the middle, and her complexion, pale as a hard-boiled egg, came into focus; writing *Little Women* within the space of a mere two months had exacted an enormous toll upon her. Louisa, once bright-eyed and vivacious, appeared to have faded and shrunk, defeated into middle age.

May straightened up and placed the clippings back into Louisa's fingers. "I'm fine."

"Let's hold off on the party anyway." Louisa folded the clippings into a neat stack in her hands. "The downstairs needs to air out from all the smoke. I'll take the nephews into town for a treat."

"Good idea. The little imps are in a lather over the prospect of candy." May marveled that her voice could sound so steady, despite the sinking sensation in her belly.

Louisa took a final look at her sister and turned back into the kitchen. Alone, May pulled off her apron and bunched it up into a wad before dropping it on the ground. The pan still lay in her path, so she gave it a small kick as she stalked away from the mess.

UPSTAIRS, IN THE privacy of her own bedroom, May rifled through her loose papers and sketchbooks from over the years. With her artwork clenched in her arms, she tiptoed back downstairs, listening for any sounds of her family, but the house was silent. They had all gone into town. Good. She dropped the pile on the kitchen floor next to the stove, squatted down beside it, and yanked open the small doorway to stoke the fire. Once the flames began to grow higher within the stove, she started ripping up her notebooks one by one. Satisfaction verging on hysteria seized her as she tore her sketches into tiny pieces and stuffed them into the stove's fire. Tears that had been threatening to fall after reading those scathing reviews evaporated with the growing heat of the fire. With trembling hands, she reached for a new sketch to shred but froze when she saw an old, yellowed self-portrait in her hands.

The young girl in the picture wore a crown of flowers, long golden plaits, and a broad smile, and held a painter's palette in one hand and her old calico cat, Flora, in the other. The poor round creature looked more like a pig than anything remotely feline (horses were still the only animal she could consistently draw well). The girl's facial features were crooked and the lines unsteady, but May remembered the pride she had taken in the sketch.

Almost twenty years later, the self-portrait certainly resembled no masterpiece, but it marked a beginning. While she was no Rembrandt, her skills had surely improved. With more prodding and discipline, progress could be possible. *Dear Lord, yes, of course progress is possible.* She traced a finger along the face on the paper, leaving sooty smudges on it, and contemplated her sketches in *Little Women*.

Louisa had confessed to basing her main characters—the March sisters—upon her own family, but added that she ironed out some of the irregularities of their lives: Anna's gracious temperament lent itself to becoming the kind and nurturing Meg; Louisa smoothed herself into the feisty rebel Jo; Lizzie's saintliness increased; and May turned into little precocious and selfish Amy. May's shoulders clenched with anger at the thought of Louisa's characterization of her as frivolous Amy March. Yes, little Amy was a mere character in a book, but everyone knew she was meant to be May. Amy's pretentious and incorrect usage of sophisticated words and the character's insufferable vanity and preoccupation with material goods— Louisa's portrayal of May galled her. An injustice, that's what it was, but she couldn't think about that now. She opened her eyes again to study her self-portrait and sighed.

When she sketched, it felt as though she had a fever, a good fever, a fever that warmed her insides and made the rest of the world melt away. Even if the results didn't look like what she pictured in her mind's eye, she persisted, making more and more, telling herself that improvement would come with time and practice. If she stopped creating, what was left? A slow slide into spinsterhood? She'd be stuck in Concord forever. With her knuckles pressed to her lips, she gazed into the opening of the stove to see pieces of drawing paper curling into black charred ribbons. No, she couldn't destroy any more work. She smoothed the edges of the self-portrait on her lap and placed it back on the pile next to her.

She needed her art—that was a certainty. But that certainty, that clench deep in her gut, it was all she had to push against everything else determined to keep her in place. She stood and picked up the remaining artwork. It would have to be enough.

Chapter 2

The following afternoon, May tossed a soapy dishcloth onto the kitchen table and pulled off her apron. Fresh air. That's what she needed. Outside the kitchen door, a red McIntosh gleamed in the dried-out grass, and she bent over to pick it up for a bite, but a constellation of wormholes cratered the fruit's surface. She groaned and hurled it at a distant tree. To her surprise, the fruit hit its target and exploded with a satisfying *crack*, sending juicy shards splattering onto the moss and crabgrass below. The pounding of hooves rumbled behind her, and May froze with a breath caught in her throat. Oh, thunder, she thought, cringing to think her temper tantrum had been witnessed.

"You never warned me about your strong arm," a familiar voice called out with a good-natured laugh. May turned. If there was one thing that could take her mind off the sharp-toothed critics, it was Joshua Bishop.

Before she could take a moment to smooth down her hair, Joshua was already leading her toward the barn, past the washing from earlier in the day hanging on the clothesline off the side of the house—two petticoats and a pair of trousers flapped in the breeze with a taunting snap. And then they were inside the barn saddling May's horse, Rosa, with the smell of tangy freshly sawed cedar shingles and the damp press of manure closing in on them.

The horse's glossy dark coat made the glint of an unfastened brass buckle on the balance strap sparkle in the low light, so she leaned in to secure it. At the same time, Joshua reached for it, and the palm of his hand suddenly rested upon the back of hers. The two paused, uncertain how to proceed, but not altogether uncomfortable with their unexpected closeness. She turned to find his light blue eyes, dazzling even in the dim light, fixed upon her.

"Let's go outside. I'll help you up."

Unable to trust her voice, she nodded and followed. While he led her horse outside the barn, May gave a surreptitious look down at her chest, convinced the pounding of her heart was visible, before biting back a giggle at her own foolishness.

Moments later, they trotted west on Lexington Road atop their saddle horses, blinking against the bright light. Recent warm days and cold nights produced vibrant foliage that surpassed anything May had seen in years. She looked out of the corner of her eye at him and felt a giddiness travel from her hand to her shoulders and then round through her, making her almost dizzy. Everything seemed to glow with unexpected brightness and intensity. Even this late in the season, leggy chokeberry bushes, luminous in a hue straight from a tube of vermilion paint, lined the dirt road. As they reached the town center, she slowed Rosa's pace and called greetings out to a couple of neighbors.

"You know everyone," Joshua said, dipping his hat to an older woman waiting to cross the road. The woman, Mrs. Pierce from over on Walden Street, allowed her eyes to travel over Joshua before giving May a knowing smile. Since the war's appalling casualties, young men were scarce in New England.

"This is Concord, not Boston. Everyone knows everyone."

Joshua laughed, conceding May's point.

It would be pleasant to live in a city, a place packed with people, a place where anonymity was possible, a place where neighbors didn't know everything about each other. But ever since Louisa published her book, more and more people beyond Concord suddenly seemed to know all about the Alcotts. A reporter from the *Boston Herald* had appeared at the family's back kitchen door the previous week hungry for scraps about the renowned authoress of Concord. Mother had shooed him off, shaking her head at his impudence, but he was just one of many. Journalists had begun arriving on the Alcotts' doorstep from as far away as Saint Louis looking for an interview with the newly famous writer of *Little Women*, pushy terriers who pretended not to understand the word *no*. Before leaving the house, May had taken to sticking her nose outside the door and sniffing the air for cigar smoke, a telltale sign a newspaperman was lying in wait down by the road.

"Hullo, Miss Alcott," a voice trilled from the steps of the white clapboard Middlesex Hotel. The innkeeper's wife gave a fervent wave. "I saw the article about your sister's book in *The Boston Evening Post*. It's so exciting to have a new celebrity in town." The older woman's chins multiplied as her head bobbed with enthusiasm.

Conversations stopped as all of the men and women on the inn's front porch turned toward the road at her. May's throat went dry. Had people read the reviews? She couldn't tell if all the faces looked at her with curiosity or pity. She gave the woman a wobbly smile, lifted her hand weakly in a halfhearted greeting, and tightened her knees into Rosa to increase their pace, eager to get beyond the crowd of neighbors. She wondered if the others at the Art Club now believed her to be an imposter. She dreaded to think of their next meeting and her halting walk up the splintery stairs of the Masonic Hall and turning the corner to see everyone's faces looking at her with disappointment. When she thought back to offering to serve as the group's leader and instructor, she winced in embarrassment at her folly. *Who did she think she was?* Perhaps she would send a note announcing she was sick for next week's meeting.

"My aunt was saying the reviews of your sister's book are favorable. She likened Louisa's success to that of Harriet Beecher Stowe's. Isn't that something?" Joshua called out as the Middlesex Hotel fell behind them.

She bit the inside of her mouth, hoping the pain would distract her from the disappointment curdling in her stomach. "Let's race."

Joshua raised his eyebrows, casting an uncertain look at her pale blue day dress, but she kept talking. "I shall race you up to the North Bridge and loop around the pasture. We can finish at the riverbank behind the old house up ahead." Without awaiting a response, she dug her heels into Rosa's sides. The horse needed little prodding to break into a gallop down the road and jump over the mossy stone wall to land them on a path along the Concord River. May's bonnet slid down her head so she yanked it off, holding it alongside the reins. With the thundering of Rosa's hooves over the North Bridge, she lost herself to the blur of big bluestem grass waving in the breeze and galloped a wide circle around the farm fields before heading back. There was nothing quite like riding fast to help shake off the humiliation that made her itch as if her clothes were full of nettles. Soon, her burning muscles and lungs were all that she could focus upon.

Once at the river, May slid off Rosa and gasped for breath as Joshua pulled up on his horse behind her. He dismounted, ambled to a shady patch of grass under a dogwood tree, and reclined on the riverbank to watch May as she walked to the river's edge and knelt. She rolled up her sleeves and dipped her hands into the river, relishing the cold current beneath the sun-warmed surface. Silver minnows streaked, darting from shadow to shadow in the crystalline depths of the water. It was easy for her to pretend she was in another world. "I wish I could just dive in," she said, looking at the bubbles of air clinging to her submerged fingers like tiny pearls.

"You wouldn't."

"What makes you so sure?" May laughed. "Someday I'd like to swim in the Atlantic."

"There are dangerous riptides."

"Still, I should like to try it someday."

"My, aren't you bricky."

Every muscle in May's body loosened in the glow of his admiration for her courage.

"Come up here." He brushed off his trousers as he stood and helped her up the riverbank and right into his arms. He brushed at her jawline gently, and her heart caught in her throat at his touch. Tiny blond hairs along his face caught the sunshine. The solidity of his shoulders tempted her to run her palm along them.

Beyond the trees, a train horn blasted, shattering the moment. Startled crows, like oily black smudges on a background of ocher-, umber-, and sienna-painted grass, flew in a rush toward the sky.

"I should get you home and ride back to my aunt's house in Lexington."

She inhaled sharply, glancing down at the grit covering her dress. Without looking at his shoulders again, she dropped her gaze and gave her skirts a good shake with both hands before mounting her horse. "When will you return to Boston?"

"The day after tomorrow."

CONCORD CENTER WAS quieter late in the afternoon, and sun the color of ripe peaches peered down through the trees. May let her body sway to the rhythm of the horse, only half listening to Joshua describe a client engaged in quarreling with a neighbor. Within minutes, the Alcotts' home appeared, and he brought his horse to a stop and looked at May intently.

"So, your sister's book's success is a good thing, is it not?"

The drone of meadow bugs filled the dirt road around them. How could she easily explain her mess of feelings about her sister's book?

"Louisa's been writing for as long as I can remember, so I'm delighted *Little Women* is being so well-received, but the critics are merciless about my illustrations in the book. They're calling them 'amateurish' and worse."

"That seems unfair. I thought they looked good."

A little sympathetic indignation on her behalf bolstered her spirits, and she smiled.

"But they like the book—that's what's important, right? And after all, you *are* an amateur."

Her smile vanished. "True, but I want to become a professional artist."

"An artist—?"

"A painter."

"And get paid for your work?"

"Yes, just like my sister gets paid for her writing."

He opened his mouth to say something, hesitated, and then gave a small shrug.

"Your sister Louisa gave up a lot to be a writer. Would you do the same?"

His question caught May off-kilter, and she floundered, wondering at his intentions toward her. Louisa's writing raised eyebrows, though her success with *Little Women* helped to patch her condition into something acceptable. While remaining unmarried like Louisa did not interest May in the slightest, she couldn't help admiring her sister's independence and success. Couldn't she marry *and* pursue her art? It galled her to have to choose. She sighed. "I shouldn't have to give anything up."

"There's a fellow down on Washington Street who runs a business painting portraits. Would an endeavor like that suit you?"

May didn't understand the workings of business. Furthermore, the *Little Women* reviews made it obvious she knew nothing about drawing people correctly—how in the world could she start painting portraits? The whole conundrum made her head hurt.

"I'm still . . . getting ideas and working out all of the details."

"I'm sure you are. You never seem short on ideas."

She wanted to lean closer to him, to feel the traces of sunshine still lingering on his shirt, but Rosa gave an impatient snort and shuffled her hooves, so instead she busied her hands with patting Rosa's neck. "I hope to see you again soon."

Again, Joshua cocked his head thoughtfully and appeared on the verge of saying something, but stopped himself and simply smiled before riding away. She watched his retreating figure from the side of the road, puzzling over their conversation before turning to face the house. She twisted the cracked leather harness strap around her hand tighter and tighter as she wondered if he would have paid any attention to the May Alcott of a year ago, before *Little Women* was published. Somehow this novel bestowed a sheen of respectability upon her family she now realized they had always lacked. Louisa's success seemed to highlight that Alcott women were known for being ambitious and not following the conventional path into wifehood and motherhood. No wonder May perplexed Joshua; she perplexed herself.

Above, Louisa's silhouette was visible in her bedroom window where she sat at her desk writing, writing, always writing. Blood pulsed and throbbed in May's fingers until she loosened the strap and walked the horse to the barn. Was there room in the family for more than one accomplished woman?

Chapter 3

A week later, a faint outline of a plan started to take shape in her mind. The steady whisper of drizzle outside brought the sisters together in the parlor to work on mending, and May sensed her opportunity.

"Louisa, I must ask you something." She took a deep breath and lowered her sewing to her lap, but a frantic knocking at the front door followed by giggles and a rustling of silk interrupted her.

Louisa rolled her eyes, dropped the letter she was reading, and fled through the dining room for the kitchen door. Moments later, she rushed past with a white cap listing to the side of her head and a white apron billowing behind her. Louisa opened the door to three young women, who leaned in and looked around expectantly, rubbing raindrops off their faces.

"Is Miss Alcott here?" one of the girls asked, clutching a copy of *Little Women* to her chest.

With a convincing Irish brogue, Louisa pretended to be an

Irish maid and explained the writer was out of town visiting friends. The front door provided stagelike framing, and Louisa readily delighted in her playacting in front of these young fans. She closed the door and sauntered into the parlor, giving her sisters a sly grin.

"You're an absolute devil," Anna said. "You should feel awful for doing that. They were so excited to meet you."

"Mercy me, I don't feel one drop of guilt." Louisa pulled off the apron with a dramatic flourish as she took a bow. "My little performance actually made me feel nostalgic for our old shows. Remember? You used to dream of being Jenny Lind."

"Oh, goodness, that was all so long ago." Anna gestured at a dingy mail sack overflowing with letters next to May. "But think back even a couple of months—did you ever imagine you would be reigning over Concord as its most celebrated author?"

"Anna, you're too good to me. A gaggle of girls fawning over my juvenile novel does not compete with the importance of Mr. Emerson, Mr. Thoreau, and Mr. Hawthorne."

Anna laughed and leaned over, sifting gently through the contents of the bag. Wobbly handwriting skittered along the envelopes like the frenetic tracks of squirrels upon snow. Since Louisa barely tolerated the fan mail that arrived in huge sacks, Anna took it upon herself to answer the letters, even delighting in signing them as *Meg March*. She pulled one out to read. "This sweet girl from Albany wants to know what she can do to become a famous writer like you."

"Well, that's an improvement over the usual drivel. I'm sick of questions about husbands for the March sisters."

"You're a dreadful curmudgeon," May said.

"I rather like being a curmudgeon. Honestly, do girls give two pins for anything beyond marriage proposals these days?" Louisa stuck her nose up in the air as she stood and gathered up her bonnet and shawl from a peg by the door. "Now, I'm off to see Lidian Emerson."

Before the front door shut, May called out to her sister's back, "It seems rather mean-spirited to complain about getting letters from admirers."

Only the decisive click of the door's latch answered.

She squinted down at her sewing, amazed that even though *Little Women* proved Louisa's writing to be successful, her sister still begrudged almost everything about it.

"Weren't you about to say something to Louisa?" Anna said. "Before those girls came to the door?"

"No, no, I must catch her in a good mood."

"Ha, that's no easy task. Lately, you two are always after each other with your claws out. You're both too competitive for your own good."

"Competitive? How can I possibly compete with her, a renowned authoress? Meanwhile, look at me." May flapped her hands around herself impatiently. "I'm still here, producing . . . I don't even know what I'm producing anymore . . . I daresay the critics would pronounce it rubbish."

"You exaggerate. I *am* looking at you, and believe me, most people would agree you have much in the way of fair assets. Come now, you and Louisa need to be more generous with each other and yourselves."

"It's easy to be generous when you're making money."

"Generosity has nothing to do with money. You know that." She reached forward and smoothed an errant curl back from May's forehead and said quietly, "You two are so similar, both so hungry for something more, but at the same time, you couldn't be more different." The dimple on Anna's right cheek deepened as she gave a warm smile to May before returning to the letter in her hands. "See? This is why I must come from Maplewood so often. You both certainly know how to make my visits lively."

May pictured the Pratts' little weathered bungalow, fifteen miles away, north of Boston, and how it strained to contain the energy of her two nephews. "Livelier than the boys?"

"They have nothing on the two of you," Anna said, tilting her head and smiling to herself as she read and ran a hand absentmindedly along the swirl of her thick dark hair's upturned twist.

LATER IN THE evening, the sisters cleaned the kitchen. May put a stack of plates in the cupboard and admired how the late afternoon sunshine fought its way through the rain-smeared windowpanes, stippling the wooden floorboards. Soon the lamps would need to be turned on. Louisa cleared her throat as she dried a glass. "Mr. Niles is after me to answer the clamoring masses and all of their questions about whom each sister marries. He thinks I ought to write a second volume—a continuation of *Little Women*."

Anna put a water pitcher down on the table, her dark eyes flashing as she spoke quickly. "Oh, you must, you definitely must write more about the Marches. When you ended it, there were so many questions needing answers. Will Meg still marry Mr. Brooke, despite Aunt March's threat of disinheritance?"

Louisa grimaced. "You're just as bad as these girls who write to me."

"Well, a second installment is a capital idea." Anna glanced at May. "What do you think?"

May turned from sorting dishes to look at her sisters. No mention had been made of her illustrations, and her shoulders tensed with the realization that Louisa did not plan to ask her for more. Outside the window beyond Louisa, shadows swallowed the yard. Anna's boys were wrestling in the grass; a blur of limbs whirled amidst the fallen, wet leaves. "I think your little blisters are undoing all of Father's raking." As she spoke, Freddy formed a dirty, sodden ball of leaves from the ground and threw it at his younger brother. Anna headed for the door to intervene in the mudslinging beginning outside.

When cleaning up from supper was complete, May left the kitchen for the parlor and sat down on the lumpy horsehair divan across from Louisa to resume her sewing. Mother joined May and ran her fingers through the long golden curls cascading down her youngest daughter's back. "I hear Joshua Bishop came courting the other afternoon. Must have been nice to go gallivanting around on his arm. I'll bet lots of tongues are wagging about you now."

If people were talking about her, May certainly hoped it was about Joshua Bishop instead of the mortifying reviews of her *Little Women* illustrations.

Mother pointed to the two rectangular pieces of velvet on May's lap. "What's this?"

"I'm making a gift for Louisa. A mood pillow."

Louisa looked up from her newspaper. "What on earth is a mood pillow?"

"It's my own creation. You can keep it down here on the divan and place it horizontally when you're in a good mood and welcoming guests. If you're feeling prickly, set it vertical as a warning to keep people away. Clearly you need it, judging by how you sent those poor girls packing earlier today."

Louisa brayed with laughter. "Well, aren't you clever? And I suppose such a gift means you want something from me?"

May stroked the cornflower-blue velvet fabric, a remnant from her favorite skirt she had ruined by spilling ink on it.

Louisa narrowed her eyes. "Out with it—what do you want?"

May turned away from her sister and, using the nickname the girls had bestowed upon Mother years ago, enlisted her help by saying, "Marmee, I've decided I must find some artistic instruction. Do you think Mr. Emerson may know of anyone in Boston open to teaching a woman?"

Marmee raised her eyebrows. "In Boston?"

"Yes, I was thinking I could live with Louisa in the city while I study and come home to help you around the house on weekends."

"What a fine idea. You can keep an eye on Louisa's health. Especially if she undertakes this second volume of *Little Women* for Mr. Niles." Marmee frowned and looked at Louisa.

"Falling into that last writing vortex of yours nearly undid us all. You cannot write all of the time. You must pace yourself."

Louisa let out a groan. "Now I see where this is all going. And I suppose I shall pay for these lessons. How much will all of this cost? Why can't you simply practice on your own?"

Indignation flared through May, and she dropped her sewing in her lap as she leaned forward to respond, but Marmee sent her a warning look and turned toward Louisa. "I know you take pride in believing you're a self-taught writer, but you've been fortunate enough to be surrounded by writers your entire life, and now you're reaping the rewards. Yes, you've practiced, but you've also seen Mr. Emerson, Mr. Thoreau, and Miss Fuller at work and heard them speak of their craft"—a small smile danced at the corners of her mouth—"often endlessly. Surely you can help your sister."

"Yes, but—"

"But nothing. Let's find an artist for May. After all, now you girls have the mood pillow." Marmee stood and walked toward the front hallway, looking back at them over her shoulder mischievously. "I'm sure it's all you need to make your new living arrangements harmonious."

THE NEXT MORNING, May clipped wet laundry to the drying line and studied the anemic gray light yawning down into the backyard. Was it getting too late in the season to dry laundry outside? She flexed her damp fingers in an attempt to bring some warmth back into them and noticed a large grease stain on a shirt Louisa had bought Father from Cambridge Dry Goods. A brand-new shirt. She would hide it from Louisa, knowing it would set off a tempest if her sister caught sight of how her benevolence was wasted.

The kitchen door creaked open to reveal the tall, thin figure of John Pratt, Anna's husband, stepping out. "May, here you are—the postmaster gave this to me as I rode through town." He stooped under the laundry line and handed her a delicate square of paper.

She opened it to find an invitation to a Christmas ball at the Bishop family's house in Boston. Her fingers tightened on the paper; an excited tingle ran up from her fingertips.

John stomped his boots on the ground to shake some of the caked mud off and peered at the paper. "Now I'm no socialite, but I'll bet this is one of the most coveted invitations of the winter social season."

May began to laugh, but her heart stopped as she saw Louisa's name listed below her own. Could she go anywhere without people being interested in Louisa these days?

John's narrow, angular face crinkled into a kind smile. "And now you're meeting the fella's family? That's a big step."

"Yes, it is." May bit her lip and felt her face flush. Excitement and uneasiness spun around inside her head. What exactly, she wondered, was she stepping into?

Chapter 4

May's valise quivered in the overhead rack as the train jostled along to Boston. The early December snow had prompted people to stay off the roads, so the train was crowded with coughing passengers and the smell of wet wool. May sat next to Louisa and eyed her battered old luggage, running an inventory of what she would need over the next few days in her mind. She had expected Louisa to complain about attending the Bishops' Christmas ball, but her sister's enthusiasm over the party had been genuine. No doubt she could use a lark after being immersed day and night in writing the sequel to *Little Women* since October.

May rubbed her chilled hands together. "Do you think this cold snap will continue?"

"How the deuce should I know?"

"I should've brought another set of woolens. I hate being cold."

"We're heading to the city. You can replace anything there."

"I have a perfectly good set at home. The last thing I want to do is spend money on a boring ol' pair of woolens."

"For Pete's sake, if it'll get you to stop fussing, I'll give you the money for some."

Louisa yanked a portfolio filled with correspondence from her satchel and sifted through it, pausing to glower at a letter tucked in with the other papers.

May stretched her neck to catch a glimpse of the letter, and her suspicions were confirmed. For as long as she could remember, due to limited resources, Father wrote his daughters letters for their birthday gifts. These letters were usually filled with praise for their virtues but also words of advice for future growth. Compared to what her sisters received, Louisa's birthday letters always weighed conspicuously heavier on advice than praise. Louisa and Father shared a birthday on November 29, and the family had celebrated them both a few days earlier.

"I wish you would stop taking Father's birthday letters so hard."

"I don't." Louisa ducked her nose deeper into the portfolio.

"Every year you're in a sulk on the day after your birthday."

Louisa drooped toward the steamed-over window and rubbed a small circle to look out at the bleak, snowy landscape sliding by. "He's never satisfied with me. After all I've done this year, I expected him to be pleased."

"He's never satisfied with anything. He's always dreaming of perfection that none of us can possibly achieve. You know this."

"Easy for you to say."

Louisa was right; it was easy for her to say. As the youngest of the family, May somehow managed to dodge her father's attention, and this suited her just fine. According to family legend, Anna's babyhood had fascinated Father, and he'd spent hours cataloging every giggle and wiggle, filling notebook after notebook with his observations. A year and a half later, Louisa's squalling arrival had not only interrupted his study of Anna's placid nature, but it threw a number of his theories out of alignment. His second daughter emerged into the world a headstrong and impulsive personality from the beginning. Father was baffled as to how two children could be so markedly different, despite sharing the exact same origins. Anna could sit and play with a pot and a spoon for an entire morning, whereas Louisa would grab the pot and promptly hit her sister over the head with it. Anna and Father would hunt hand in hand for alphabet letters in the signage scattered throughout Abbot's General Store, yet Louisa disappeared whenever he turned his back on her. Father never gave up attempting to curb Louisa's temper and independent streak, and it put the two of them on a lifetime trajectory of frustration with one another.

On the evening of the ball, there was no missing the location of the party, for the Bishops' block was backed up with a line of hackneys, hansom cabs, and coupe carriages. Women festooned in the latest winter fashions, and men in formal black suits and tall beaver hats lined up outside the front doorway which was bedecked in garlands of evergreen. May bit her lip and nudged her shaking hands deep into her ermine muff. The sound of a violin beginning a Viennese waltz floated past them. A maid took their outerwear and the women were ushered along the black-and-white tiled foyer into the great hall pulsing with activity. An orchestra played next to the staircase which rose along one wall, leading upstairs to a gallery mobbed with partygoers looking down on the dancing below.

Surrounded by delicate, swanlike women gliding around the room in glittering jet beads and seed pearls, May felt too tall, her shoulders too broad, her nose too wide, her skin too freckled. Gowns, unwrinkled and crisp from the ateliers of the city's most sought-after dressmakers, brushed past. She edged a look down at her robin's egg–blue gown, checking all traces of white tailor's chalk were gone. She had spent hours resewing the flounces of her older dress's voluminous skirt into a basque to achieve the latest bustled silhouette.

Joshua, debonair in a black evening dress jacket, appeared at May's elbow. Every inch of him looked perfectly pressed and polished. Aware that people were watching them, she stood tall and threw back her shoulders. After all, he was grinning at her, not at the fawning, powdered faces encircling them.

Like the figurehead at the prow of a great ship, Mrs. Bishop plowed through the center of the room toward Joshua, steering Mr. Bishop alongside her. There was no mistaking Joshua's father, for the resemblance was obvious, except for a faint looseness of the jowls on the older man, a thickening around the waist, and a ruddiness to his complexion—telltale signs of years of fine dining and smoking cigars late into the night.

"Miss Alcott"—Mrs. Bishop directed her comments toward

Louisa—"our daughter Nellie cannot stop talking about your book. She has read parts to me aloud. I must say it's a joy to hear a novel that demonstrates such a profound understanding of New England's values. It's a shining example to our young women of the importance of duty and family."

Guests strained their necks to observe Louisa.

Mrs. Bishop shifted her gaze and coolly appraised May up and down. "And you must be the lovely reason why Joshua travels all the way out to Concord." Her lofty tone implied the Alcotts might as well live in the Yukon. The older woman nodded slightly and then turned back to Louisa to begin introducing her to the other guests standing nearby, wielding Louisa's literary fame as though it were her own.

Joshua eased May out of the circle. "I hoped Louisa would distract everyone and allow me more time with you," he said into her ear. Her head swam in the smell of cloves and roasting goose, the press of bodies, and the clamor of voices and music. She had not expected to be eclipsed by her sister so quickly. Normally Louisa lurked on the fringes of parties, avoiding idle chitchat while May circled in the center of the action. She had worked hard over the years to ensure her spot on guest lists by knowing the latest dances and being a lively conversationalist. After all, paying attention to social graces cost her nothing, and she needed a line of defense against the girls whose allures were buttressed by promising dowries. But now the unavoidable beam of Louisa's rising star drew the crowds to her through no charm of her own, and May realized she needed more than a few graceful chassés to keep up with Louisa.

"Care to dance?" Joshua disrupted May's thoughts by raising her arm to give her a twirl. The brightness of his Delft-blue eyes made her take a deep breath, smile, and step into his arms to begin a waltz, their feet easily gliding into the familiar steps of "The Blue Danube."

They spun around the dance floor for ages it seemed. When May's heel burned from a blister, Joshua smuggled her out of the crowd and into his father's study. There, within the dry smell of leather-bound books and tobacco, away from the sounds of voices and music, she pulled off a glove and reached out to straighten his pale green cravat. Her fingers lingered on the silkiness of the fabric. With the two of them alone, the small gesture felt headier than when they were crushed together moments earlier in the great hall. She realized she was holding her breath and let out a nervous gasp.

Joshua smiled and removed her fingers from his chest, holding them in his own. Without saying a word, he pulled May to him and kissed her. A deep, languorous kiss that tasted of brandy and felt like summer sunshine. Everything outside of them blurred as he pulled her deeper into his chest. Deeper into that kiss. She eventually pulled back, but the lace at her neckline caught on one of his waistcoat's pearl buttons. They stood, tied together, faces inches apart.

"Let's not tear your dress." His voice, low in May's ear, made her lean in close enough to see the softness of his freshly shaven cheeks and smell lemon verbena soap on his skin. She refocused on the knot between them.

"Yes, that would certainly raise eyebrows." Her hands rose,

quivering, to work at the snarled lace. Resting her forehead against his chin, she tried to ignore his breath tickling her ear as she worked to free her dress from his suit, though it tempted her to remain knotted together. She stepped back and looked up at his solemn expression. A blast of French horn blared in the distance. Laughter warbled outside the door.

"Everyone must be wondering where you are," May whispered.

"Let's hide out here," he said, reaching to bring her close again.

"No, I don't dare." She giggled, wriggling from his arms. "I don't trust myself to stay."

The two exited the library into a horde of servants darting in and out of the path to the kitchen. They continued into the throngs of the great hall, but a small blond woman moved into their path to block the way. Joshua laughed. "Why, Alice Bartol—what a pleasant surprise! I haven't see you in ages. Do you plan to challenge me to a snowball duel?"

Alice shook her head in consternation at his jesting. "You always were the neighborhood menace. And now it appears you've tricked someone into thinking you're respectable." She smiled and gave May a friendly nod. "I live around the corner and have known this ruffian for as long as I can remember."

The woman possessed a head full of curls, a plump appealing figure, and the smooth complexion of a china doll; in fact, her petite size made her seem a bit like a doll. She had a perky narrow nose that would have been perfect—May, always feeling her nose was too broad, kept a lookout for perfect noses—except the line of it shifted slightly at a small bump on its bridge. May felt drawn to her for reasons she could not have readily explained.

"How do you know the Bishops?" Alice asked.

"Joshua and I met at a badminton competition at Harvard College—"

"—that we won," Joshua cut in with a smug grin at Alice.

May laughed, for it still felt as though their meeting at the tournament was yesterday, not several months before. They had proven to be a formidable pairing and were still contenders in the tournament late into the sweltering August afternoon. Their crisp badminton whites had become increasingly grass-stained and damp as the matches continued, yet there was an unmistakable energy between the two that didn't waver, even as they tired. Joshua displayed a knack for placing the shuttle-cock just out of reach of their opponents. He was quick to compliment a good shot but also shrugged off any disputes over line calls graciously; his gallantry impressed May. She smiled at the memory of how they had linked arms and bent toward one another, toasting their victory over sweating coupes of chilled champagne.

"Well, three cheers and a tiger for you." Alice laughed at Joshua's boasting. "I see nothing's changed. You're still an incorrigible braggart."

"True. So, let me guess the reason I haven't see you lately," said Joshua, folding his fist in mock seriousness underneath his chin. "Hmm, some lucky fellow has swept you off your feet, and you're absorbed with planning the wedding of the season."

Alice's eyes tightened around the corners, but her smile remained unchanged. "Hardly. I've been taking art classes."

"Well now, another aspiring artist. I had no idea studying art had become so fashionable amongst the lovely ladies of Boston."

Alice flushed. "I've been taking them for a couple of years now."

The woolly-headed feeling that had descended upon May since her kiss with Joshua evaporated. She tried to steady herself; she didn't want to frighten this woman off with too much enthusiasm, not that Alice seemed like the type to flinch from enthusiasm. "I've been drawing and painting for years too, but I need lessons. Where do you take them?"

"There's a man in the Studio Building in Park Square who gives classes to women—Dr. Rimmer. You should join us."

By the time cigar smoke drifted overhead and the crowd thinned, Alice had made May promise to join her at Dr. Rimmer's class in the new year.

Joshua escorted May and Louisa outside and insisted on hailing a hackney. "When will I see you next?"

May's breath caught somewhere in her chest as she looked up at his face, backlit by the glow of the street's lanterns. "Soon. With the holidays, I shall return to Concord, but I'll be back."

He held on to her arm a beat longer than was required to help her step up into the carriage and slipped something into her gloved hand. May folded into her seat and opened her fingers to reveal a tiny pearl button gleaming in the light of the lantern hanging from the carriage. From his spot outside her window, he pointed to his vest where the button should have been, where they were tangled together earlier. Ears ringing with the sudden quiet of the late-night city street, she tightened her grip around the button as the horses carried them away.

"What a tip-top evening. It's funny—I used to detest parties. I had no interest in discussing ball gowns or promising pairings, but now people want to discuss more substantial things with me. People see me as a figure of reckoning. I like it." Louisa tucked herself under the carriage blanket before a quizzical look passed over her face. "I lost you for a bit in there."

May swallowed and leaned her head back against the carriage seat, turning her face to the blackness of night outside the window to hide the delight she knew was stamped all over her face. "I sat out some of the dancing because of a pesky blister. But I recovered."

"Yes, Joshua's a fine tonic for any ailment, I imagine." Louisa closed her eyes and rested her head on May's shoulder. "He's a lucky find. What an evening."

What an evening indeed. Since they were children, Louisa had complained of her young sister's luck, but now it wasn't that simple. May peered down at her fist again. She made her own luck. Without taking off the glove, she knew the button had already left an imprint on the center of her upturned palm.

Chapter 5

January 2, 1869
Boston

Dear May,

I'm not surprised Dr. Rimmer has invited you to attend
his class—you have a knack for getting what you want.
Although it's a good deal fancier than what I usually look
for in my living quarters, I've taken the sky parlor at the
Bellevue Hotel so the two of us can lord over Beacon Hill
together. I'm partial to being able to order sorbet from the
Marble Café at any hour, but the passenger elevator is my
favorite luxury here. Yesterday I found myself stuck at a
place in my manuscript, so I spent several hours riding
up and down in the contraption, trawling for story ideas
by eavesdropping on the conversations of fellow passen-

gers. The saucy things people discuss in public never fail
to amaze me.

I don't see how Mr. Niles expects me to spin 400 more
pages of this "Little Women" hokum, but I suppose I must.
He vexes me to no end with all of his suggested titles—
"Wedding Marches" is the latest stupidity. He thinks it's
clever since all of the sisters pair off. Obviously, I don't approve one bit, but I've become quite the mercenary. As long
as these publishers keep writing me checks, I'll keep writing what they want. But I'll be getting the last laugh—I've
given in to perversity and have made a quirky husband for
Jo March.

Be sure to bring my favorite heating pad from Apple
Slump. My joints have been acting up dreadfully. See you
within the week.

Yours,
Louisa

Snow had been falling since May's arrival in the city at the
turn of the new year, but it finally stopped. The sky emptied
out to a bright blue. Sun cleaved through the clouds. A perfect
day for a sleigh ride around the Common. Since receiving the
invitation from Joshua earlier that morning, she couldn't count
how many times she had checked the clock. *When would it be
three o'clock?* Near the entry to the Bellevue, porters in smart
red jackets called out room directions while May waited for
Joshua's arrival by the lobby's fireplace.

A gust of biting January cold air billowed through the lobby as he burst through the hotel's doors. He loosened a dark crimson muffler from around his neck to reveal an open smile that looked so unguardedly pleased to see her, it split her in two. "Ready?"

"Yes, I'm sick to death of being cooped up inside." Outside the building, the cold air made her lungs ache, but after weeks and weeks of gray gloomy weather, the sun felt glorious.

"Careful, I've just greased the runners. She runs like a hot knife through butter," he said, helping her under several layers of woolen carriage blankets. Once they were settled, he gave a snap to the reins, making a merry tinkle of bells ring out as his white, shaggy horse kicked up its hooves. The sleigh was just big enough for the two of them, and May nestled deeper into the seat, closer to Joshua's warmth. The sleigh swerved slightly; its runners sank deeper into the snow. The pace of the sled increased, causing clumps of snow to spit into the air. She clutched the seat for balance. They reached the Common, and acres of untouched whiteness stretched before them while a lacy filigree of snow-covered tree branches arched overhead.

A team pulling an omnibus headed toward them, and May inhaled sharply. He gave a sharp tug on the reins to steer the sleigh into a clear straightaway.

She tried to relax as the sleigh careened along the snow. "I can barely wait for my art classes to begin. Alice has been so helpful, giving me all of the information about supplies. What a lovely woman."

Joshua frowned and pulled his wool cap down lower on his forehead. "Well, don't get me wrong, I've known Alice for years, but she has some . . . well, Alice is a bit different."

May pictured the small, pretty woman at the party. "How is she different?"

But Joshua kept talking as if he hadn't heard her. "And anyway, why tie yourself down to all of those classes? You don't want to illustrate another one of your sister's books, do you? The first one brought you so much heartache. I'd hate to see you go through that again. Why keep punishing yourself? Artists appear to be a miserable lot, and that's not you."

Her right mittened hand clenched the rim of the sleigh. Who was he to tell her how she should feel about art? She opened her mouth to speak but realized the storefronts on Boylston were blurring past them. We're going too fast for a busy area, she thought.

They veered onto Tremont Street, and an icy patch glistened ahead in the snowy sludge. Before May could say anything, they were fishtailing along the ice on the road. Their horse staggered, its rear legs sliding out from underneath it. Everything held suspended for a moment before a shriek of splintering wood snapped through the air with a sickening crack. The sleigh whipped sideways while remaining upright. May pitched to the right, jammed between the rim of the sleigh and Joshua's weight. Her mouth, open with a silent scream, clamped shut with a bone-tingling click of tooth upon tooth from the impact of their sudden stop. But there was no time to assess injuries.

"Get out, get out!" Joshua shouted. She needed no urging and fought the drag of her skirts to scramble over the high back of the sleigh. Without thinking, she circled forward to grasp the horse's harness. The poor beast had regained its footing and stood enveloped in wreaths of vapor from its heavy breathing, kicking its hind legs in agitation. A broken wooden shaft hung awkwardly off the sleigh. The creature's hooves continued to drill into it, sending splinters flying through the air like shrapnel to litter the snow behind them.

"He's free—move him away, move him!" Joshua yelled from somewhere beyond May's vision.

Without taking her eyes off the horse, she backed away from the sleigh, bringing the animal with her. The whites of the creature's eyes settled, its big brown eyes rested on her. May let out a shuddering exhalation.

Joshua came around the animal, bent over and checked its legs before rising to look at her with a sheepish and shaken look on his face. A thin, red scrape blazed across his cheek. "Are you hurt?"

Was she? No, she felt alive. More alive than she had in ages. The cold air tingled against her face, and the brightness of the day left her blinking furiously. She shook her head. "Are you?"

"No, but I was sure I was going to end up like a pincushion with all of those shards stuck in me while I unharnessed him." Joshua gestured at the sleigh; its ruined shaft bristled with splinters.

She nodded, trying to sort out what had happened just as a horse-drawn cart stopped next to them. Voices called out offers for help. Wide-eyed faces orbited, curious for a glimpse of excitement. Shaking, she crossed her arms over her chest and backpedaled out of the circle of onlookers.

"Let me arrange a ride home for you," Joshua said, following her attempt at escape.

"No, I'm fine, but I need to stay on my feet." She mustered a confident smile. "The walk home will settle me."

Already a swarm of men had descended upon Joshua, and he nodded back at her distractedly. She turned, pulling her wool cloak around her, and set off into a packed-down path of snow to cross the Common. About three-quarters of the way across, she began to regret walking. Within her wet leather boots, her feet stiffened into frozen blocks. Her neck ached, and she suspected a spot upon her right hip was ripening into a juicy bruise. She arrived back at the Bellevue to find their rooms dark and cavernous. With icy, numb fingers, she wriggled out of layers of clothes and collapsed into bed.

Shivering under the quilts, she thought back to the sleigh ride, before the crash. What had they been discussing? Joshua had discouraged her from a friendship with Alice and pursuing her art. He didn't appear to take May's aspirations seriously at all. Did he think her art would disappear as her affections for him grew? Art was no passing fancy; it was no phase to be outgrown like wearing plaits and pinafores. She burrowed deeper down in the sheets and fell into a restless sleep.

"WELL, YOU LEFT the sitting room in quite a state last night. I spent ages sorting through your soggy clothes and hanging everything up to dry," Louisa grumbled from her desk the next morning when May limped out of the bedroom, but her eyes widened as she looked her sister up and down. "Good Lord, what happened?"

May dropped onto the chintz love seat next to the fireplace and relayed an account of the unfortunate sleigh ride while Louisa tucked a blanket around her. May brushed some loose papers on the seat out of her way, but stopped to study one.

"Who's A. M. Barnard?"

Louisa mumbled something unintelligible as she wrapped a shawl around May's shoulders.

"What?"

"I'm A. M. Barnard."

"You are?"

"Mr. Niles told me I can't write any more of my blood and thunder stories as Louisa May Alcott," she said. "People expect wholesome fare from me now. A. M. Barnard is my pen name for when I want to write more salacious stories."

May stared at her sister as she let this sink in. "So, you're finished with the second novel?"

"Yes. I finally sent in the galley proofs for part two of *Little Women* yesterday. Mr. Niles confessed they want to entitle it *Good Wives*. I told him that was the most feebleminded title I ever heard and threatened to not pen another word for him ever again. They should just call it *Little Women Part Two*. Eventually they can just print both of them as one book. Ugh, *Good Wives*. What malarkey."

"So, what becomes of Amy March? What should I expect from my fictional counterpart in this one?"

Louisa sat in a chair and gave her sister a smug smile. "Well, I know you felt I did you a great disservice with young Amy March, but I think you'll be quite pleased with how she grows up. Aunt March sends Amy to Europe to study art. Back at home, Laurie professes his love to Jo, but she rejects him, so he travels to France where he and Amy fall in love and marry. So, Amy March ends up being wealthy and able to pursue her art."

Disappointment deadened May's limbs. She certainly didn't want a cast-off suitor from her older sister.

Louisa gave a triumphant smile. "I knew you'd like it. You get to be an artist."

May's breath stopped somewhere deep inside. All these years, her family had humored her artistic aspirations: Father built her a tiny art studio off his office; Marmee let her draw on the walls of her bedroom; Louisa permitted her to illustrate *Little Women*. But May always suspected, deep down, they didn't believe she was an artist, not in the same way that Louisa had always been considered one. Was it because Louisa suffered for her writing? Must one suffer for art? May certainly hoped not. Creating beauty through art made her happy. And being happy seemed to be her natural state, a state Louisa seemed to view with suspicion. And now it seemed Joshua also equated art with misery. She massaged her sternum and found her voice.

"Why do you write? To make money?"

Louisa looked surprised. "I suppose I write because stories and characters rattle around my head day and night."

"But did you start to feel like a real writer once you began to make money from it?"

"No, I always believed I was meant to be a writer, but after years of eking out a slight existence, it feels awfully satisfying to make some coin from all of this, even if I'm not writing exactly what I want. This juvenile fare bores me to tears sometimes. But I'll get to write more of what I want. Someday." Louisa poured a cup of tea from the pot on her writing desk and stirred at it with a silver spoon. Both sisters watched the gleam of the metal flash in the low lighting of the room.

"Are you ever lonely?"

"How could I be when I've got you around?" Louisa stood and walked to the window and pointed to the street below. "We've never been up so high up before. I love this view."

May rose and joined her. Seven stories down, people the size of thimbles went about their business, bustling from storefront to storefront, loading in and out of carriages. It was another world up here. The State House rose in the distance with the empty space of the Common farther away to the left, paths scarring its snowy expanse. Her eyes left the drab blocks of brick buildings, traveling along the cirrus clouds feathering the vast cerulean blue sky extending out in front of them. "It's a far cry from our attic window back in Concord, that's for sure."

Louisa turned away with a fit of coughing and circled back to her seat. "I simply can't imagine a life that didn't include writing. Caring for a husband and a flock of babies just never interested me." She gave her sister a level look before tilting her head from side to side to stretch the cords of her neck.

May stayed at the window, studying the frozen landscape below. She remembered a time, years ago, when she was playing in the barn with her sisters. A well-placed barb had provoked Louisa into pulling one of May's golden braids and hissing, "See how you're the only fair-haired member of this family? See? It's because you are not one of us. As a little mite, you were abandoned on our doorstep one morning, and Marmee took you in. Now we're stuck with you." Louisa had leaned back from her tirade with a look of vengeful delight, expecting to see her younger sister crumble into a teary puddle, but May felt only a sense of freeing clarity. So *that's* why she was so markedly different from everyone else in the household, why she didn't accept hardship as readily as the rest of them.

During the previous winter, Marmee and Lizzie had dragged five-year-old May to a decrepit tenement in the city's West End. She remembered her eyes watering at the rank smell of onions in the dark press of the room and the chilling, listless stare of the baby whose twig arms dangled from the grasp of its mother. The woman's surrendered expression had been that of a dingy, moth-eaten flag lying on the floor, and May had counted to three hundred to steady her quaking legs, while willing Marmee and Lizzie to speed up their patient conversation with the woman. May had kept counting and tried to keep from looking at the nearby table covered in dead flies dotting unidentifiable stains. When she had tried to sleep that night, it wasn't the image of the neglected woman and her baby keeping her awake, it was the fear that the Alcotts often seemed close to finding themselves in a similar predicament. She swore to never visit the poor with Marmee again. Father's philosophies set them apart from everyone, and while her sisters and Marmee supported his radical views, and even added some of their own, May did not subscribe to any of them so readily, and it often felt as though her family believed her desires for comfort, happiness, and stability to be shortcomings, moral failures, signs of selfishness.

For months after Louisa's sly story, she had imagined her other family out there—her *real* family—living in a lovely home, somewhere far from the privations of the Alcotts' quirkiness. *It all made sense.* Of course, this all made *no sense*, but her overeager imagination seized on the idea and sugar-spun it into a fantasy far from the realities of her day-to-day toil. The dream lost some of its clarity in the years that followed, but it morphed into something more toxic: a belief she was an outlier within her own family.

May sighed. Snippets of Joshua's dismissal of her artistic ambitions in the sleigh came back to her. Well, she could do better than what everyone else imagined. Much better. Soon no one would question her artistic aspirations. And she'd do it sensibly without sinking into vortexes and making herself miserable. Somehow she would become an artist in her own right. Though it went against every instinct, May leaned in closer to the window and peered out. Dizziness struck her, but she rested her forehead against the cool glass and continued to study the city below, ignoring the vertigo rising inside.

Chapter 6

r. Rimmer, please allow me to present Miss Alcott."

The trim man with dark hair pomaded with architectural precision paused and gave a curt nod. "May I check to see you have the correct supplies?" May fumbled for her shawl strap and pulled out the paper, drawing pencils, and charcoal he specified in his letter. Dr. Rimmer ticked off the items she brought against a list he produced from his breast pocket. "Excellent, welcome." He hurried to resume his spot at a long table in front of the room. With easels lined up in perfect lines and whitewashed walls, bare except for the occasional anatomical study of the human body, the space looked less like an artist's studio and more like a surgical theater.

Without lingering on a long introduction to the day's subject—the study of hands—Dr. Rimmer lectured about the relevant bones and musculature while the women followed along taking notes. Aside from his voice, only the scratching of pencils on paper could be heard. May smiled as she looked at all of the women around her, solemnly bent over their work. This was no class for debutantes looking to fritter the day away by painting and gossiping with friends. Now, *this* was a real art class!

While May worked, she became conscious of her own hands. Chapped, despite her constant attempts to keep them smooth with cold cream, they knew their way around a laundry scrubbing board. Marmee, Louisa, Anna, and May all shared the same weathered hands, whereas Father's were graceful with tapered, long fingers. Sometimes a dark crescent of soil ran along the top of his fingernails from his work in the garden, but May often eyed the contrast of Father's enviably unmarred hands to her own with dismay. His attempts at writing essays about his beliefs fell short, and to complicate things further, he didn't believe in being paid for his labor, yet he seemed not to notice that the women in his family held no such compunction and accepted employment as nurses, cleaners, and teachers to bring in much-needed income to the family coffers. The impracticality of his ideas aggravated her to no end.

May couldn't help dwelling on Lizzie as she worked the contouring of a thumb joint. She had inherited Father's graceful hands. It was hard to believe thirteen years had passed since her death. Marmee had been caring for a destitute family crammed into a squalid room perched over a pig shed and unwittingly brought scarlet fever home with her. Both Lizzie and May had fallen ill. Guilt always nagged at May over the fact that she recovered quickly, while her sister never recuperated. Lizzie had spent two years languishing in poor health before dying a few months short of her twenty-third birthday. The memory made May drop her charcoal into the rim at the bottom of the easel and exhale loudly.

Dr. Rimmer appeared at her side. "Miss Alcott, may I recommend using a more circular technique for rendering a smoother gradation of value?" He held out his hand for her pencil and demonstrated using tiny meticulous circles to build shadows, before handing the pencil back. His nails were clipped short, his hands unmarred. May tried to imitate his method, banishing all thoughts of Lizzie from her mind.

"Better." He nodded. "When in doubt, think back to the basic shapes to guide your work—triangles, circles, rectangles— there's a system." She looked down at her drawing, and her eyes caught a flash of gleaming black leather boots on the floor beside her. She suspected Dr. Rimmer polished them himself, for he seemed like the type of man who didn't trust others to get things just right.

"Yes, a system," she echoed.

Dr. Rimmer continued down the row, inspecting the other easels, making corrections and adjustments to the work of his students. May's hands were smudged, and she was sure charcoal streaked her cheeks and forehead. Unused to sitting for so long, her back felt stiff and her eyes burned. Dr. Rimmer's white shirt still looked crisp and unblemished, and he held the posture of a military general, even late in the day.

He resumed command in front of the room and held a plaster sculpture of a hand. Pointing to the three phalanges comprising each finger, he lectured the women on the importance of shadowing these contours correctly. May could not remember a time she worked for so many hours in a row. Next to her jumble of lines, Alice's sketches of hands looked convincing. As the outside light faded, Dr. Rimmer noted the time and announced the end of class.

SEVERAL WEEKS LATER, May and Alice ambled along the brick sidewalks of Hamilton Place, eager to stretch their limbs after a long day in class with Dr. Rimmer. They dodged piles of filthy snow, remnants of the long winter that seemed to be nearing its end. In all their time together, May had been studying her friend closely, looking for a sign, a hint of why Joshua had described Alice as *different*, but she remained confounded.

Alice grabbed May's arm and pointed at a feathered bonnet visible in the window of a milliner's tiny shop. "What a confection! I must have that for spring," she said, tugging May into the store.

The milliner moved a pincushion aside on the counter to showcase the hat for Alice. "Colored feathers are all the thing for next season. They've arrived straight from Paris, miss."

"This is divine." Alice held the pearl-gray satin bonnet up and ran a finger along one of the emerald-colored feathers sprouting from a cluster of lilies of the valley.

May nodded, unable to assemble enthusiasm for the extravagant purchase. She squinted into a far corner of the milliner's shop—in the low light, the silhouette of a dress form reduced itself to basic shapes. Dr. Rimmer's words about bodies being composed of a system of lines and angles crystallized in her mind as she studied the beautiful simplicity of the triangle of the shoulders down to the torso and the same shape mirrored downward from the waist to the hips. It was easy to get distracted by the details of musculature and facial features, but finally, she could see the body in its most elemental form. Dr. Rimmer was right. She laughed out loud at the simplicity of her newfound sight.

"Oooo, that's a beauty, too," said Alice, pointing to the hat atop the dress form.

"Would you believe I hadn't even noticed the hat? I was too busy recognizing that Dr. Rimmer actually knows what he's talking about. He keeps telling me to focus on simple shapes, yet I'm always trying to make things more difficult for myself."

Absorbed with her newest find, Alice lifted the fancy basket-weave hat with a bow of pale yellow silk moiré ribbons off the dress form and placed it on her head. She ended up purchasing both hats. "Since we don't have class tomorrow, would you like to join me at the new tearoom on Newbury?"

While May explained she had to go out to Concord to check on her parents, she watched Alice wad her change back into her purse without counting it. May couldn't afford an outing to the newest tearoom, even if she could have stayed in the city for the weekend. She wondered how it would feel to be like Alice and do whatever she pleased without any concerns about money or taking care of anyone. But wait—was this it? Alice enjoyed a far greater degree of independence than most women. Was this what unsettled Joshua?

On the sidewalk outside the shop, May asked, "Alice, how is it you're still unmarried?"

"Oh, goodness, it all started as bad luck." Alice shifted the hatboxes in her hands before they set off toward Beacon Hill. "Well, I lost my mother when I was ten. Five years later my cousin Francis died of consumption. I was young but always pictured myself marrying him. And then right before the war, I met a young man who worked for my father. I thought we might have a future, but he died at Fredericksburg. By that point, I was thoroughly tired of losing people and swore off opening myself up to disappointment again. I'm sure all of the other women on Beacon Hill find it odd, but my father fully supports my unconventionality." She raised up her chin with a decisive nod. "So this is it. It's a surprising relief. And how would I pursue art if I was married with children?"

May nodded, and her mind raced. *Yes, how indeed?*

CLAVICLES. SCAPULAS. OBLIQUE muscles. Metacarpal bones. May wondered if she was studying to become a doctor or a painter? Every day with Dr. Rimmer was an exploration of the body: the articulation of the wrist; the bony landmarks of the leg; the proper proportions of the torso. As the weeks became a blur of sketching, she began to see improvement in her work; a relief, for she was ravenous to catch up to her classmates, many of whom had been taking lessons for several years. She spent hours copying from sketches tacked to the front of the room and poring over plaster casts of femurs, the skull, and the pelvis.

May became a watcher of people. She no longer listened to what people said, but studied how faces moved when speaking, altering from one expression to the next, and it amazed her to think of the sea of muscles—contracting, elongating, and slackening—existing under the smooth planes of the face. Even in the hinterlands of sleep, her dreams were strangely fantastical with talking skeletons and bodies that could peel off skin as easily as removing a layer of clothing. The dreams left her bleary, but, unlike Louisa whose spells of compulsive writing diminished her, May thrived on her obsession. She lived in a state of radiant exhaustion.

Chapter 7

Winter passed. The days lengthened. One afternoon spring-time sunlight poured through the windows of the Studio Building, making Dr. Rimmer's room stifling hot. From the voice instructor's studio next door, the endless trill of a soprano practicing scales gave the afternoon a tedious edge. May erased some unsightly attempts at sketching a reclined figure and promptly wore a hole through her paper.

Impatience had hounded her all week. On Monday, she met Joshua and his younger sister, Nellie, for tea in the Marble Café at the Bellevue Hotel. Amid potted maidenhead ferns and oyster-colored table linens, May greeted them with a signed copy of the newest edition of *Little Women*. The girl, shining in a stylish primrose pink velvet dress, could barely contain her joy over meeting one of the Alcott sisters.

"Since reading the first part of *Little Women*, I feel as if I already know you!" Nellie gushed, plucking the book from May's grip and hugging it tightly under her chin. "I can't wait to see who all the girls marry." Nellie rifled through the book's pages and continued without taking a breath. "Isn't it strange your life has been published for the entire world to read? If Joshua wrote a book about me, I'd be thumping mad."

"I only take credit for Amy March's more gracious moments. It can be odd at times, but *Little Women* really isn't my life. My sister made up those stories," May said without elaborating on the truth behind that particular fiction. "Though once I burned a manuscript of Louisa's after an argument, just like in the book."

Nellie let out a whoop of laughter that would surely have resulted in a reprimand at her finishing school. "I loved that part. It was so mean of Jo to prevent Amy from going to the theater. She had it coming. I'm glad Amy got her revenge."

Joshua chuckled and raised his eyebrows. "I really must read this book for a better understanding of you."

"One shouldn't need a book to understand me." May smiled back at him over the rim of her teacup.

Before parting, Joshua insisted May join his family for dinner. With Nellie nodding her head furiously in agreement, he said, "I shall speak to Mother tonight. We shall have you over on Thursday night. Expect a note with the particulars to arrive later this evening."

Well, that had been on Monday, and it was now Thursday. No note arrived. Every morning May checked with the front desk at the hotel but to no avail. No note.

May frowned at her ruined sketch. Next to her Alice moaned, crumpled her paper, and threw it to the ground.

"Let's get out of here," May said. Without further discussion, the women tossed their supplies into their shawl straps and stumbled downstairs, past the mind-numbing hum of the sewing machine store on the first floor, and outside onto Boylston Street.

"Oh, thank goodness for the breeze," sighed Alice, reaching up to re-pin her hat. "Where shall we go?"

"Let's go to the show at Williams & Everett that Dr. Rimmer mentioned this morning—what was the woman's name?"

"The woman from New Hampshire? Jane Gardner."

May nodded. "Did you catch that she lives in Paris?"

"Imagine that."

"I feel as if I spent all morning doing just that—imagining myself living in Paris. I could desperately use some inspiration and distraction. Let's go."

INSIDE THE MAIN gallery of the oak-paneled walls of Williams & Everett, a woman, glowing in a plum-colored silk day dress, held court. A cluster of somber-suited critics and dealers surrounded her. It could be none other than Jane Gardner.

May and Alice inched through the crowd to get closer to the woman. They were blocked by a pale lanky fellow with an oversized Adam's apple, who stroked his chin, bristling with red whiskers. He nodded approvingly. "Miss Gardner's animals are surprisingly good. They remind me of Rosa Bonheur's."

The man next to him gave a low laugh and replied, "Do you think she perfected her technique by sketching haunches and cuts of ribs in a Parisian butcher's meat locker like Bonheur?" The man caught sight of May tilting her head to listen to them, and his walrus-like drooping mustache twitched as he frowned. "Women artists are unseemly."

"Well, if it gives me more work to sell, I'm all for it." Still stroking his chin, the tall man moved away to inspect the paintings lining the walls, leaving a space for May and Alice to edge in closer to Miss Gardner.

A man with a pipe in his mouth said loudly, "Whenever I visit Miss Gardner's studio, there's quite a menagerie."

May couldn't tell if he added this information to talk about animals or to stake some sort of claim on the woman.

"It's true, I adore animals and have two dogs, a cat, and an assortment of birds," Miss Gardner said. With glittering eyes, she lowered her voice and leaned into the crowd. "But once I used a lion as a model."

May watched the artist describe how she went to a ratty little zoo on the outskirts of Paris where she cajoled the zoo master into letting her draw their lion, but of course, the lion was ill; yet she used this as the perfect opportunity to study his anatomy. The poor creature was so bony she could practically see right through him, and so she sketched the pitiable flea-infested waste of a lion until he died; but even then she was not done with him; the plucky artist managed to locate a cart into which she loaded the pathetic beast and wheeled her specimen along the avenues of Paris, until she arrived at her studio where she dumped the corpse and painted him until the fetid stink of the sad creature defeated her.

It was as if she had thrown bread crumbs into a gaggle of

geese, for the men all erupted into equal parts agitation and titillation. No one could have ever considered her a conventional beauty—the woman was slight with a narrow face, sharp nose, and thin dark hair pulled back into a bun—yet she had these men enthralled.

"Your human figures are equally convincing," said the walrus-mustached man, pointing at one of her paintings on the wall. Although he didn't say it, the obvious implication was: *How does a woman manage to achieve such lifelike paintings?*

His insinuation was not lost on Jane Gardner. She looked him straight in the eye. "I dressed like a man to have access to one of the government-run schools, so I could work from nude models. I'd been ill and my hair was cut very short. My classmates figured out my ruse quickly, but no one seemed to mind."

She shrugged as she spoke, but her nonchalance was feigned. She was alert, watchful, and nimble with her command over her audience. "I speak French fluently, so I fit right in."

Again, her audience clucked and deluged her with comments.

May and Alice wandered the gallery, awaiting an opportunity to speak with the artist. A dead lion in her studio? Dressing as a man? Nude models? Miss Gardner remained besieged by the men, so eventually May and Alice gave up and reluctantly climbed the stairs to the lobby.

Bent over to sign the guest book, both women failed to notice Miss Gardner slip out the front door of the gallery. It wasn't until they walked outside that they found her alone. She stood on the sidewalk, immersed with sprinkling some tobacco onto a small white paper resting on her palm. After rolling the paper up to make a cigarette, she ran her small pink tongue along the edge to seal it and noticed May and Alice.

"If you wanted to speak with me, you needed to be pushier in there. All those fellas have no problem interrupting one another to get at me." She flicked a match down the side of the brick building to light her cigarette, took in their art satchels, and exhaled a ring of smoke slowly. "So, now there are opportunities to study here in Boston? I left because there was nothing for women."

"Miss Gardner, how have you learned . . . ?" May waved her hand at the gallery's entrance, lost for words. "Your work—it's so *real*. The composition, the—"

The woman shrugged. "I started off by copying the masters in the museums in Paris. Over time, I developed clients willing to buy my copies so I could afford private instruction. But really, copying was how I learned the most."

"But studying with master painters—" Alice began, but Jane cut her off with an impatient shake of her head.

"The masters are a mixed lot. Some practically run opium dens. They're like parasites, bleeding naïve American students dry of all their cash. But they do have connections to dealers and critics, and those are the fellows you need to sell your work. But really, first you need to have something to sell. I do nothing but paint and meet with potential clients."

A woman in a chocolate-brown velvet jacket sidled past them on the sidewalk, scowling pointedly at Jane's smoking, but the painter ignored her. "The men all waste their days meeting

in the cafés to drink with each other, but I work all of the time."
She looked back over her shoulder at the gallery and dropped
her cigarette to the sidewalk to snuff it out. "Speaking of work, I
should probably get back in there to mingle with those wretched
sharks. Well, aren't you going to introduce yourselves?"

Flustered, both May and Alice rooted through their bags for
their cards and made introductions.

"Be sure to call on my studio when you arrive in Paris."
Miss Gardner held the cards aloft and sauntered back into the
shadow of Williams & Everett's doorway.

"*When* we arrive in Paris?" Alice watched the woman with
a glum expression. "I think she means *if* we arrive in Paris."

May breathed in the smell of tobacco and exhaled slowly.
"No, she knows what she means. We must get to Paris somehow."

Chapter 8

May exited the main entrance of the Athenaeum onto Beacon Street with thoughts of Greenough's *Venus Victrix* filling her mind. She had taken to leaving Dr. Rimmer's class some afternoons to sketch in the Athenaeum's sculpture gallery. The marble statues served as feeble substitutes for a live human model to be sure, but they beat copying endless anatomical sketches. The prospect of studying from live models had gripped the women artists since winter. After all, women were earning medical degrees at the New England Female Medical College over on Stoughton Street—surely these women studied the human form. Why not the women in the Studio Building? Yet Dr. Rimmer remained clear that there would be none of that in his class. Not in a class for ladies.

Since seeing Miss Gardner's show the previous week, May had been consumed with thoughts of traveling to Paris. Was she getting ahead of herself? After all, she needed to spend more time under Dr. Rimmer's tutelage learning the fundamentals of figure drawing, and really, drawing everything for that matter. Uprooting herself from everything she knew and voyaging to France was daunting. For mercy's sake, she didn't even speak a lick of French, thanks to her unorthodox education. But if asked to copy one more set of feet from a sketch of Dr. Rimmer's, she was going to eat her bonnet.

"Miss Alcott!"

She looked up to see Joshua approaching her on the sidewalk, his mother at his side.

With a contrite expression, he said, "I apologize for not sending over a note sooner—I've been tied up with a dreadful case at work, but isn't this a happy coincidence? Mother, you remember Miss Alcott?"

Mrs. Bishop studied her son and her face bloomed, transforming from haughty to doting in an instant. "Such a good son. Even busy, he still makes time for his mother." The older woman looked at the sandstone façade of the Athenaeum. "You were in there?" she asked May, raising her hand to her heart, as if visiting the Athenaeum was on par with frequenting grog shops down by the wharves.

"My sister was recently granted lending privileges, so I'm able to visit the art and sculpture galleries as her guest." May ran her fingers over the sketchbook tucked into her satchel as she spoke. The last thing she needed was her sketches of unclothed figures to tumble down onto the sidewalk in front of them.

Mrs. Bishop sniffed. "A library is no place for women."

May refrained from pointing out that her family believed

that a library was the perfect place for women—she had no desire to emphasize the singularity of her parents and their views.

Oblivious to the cool looks passing between the women, Joshua said, "Mother, Miss Alcott must join us for dinner."

The older woman's nostrils flared. "Of course, that would be lovely. You must. Shall we say this Friday evening?"

Joshua nodded. "Perfect, it's settled."

May accepted gracefully, but doubts screamed inside her head. Wrapped in a mink stole, Mrs. Bishop resembled a large creature of prey. May thought back to moments earlier when the woman's face had conveyed such pure joy when she looked at Joshua. May wondered if hers did the same thing. It probably did—he could have that effect upon a woman.

Perhaps this was why Mrs. Bishop disliked her.

THE BISHOPS' LONG dining room table was crowded with Bristol glass candlesticks and a bouquet of hothouse roses, mignonette, and pansies. Silver forks and spoons of every length gleamed at each place setting—more than May had ever seen. What would she do with all of them? She thought of her attempts to brighten up her family's table at home with garlands of autumn leaves and vases of wildflowers and shrank in her seat.

The burl-veneered panels of the sideboard gleamed underneath steaming plates of veal pies, steak, scrod, rolls, and baked beans bathed in brown sugar and molasses. The table practically groaned with abundance; there was no way the five of them could possibly consume everything. She thought of the food baskets Marmee delivered to the poor. How many baskets could she make from this meal to deliver to families in the slums of Boston's West End? Her family had its weaknesses but squandering blessings was not one of them.

From her spot at the end of the table, Mrs. Bishop appeared to pick at her food. "Your mother must have been sorry to see you move to Boston. She has no objections to you living on your own and studying art?"

"My parents have always encouraged us to be independent."

"I'll say. You're lucky," Nellie said.

May smiled at her, relieved by the presence of her young ally.

"Nellie, if this evening is too much for you, you can have all the independence you want and eat alone in your room." Mrs. Bishop's grim warning served its intended effect; the girl looked crestfallen and clamped her mouth shut.

"Our eldest, Charlotte, studied watercolors briefly but found needlepoint more to her liking," Mrs. Bishop said. "But she has no time for frivolities like that now. Once you're a wife, running a household and raising a family takes over."

Frivolities. May reminded herself not to rise to her hostess's bait. "Well, there were few options for me to study art in Concord, whereas here I can take drawing classes with Dr. Rimmer over in the Studio Building in Park Square."

"He's a doctor. And an artist? How peculiar."

"Dr. Rimmer is a trained medical doctor and an artist. His classes focus on anatomy."

"Anatomy." Mrs. Bishop repeated the word with a grimace as if something rotten sat in her mouth.

"We study musculature and bone structure from his sketches and plaster casts."

Mrs. Bishop placed her fork down carefully and glared across the table at her husband. Mr. Bishop studied a spot on the wallpaper above his wife's head. May looked to Joshua for support, but he buttered a roll with such grave concentration, it seemed he was removing a bullet from a gunshot wound. Only Nellie dared to look at May. When their gaze met, the girl smiled slightly as a sign of commiseration.

"And do you want to be a professional?" Mrs. Bishop's tone indicated being a professional implied only one thing for a woman.

"A professional artist, yes."

The drumming of Mr. Bishop's fingers on the table was the only sound in the room for a moment.

"And Nellie mentioned you're interested in Paris? It seems terribly narrow-minded to think *only* Europe has culture."

"If I'm serious about becoming a painter—"

Mr. Bishop shook his head. "Show me a Frenchman who wouldn't cheat his own mother out of her pension or marry his sister if it suited him; there's not a single plain dealer in the entire country. No American in his right mind would go there. It's much better to stay here in Boston. Why, the area is thriving."

His wife nodded her head in approval, and May blinked in surprise at how precisely she was cut down.

Joshua pivoted the discussion to describing the commercial development of the Back Bay, but May could barely hear him over the pounding of her heart in her ears. Mrs. Bishop's *narrow-minded* accusation rankled. Anger roiled inside her, but the table conversation sailed along without her. On her plate, a viscous film of fat had arisen where the beef remains lay. Her food congealed.

"The whole area has been modeled on Parisian avenues," Joshua said, finally looking over at May. "See? You can enjoy France's finer points without even leaving home." He nodded with delight at his own idea and swirled dark red wine in his glass—a wine from Burgundy, no less.

May stared at him and wondered if she really knew anything about him. *Did he really think a Boston neighborhood affecting French architecture could solve everything?*

AFTER DINNER, THEY retired to the drawing room for coffee, and Mrs. Bishop complained about the houses springing up by Marlborough Street. Too newfangled, she called them. May's temples throbbed, and she looked around the drawing room, searching for a distraction. One of the serving girls hovered next to a bookshelf watching Joshua intensely. The girl's cheeks were marred with a smattering of pockmarks, a remnant perhaps from a bout of scarlet fever. Joshua signaled to her for coffee. With the steaming sterling silver coffeepot trained over his cup, her shaking hand caused her to spill it on his right forearm. He jumped from his seat and let out a yelp of surprise.

"Ach, sorry, I'm so sorry," the girl called out, spraying more coffee along the Aubusson carpet in terror. Another maid swooped in with a white towel to clean it. As Mrs. Bishop let loose a tirade against her, the girl's eyes filled with tears, and red splotches rose up her neck and across her cheeks, before she fled the room, trailing a stream of coffee splatters behind her.

During the entire mishap, May held her breath. Unfazed, Joshua resumed sitting and continued to stir his coffee. None of the Bishops seemed to care about the incident, whereas May's hands trembled as if she were the one to suffer the rebuke.

"WELL, WASN'T THAT a pleasant evening?" Joshua plucked a dark purple pansy from a neighbor's flower box and tucked it into his lapel, as he and May walked back to the Bellevue Hotel after dinner. "Now Nellie will probably want to be an artist."

"A pleasant evening? Were we at the same dinner?" All of the pressure building in May's head exploded. "I can't believe you didn't defend me back there."

"Excuse me?" Joshua stopped walking to stare at her.

"Your mother made it abundantly clear that my interest in becoming an artist is beyond my purview."

"Why do you insist on stirring up a hornet's nest? If you simply eased off your talk about anatomy and Paris, it would all be fine. Mother can be a little slow to embrace new ideas. But she'll come around. It's not as if she disapproves of your sister and her writing."

May walked away from him, saying over her shoulder, "Well then, maybe you should court my sister."

Joshua laughed and caught up to her, taking her elbow gently. "Don't be such a pepper pot. By the next time she sees you, Mother will have forgotten all about this."

"But I won't." May lowered her voice as they reached the brisk comings and goings of the Bellevue Hotel's front entrance.

"Well, you should. Honestly, what am I going to do with you? Stop worrying. I'll see you soon."

He smiled, and May couldn't help letting her frown weaken as she said good-bye—somehow with his handsomeness, he exercised the calming powers of a snake charmer. She chewed her lip as she watched him stroll down the block, tossing his pocket watch around in circles, completely immune to the wreckage of the evening still smoldering in her head.

Disappointment's jagged edges caught in her throat. It was as if they all had ignored the script for the evening. When they bungled their lines, no director stepped in and asked them to start over. And the night's script was supposed to include a happy ending—May always favored happy endings—but somehow it all ended in a most unsatisfactory manner. The Bishops were supposed to have been eager to welcome her into their family—instead, it seemed she was all but banished. But the feeling was mutual—her own disenchantment was the biggest disappointment of all. She did not approve of the insularity of their sphere and the casual disregard with which they treated each other one bit. There was no chance she wanted be a part of that family, no matter how charismatic and promising Joshua could appear. The realization of what she needed to do struck her with the force of a kick to the shins.

She hurried to the front desk inside the hotel lobby and scribbled a quick note. She slid it, along with some coins, across the counter to the manager and said good night.

Chapter 9

The Public Garden emptied of people eager to get inside before the storm began, but May stood rooted to her spot on the bridge over the lagoon, watching Joshua clench and unclench his hands on the railing. He looked at her in disbelief. "You want to go to Paris to study art regardless of what I think?"

She nodded.

"You're relentless. Those reviews from your sister's book would have been enough to sink most people. But not you." Joshua looked away, and his gaze swept the lagoon in front of them, his jaw shifting back and forth to assume an expression of control. "Remember the day we met playing badminton? I liked your spirit of adventure. I'm just sorry the very qualities that drew me to you now work against me."

"I was so hopeful—" May's voice broke. She clutched the railing on the bridge to steady her shaking hands.

They both looked out over the water. Thunder rumbled in the distance. "We should go," he said in a low tone. Although people surrounded them, it felt as though they were the only two people left on earth. "Is this because of last night? Because I didn't say something to the servant? To my mother?"

Last night put their relationship into perspective for her, but she knew he would never understand her dissatisfaction. The time to solve anything that needed fixing had passed. "No, I need to pursue my art. I need to leave Boston for a while. Now I have the courage to go."

"It's about to rain. I should walk you home."

"I'll be fine on my own, but thank you."

He hunched up his shoulders in his jacket, looking chagrined. "Of course, you will."

"Joshua, I'm so—"

"No, you're right to end this, it's for the best." He gave a quick nod of his head, turned, and walked briskly toward Charles Street.

She tugged at a button from the wrist of her glove and it pulled off, slipped through her fingers to the ground, and danced around the hem of her skirt. A limp nub of thread marked the spot where the button had been attached; she pulled at the loose thread, and it came out easily, leaving no mark that it had ever been there. She bent over to pick up the button and stared at it, thinking of the night of the Christmas ball. That evening felt like a lifetime ago. She wound up her right arm and threw the button far into the lagoon.

"WHAT A SURPRISE—DO you need a place to ride out the storm?" Alice took May by the arm and led her to the drawing room.

May winced at a crash of thunder overhead. She had barely made it to Alice's front door before rain began to fall furiously. "My life is a storm, I'm afraid." She went on to describe her encounter with Joshua in the park as a maid entered the drawing room with a steaming teapot and a tray of sandwiches. The maid placed it all down on a marble-topped table and proceeded to pour them both cups of tea.

Once she left, Alice stood and walked over to a cabinet to retrieve a bottle of sherry and two dainty crystal glasses. While Alice poured each of them a small amount, May looked around at the well-apportioned room and suppressed a pang of envy—a Sèvres vase on the mantel, exquisite Flemish china statuary on the bookshelf, three Chinese fans hanging artfully on the wall. Why did Father take transcendentalism so much further than his colleagues? Why did he have to take *every-thing* so much further than *everyone*? Sitting in Alice's elegant drawing room, May could almost imagine what her life would have been like if her family hadn't been all but exiled from Boston back when Father invited several Negro children to join his classroom. Even Bostonians filled with abolitionist fervor were not prepared to accept educating black and white children side by side.

The pungent smokiness of Lapsang souchong floated up to May's face on the steam from her teacup, and she savored the woodsy smell as she thought about Concord. Thank goodness for dear Mr. Emerson and his sponsorship over the years. If it hadn't been for him, how would they have made it through all of those lean years? Certainly Marmee's small inheritance wasn't enough. Driven from the city, her family had arrived in Concord at Mr. Emerson's invitation with little in their possession except the stain of scandal. After the tall philosopher would stop by for a visit with Father, a few dollar notes would appear on the mantel next to a vase. Mortifying, but necessary.

Alice handed May a glass of sherry, and they both sipped from their drinks. Rain lashed at the windows. "The Bishops are quite set in their ways. I can only imagine what Mrs. Bishop made of you."

"When she heard I sometimes visit the Athenaeum, she practically threw a conniption fit."

"Of course. She doesn't want Nellie to develop any ambitions beyond landing a prosperous husband. Perish the thought that Nellie could catch whatever affliction you've got."

"I don't think Joshua ever really understood who I am."

"Or maybe you're just starting to understand who you really are."

May nodded slowly, but Alice gave her no time to ponder the remark and continued briskly, "Well, he'll be a good sort for the right woman." She gestured toward the serving plate's stack of sandwiches. "Try the one with cucumber and pear."

May studied the luxurious soft white bread and took a bite. The tanginess of mint filled her mouth, and she smiled.

"So, what will you do now?" Alice asked.

"That's why I came to see you. I've been thinking—"

"A thinking woman? Sounds dangerous." Alice sat upright with a broad grin and leaned in.

Part 2
April 1870–February 1873

Europe

Chapter 10

*M*ay awoke to the sound of groaning. It took her a moment to realize the sounds of misery had come from her. *Lafayette's* lurching, rolling, and creaking convinced her the ship was on the verge of disintegrating, a thought that left her shivering in a cold sweat. When Marie, their stewardess, showed them the features of their stateroom the day before, she'd pointed out a bucket discreetly tucked under the sink. Now May fumbled in the dark to retrieve it with desperation. The ship's violent rocking created a disorientation that made it impossible to locate the direction of the floor. She clambered out of her bunk and landed with a thud, hitting her elbow as she went down. She crawled along in the darkness, and her knee hit up against something.

"Ouch!"

"Louisa?"

A moan confirmed her sister lay on the floor of the cabin. A pungent sour smell indicated where the bucket stood and that her sister had beaten her to it. May huddled in beside her and used the bucket to vomit.

The voyage had begun innocently enough the day before. When May, Louisa, and Alice stood on *Lafayette*'s deck, both the mother-of-pearl sky overhead and the leaden water below seemed to indicate an unremarkable crossing ahead. White handkerchiefs whirled around the ship's deck like snowflakes. Seagulls shrieked. The bristle of ship masts loomed over the low clusters of New York City's buildings. May longed for her watercolors to capture the steel-colored day. As the steamship pulled away from the docks, her spirits surged with anticipation.

"Next stop: France," she said, pulling Louisa and Alice close to her. The three women beamed at each other with the giddiness of embarking on a new adventure. It had taken almost a year, but they were on their way to Europe at last.

Sitting aboard the train from Boston to New York City earlier that morning, a sales boy had waved a copy of *An Old-Fashioned Girl* in front of Louisa, saying, "Bully book, ma'am! It just came out this morning. Better get one. I've been selling tons all morning!"

John Pratt, who had been escorting his sisters-in-law to their ship, had stifled a chuckle. "Believe it or not, but you're addressing the author of that very book."

The freckled young shaver had looked back and forth from Louisa to the book in his hand. "Really?"

"Yes, it's my latest, but you're not to go telling everyone on this train that I'm here, do you understand?" Louisa had handed him a few coins to ensure his loyalty.

"Thank you, ma'am. I won't breathe a word." The boy had left them looking suitably impressed.

The encounter with the newsboy put the travel party in high spirits. Those same high spirits seemed like a lifetime ago to May now as she hunched over the bucket.

The door opened to reveal Marie surrounded by a dingy morning light. Somehow she carried a tray tinkling with clattering china. The smell of butter and fragrant black tea made the sisters bump their heads together over the bucket and retch.

Marie peered in at Louisa and May, shaking her head. "Hmm, I'm afraid we're experiencing some dirty weather today."

"How in the world did you manage to carry the tray while this infernal ship is bucking about?" Louisa lay on her back next to the bucket on the floor. May looked at her sister's wan face surrounded by stringy hair and assumed she looked no better.

A steep roll of the ship sent a hairbrush sliding down the length of the enameled sink to hit May on the back of the head as she kneeled over the bucket again. "Can you die of seasickness?" Her voice echoed off the edges of the bucket.

"*Mademoiselles, je suis désolé.* Being seasick is miserable, but I'm sure it will pass in a day or so. As we reach deeper waters off the coast of Newfoundland, conditions settle down." She handed Louisa a small teacup of weak tea, only half-full in consideration of the ship's violent movements. "We need to get you shipshape. Your fans have been waiting outside this door since yesterday, hoping to get an audience with you."

"No visitors," Louisa groaned. "Just *please* get this god-awful ship to stop rolling."

The next few days were spent in a state of constant nausea for both May and Louisa, although somehow Alice remained unaffected by the high seas and would pop her head in occasionally to check on them. *I just need to make it to Paris*, May chanted in her head as she lay in her berth swallowing back nausea. *Paris. Paris. Paris*. Days slid into nights that slid back into days. By day five at sea, May awoke and found herself hollow and light-headed from hunger. When she ran her fingers along her ribs under her nightgown, her stomach felt concave and stripped of any extra flesh.

Louisa remained incapacitated and wrapped in sheets like a mummy in a tomb. "I hurt all over," she moaned from underneath a swaddle of blankets. "The sooner I get off this boat, the better. They have named boats *Malta*, *Africa*, and *Oceania*. This one should be rechristened *Nausea*."

May tucked into a bowl of porridge before dropping out of her berth on weak, shaky legs. Her reflection in the small mirror above the washing bowl appalled her. She wanted to burn the filthy nightgown she had been wearing for close to a week. Marie helped to dress her in a navy blue skirt and gray jacket of boiled wool.

"I need to get outside—isn't sea air supposed to be restorative?" May asked. Marie nodded and led her out the door to the empty hallway. "Where are all the girls? They've given up their vigil?"

Marie's face puckered with concern, and she followed May out of the stateroom, shutting the door behind her. "I don't want to alarm your sister."

"About what?"

Marie's gaze traveled up and down the corridor before landing on May. "There's a smallpox outbreak aboard the ship."

"Smallpox? Are you sure?"

"I'm afraid so. The captain recommends passengers remain in their staterooms as much as possible. Go to the deck for some air, but then come back here straightaway. Talk to no one."

"Miss Bartol is fine?"

"She is."

"I'm worried about my sister, she's so weak already. She cannot get the fever." Fear stabbed at May.

"I know. Hurry back."

Only when May was outside on the deck did she realize she had been holding her breath since leaving Marie. She clasped the rail, feeling depleted and raw in the bright sunshine. The sky was a clear blue with thin clouds lining the sky like fish bones. A breeze tugged at her hair and pulled at the rim of her bonnet. A keening sound hummed in the distance, but it took May a moment to register it. The ship was too far out into the middle of the Atlantic to have seabirds squawking overhead. She squinted her eyes against the day's brightness, looking fore and aft. A cluster of people stood at the stern of the ship around a man who hoisted a small white parcel over the railing of the ship and flung it overboard. It fell toward the water, turning end over end in slow circles until it dropped into the sea in a halo of white foam before vanishing below.

She let out a small cry of horror when she realized what she had just seen: a body buried at sea. Judging by the compact size of the package, it was a child. Another rectangular package was hauled over the side. The second bundle tumbled down into the ocean below. And then it happened again. After the third body dropped overboard, she could hear a smattering of voices raised in a hymn. The group dispersed and moved back inside the ship.

May looked at the ocean with fresh eyes. She had floated above it all, thinking only about what lay ahead, with little thought of all that lay below. Now she understood that underneath the smooth sheet of blue lay all sorts of beauties and horrors: fish, monsters of the deep, debris, wrecked ships, and bodies. There was a whole other world underneath her with a landscape of its own. Although the surface looked placid and lovely, she was surrounded by an unexpected wilderness, dangerous because of its seeming innocuousness. She wondered if their voyage was too ambitious. Perhaps she should have stayed in Boston and led a comfortable life as Joshua Bishop's wife.

She turned and hurried back inside. On her way to their stateroom, she passed the ship's rheumy-eyed physician. His shoulder knocked into hers, leaving her enveloped in fumes of rum as he staggered by her in a path as crooked as a Virginia fence line. May picked up her skirts and ran directly to their stateroom, slamming the door behind her.

"Why did you do that? I was sleeping," Louisa mumbled, opening one eye to squint up at her sister, who leaned against the door, panting.

"Sorry, I lost my balance and knocked into the door."

Louisa didn't notice the tremor in May's voice and rolled onto her other side. Within moments, she was lightly snoring.

May steadied the shaking in her hands with deep breaths and sat on the bench to watch over her sister.

THERE WAS A faint rapping at the door. May opened it to see Alice looking jubilant.

"Good news, the coast of France is visible. We'll be in port soon."

May's legs wobbled as relief flooded her. She grabbed for the doorframe. "Thank God."

Alice frowned. "Have you gotten any sleep?"

May shrugged. She couldn't remember the last time she had slept. Even in the dark, she had stared ahead, listening to her sister's even breathing. The last five days had been spent watching her sister for any sign of fever. Every time Louisa emerged from her bundles of bedding, May inspected her sister's face, looking for any of the telltale signs of rash. It seemed they had been spared.

After ten days at sea, Louisa hobbled off *Lafayette* between Alice and May, determined not to give away her poor health to the assemblage of fans and journalists awaiting her arrival in France. She signed a few books for girls aboard the ship before the women looked for a carriage to take them somewhere to clean up.

May could have kneeled down and kissed the solid ground beneath them. She never mentioned the bundles buried at sea to anyone.

Chapter 11

May 15, 1870
Dinan, France

Dearest family,

I'm delighted to report that I'm in a perfect state of bliss. France surpasses even my most optimistic dreams. For one thing, the light here is suffused with a golden tinge that gives the gray stones of the village a lavender and rosy hue, depending on the time of day. You probably think I'm embellishing, yet Louisa and Alice both confirm that the atmosphere is extraordinarily picturesque.

Alice continues to be a perfect travel companion, although I'll never forgive her for remaining perfectly chipper the entire time we were at sea—a little sympathetic seasickness would have been appreciated by all of us who were flattened. She surprised Louisa and me by bringing home a bright green parakeet yesterday. He's a dapper little fellow and his endless songs give our apartment a jolly atmosphere, which is particularly pleasant for Louisa, who has been staying behind to rest while Alice and I sashay around town. (Anna, I've found a shop with kid gloves on sale for a mere pittance—I shall stock up and send some home to you.)

Alice and I discovered a swimming hole nearby, and we've been able to rent some donkeys to tow us in garden chairs to the small sandy beach along the riverbank. The only downside is that my stomach always ends up aching dreadfully from laughing so hard. I suppose it's a small price to pay for such a lark. Louisa has been under the weather with aching joints and insomnia but a local doctor prescribed some laudanum to help her.

You would not believe the lovely vistas that abound. Alice and I simply don't even know where to start with our sketching. There are some charming thirteenth-century ruins nearby called Anne of Brittany's Round Tower. From the top, we can see sweeping views of the village and valley below. Alice's hat blew off when we were up there yesterday, and we must have made quite a sight as we chased it along the gardens below. A viaduct said to be one of the best preserved examples of Roman engineering in the country towers above the village. I'll be sure to send along some sketches of all these marvels as soon as I can.

My favorite spot so far is the rue du Jerzual with its gabled stories of timbered shops crowding out over the

*steep and narrow cobblestoned street. It's here I'm likely
to encounter local peasant women clomping along in
their wooden sabot clogs and sweet-faced children in their
white Communion dresses and suits traipsing along after
a priest.*

*Despite all of the village's charms, I practically ache to
go to Paris, but we've learned that all of the master painters
leave the city during the hot months of summer. Fall will be
the ideal time to arrive in the city to study art, so I'm forced
to be patient. In the meantime, I'm working on my French
with an old widow from down the street whom Alice enlisted
to tutor me. The old biddy picks at her long, yellowed teeth
with a hairpin as she runs me through endless verb conju-
gations. If that's not incentive for me to improve my French
enough to be done with lessons, I don't know what is.*

Love,

May

The Pension de Madame Coste on Place Saint Louis became
their new home. Tucked next to the ancient fortified stone
walls of the medieval city, their new quarters provided a con-
venient location for the women to explore both the town and
the surrounding area. The spring air was warm and unusually
mild, according to Madame Coste. The fragrance of peaches
and peonies wafted up to the ivy-covered walls from the garden below. While May and Alice adventured, Louisa liked
nothing more than to sit in the salon window overlooking the
street. Farmers in straw hats and striped shirts trudged along

the cobblestones to escort their pigs to market. Priests, blessed with rotund figures, ambled to Mass smoking long, aromatic pipes. Louisa did not write a word, but simply sat at the window, taking it all in. Although she was paying for this trip, she could barely muster the energy to leave Madame Coste's.

When May suggested meeting with an English doctor who was staying in town, Louisa grimaced. "Who knows what ruinous measures he'll prescribe?"

"Hopefully more French wine. Come on, you must try."

In fact, the doctor recommended more rest and a prescription of iodine to treat what he suspected were the aftereffects of the mercury treatment Louisa had received following a nearly deadly encounter with typhoid fever several years earlier when serving as an army nurse in the nation's capital during the war. Soon, Louisa recovered her vigor and itched for a change of scenery.

By June, the three women left Dinan and crossed the country for the clear air of Switzerland. Once settled into the Pension Paradis in Vevey, they indulged in boating excursions along the lake and hunting through the area's shops for trinkets. May spent her mornings exploring the nearby countryside. One afternoon toward the end of summer, she arrived back at the hotel breathless after an alpine hike with some other American travelers and found Louisa and Alice in the hotel's tearoom.

"Goodness, I'm in quite a drip. As we got higher and higher, it just kept getting hotter and hotter." May dropped into a chair at a small table across from Louisa and Alice, pulled off her bonnet, and fanned at her face as she looked around the parlor's cluster of guests demurely drinking tea. "Hmm, perhaps I should run upstairs and clean myself up." She started to rise.

"Wait," Louisa said, reaching out to put a firm hand on May's forearm.

"What?"

Louisa exchanged a long look with Alice before speaking again. "Read this." She swept the pile of newspapers toward May. "The Prussians are on the move and marching deeper into France."

"Can this wait a moment? I really don't want to run into anyone looking like this." May looked around for a familiar face at the tables around them.

"No, this is serious." Louisa's dark eyes glinted down to the newspapers.

"Is this about the Prussians and the French? Isn't all of this nonsense confined to the Rhine? Why should we be worried? While everyone else is mad as hops, the Swiss have kept their heads." May brushed the papers aside and looked back and forth at her companions.

"True, but the papers are reporting that masses of refugees are beginning to flood this area," Alice said, fingering the edge of the lace tablecloth.

"But there are plenty of places for people to stay. Remember all of the lovely rooms to rent in Bex?"

Louisa leaned toward May and tapped her finger on the front page. "Bismarck just flattened Strasbourg, and he's now laying siege to Paris. It's inadvisable to visit the capital. The newspapers are reporting that Parisians are now eating rats to survive."

May opened her mouth but nothing came out. She looked to the row of windows along the wall beyond the hotel's guests idly gossiping over tea and sandwiches and could see Lake Geneva shining like a jewel under the relentless August sun. "Rats?" she asked in a tight voice.

"We must reassess our plans." Louisa spoke calmly and sat back, seeming to draw out the moment now that she had May's full attention.

The realization she would not be going to Paris dropped swiftly through May like a stone sinking in water. She willed herself not to cry. "So, what now?"

"Well, there's some uncertainty about money. I'm going to look into getting a line of English credit here because the value of the franc is dropping." Louisa crossed her arms and chewed on her lower lip, lost in thought.

"I'm going to England with plans to return to Boston as quickly as possible," Alice said quietly.

"You are?" May's eyes widened. "Don't you think that's rash?"

"No, I'd feel better returning home. And I'm not alone. I spoke with the Monroes and the Wallaces this morning—they're all leaving."

May sagged back in her chair defeated, all concerns about her appearance forgotten. The mere prospect of boarding a ship anytime soon made her stomach roil.

Louisa nodded. "Alice, I think your plan is a prudent one—"

"No." May dropped her hand on the table with a thump. "I will not get back on a ship. Not yet." Louisa and Alice looked at her in shock, and May gave them a defiant thrust of her chin in return. Who knew when she would have the opportunity to return to Europe again? It was bad enough that travel to Paris was impossible; she was not about to concede the rest of her trip. "Until Bismarck himself shows up at our door with a bayonet in his hand, I'm not going anywhere."

Louisa gave a weary sigh, but May thought she could see her sister hiding an amused smile. "Well, what do you suggest?"

May took a deep breath and looked around the room. Where else could she go to study art? Dresden, Düsseldorf . . . German cities were out of the question with the Prussians riled up over unification. Her eyes landed on a delicate gold cross resting on the collarbone of one of the women sitting at the table next to their own. "Rome. Let's go to Italy. Aren't they neutral in this whole thing?"

Louisa raised an eyebrow at her, and May shook her head in indignation. "Don't look at me like that. I haven't been completely ignoring what's going on. I just try not to dwell on bad news."

"Very well. I'm not opposed to heading south to Italy." Louisa took a sip of tea. "Spending the winter in a warm place will be good for my joints."

Chapter 12

November 10, 1870
Rome

Dearest family,

Rome has welcomed us with open arms. We have a divine view of Saint Peter's dome from our parlor's windows and a balcony overlooking the piazza and its glorious seventeenth-century fountain of Triton. The towering muscled merman and his spouting conch shell once delivered water in spectacular fashion to the residents of the Piazza Barberini, but I confess to being disappointed to learn that the far more basic and boring Fontana delle Api (in the corner of the piazza) was built when it became evident the mighty Triton sprayed water all over the women seeking to fill their water jugs on windy days. Apparently the Italians have a bit of practicality in them after all.

Our cook informed us that unknown corpses were carted out to the piazza below our balcony for public identification until the eighteenth century. Of course, this morbid historical fact made Louisa's dark eyes brighten up considerably. She's been sleeping better and barely even touched Dr. Kane's laudanum lately. I wouldn't be surprised if she begins to write again soon.

The other morning we awoke to find icicles hanging off our Triton. Fortunately we bought new furs in Florence, so we bundled up and walked the paths of Borghese Gardens and the damp halls of the Capitoline Museum while snacking on hazelnut truffles purchased from toothless old widows stoking braziers of roasting chestnuts.

I bought a copy of Mr. Hawthorne's novel "The Marble Faun" along the Corso and have delighted in following the custom of using the novel as a travel guide of Rome. Louisa has been helping me collect touristic photographs to insert in the novel at corresponding passages.

Rome's filled with treasures, and the fact that they're cracked and crumbling does little to diminish their charm. Around the piazza, a jumble of terra-cotta-colored buildings, all in varying states of deterioration, tumble on top of one another, but rather than giving off an aura of decay, the whole area seethes with daily activity. I've been telling myself that I must start sketching regularly, but I've been too busy exploring our new home.

Yours,
May

On a chilly morning late in November, May sat down at the table in the parlor for some coffee and toast. From across the table, Louisa flipped through a newspaper. American papers were always a couple of weeks old, but the sisters welcomed any news from home. Rain had fallen all night, and May huddled into her housecoat to fend off the unavoidable dampness permeating their rooms. She exhaled as warm coffee seeped through her body, but her enjoyment stalled when Louisa let out a small cry and clutched the newspaper, pulling it closer to her face.

"What happened?"

Louisa stared in fixation at the newspaper before dropping it to the table as if stung. "It says . . ." She spoke in a dazed tone. "It says our dear John Pratt died."

Louisa's words were slow to puncture the drowsy protection of morning, and May struggled to comprehend the news. "But . . . what? How did this happen?" Pings of rain tapped against the balcony's French doors. Lavinia, their housekeeper, mumbled to herself from the kitchen, as she yanked and tugged at swollen sticking wooden drawers. "Could it be wrong? Is it really *our* John?"

"It says he died of pneumonia and was buried in Sleepy Hollow. The paper is dated from November eighteenth," Louisa said.

May reached for the newspaper, but Louisa knocked it to the floor.

May burst from her seat and fled to the small table in the

corner and tore at the papers scattered across it. "Where's our mail? Why have we not heard about this in a letter already? How did this happen weeks ago without us knowing?" Her hands flapped over the desk and her voice rose in panic. "It seems like we should have felt this somehow. We should have been . . ." She shook her head as her voice faltered. "We should have been there," she whispered.

It was inconceivable to think they had spent the past few weeks visiting friends and sightseeing while their family suffered across the Atlantic. The depth of Anna's grief was unimaginable. May remembered the look of pride John had given his wife over newly born Freddy swaddled in his arms. Anna's cheeks, already flushed from the exertions of childbirth, had reddened even darker as she returned his gaze with a contented smile.

Louisa closed her eyes. "It feels impossible John's gone." She stood and walked to the French doors to look out onto the empty piazza. "Blast the Atlantic. I wish we were home now."

"Should we go? Go home?" A part of her hoped Louisa would say yes. To go home and give comfort to her family, to fall in easy step with what fate was trying to tell her. It was tempting to give in to the familiarity of home. At the same time, she hoped Louisa would say no. She wasn't ready to leave Europe, wasn't ready to return to her former life. *How can I feel such contradictions?* May pressed the heels of her hands to her eyes.

Raindrops sluiced down the windows, the rivulets mesmerizing Louisa. Color started to come back to her face. "No. We'll stay."

"Are you sure?"

"Yes, of course. Our sister is husbandless. She shall not be penniless."

"WEREN'T YOU FRIENDS with Anne Whitney back in Boston?"

"The sculptor?" Louisa's nose hovered a couple of inches off the page in front of her as she wrote furiously. Less than a week had passed since learning of John's death, and already Louisa was immersed in writing a new novel. "Calling her a friend might be a bit of a stretch."

"Was she not a member of your abolitionists group?"

Louisa raised her head. Her dull eyes, along with a smudge of ink on her cheekbone, made her look weary and battered. "She was quite a bit older than me, but yes, we worked on a few projects together. Her bossiness wore on me. She got all puffed up after her sculpture *Africa* became well-known."

"Apparently she's here in Rome now." May held up the newspaper she was reading. "This Boston paper mentions a small show of her work in a gallery on Piazza di Spagna. If you write me a letter of introduction, I'd like to go meet her."

"She's very serious and not one for social visits. I doubt you'll have much in common with her."

May stifled her impatience. Why did Louisa always think May lacked dedication to her work? "I can be serious about art. Maybe she'll have some ideas for me about finding an instructor."

"Why do you need an instructor? Just work on your own."

"But it has gotten so cold, I'll have rheumatism in no time if I copy in the Ludovisi. Remember how few of those tiny heaters were scattered around the hallways? I could use a studio. And it would be nice to work with some models. Finding an instructor really is the best way to do this. It's certainly the most cost-effective . . ." May's voice trailed off as Louisa gave her a long stare.

"I'll write the letter this evening."

"Thank you."

Without another glance, Louisa hunched back over her writing and continued working. May knew she was already blurring into the background of her sister's mind. May envied her sister's ability to escape her grief by burying herself in writing. Even in Dr. Rimmer's class, May had never felt completely absorbed in her art the way Louisa seemed to lose herself in writing. Responsibility weighed on May—she had to take care of Louisa, their parents, the care of Apple Slump. Somehow Louisa pushed aside all domestic pressures and thoughts of the outside world while she worked. Her single-mindedness verged on obsession, leaving her ill, exhausted, and difficult. May certainly didn't want to behave the same way, but nevertheless, she couldn't help but wonder: Did her lack of obsession make her less serious, less of an artist? She had managed to squeeze in some quick sketching sessions here and there, but it had been months since May had dedicated herself to a daily practice of creating art. Could she have lost all of the progress she had made in Boston? She needed to find out.

Chapter 13

Anne Whitney, a sturdy woman with white frizzled hair, greeted May into her studio on Via di San Nicola da Tolentino and gestured her toward a circle of chairs set up around a small table in a corner near the fireplace. "Addy?" She called over her shoulder toward the back of the studio. "Remember my friend Miss Alcott, the writer? Come and meet the other Alcott sister." She turned back to May, revealing spatters of clay dotting her black silk dress. "Sorry, for the spartan entertaining quarters. I don't like to host salons when I should be working."

May, with her fair hair curled into ringlets running down her spine, realized she probably looked as though she was on her way to a salon. In her navy blue silk dress bedecked with fashionable braid trim (to hide a fraying hem) and a purse that coordinated too much with her outfit—no doubt she resembled a dilettante. She regretted spending so much time at her toilette, but then shook off her doubts. What was she supposed to do? Smear some paint on her dress to make her more acceptable to Miss Whitney? She sat up straighter and smoothed down the bodice of her dress, ignoring Anne's impatient greeting. "You have a pleasant spot. The lighting is good."

The walls were crowded with lithographs, photographs, and sketches, some framed, others simply tacked up. A damp, earthy smell of clay hung in the air.

Anne eyed May suspiciously as if she could see right through her. "Where are you two living?"

"We took some rooms off the Piazza Barberini."

Anne raised her bushy eyebrows. "You picked a fashionable area." She said it in a tone that implied fashion was to be avoided at all costs. "It took us a while to figure out renting an apartment is the most economical way to live around here. We used an American agent. I don't trust the Italians as far as I can throw them."

May ran a hand over her mouth to hide a smile; Anne's broad shoulders and stout build made the sculptor appear to be quite capable of giving most Italians a sizable toss. "A friend of ours recommended the neighborhood."

Anne narrowed her eyes. "Who?"

"George Healy. He painted my sister's portrait when we first arrived."

"Did she like the final painting?"

"Oh, yes, she took quite a shine to him. He has such a lively studio." A visit to Mr. Healy's studio always promised great fun, for he regaled the sisters endlessly with gossip about everyone in Rome. Unfortunately for May, demand for his portraiture services prevented him from offering lessons. "Since we will be staying here for a bit while Louisa writes a new book, I'm looking for some art instruction. Do you know of anyone offering lessons?"

"Well, there's young Frederic Crownover from Boston. He's part of a three-ring circus involving many of the male artists over on Via Margutta." Anne looked dour. "It's a wonder he has any time to paint. These men, they're a bunch of rowdies, but I've heard he takes students. Or he may know of someone else who does."

The conversation was interrupted by a younger woman joining them. She wiped her charcoal-smudged hands on a rag, smoothed down her dark hair, and gave May a kind smile. Anne introduced her as Adeline Manning.

"Shall we give her a taste of home?" Miss Manning asked Anne.

The older woman gave a gruff assent. "Loretta can make a serviceable Indian pie." Sure enough, their Italian maid brought out a round dish of corn bread. "I've been working with her to create a repertoire of American foods for us to eat. How do you find the food here?"

"I like Roman food more than I liked French food, though when we first arrived, we tried some of those restaurant meals that arrive in tins."

"Those can be pretty dreadful," Addy said, with a sympathetic grimace as she took a seat next to May.

"True, they inspired us to find a housekeeper, who is a marvelous cook. I've become quite addicted to eating the artichokes our Lavinia prepares."

"I'm not sure saying Italian food is better than the Frenchie's is saying much." Anne leaned back while she waited for Loretta to slice up the corn bread. Their housekeeper handed out pieces of bread with a blank expression while the American women talked about Louisa's recent successes for several minutes. "So, your sister wrote that you paint. What kind of painting do you do?"

"Mostly watercolor landscapes."

"Watercolor landscapes?" Anne stopped with a forkful of corn bread midway to her mouth. "And what do you bring to these?"

May wondered what in the world she was supposed to say.

"Well, what's the *point* of your landscapes? Are you experimenting with a new composition or technique? Anyone can paint watercolor landscapes."

Addy gave a scolding look to Anne, who ignored her.

May wanted to rise and leave without saying another word. Visiting this old harpy was a terrible idea. Did May need a political cause behind her art? A message about the state of humanity? "I'm trying to record the beauty of what's around me," she said lamely.

"You're going to need more than a wishy-washy idea of beauty if you're really trying to make a career as an artist." Several crumbs of corn bread remained caught in the white whiskery hairs above her upper lip, and Addy leaned in toward Anne, brushing the crumbs from the older woman's face gently. Anne tossed her linen napkin onto the table and rubbed at her fingers as if to emphasize that the physicality of sculpture was exhausting. More exhausting than painting, of course. "Now, let's take a tour of my studio. I have important work to show you."

WHEN SHE RETURNED home that evening, May picked at her dinner while Louisa sat at her desk, massaging her left shoulder with her right hand. "These awful steel-nibbed pens are making my right thumb go numb, so I've taught myself to write with my left hand. It's still a little awkward, but I'm getting better."

May looked over at the handwriting on the page in front of her sister and saw it was legible—a bit of a scrawl, but definitely legible.

"Now I can switch back and forth between hands. When one gets tired, I just switch to the other."

"So now you really can write all day and all night." May rubbed her temples. "Come on, take a break with me."

The two women curled up on the love seat in front of the fireplace. May took her sister's feet onto her lap and massaged some circulation into them.

"Did you get a letter of introduction for Crownover?"

"No, I couldn't take a single favor from that woman. I'll figure something out."

"You can be too proud. She could help you, if you let her."

"I know, you're right, but I just couldn't help myself. Anne was tiresome, but the thing is . . . when I looked at her sculptures today, I felt so . . . so inconsequential."

May thought back to the moment earlier in the day when

the sculptor had pulled a clay-streaked cloth off a lump on the table in her studio to reveal the figure of a seated old woman carved in clay. Anne spluttered her disgust at how the Romans frittered away money on building one palazzo after another while ignoring the needs of the poor and elderly. "That money—*church* money"—Anne had shaken a fist as she spoke—"the Papists should be using it to serve those in need. These Papists are a load of hypocrites."

The Catholic excesses in the city went against everything in May's Protestant upbringing, but still, she could not help but be fascinated by the pomp of the ceremonies, and the endless *festivals* clogging Rome's streets, and the mangy relics. (*Really, how many digits did some of these saints have? And how many pieces of the cross could there possibly be?*) She loved to sit in the pews of Rome's many cathedrals and stare up at the *putti* flitting around on a soaring dome overhead. She would imagine herself back in the Renaissance and feel the awe a peasant from the countryside must have felt when entering one of these magnificent buildings for the first time. Yes, it was all overdone, but May could see why people believed in God when she absorbed the beauty of Rome's churches and cathedrals.

May grabbed a poker and stoked the fire from her spot next to the fireplace. "It's just that she's creating work of importance. It's all infused with meaning and morality, it all has a message. And I've just been scratching away at landscapes." She closed her eyes, trying to find comfort in the warmth of the blaze across her face.

"Being political all of the time is overvalued. Look where it took Father."

"I know. And really, it's just not in me to be political. All I want to do is create beauty."

"So? Create beauty. The world needs more of it." The embers crumbled, and the fire shifted and sighed. A series of cat screeches outside of the window pierced the night.

"Miss Whitney pegged me as a mere dabbler."

"Don't mind her. Anne's always been self-important. Back in the day, she'd carry on at those abolitionist meetings endlessly. She was a poet at the time. Few people think they're more profound than poets." Louisa chuckled and turned away from May, her face hidden in the dark. "This fellow Crownover will accept you. People always want to help you."

"Me? People are interested in *you*. I'm merely the other Alcott."

"I'm famous for writing a book I would never have chosen to write. And everyone expects to meet Jo March when they meet me. Then they see I'm not the vivacious girl they've pictured. I'm old and plain and certainly not as pretty as you." She pulled her feet off May's lap and wrapped her arms around her knees. "And now I'm giving them even more with this new manuscript."

"More of what?"

"More reasons to lurk in our yard staring up at the door, more reasons to flood me with requests to baptize babies. More reasons to meet me and be disappointed with what they find, I suppose. I'm continuing with the character Jo March, and she has started a school with her husband. I'm thinking of calling it *Little Men*."

"Is Amy March in this one?"

Louisa sighed and leaned her head against the back of the couch. "I'm sorry you've never liked her."

"But do you really think I'm like her?"

Louisa stretched her arms over her head and shuddered as several joints cracked. "I needed a comedic character, a foil to Jo. Using Amy seemed like a good idea. You've always been so golden, so popular, so resilient. I didn't think you'd mind. Don't forget every sister, with the exception of Beth, has some humbling moments in the story. You've taken Amy March too personally. So, to answer your original question, no, Amy March isn't in this story. You're free to live your real life. No more fiction."

May contemplated a life without *Little Women*. Where would she be if Amy March did not exist? Probably back in Concord calling one of her old Art Club meetings to order. Although May hated to admit it, Louisa's book set her off on a path from which there was no deviating now that she understood what was possible in the world. "You must enjoy your success and stop worrying."

"But that's impossible while you all depend on me."

Louisa's matter-of-fact words woke May to the reality of their situation as if she had been carried outside and dumped into the icy waters of the Triton fountain. Louisa was at the center of the family; her income supported them all. As Anne

Whitney had made all too clear, May was out of her depth and depended entirely upon her sister. Her parents did, too. Father's lectures received fresh life from Louisa's rise to literary fame; on his lecture pamphlets, he always made sure to include wording to emphasize he was the father of the famous authoress. And now Anna and her children were dependent.

"Once I'm an artist, I'll be able to help the family out, too. I really will."

"But aren't you an artist now? When will you—as you say—*become* an artist?"

May fiddled with the fabric of her skirt. "I need more training."

"We all probably need more training. At a certain point, you just have to move forward and hope for the best. You have talent. For more than just art. I envy your ability to rise along over the waves that threaten to tug the rest of us down. You're unsinkable."

May pulled at a tassel on the shawl around her shoulders. There was so much she did not know how to do. The reviews of *Little Women* made that clear to her, and everyone else, for that matter. When would she feel ready to declare herself an artist? When would the moment of transformation occur? At what point would she feel as though she knew what she was doing? The first time she sold a painting? May tried to think back to a demarcation between Louisa's dreaming of being a writer and when her ambitions were realized and could come up with nothing.

Chapter 14

May searched the placards next to each door along the Via Margutta, pushing tentacles of ivy away from house numbers on the ocher-colored stucco walls. Planks of wood leaned next to a doorway, waiting to be hammered into canvas frames. The clink of chiseling emerged from an open window. The neighborhood boasted a long history dating back to the Middle Ages of being an enclave of artists and craftsmen from all over Europe. When she found a small tile painted with *F. Crownover* next to a dark green door, she almost did a jig, right there on the cobblestoned street.

It seemed mad to simply show up at the doorstep of his studio, but she took a deep breath and knocked anyway. A young man with dark blond hair and a Vandyke beard answered the door and raised his eyebrows at her.

"Good day, I'm looking for Mr. Crownover."

The man appeared perplexed, but grinned good-naturedly. "Well, look no farther. You've found him." The artist signaled

May to come in as she spoke. Behind him, on a white sheet, a plump gurgling baby lay on his back, perched on a long table. "My son is modeling for me today," he explained. An attractive woman with copper-colored hair pulled into a chignon appeared at his elbow.

"How do you do? I'm May Alcott, from Boston." May paused, unsure how to proceed, and looked down at the baby trying to wrangle a pudgy foot into his mouth. "I . . . I'm spending the winter here in Rome and am looking for some art instruction."

Crownover shook his head. "Sorry, I don't take students."

May blinked and struggled for something to say. She needed this plan to work. She couldn't leave empty-handed.

His wife stepped forward, looking intently at May. "Your last name is Alcott? Did you say you're from Boston? What are you doing here in Rome?"

May explained she was in Europe for the first time, traveling with her sister.

The woman nodded with a satisfied smile. "Welcome, I'm Helen Crownover. Frederic, we can't possibly leave a fellow Bostonian in the lurch. At least, let's see your portfolio, shall we?" She led May farther into the room with whitewashed exposed brick walls. "Tell us about how you got here."

May described her lessons in Boston and itinerary through Europe while spreading out her work. Mr. Crownover hung her best sketches on clips strung along the wall. May studied the selection of what he had chosen and chewed the inside of her cheek. *Were the lines too wobbly on her landscape sketches of the viaduct in Dinan? How had she never noticed the neck was* too long on that figure study from Rimmer's class—why had she included it in her portfolio? She tried to steal a sideways glance at the man to gauge what he was thinking.

He raised his hand to rub his beard. "I studied with Rimmer, too, before leaving for Europe."

"You two have such similar backgrounds," Helen Crownover said. "It seems a shame not to work together. Frederic, weren't you just saying how you wanted to teach?"

He looked at his wife in bewilderment. "I need time to work on some commissions at the moment."

"But it's so rare to have people from home knocking on our door for help. It seems the least we can do, don't you think?" Mrs. Crownover persisted, taking her husband's arm and leading him to their back room. "Miss Alcott, please excuse us for a moment."

May nodded, looking back and forth from husband to wife, grateful to find Mrs. Crownover to be such an advocate. While the baby continued to gurgle to himself next to Mr. Crownover's sketchbook on the table, she took in the well-organized studio. The windows were polished and free of smudges, allowing daylight to flow in. Several easels rested in a far corner. Brushes stood in clean glass jars on a wooden shelf.

After several minutes, the Crownovers reappeared. "I suppose we can work out an arrangement for instruction," he said slowly.

May brought her hands together gratefully, not pausing to wonder at his change of mind.

THE NEXT DAY, May returned to the Via Margutta to begin her studies with Mr. Crownover, but her new teacher steered her away from the easels in his studio and beckoned her outside.

"In Paris and London, art lives in the galleries and museums, but here, in Rome, it's everywhere." Outside his door, he pointed to a marble fountain with elaborate faces carved above the pool of water. "We can see the art where the artists meant for it to be. Rome is filled with constant intersections between art and daily life. And the sense of discovery and wonder that marks art from the Renaissance—I just love the energy of it." He looked at May for agreement. She nodded. Finally, someone who spoke her language!

Crownover led her down Via Margutta toward the Piazza del Popolo. The easy manner in which he leaned in to point out the carvings on a wooden doorway gave May the sense he was aware of his charm, yet his unaffected manner made it hard to fault him for his confidence.

When they reached the twin churches of Santa Maria di Montesanto and Santa Maria dei Miracoli, they went in the one on the left. The calls of street vendors and racket of carriages disappeared once they entered the hush of the sanctuary. Crownover described the artwork on the altarpiece and pointed up to the fresco adorning the cupola. As he described the technique used by Gimignani to paint the ceiling, he ran his hands through his hair, making the dark blond hair disheveled, tousled, and boyish. He walked up close to a carved altarpiece and traced his fingers along the lines of the figures. His whole being exuded a sense of tactile exploration and energy, and May was drawn to the disarming joy he took in discussing art. Here was a man who loved beauty as she did.

Her head swam with the mixture of the cloying orange-blossom scent of frankincense and vertigo from looking up at the ceiling. Crownover led her from the church as quickly as they entered, and they strolled back to his studio. In all this time, May barely uttered a word, so swift was his commentary. He spoke as if thinking aloud and left no room for questions.

When they arrived back in his studio, he handed her back her art box and gave a small bow. "I shall look forward to seeing you tomorrow."

May took it back slowly, making no movement toward the door. "Are we not sketching today? Or painting?"

"Not today. I want you to think about what we've seen. Take a long, scenic walk back to your rooms. Look around you. More than anything, we need to work on how we *see* our surroundings. Beauty is everywhere, and it's up to us to find it and communicate it in our art so others may see it."

"Will we sketch tomorrow?"

He gave her a mischievous grin. "Maybe." Discouragement must have shown on her face, because he nodded. "I believe you have a good eye. We'll be sketching soon, don't worry."

She nodded and took her leave with a small wave. Outside on the Via Margutta, a shaft of late-day sunlight cut a sliver of brightness along the stucco walls, giving the stucco a warm golden glow that masked the cracks and water stains. Ivy draped across the alley ahead connecting one side of the stucco walls to another, creating a dark curtain of graceful greenery. May paused for a moment, holding her art box to her chest, and looked at the patchwork of texture and tone created by the different planes of stucco walls facing into the alley and visible in the distance beyond. She could create several small landscape studies just in the space around her in front of Crownover's studio without traveling any farther to see a chapel or fountain. She smiled to herself.

OVER THE NEXT month, May and Crownover traveled the sights of the Eternal City together, roaming the sprawling Colosseum and exploring Saint Peter's Basilica. They also wandered down shopping avenues and sat next to markets, always on the watch for interesting subjects. They sketched studies of strings of garlic and crates filled with glistening piles of anchovies. May filled one sketchbook after another with scenes—both big and small—of Rome. Crownover seemed to know everyone, and they moved around the city with ease, singing out greetings in enthusiastic Italian to shopkeepers and café owners.

One warmish day in January, the two sat on their camp stools in the Borghese Gardens, overlooking the Temple of Asclepius. May peeled a Sicilian orange, and the sweet smell of citrus rose from the fruit as she split it in half and handed a portion to Crownover. He took it with a distracted nod and stared at his box of pastels as he put a slice into his mouth. They each chewed in silence.

May held up the final section of her orange and studied the light behind the fruit and how it made the veiny innards glow.

"It's a shame I've eaten this so quickly. The color of the fruit is so lovely. These slices could have been the subject of a quick still life."

Crownover grunted as he reached up to adjust his hat.

May munched the last of her fruit, watching as Crownover slowly set up his materials.

"You're unusually quiet. Are you feeling well?"

Crownover nodded morosely. "My brother Frank died of consumption a little over four years ago. Some mornings I wake up, and he is all I can think about. I'm afraid today is one of those days."

May closed her eyes briefly and winced. "Oh, I'm terribly sorry for prying. We don't need to work today."

"No, no, you weren't prying. How were you to know? And I actually feel better working. It's good to be in motion."

She thought of Lizzie and John Pratt as she looked toward the smooth water of the lagoon in front of them. The only sound around them was from a pair of gray gulls splashing in the water nearby. "I'm so sorry."

"Thank you. I left Harvard before graduation to spend time with him before he passed, but the experience left me . . . well, I think about him every day."

"Yes, I understand. One of my sisters died twelve years ago."

The two drew in silence for several minutes before Crownover spoke again. "I feel closest to Frank when I'm creating art. Sometimes I can fall into a state of creation where the work just happens on its own, as if a spirit is guiding me. These moments can be quite rare, but when they happen, they feel sacred. It always seems as though Frank is with me when this happens." He took off his hat and rubbed his hands through his hair. "Excuse me, you must think me maudlin. Don't worry, I'm not about to suggest a séance."

"No, I think I understand." May had never heard it expressed like that, but she knew what he meant. She had experienced moments like those in Dr. Rimmer's class and, most recently, a few afternoons in Dinan. Art simply flowed from her. She felt a heightened awareness of everything around her, while at the same time, she was distracted by nothing except for the work in front of her. "I try to find that feeling, too, but it's been a while."

"Yes, long spells can pass in between, but I persist. Sometimes I think I practice, not so much to advance my skills—although obviously this is part of it—but really, because I want to be able to tap into the feeling more often and hold on to it for a little longer." He shook his head. "I sound mad."

May laughed. "We're all a bit mad. You're in good company." The conversation comforted her, for now she was not the only one stumbling through the dark looking for an elusive sense of connection with the wider world.

Since Louisa was cooped up with her writing, May spent as much time as possible at Crownover's studio, not just sketching, but also socializing. She played with his two small children and taught Suzette, the five-year-old, how to jump rope. She sat in the studio with Helen and discussed life back in Boston while munching on small dishes of dried figs, salted almonds, and slices of crusty, golden bread dipped in olive tapenade, never stopping to contemplate if their triangular arrangement was becoming too familiar. Both women gazed upon Crownover fondly, but May felt no competition with his wife. She watched Helen carefully, the way a small furrow creased between her eyes as she studied a new canvas of her husband's and told him what she liked about it and the way she always brought her husband plates of food while he worked. May noticed how Crownover smiled when his wife threw back her head to laugh. If anything, spending time in the glow of the Crownovers gave her hope, and she allowed herself to believe that she could find a similar relationship if she just watched and learned from both of them.

She never was a devoted churchgoer. Her visits to the Unitarian Church in Concord were based more on being part of a community than an overwhelming preoccupation with dogma, but she understood the ecstasy pilgrims felt as they stood in front of Saint Peter's Basilica. May found religion in the form of art, and Crownover was her leader. She followed him with a thrilling fervor that terrified her, because she was aware of a shadow lurking in the brightness of her excitement, though it slithered out of sight every time she tried to scrutinize it. Reluctance drew her back from examining the shadow closely for she feared what it might reveal.

Chapter 15

At the beginning of February, Crownover announced he needed to work on his life-drawing skills for a commission he hoped to win, so he hired a model. The prospect of working from a live model made May's stomach flip in circles of anxiety, though it was an opportunity she had been waiting for since meeting Jane Gardner. When May arrived at the studio one cold morning at the end of January, she could hear Crownover talking in his small back room. The brazier burned brightly to heat up the room for the model. May's hands trembled as she set up an easel and took out her sketching materials. She tried to remember all of Dr. Rimmer's instructions on using basic shapes to create the human form.

Crownover emerged from the back room with a woman wrapped in loose drapery, snaking around her torso to reveal views of her décolletage and glimpses of her bare midriff before the fabric trailed off one hip and down her legs. May inhaled deeply, trying to still the apprehension she felt at seeing the woman's long bare arms and legs. She had never been so close to an unclothed person who was not one of her sisters and could not bring herself to look into the woman's eyes.

"Start with two trapezoids to depict the torso," Crownover said from his easel beside May. The model looked classically Roman with an olive complexion, long dark hair, and a solid build; she fit the proportions May had learned in Boston. Dr. Rimmer's system of basic shapes to delineate the head, shoulders, rib cage, waist, and hips all came back to her. May finished a rough sketch and nodded to herself as a sense of momentum unfurled inside of her. She could do this. Glancing toward the model, she sketched in the curve of the woman's breasts and hips. She paused to get the weight distribution of the legs correct before standing back to check her basic lines. Her sketch looked convincing. The only sounds were the occasional shifting of the model, as she adjusted to Crownover's commands, the occasional flap of paper moving, and the scrawl of pencil.

At the end of the session, the model stood on her toes and stretched her arms unselfconsciously toward the ceiling before walking back through the studio to dress. Crownover moved closer to May to study her work. She became all too aware of the rise and fall of his chest next to hers. She dared not look over at him and could feel her face flushing. With the model gone, she felt an awkward sense of intimacy arise between the two of them.

"You created convincing volume in these latter sketches," he said. May leaned in closer to him, under the pretense of studying her work. She breathed in his scent of coffee and sweat.

"Pay attention to which line goes in front for a sense of which body parts are closer than others." His finger landed on the intersection of where the figure's rib cage met her hips, but he turned and looked at May. She became aware of every square inch of her body. The boning of her corset stays dug into her waist; the lace on her collar made her chin itch. Her legs trembled under the swathes of petticoats and skirts.

The door at the back of the room sighed as it opened, and the model sauntered back in. As Crownover busied himself with paying the woman, May let out a long breath—her shoulders collapsed in toward her chest with exhaustion. It felt like she had not breathed for hours.

She packed up her art box and fled the studio, mind racing. Nothing improper had occurred in the studio. They worked. They sketched. They talked. Nothing would have been different if Helen remained in the studio. But then why did May's cheeks burn at the memory of Crownover looking at her sketches? Why was she imagining how it would feel to have his fingertips sliding along her bare waist, across her belly and downward? She walked the slick, rainy unfamiliar streets until an exhausted burning in her quadriceps replaced the nervous quivering she felt in them when she'd left the studio. Only once she felt steadied did she turn to retrace her way back to recognizable territory.

MAY BEGAN TO return empty-handed from shopping trips after forgetting what she had planned to buy. She would write a letter home but stop midway through, after losing track of what she wanted to report. Her new mentor consumed her thoughts. Each time they sketched from a model, May would feel the same charged energy between them that had occurred the first time, and the sessions ended with the same sense of ragged confusion. She told herself it was admiration for him, but she felt a little breathless when he pointed to the parts of models to explain how to pose a body. But her attraction was more all-encompassing than simply being enamored with her teacher; she felt certain they experienced a true meeting of the minds.

One afternoon he asked if he could sketch a portrait of her. He held her chin gently while turning her face from side to side to find the correct angle for his composition. He brushed some of her hair from her cheekbones, and her face felt branded from where he touched her. She felt sure he could see the questions burning through her eyes, but he merely tilted her head and spent an hour sketching her profile, while discussing a village near Albano he planned to visit that summer. May did not know what to think.

After countless invitations from Helen to visit the studio, Louisa finally stopped by the Via Margutta one afternoon to admire May's work. Walking home, Louisa said, "It's funny he's the instructor. To be honest, your work's quality is not far behind his. But I suppose it's the typical arrangement: man as teacher, woman as student."

May ignored her sister, but her fingers tapped the basket she carried impatiently. Louisa could complain all evening long, but May told herself Crownover represented everything she wanted: he created beauty and taught in a lively studio, surrounded by friends and family.

Louisa cut into her sister's musings. "I see the way you watch him. Don't let yourself be fooled into thinking he could ever be yours. He's married."

May stopped in her tracks. "I can't believe you would say that."

"Why? Because I'm wrong? Or because you thought no one noticed?"

May tightened her lips together and strode past her sister. "I know he's married," she said through gritted teeth.

"Good, don't lose sight of this unmistakable fact."

Louisa followed her down the sidewalk, but May whirled around to face her, seething. "Don't you think I know he's married? I envy him for it. I envy him for being able to be an artist with a spouse who supports him and encourages him. Don't you think I would love to have what he has?" May choked through her tears. "I'm not like you. I want to marry—I just can't find the right one." She was glad for the darkness of evening because it hid her tears, though a weeping woman on the street was nothing unusual within the daily dramas unfolding in Rome.

"Come now, no need to be so dramatic. You've had plenty of compelling offers over the years from various suitors. I'm still surprised you didn't accept any of them. And what of Joshua Bishop? He seemed to have everything you wanted."

"How is it that you always think you know exactly what I want? *You've* made things simple for yourself. You've frowned off any prospect of marriage and you answer to no one, but here you are writing about imagined romances! Don't you wish you had experienced any romance yourself?" Louisa began to speak, but May cut her off. "No, I will not end up as a cranky spinster like you, but I also don't want to end up like Marmee, educated and ambitious yet toiling away like a beast of burden. And then there's Lidian Emerson and Sophia Hawthorne. Think of all the intelligent women we know who seemed to think they had met their academic equal—we've watched them all end up frustrated and unhappy, relegated to domestic duties. By not marrying, you've taken the easy path of renouncing it all, yet you're *still* frustrated and unhappy. I plan to be happy and find someone who loves me *and* loves my art."

"You know it's not really that easy."

"Of course, I do. But I must hope. Or else . . ." May dropped her hands to her sides in resignation.

Louisa stepped forward and patted May's shoulder with contrition. "Am I really that difficult?"

May grimaced under her tears and wiped her cheeks with her handkerchief. "Yes."

"Well, I'm sorry. I didn't mean to get you so upset."

"I'll be fine. You always underestimate me."

"Believe it or not, but I know how it feels to be underestimated." Louisa let out a bark of a laugh. "I believe that's why I'm so cranky."

The two women walked on, but Louisa put her hand over her sister's when May reached for the front door to their apartment building. "Just be careful. Don't get caught up in anything you could regret with the Crownovers."

"I won't. I would never do something like that." Saying the words aloud helped to strengthen May's conviction.

"Of course you wouldn't."

Once May climbed into bed that evening, she closed her eyes and thought back through her string of suitors. Of course, there had been fellows back in Concord over the years, but none of them had understood she needed more than a pretty farmhouse with a view of the Sudbury River. All of them assumed she would put away her art once she married. Joshua Bishop had seemed so promising with his city ways, but even he didn't understand her aspirations. She hadn't fully understood them either, but now she did.

Meanwhile, the stack of paper for Louisa's new novel grew taller and taller with every passing day. May knew her sister would finish her book soon, and they would return to America. May's sketches showed improvement, but she wasn't ready to go home. Thoughts of Crownover overshadowed everything, despite her attempts to think of anything but him.

ONE MORNING AT the end of February, she arrived at the studio to find her teacher standing over some sketches. Helen sat in the corner looking out the window, idly thumbing through a newspaper. Little Suzette sat on the floor surrounded by some colored pencils and paper, while the baby lay on his belly gnawing on a stub of charcoal. A line of drool dripped from his mouth, sparkling like a string of diamonds.

"Helen, the baby—" May pointed to the self-satisfied grin on the baby's smudged face.

Helen cried out and plucked the charcoal away, prompting a wail of anger that reverberated off the walls of the room. Crownover glanced up at Helen in annoyance while she shushed the petulant baby. May moved next to Crownover and studied his sketches.

"I've landed a commission from Mr. Herriman to work on a landscape of the Colosseum."

"Wonderful."

"Yes, but when I suggested a historical scene, he criticized my life drawing."

The front door banged open, letting in a gust of cold air, and Mr. Vedder, another American painter with a studio several doors down from Crownover's, stuck his head into the studio. The two men went to life drawing sessions at a studio up the street one night each week, but never offered to bring May.

He nodded at Helen and May before directing himself to Crownover. "Hullo! Sorry, but I can't make it to Gigi's studio tonight."

"Too bad, it'll just be me and the Italians."

"Maybe Harville will go." Vedder shrugged apologetically and disappeared.

"Little good bloody Harville is," Crownover said to himself.

"You should bring May with you. She might like the life drawing practice, too," Helen said, her eyes on the baby.

Crownover nodded, squinting as he stepped back to look at his work.

"Frederic," Helen persisted. He looked up at her in surprise. "Bring May tonight."

"Oh, right." Crownover looked over at May with an unreadable expression. "It's usually only men. And it could be a male model. Do you want to go?"

Helen nodded encouragingly at her. "Of course she wants to go. She wants more practice, don't you, May?"

"I could certainly use more practice, but . . ." May looked back and forth between the Crownovers. His usual smile was gone as he watched his wife warily.

"You're not worried that it will be men, are you? If there's anyone who is confident enough to handle a room full of men, it's you." Helen's eyes glittered with steely resolution.

May was unable to decipher why the issue seemed to matter to Helen so much, but any misgivings she felt were overshadowed by a twinge of excitement to be with Crownover on her own. She tamped down the traitorous thought, reminding herself it was just a sketching session. Yet it was a sketching session with a group of artists, many of whom ran thriving art studios of their own. She would be in the company of some of Rome's most successful painters. Why not try it? There was the issue of the male model, but May felt confident her background in anatomy enabled her to handle it, although now she understood why Crownover never invited her to Gigi's. While in Europe, certain standards could be relaxed by an American instructor, but bringing an American woman to see an unclothed male model was a bold proposition. She forced a casual shrug. "Yes, I can go."

She watched Crownover carefully to see if he balked, but other than an initial pained look, he carried on as if nothing was amiss. Excitement prickled through her at the challenge ahead.

"I can feed you both supper so you can just go straight there." Helen appeared relieved. "Should we send a note to your sister so she knows where you'll be?"

"No need. Louisa's engrossed in her manuscript. I could sail back to Boston tonight and it would be weeks before my absence would register with her."

"Your sister's such a hard worker. She needs to take a break sometime and come and visit us again."

Crownover ignored his wife's pointed look at him and carried some canvases to the back room.

May set up to work on a landscape she had begun the previous week.

"Frederic is worried about this commission." Helen said quietly.

"Why? Are they still negotiating the terms?"

"No, it's his. But we really need it to go well. He wants the recognition."

In the almost four months May had worked with Crownover, he had not been awarded any commissions until now. May wondered if money was an issue. Her teaching payments hardly amounted to anything substantial. Based on a few of Helen's past comments, May knew she had brought inherited money to their marriage, and it was certainly much cheaper to live in Rome than Boston, but a tension had arisen between the husband and wife, and May could not discern the source of it. Crownover's other painter friends were always busy with various commissions and lived in grand rooms with attending staff while the Crownovers led a far more frugal existence by renting a modest apartment, avoiding travel, and relying on Helen's mother, who lived with them, to care for the children.

Helen's voice interrupted her thoughts. "Make sure he stays focused tonight."

"I'll keep us on track."

She gave May a grateful smile. "I know you will, thank you."

May resolved to focus her excitement only on the prospect of working with a new group of artists that evening. This commission was important to the Crownovers, and his wife had tasked her with keeping him working. Going somewhere alone with Crownover meant nothing. After all, he was her teacher.

Chapter 16

Later that evening, Crownover and May strolled down the Via Margutta to Gigi's Academy. A light rain had fallen throughout the day, and now patches of fog hung low, edging their way down the streets like little lost clouds. Having her mentor to herself stoked giddiness within May. She breathed in the chilly, damp air and shivered with excitement.

"Are you cold?"

"Not really. It's a short walk." In truth, May was on fire and welcomed the cool air.

"Take this." In one fluid motion, Crownover stopped, pulled off his wool coat, and swung it around May's shoulders. The wool collar scratched lightly against her lips. She dropped her art box, gasping as she wrapped herself deeper into the warmth—*his* warmth—and hugged it around herself. She practically skipped down the sidewalk to keep up with him. His eyes were fixated on the ground and distracted when she reached his side, so she checked her excitement, remembering her promises to Louisa and Helen. She resolved to think about art. Only art.

They entered Gigi's basement studio to find a handful of men milling around the room, drinking Chianti out of tumblers. The other artists raised their eyebrows at May's entry, but Crownover's introduction allayed any comments, at least as far as May could tell. Easels circled the model's space in a close ring. The room was a humid fug of sweat, wet dog, and the pinch of red wine. May reluctantly peeled off both Crownover's coat and her own velvet jacket and looked around for a place to hang them. Her eyes caught on Crownover rolling up his shirtsleeves, unbuttoning the top of his collar, and unfastening his cravat. She diverted her eyes from the triangle of skin appearing at his throat and hurried away to the hooks near the door to hang their jackets. With the door still open, May lingered, welcoming the cool breeze on her face before heading back to the easels.

She could overhear James Harville, the English painter, talking to Crownover about his new commission, but then the sound of her name floated toward her, prompting her to listen more closely.

"The woman is your student? Since when did you begin taking students?"

Crownover mumbled and shook his head, running his hands through his hair. "She's got a wealthy sister. I've been hoping to land a commission from her. God knows, we could use the money."

May froze.

"So, she's only your student? I could think of a few other ways to put her to use."

"No. Not my type."

Both men laughed.

She could not find her breath. It was like when she was eighteen years old and thrown from Rosa's back while jumping a fence. She had found herself lying flat on her back, staring at the sky, wondering if she was alive. The same shock paralyzed her now. *Crownover's only interested in me because of Louisa.* This thought kept repeating itself in her mind. Over and over. Each time, her lungs flattened a little more. Every doting thought of him she had entertained now shamed her. How could she be so naïve? Rage filled the empty space inside her. And Helen, a woman whom she counted on as her friend—was she a friend? All the times Helen encouraged Louisa's presence—it all became clear. Painfully clear.

A door flung open from the far wall of the studio and a shirtless man swaggered out, followed by another man with an eye patch, presumably Gigi, the owner of the studio. May guessed the first man to be the evening's model. Clad only in trousers, he had a swarthy countenance and a compact, athletic build with perfectly defined abdominal muscles. Since Rome's paintings and sculptures were the closest May ever came to naked men, she could not help but stare. He took his place in the center of the easels and reached down to unbutton his pants, kicking them off behind him while talking and laughing with one of the other artists. As she was standing in the back of the room, he didn't even notice her. Without being aware her feet moved, May stepped to her easel, drawn to the model, momentarily distracted from her anger at her mentor.

"Good, we've got Paolo tonight," Crownover said, smiling to himself as he arranged his sketchbook on the easel.

May seethed at the sound of Crownover's voice, but the other artists called out directives for the model's first pose. She turned back toward the model, not wanting to miss a thing. He remained engrossed in the painters in front of him.

The Italian voices all reduced to background noise as she studied the man before her.

He settled on a pose with one foot forward and a hand on his hip. From May's position, she could view him from the side and did not have to look at his face. This turned out to be a blessing, for he was not the type of model to look out over the heads of his audience with an air of detachment; rather, he made a point of trying to catch the eyes of artists and engage them with a rakish angling of his brow, a suggestive shift of his jaw, or an insolent flare of his nostrils. This caused a certain amount of involvement with his audience and prompted a steady stream of conversation.

A bead of sweat trickled down her hairline, and she tugged at the collar of her dress in a futile attempt to cool down. She cast an envious eye toward the tumblers of wine parked around the room but then thrust all thoughts of the stuffy room from her mind. She focused on the model and tried to summon all of the lessons with Dr. Rimmer to the forefront of her mind. *I have a job to do.* She ignored the distractions and absorbed herself in the long lines of his basic contour. He did not hold poses for long. Instead of a clock or hourglass, the only measure of time passing was the plummeting levels of wine in the dark green bottles on the benches surrounding May.

At a certain point, the tone of the room shifted. Voices became louder, the laughter raucous. The model turned, noticing her for the first time, and she found herself looking straight into the naked man's dark eyes. He reconfigured himself into a new pose, facing her straight on. A wolfish leer spread across his face, and he thrust out his pelvis toward her while throwing back his shoulders, spreading out his arms with open palms, daring her to look down to the line of hair traveling from his navel into the unmistakable bulge under the loincloth. Somehow May maintained an impassive gaze back at the man and sketched. Half-aware the other artists had abandoned their own work and were watching her, she refused to stop sketching. A sliver of fear wormed its way into her. She became aware of every snigger and chuff in the room and stood alone, surrounded by men, none of whom cared a whit for her. She tilted her chin upward and clenched her jaw; if they expected to frighten her off with some foolishness, they were sorely mistaken. Passion ignited in her as her hand flung across the canvas, tracing the contour lines of the model before her.

Without looking at his face, she sketched the model's basic form. In her mind, May repeated the instructions about grafting the bone and muscle combinations of the arm to the shoulder and torso. She sent out a silent blessing to Dr. Rimmer for spending so many hours of class drilling them on the minutiae of how the pelvis fuses together. *Ilium, pubis, ischium*, she breathed to herself to maintain a smooth rhythm.

When taunting May didn't elicit any reward, the men returned to their sketches with an air of disappointment. The model wasn't giving up so easily. For his next pose, the man gave a smug smile, and turned in the opposite direction so she viewed his tight buttocks. Transfixed, May ran a hand across her forehead and found it damp. She pushed up her sleeves as high as they would go.

A bottle stood on a bench near her with an abandoned tumbler next to it. She left her easel, walked over, and poured a glass, hoping none of the men noticed the shakiness of her pour and the droplets of bloodred wine that spilled onto the floor. A couple of the painters raised their glasses to her. *Salud.* May raised the wine to her lips, ignoring the haze of vinegar that overwhelmed her, stinging her nostrils. She took long, deep gulps of the stuff trying to slow her galloping heart. One of the Italian painters walked over to observe her canvas and nodded approvingly. She nodded back at the fellow painter and took another swig. With the tumbler emptied, she wiped the back of her hand across her mouth and returned to her easel. Seeing Crownover fully absorbed in the model made her fume. At the same time, confidence grew in her; her work was good enough for her to remain. She turned to her easel and continued to sketch, plotting the confrontation she planned to have with her teacher after they were done.

She pondered the nature of her accusations to Crownover

as she painted. What exactly were the charges she planned to level upon him? He used her for access to Louisa? It was hard to fault a man for trying to support his family. How about leading her on with advances? When she pictured the last few months in her mind's eye, she knew the advances were all hers. Maybe it was the wine, maybe her anger, maybe it was her increasing embarrassment, but now her strokes were big and loose. It felt freeing to simply lose herself in sketching.

And then, suddenly, it was over. With a secret cue they all seemed to understand, the model stood up straight and stretched. The men drifted from their easels to talk in small clusters. Harville packed his pencils into his satchel. May turned to say something to Crownover, but he was bent over, picking up some paper he dropped on the floor. She walked back to the coatrack by the door, trying to settle her muddled thoughts, but by the time she returned to her easel, her mentor had disappeared. She looked around the room. There he was, in the far corner of the room, huddled by the model. The two men slipped into the door of the office—without so much as a backward glance—Crownover's hand in plain view resting on the model's bare shoulder before dropping to caress the man's spine at the small of his back. May stared. The door shut behind the two of them. Perhaps the wine was making her hallucinate—but as her gaze traveled around the room, she could see nothing else amiss. Mr. Harville glanced over at her, smoothed down his thinning pale blond hair, and gave a hopeful smile. "Shall I escort you home?"

"Ummm . . ." May, still stunned by the sight of Crownover skulking into the back room with the model, could only stare.

"The streets are not as safe as London's, I'm afraid."

May nodded acceptance and lifted her art box. Harville appeared delighted by the possible dangers lurking in Rome's streets and stuck out his hand to take May's art box.

"Oh, no, thank you. I can carry it."

His smiled wavered momentarily, but he escorted her outside of Gigi's.

Once out the door, she inhaled deeply, shivering against the sting of night air traveling down her throat and into her chest. She felt hollow. In all her born days, she would never have foreseen the evening's happenings. While they walked, Harville chronicled a running history of each piazza they traversed on their way to May and Louisa's rooms. He appeared happy to lecture, and she was grateful not to have to comment. At her door, he paused before saying, "If you'd like, I'd be happy to take you to my favorite sites and tell you more about the history of the city."

"That would be lovely."

He stood up straighter. "Wonderful, shall I call on you this Saturday?"

"I'll need to see what my sister has planned. I can send you a note about getting an outing on the calendar."

His smile fell slightly, but he nodded, tipped his hat, and politely took his leave.

She closed the oversized wooden door behind her with relief and leaned against it before mounting the stairs. "I'd better hope my art is better than my read of men," she said to herself, shaking her head in disbelief.

Upstairs she found Louisa waiting up for her. "I'm done with my book. Let's go home." Louisa started to list out all of the tasks they needed to complete before leaving, but stopped when she got a good look at her sister's expression. "What's wrong?"

Depleted by the agonies of the day, May simply leaned an arm out to the doorway of her bedroom and turned to Louisa. "Dash it all, I barely know where to start." She decided not to mention anything of the Crownovers using her for access to her sister. That indignity was all too painful. "Suffice it to say, nothing indecorous was ever going to happen between Crownover and me."

Louisa stared at her sister in bewilderment.

"It appears he's drawn to strapping Roman bucks."

Louisa's eyes widened, and she clapped her hand over her mouth in surprise, before bursting out in laughter. "Oh, goodness. Dare I even ask how you discovered this?"

"Please, don't." May pulled a couple of pins from her hair. "Now, if you'll excuse me, I'm ready to retire—my emotional resources are exhausted for the day."

"I can imagine."

But before Louisa turned to walk away, May reached for her sister and hugged her close, resting her chin against her sister's dark hair and inhaling the familiar scent of lavender and powder.

"Oh, dearest girl," said Louisa from their embrace. "You'll be all right?"

May let go of her sister and put her hands on her hips. "Of course. It'll take more than a few shenanigans to bring me to my knees, but I'm ready to return home now. Good night."

Chapter 17

"Mama, we're hungry." Freddy looked up from the game of tin soldiers he played with his brother. Anna turned her head from the window, and her gaze wandered along the paintings on the walls and to the small vase of bluebells on top of the piano, before settling on her boys with an empty expression. They looked up at their mother expectantly and reminded May of baby rabbits with bright eyes and postures tensed, as if on the verge of lifting their noses to test the wind for predators. Anna said nothing.

May fixed a smile at her nephews. "Anna, stay where you are. I'll make them some supper. Boys, what would you like? Snail sandwiches? Perhaps a worm pie?"

They giggled. May's heart ached as she watched their thin knobby shoulders rise and fall as they bent toward each other and whispered.

She stood from patching a pair of Freddy's pants on the sofa and bent over to kiss Anna's dry cheek on her way to the kitchen. As May drew back, Anna looked up at her in surprise. Her once dark hair was now streaked with gray. Gaunt and distracted, sadness had settled over Anna like a shroud since John's death. May hovered over her sister and picked up the abandoned embroidery resting on Anna's lap. "This is pretty. I'll frame it when you're done. You've always had such a good eye for sewing."

"It's not much."

"But it is. You must keep with it." May stood up, turned to the boys, and clapped her hands. "Come on, fellas. Let's get some food in those bellies of yours."

Freddy and Johnny scurried ahead of her into the kitchen, and the smell of the baked beans May had started cooking earlier in the day wafted over them.

"Auntie May, did you put extra brown sugar in the pot?"

"Don't I always?"

Both boys looked up at her with bright grins and took seats on the stools next to the window. Johnny wore unmatched socks. Freddy's vest was buttoned unevenly.

"Freddy, come here, let me fix the buttons on your vest. See how they're crooked?"

The boy shrugged. "No one seems to mind."

"Well, I mind. You've got to look sharp, my handsome little man."

"Thanks, Auntie May. I'm so happy you're home."

May bit the inside of her cheek to keep a lump from rising in her throat. "So am I."

Their little voices nattered on while May turned and sliced

off some hunks of brown crusty bread. She had arrived back in Concord to find the town fully ripened with summer. Strawberries the size of May's thumb hung off bushes at the side of the road. The cucumber vines dragged to the ground under the heft of gigantic vegetables. Lush greenery swathed the yard. Yet in the midst of all of this bounty, her family appeared diminished and forlorn.

"Here you go." May placed steaming bowls of beans in front of her nephews before putting a plate of bread on the table. Each boy grabbed a slice of bread and dipped it into their beans.

"This is my favorite meal," Johnny said, his mouth full of food.

May held back from scolding him about his manners. "What about my carrot muffins? Last week you said those were your favorites."

"I like those, too. Can I pull more carrots from Grandfather's garden so you can make more?"

"Yes, after you've eaten." May crossed her arms and leaned back against the wall, watching the boys inhale their food. Anna never used to forget to make meals. Since arriving home six weeks ago, May barely had time for her art, so consuming were the household tasks that filled her days. After John's death, Anna had sold the house in Maplewood and moved back in with Marmee and Father. The household, expanded with two young boys, appeared to overwhelm Marmee. Her gait was halting and even the smallest household tasks created struggles for her. The only family member who appeared unaffected by grief was Father. If anything, he became sprier and more productive than ever. Clouds of white hair circled his head, immune to the forces of gravity. Louisa's success was feeding his own.

When Father and Mr. Niles had met Louisa and May at the docks in Boston, they rode in a buggy garnished with a sign on top advertising *Little Men*. The sisters, weary and reeling from another rough Atlantic crossing, had been besieged by fans seeking signatures of the famous authoress. Mr. Niles had fished them out of the crowd threatening to drown them and deposited the sisters on the back seat of the buggy; all the while, Father had waved and handed out pamphlets promoting his next string of lectures throughout Massachusetts.

Freddy's spoon clattered against the wooden table. "All done. Now can we go outside?"

"Yes."

"Can I bring a jar outside? I'm going to look for treasures." Johnny stood up next to his brother.

"Sure, here you go." May reached for one up off a high shelf and handed it over to Johnny. "Just be careful not to smash it."

"We will." The boys ran outside, knocking over one of the stools in their haste. Rather than telling them to slow down and pick up the stool, May simply watched them go.

LATER THAT EVENING, May left the kitchen through the back door and walked out into the warm evening. Streaks of movement flickered through the stalks of corn standing tall in one corner of the garden, and laughter floated through the air. Like a drop of ink spilled into water, dusk seeped across the orchard, darkening the air and reducing all of the trees and shrubbery into simple, flat shapes.

"Boys, come on in and get ready for bed. Grandmother is waiting to read to you both." She could hear the boys hushing each other into silence and the pattering of their footsteps stopped. "Oh, do you plan to hide from me? I'll find you." May raised up her arms and swooped into the garden as if she were a great owl, chasing them. The boys shrieked and pulled away from her outstretched hands, giggling as they jumped to their feet and tore toward the back door, vanishing into the house. She sighed, her enthusiasm feigned. Although she acted lively with her family, in reality, everything she had been working toward in Europe seemed to be drifting away from her. Here, the oak trees hemmed her in, the dust of summer weighed on her, and the repetitiveness of the days made her want to scream. Time stretched before her in an endless, predictable path of banal routines—preparing and cooking meals, cleaning up the same daily disorder of the house, and discussing the weather with neighbors.

Ahead of her in the dark yard, something glimmered on the ground, and May walked over to see Johnny's jar lying in the grass, abandoned. She picked it up and a croak echoed out from the glass. Something landed on her arm, causing her to shriek. A brown frog perched on her forearm, its little chest heaving in and out rapidly. She held her arm still and stooped over. The small frog leapt off her arm and hopped away across the yard into the darkness. "Go frog, go," May said, quietly.

IN EARLY AUGUST, Alice Bartol visited May on her way up to a friend's summerhouse in New Hampshire. May needed the visit desperately. The oppressive summer heat, her family packed under one roof—she felt on the verge of madness.

Alice said, "I find sketching trees to be terribly hard. It's just so difficult to get the lines of all of the branches to look natural and graceful."

"It is."

"I've missed you this summer. I've been visiting lots of friends from Dr. Rimmer's class. Sarah Whitman and I traveled up the coast to visit Elizabeth Boott—do you remember her? She's quite a beauty. Oh, wait, she wasn't in Dr. Rimmer's class when you were there. She joined while you were in Europe."

Alice stopped talking when she noticed May's weary expression. "It's been pretty miserable here, hasn't it?"

"Yes, quite grim."

"I'm sorry. Poor Anna. Her boys are darling."

"Aren't they? It's been heartbreaking to see her brought so low."

"How's Louisa?"

May groaned.

"That bad?"

"You'd think being the top-selling author in the country would put her in a fine mood, but it doesn't."

The previous day, Louisa had accused May of losing a mailbag filled with important correspondence. She had dragged

May up to her bedroom and pointed an ink-stained index finger at the mailbags lined against the wall. "When Father and I picked them up from the post office, there were *eight* bags. Now there are *seven*. See?"

She'd continued to rail about the missing mail while May searched the house, high and low. Father eventually located it in the barn—the bag was simply overlooked when they were all brought inside. But its recovery had done nothing to placate Louisa. "You're just jealous of all my success!" Louisa had stormed, slamming her bedroom door on May.

The worse part was that Louisa was correct; May did envy her sister. Cards with requests for speaking engagements and interviews littered the dining room table. Each day visitors arrived at Orchard House looking for the writer. May watched her sister's star rise with a sinking feeling of being left behind. Louisa planned to move back to Boston at the end of August, and the date couldn't arrive soon enough, as far as May was concerned.

Alice bent over her sketchbook to draw in some small lichen patches on the tree trunk. "You two make me glad I'm an only child. But listen, I've been looking forward to telling you some good news. There's this new fellow in town, William Morris Hunt. He spent years in France studying under Millet and Couture and runs a thriving portraiture business in the city. Beginning in the fall, he's offering art classes to women."

May looked up from her sketch pad.

"He's taking Boston by storm. We must get into his class," Alice said.

"What do we need to do?"

"Well, I won't lie—the whole process sounds rather intimidating. On September fifth, we must drop off ten sketches by nine o'clock and wait for our work to be reviewed. If he likes what he sees, we'll be called in for a brief interview and learn if we've been accepted."

"Only sketches? No watercolors?"

"Only sketches. He wants everyone to demonstrate exceptional drawing skills."

"My drawing skills have improved . . . but still," May said, holding up her worn eraser, "I have to use this more often than I ought to."

"I know. Me, too."

"But if we don't get in, we can always go back to Dr. Rimmer."

"Well, there's the rub: we can't. Rimmer left for New York City last spring and took a teaching job down there."

"So, this Mr. Hunt is the biggest toad in the puddle." May tapped her lip with her eraser.

"He's the only toad in the puddle."

May stood and smoothed out her skirt as she pondered preparing for her audition with Mr. Hunt. She winced, thinking about how she would need to move back to Boston if she got into this class.

"Are you all right?"

"Yes," May said. She couldn't let a few arguments with Louisa get in the way of advancing her art; she would have to make amends with her sister. "Well then, we must impress this man with everything we've got."

A WEEK LATER, May walked into the barn looking for nails to hang up some sketches on her bedroom wall, and she encountered Rosa, standing in her stall. The horse looked at May balefully. "I know you want a good long ride, old girl. Sorry, I'll get you out there soon." She rubbed her fingers over the horse's bristly nose, feeling the warm exhalations on the palm of her hand, before continuing her search for nails.

Since Alice's visit, May's bedroom walls had become covered with sketches while she considered what to put in her portfolio for Mr. Hunt. She would awaken at night, light her lamp, and sit on the floor with her work spread out around her. Her eyes burned from the lack of sleep, and she could barely stomach anything to eat. After all of the effort and expense put toward her artistic training, May could not bear to consider how she would survive the shame of being denied entry to Mr. Hunt's class. How would she be able to live with herself if she failed? But another question niggled at her: What would she do if she got in?

Chapter 18

*Y*our dress is terribly impractical for this weather. You'll arrive looking like a drowned cat," Louisa said. Rain sprayed at the windows of Louisa's Allston Street boardinghouse room where May had spent the night before her interview with Mr. Hunt.

"Yes, but wearing blue seems to bring me luck, so I shall stick with it and hope for the best. Maybe it will stop raining."

From her writing desk, Louisa sighed. "Your optimism will be the death of you. There"—she pointed at her purse—"take some money so you can take a carriage. And take my black umbrella."

May didn't even attempt to argue. The muddy streets left the morning's traffic in a snarl. She fretted about being late the entire time she sat in the hackney with her portfolio clasped in front of her. The cab's wheel got stuck in a pothole and pitched her forward. Her portfolio flew from her fingers and fell to the floor. She scrambled to pick it up and then wiped the sludge off the black leather sides. Once she was assured her work was undamaged, she closed her eyes and hugged it to her.

The night before, she had pulled up a chair to Louisa's writing desk. "If I'm granted permission to join Hunt's class, I'm going to move back into the city."

Louisa had dipped her pen into the inkwell and paused to look at May. "Now that we're back from Europe, you're in charge of caring for the family. I must keep writing."

Over the summer, Louisa had installed a new furnace to keep their Marmee's rheumatism at bay, so May felt emboldened. "What about hiring a cook and a housekeeper to help back at the house?"

Louisa put down her pen, crossed her arms, and frowned in response.

"What good is having money if you can't spend it on making life more enjoyable?" May asked.

"I hate spending my hard-earned money on stuff like that."

"Stuff like what? Useful stuff? Come on, we'll both be swaybacked old mares soon if we keep trying to do everything. Don't worry. I'll go out to Concord every few days."

"I hate the idea of servants' gossip. Soon the *Boston Globe* will be carrying stories about what I like to eat for dinner and what's in my dresser drawers. I can only trust family. You must do it."

"I cannot do everything."

"You mean you *won't* do everything." Glowering, Louisa

pressed her palm to her temple. "I suppose we can *try* the arrangement. But if the help breathes a word about me—*anything* about me—to the press, I'll hold you responsible."

May nodded her head wearily. Ever since they were in Switzerland and some of Louisa's discarded correspondence with her publisher led to some newspapers publishing accounts of her earnings, she had become obsessive about burning her letters. "I'll also speak to Father about filing his letters away instead of leaving them all over his desk."

Louisa gave an assenting grumble. "And where are you going to live?"

"I'm looking into taking a room in your old boardinghouse on Beacon Street."

"Nonsense, you will live here with me."

"But I've—"

"You have no income to speak of. You'll live with me." Louisa had bent back over her writing to indicate the discussion was over. May knew her sister to be correct; May didn't have the means to be independent. Not yet, at least.

The carriage finally rattled to a stop in front of Mr. Hunt's Mercantile Building studio on Summer Street. Inside, the hallways were crowded with anxious women. She turned in her portfolio and wormed her way out through the sea of bodies to find a place next to Alice for the long wait. May knit to occupy her hands, but it did little to still the anxiety slithering around inside her mind. The hands on the clock on the wall slowly ticked forward. One by one, names were called. Some exited Hunt's studio looking pleased; many left blinking back tears.

May's stomach dropped when Alice emerged from the interview looking gleeful. What if she failed?

How much more time passed? One minute? Ten? An hour? A year?

Finally May's name was called. A plain-faced woman gave a terse greeting at the door of Mr. Hunt's studio. "I'm Miss Helen Knowlton and serve as Mr. Hunt's deputy," she said, inspecting May with unblinking eyes. May kept her face composed but wanted to giggle nervously at the woman's self-important usage of the word *deputy*. "Please, set out your work for inspection."

May followed the woman to a counter, piled high with heaps of canvases, and lifted her portfolio onto a cleared-off section. She towered over the wisp of a woman. Miss Knowlton surveyed May's presentation of work from Europe with a deliberation that left May wondering if she underestimated the woman's jurisdiction over the studio. "You have a confident line and your drafting skills appear solid," Miss Knowlton said. May felt surprised by the relief she took in the woman's approval.

Heavy footsteps signaled the arrival of Mr. Hunt, and May turned to find an older, lanky man in a dark suit striding across the room to join them. While Miss Knowlton stood barely five feet tall with silvery blond hair pulled back into a practical bun at the nape of her neck, Mr. Hunt loomed a couple of inches over six feet tall with a long straight nose, balding head, and bright blue eyes looking out from over an unwieldy white beard that practically reached his chest. "Miss Alcott? Based on the landmarks in some of your sketches, it appears you've spent some time in Europe."

"I did. A year, sir."

"Yes, yes, I can see it made an impression on you." He pulled at his beard as he studied May's sketches. "European travel is always transformative for any artist. I myself studied in the studios of Millet and Couture. Those experiences left me a changed man."

She nodded, but Mr. Hunt looked up from her sketches expectantly, making her feel the need to say something. "Unfortunately, Napoleon's war changed our itinerary. We were forced to avoid Paris."

"Ah yes, it's a pity so many critical works were destroyed." He sighed. "And now the remains must be assessed, and Paris will recover. She always does. But still, what a senseless waste."

"We made the best of it and went to Rome instead."

"I studied art in Rome years ago. While certainly different from the fine ateliers and collections in Paris, it offers its own charms and lessons in art history."

"Yes, we made do in Rome, second-rate sorry art capital that it is." This flippant response somehow bubbled up within her anxiety; she froze as the words left her mouth. Miss Knowlton's eyes widened.

To her immense relief, the wrinkles on Hunt's face crinkled, and he gave a shout of laughter, pounding his hand on the table where her portfolio lay. "Ha! Quite so, quite so. Good for you. Don't let us get too uppity here in Boston." He continued to chuckle as he paged through samples of May's work, and then he looked up at her with a squint in his eye. "I like to see humility and a good head on an art student's shoulders. After all, artists and their pretensions hold no tender with New Englanders. Let me guess, did you study with Dr. Rimmer?"

May nodded.

"He can be a bit of a schoolmarm at times, but I daresay, he's a fine instructor. Did you hear he's teaching down in New York City now? Miss Knowlton, what's the name of the place?" He reminded May of an actor with a forgotten line, as he waved a hand at his deputy for a cue without looking at her.

"Cooper Union School of Design for Women, sir."

"Right, right, that's right. Well, your figures are true to proportion and configured correctly, but look a bit stiff. Nothing a bit more time with a live model can't solve. Your landscapes demonstrate a lively line and competent understanding of light and shadow." He turned to Miss Knowlton and nodded before taking his leave from May with a small bow.

"Well, there we are," Miss Knowlton said, tightening her lips into a line. She pulled a ledger from a drawer under the desk upon which May's portfolio rested and banged the drawer shut.

"This is a class exclusively for women. Mr. Hunt doesn't believe a woman's capabilities should be considered inferior in any way to a man's, and he's committed to cultivating the talent of the women of Boston. In this class, I trust you understand models are partially draped to maintain decency. All students will commence with drawing until they are granted permission to move along to oils. Once we have established you are prepared to start with painting, I'll begin painting basics with you until you're ready to join those who have already advanced to that stage. Mr. Hunt provides critique and general instruction to every student regardless if a student is painting or sketching."

"Thank you." May gathered up her portfolio with hands trembling in excitement.

"I believe you will find Mr. Hunt's instruction to be transformative. But I have a word of warning: your name precedes you. Just because your sister is famous, don't expect any special status within this classroom. You must earn your way ahead, like everyone else." Miss Knowlton's gray, unblinking eyes bore into her. Her complexion was pale, almost to the point of transparency, and threads of blue veins running under the surface of her skin were visible, giving the woman a cold, otherworldly countenance.

May opened and closed her mouth several times, but nothing came out.

"You may go." Miss Knowlton's sharp little chin bobbed toward the door. May walked out of the door, reeling. She did not see the faces turned toward her as she numbly walked down the hallway. Once she reached the stairwell, she paused and reached for the railing, realizing the task ahead. She needed to prove herself to Miss Knowlton, and presumably others. She would work so hard that no one would ever mistake her for Amy March again.

Chapter 19

May was assigned an easel at the back of the studio. From a spot at the front of the room, Alice waved to her. A few other women turned and nodded pleasantly as May winched her sketchbook into place. In the group of about thirty women, she recognized several familiar faces from Dr. Rimmer's class. Many of the women were surrounded by oils, whereas May only had charcoal. She hoped for a swift promotion from sketching to painting so she could sit at the front of the class with her friend.

A sudden hush fell through the ranks as Mr. Hunt strode into the room. "Ladies, please take out your sketching supplies. I'd like to see you do a drawing from memory. Don't agonize over the details. You have ten minutes to provide me with a view of something you saw this morning."

There was a flurry on all sides that reminded May of a flock of birds preparing for flight and then only the scratching of charcoal and rustle of paper. She stared at the sheet of paper in front of her. Her charcoal met the page, and she outlined a lamppost out in front of the Common and sketched the newsboy who always stood at the corner of Tremont and Park Street. Mr. Hunt prowled around the other side of the room. May dashed in some shading lines to try to illustrate the morning's stark light out on the street.

"Stop agonizing over every minute detail. Poetry is *not* in the details," Mr. Hunt called out to the class. "Consider the values of what you are sketching."

His steps neared May and paused behind her. "Where's the light? Where are the shadows?"

She sketched in the angle of the visor on the boy's hat, accentuating the bent line of it. Hunt moved on. May's heart pounded loudly in her ears, as she drew over her original sketch.

When the ten minutes were up, everyone leaned back from their easels and looked at the work around them. May's sketch pad revealed a tangle of blurred charcoal lines. Miss Knowlton passed by her easel, pausing to frown.

"Start with the line of the figure's balance first—don't muddle it in afterward. The contrast of his body line should be obvious against the straight lamppost. The central themes of any piece of work should not be treated as an afterthought."

May nodded in Miss Knowlton's direction, but wistfully watched Alice put away her sketch and take out her paints.

AFTER A FEW months, Mr. Hunt delighted his students when he announced the class would begin to work from live models. On the appointed day, a model entered the room wearing a diaphanous gray pelisse as a toga. The screech of wooden easels being dragged into position quieted as women positioned themselves around the model. May edged her easel forward, but Miss Knowlton stopped her.

"Miss Alcott, I'd like you to work with a charcoal study of this Dürer print. Please, think about value. Work your light and shade thoughtfully."

May took the Dürer print, trying to ignore the frustration rising in her.

A handful of women remained hanging back with May, working on studies clipped to the sides of their easels. Alice moved up to sketch from the model.

Tears pricked at May's eyes. She blinked them back and prayed no one noticed as she kept her head down. She ignored the ache in her chest and studied the Dürer.

When she got home that evening, she found Louisa lying in bed, reading a newspaper. May dropped her art satchel to the floor. Charcoal pencils spilled out of the top and rolled around her feet.

"It seems as though everyone is painting but me."

Louisa peered at her sister over the top edge of her newspaper. "Some of those women—Alice included—have been studying longer than you."

May glowered and withheld from telling Louisa about Miss Knowlton's warning before class. She sat down on the side of her bed and kicked a pencil across the room with her stockinged toe.

Louisa frowned as she read the paper. "Remember Anne Whitney?"

"How could I forget her? She made me feel dreadful about my art in Rome."

"Well, there's an article about how the Boston Arts Committee just denied her an award for a sculpture after the judges discovered it was created by a woman."

May began to unpin her curls and groaned. "How unfair."

Louisa climbed out of bed and handed May the newspaper. "I'm going to go visit her in the morning." She pulled a black velvet dress out of the wardrobe and smoothed the lace collar down before facing her sister.

"And the sooner you abandon the idea that life is fair, you will be more productive. This world doesn't owe us a thing."

MAY TRIED TO be patient and improve her skills. With the new year, Miss Knowlton finally—with a rather reluctant nod of her head, May thought—endorsed May's promotion from master studies to life drawing, but still, she wanted to paint. Week after week of that frigid winter, May huddled against her easel and created sketch after sketch while growing increasingly confused.

"Watch your semi-tones," Miss Knowlton would say, leaning over May's shoulder, pointing to a body part. "Don't be so aggressive with your dark lines."

"Attack your subject!" Mr. Hunt would say. "Be spontaneous! You should be less concerned about technique and focus more on your great idea. What truths are you trying to reveal?"

May drew and drew.

"Your proportions are off on this model. Not everyone has the ideal form you learned from Dr. Rimmer." Miss Knowlton would shake her head. "Draw what you *see*."

May ricocheted between Mr. Hunt's grand words of inspiration and Miss Knowlton's practical criticism and steered for the middle. She began to doubt all of her efforts.

"LADIES, PLEASE WELCOME our guest lecturer to class today." Mr. Hunt stood on a podium beside the model and gestured toward the front row of class. "This is Miss Gardner. She hails originally from Exeter, New Hampshire, but has studied in Paris for the last several years."

May leaned out from behind her easel, eager to catch a glimpse of the painter she met two years prior at the Williams & Everett gallery show. The same thin, dark-haired woman stood and turned to face the students.

"I must leave class in a bit to meet with a client, so you'll all have the pleasure of Miss Gardner's instruction today. In the meantime, let's get started. Miss Knowlton, please hand everyone a stub of charcoal. Not a pencil, a stub." Miss Knowlton darted around the room with a pail of charcoal castoffs. The glass rattled in the windows at the back of the room from February's gusty wind. May shivered and surveyed the nubby thumb of charcoal in her hand with doubt.

"You're all too consumed with details," Hunt said. "Use the charcoal to capture the essence of the model's basic line and values of light to dark."

All of the women who had studied under Dr. Rimmer balked at Hunt's commands and stared at their blank papers. The idea that details created realism had been drilled into them. How could they let that all go? It was like they stood on a beach being pounded with heavy surf and were expected to dive right in.

"Go on," Hunt ordered from the front of the room.

May pushed some stray hairs out of her line of vision, raised the stump of charcoal to her paper, and created a contour line of the model at the front of the room. She squinted to simplify the model to a range of tonal shades and got to work.

Perhaps half an hour passed. "Stop working. Please walk around and see the difference in what you have all produced by just focusing on the basics."

As a whole, the studies with thick charcoal were a truer representation of form and volume. A giddy sense of freedom overtook the women, and whispers replaced the silence of the room.

"Yes." Hunt folded his arms in front of him and looked down at his students from where he stood next to the model. "Remember, are you creating something believable and interesting? I once worked on a portrait of one of our esteemed judges, and a viewer attempted to use calipers to determine if my representation of the man's nose was exact. 'Sir!' I exclaimed, 'is Mr. Sumner's character confined to his nose? No measuring is needed in my studio!'"

The class laughed along with Mr. Hunt's reenacted indignation, and May realized no one—aside from Miss Knowlton, of course—appeared to be preoccupied with anything outside of Mr. Hunt and their own easels. The knot in her chest untied a little, and she took out a fresh piece of paper.

"Now continue working from the model but don't forget to continually consider the entirety of what you are attempting to depict. If we were striving for exact likeness, we could go down to Mr. Harold's Photographic Emporium on Copley and pose in front of a camera. You must search for the inner truth of your subject. And with that final word, I'm off. Miss Gardner, the class is all yours."

Miss Gardner nodded from a spot amidst the easels and called out. "Ladies, please keep working."

The model shifted her pose, and May started a new drawing. Miss Gardner continued to circulate around the room until eventually stepping up onto the podium. "With all due respect to Mr. Hunt's instruction, it seems some of you are pushing this new discovery of inner truth too far. While it's tempting to throw away those measurement calipers, clients will want to see something recognizable on the canvas when they hire you."

A hum of confusion ran through the women, and Miss Gardner raised her hands to silence everyone with a severe look. "When you're working with clients—and I assume it's your goal to make some money from this endeavor—you better demonstrate a firm grasp of being able to paint what is right in front of you convincingly."

A woman in the second row raised her hand. "Are you advising us to paint exactly what we see without any reflection of character?"

Miss Gardner gave a sly grin. "I'm advising you to find the balance between painting your subject with mastery and sensitivity. In other words, if a client hires you to paint a portrait of his horse-faced wife, you better find a way to make those horsey features attractive."

She began lecturing about lighting and perspective and quickly immersed herself in sketching from the model to demonstrate what she meant. Without preamble, she hauled another easel up to the front, explaining that she wanted Miss Knowlton to demonstrate techniques for posing models.

"Landscapes are my specialty. I'm afraid portraiture is not my forte," protested Miss Knowlton, looking at the podium reluctantly.

"Nonsense, I know your work. Of course you can teach basic posing strategies. Now please, come up here."

Soon the class was watching both women at work. A hush fell over the class as the women watched, mesmerized by the demonstration and Miss Gardner's tactical words of advice while she sketched. May suspected many of her classmates hadn't considered actually trying to make a living from their work until now. Mr. Hunt took all of his women students seriously, but he had never spoken so frankly about running a business from art as Miss Gardner did.

When class was over for the day, May walked back to her sketchbook and sighed at her attempts at figure drawing. She closed her strained eyes and rubbed at them.

"It's not that bad," a voice said. May opened her eyes to see Miss Gardner standing next to her with a hand on her hip. She pointed at May's sketch. "Look, if you work more on weight distribution starting in the lower back and pelvis, it should solve some of your figure's stiff-legged look."

May cocked her head and could see what Miss Gardner meant. "Yes, thank you. Today's lesson was incredibly helpful. To watch a demonstration—"

Miss Gardner interrupted and grinned. "Yes, I'm under the impression there's a lot of talk in this room. Now I need to be at a friend's house on Beacon Hill in twenty minutes and could use some help with directions. Walk with me?"

Eagerly, May packed up her possessions, and the two women walked toward the Common against a piercing headwind.

"These New England winters are brutal." Miss Gardner pulled her hood up. "Now tell me, what is Hunt's class really like?"

"It's marvelous to have an opportunity to study with someone who believes in our abilities, but I'm terribly far behind my other classmates. I know this will sound like petty grumbling, but I swear Miss Knowlton will never promote me to painting. I'll never become an artist at this rate."

"What in the world do you mean? Don't wait for anyone else to call you an artist. You spend hours trying to improve your art, day after day. You may not make any money off it, but I'd say you're an artist. When I left home to study art in Paris, people thought I was mad. But you have to ignore all of that and work endlessly to make your visions a reality. Stake a claim on your ambitions. If you wait around for other people to define you, you'll be saddled with their expectations—and that's dangerous territory for a woman." Panting, Miss Gardner fanned her face with her hands. "Good lord, please slow down. I don't have your long legs."

"Sorry, it's just that I . . . I know a man who lives there." May nodded her head toward the brick house of the Bishops as they strode along Louisburg Square. "Normally I avoid this block, but it's the quickest way to your destination on Revere, and it's too cold out here to take a longer route."

Miss Gardner slowed down and studied the house. "Looks like you wouldn't have been wanting for much in that household."

"I would have been wanting for someone who took my artistic ambitions seriously. In fact, I met you a couple of years ago at a show of your work at Williams & Everett Gallery. After meeting you, I decided I needed to end my relationship with him. You opened my eyes to a different path."

Miss Gardner let out a wry laugh. "Sorry, I set you off on such a wild-goose chase."

May's eyes widened. "No, meeting you was one of the best things that happened to me. You gave me the confidence to try to be an artist."

"Funny, I barely recall our meeting. But it's interesting how one chance encounter can make such a difference. It just goes to show the importance of living the life you want to lead. Not only does it benefit the person living that life, but it can also inspire others to try the same. I'd never thought of it that way."

The women reached the boardinghouse in which Miss Gardner was staying with a friend. She surprised May by thrusting out her hand to shake it as if they were men and said, "Now chin up on this whole Knowlton thing. Remember, you're an artist. You'll be promoted to oils soon. But listen to her. Follow her suggestions. She's the one with real artistic instruction in that studio. Hunt's just the big name who takes all the credit."

May knew the woman was right. There was no more time to nurse grievances against Miss Knowlton.

The following day, she took note of every comment Miss Knowlton gave her and revised her work accordingly.

On a warm March afternoon, with street noise rising up through the open windows, Miss Knowlton finally gave her the news she waited for: "After much consideration, Mr. Hunt believes you are ready to advance to the fundamentals of oil painting. I have composed a list of the materials you should bring on Monday so we may commence the next stage of your artistic development."

May smiled and took the supply list. She was so ecstatic she did not even mind Miss Knowlton's pretentious little speech. It seemed nothing could stop her now.

Chapter 20

On a chilly evening the following November, May lay on the couch with a cool compress over her tired eyes, listening to Louisa read one of her newest stories aloud when the neighborhood fire bells started clanging outside their boardinghouse. Louisa looked out the window expecting to see flames rising from surrounding rooftops, but not a puff of smoke could be seen.

The sisters prepared for bed, but a loud knocking at the door made them pause.

A man's voice called from the other side of the door. "Missus, missus, the city's on fire!" The bells clanged with increasing urgency as if to punctuate his words.

The sisters threw their dresses back on, not bothering to fasten buttons properly, and hurried outside. The area farther east, deeper into the city, where Mr. Hunt's portrait studio was located, appeared to be engulfed in towers of flames.

They ran down the sidewalk, but May slowed, mesmerized

by the red-and-orange fire against the blackness of night. "It's almost beautiful, isn't it?"

She was reminded of J. M. W. Turner's *The Burning of the Houses of Lords and Commons* that Mr. Hunt had shown the class as a fine example of spontaneity and expressive painting. Now watching a giant plume of flames illuminating Boston's nighttime skyline, she could see the terrifying appeal of the composition. Despite its savagery, the fire itself worked in eerie near-silence—the sound of wood snapping and collapsing echoed along the street—but the flames merely sighed over and over as they consumed everything in its path.

"Come on, this is no time to daydream." Louisa pulled her skirt up to run faster.

The women rushed to the Common and found a scene of chaos. Shopkeepers ran back and forth, piling the contents of their stores into the park. Towers of books rose amidst heaps of housewares, silks and laces, and crates of china. Young boys ran back and forth with bundles and carts of goods, as the flames rose from Franklin Street. Burning wood and tar stung the women's nostrils and made them gasp. The skin on their faces stiffened from the heat. The fire sucked all moisture from the air.

Boylston Street, where Mr. Hunt taught May's classes at the Studio Building, appeared to be safe, but smoke coiled up out of Trinity Church's windows, its blocks of stone oozing and melting in the heat. May's eyeballs dried when she faced the conflagration. Flakes of black soot flitted to the ground around them like snow. A sudden boom sent the ground lurching underneath them.

"This must be what the final moments of Pompeii were like," Louisa said wide-eyed.

"Dunno anything 'bout that, ma'am." An errand boy dropped a load of shawls next to the sisters. "They're blowing buildings up, tryin' to stop the fire's path." He gestured down to the pile by his feet. "You can take some if you like. The boss told us to take whatever we want 'fore it's destroyed."

Fear muscled into May's heart. She grabbed the boy by the shoulders. "Do you know what's happening on Summer Street?"

"That's the heart of the fire, ma'am." The boy grimaced. "Ouch."

May realized she was digging her nails into the poor lad's shoulders and let go.

"Louisa, I must go check on Mr. Hunt's studio. He may be there and need help—his current work, his collection . . ."

Louisa looked at her in disbelief. "Are you mad? Did you hear what the boy said? It's the heart of the fire. You'll do no such thing—"

But May didn't wait to hear the rest of what her sister had to say and ran toward Temple Street where only occasional flames sprang from the rooftops. Shadowy figures ran in and out of buildings. Glass windows shattered from the heat. She tucked her arm around her face to protect it, leaving only her watering eyes uncovered. Her lungs stung. A cramp pinched at her side. She ran deeper into the heat, dodging piles of store goods lit-

tering the streets and almost collided with a shop boy nosing a
cart of men's boots along the road.

May stopped at an intersection and winced at the sound of
wood splintering as a mansard roof on Washington Street collapsed in on itself. The air thickened with smoke, parching her
mouth and eyes. She reached another intersection and paused,
spinning around to look for street signs. Visibility diminished
to a few mere feet.

Something hit her side, and she spun around to find a man
grasping her upper arm. The red-rimmed whites of his eyes
glowed in the darkness, wide with urgency. "Whaddya think
you're doing? Git outta here," the man yelled in a thick Irish
accent.

"I must get to the Mercantile Building!"

"You'll do no such thing." He pulled her backward.

"Let go," she cried, pulling away. The man clapped his hand
over her mouth, and May started kicking.

Despite her efforts to fight back, a deadening heaviness
came over her. The man tied a handkerchief around her nose
and mouth. He dragged her backward. A roar filled the air
around them. The skin of May's forehead prickled as if needles
were being stuck into her. She could see nothing. May doubled
over as she was dragged backward.

"Come on, move yer feet. Faster! Come on!"

Reeling, May lifted her head. Burning planks of wood surrounded them. They had almost been buried in the remains of
a collapsed building.

"That was close. Let's not push our luck again, lady." The

man's hoarse shouting rang in her ears. May blinked her eyes furiously. She straightened up and started to run beside him. The smoke made it impossible to see beyond the hem of her skirt. *Where in God's name are we going?*

She tried to hold her breath to avoid the burning sensation of smoke in her lungs, but that just brought on a wave of coughing. All she could do was focus on moving one foot in front of the other as quickly as possible. Gusts of heat blew at their backsides. Hopefully the fire was behind them. At one point, they both stopped to bat at May's skirt as her hem smoldered. Storefronts on either side of them became visible. They slowed down. The man let go of May's arm, coughing and spluttering.

"You'll be fine. Keep going." He pushed her forward.

"Aren't you coming?"

But he had vanished back into the smoke behind them.

May stumbled back to the Common and wandered, dazed, amidst the piles of furniture, books, and home goods littering the field.

"May Alcott!" Louisa marched around a pile of discarded washtubs to reach her sister. "What in the world were you thinking?" Before May could answer, Louisa reached around her sister and pulled her close into a tight embrace. Louisa's back shuddered. May realized her sister was sobbing.

"I'm fine."

"You terrified me." Louisa pulled back to look at her sister, sniffing and wiping her eyes. "Goodness, you're a mess!"

"I don't know what I was thinking, but—" Panting, May hunched over and rested her hands on her knees. "I couldn't bear to think of him losing everything." Her raw throat made her stop to cough. Hunt's collection of paintings by Millet, Rembrandt, Velázquez, Turner . . . all gone, most likely.

"What was it like?"

"What?"

"The fire—what was it like?"

"Are you already priming me for a full reporting?" May wiped at her face and could see soot covering the palms of her hands. "This will all work its way into one of your stories, won't it?"

"It's a bit like I've always imagined the underworld. Smoke, pools of fire, the ground trembling underfoot . . ." Louisa's eyes looked up to the glow of the fire above the rooftops and wrapped her arm around May's waist. "Thank goodness, you're safe."

Chapter 21

When the fire stopped two days later, a large swath of Boston's downtown and financial district lay in smoking rubble. Mr. Hunt's portrait studio burned to the ground and with it, his collection of masterworks.

May returned to Concord at the end of November, since Mr. Hunt canceled his classes to shore up the remains of his business. A crusty scab of snow settled over the small town. Inside the house, an obstinate draft always managed to locate the inch of exposed skin between the back of May's collar and her hairline. A chill seeped down her spine no matter how warmly she dressed.

Winter slammed into the area in earnest with storms enveloping the town, deepening the snow with every passing week. May chafed at her snowy prison. She longed to ride her horse. Or ice skate. Or walk to the town center. Instead she cleaned out the storage bins in the kitchen, emptied the fireplaces, and mended countless quilts. She knit a pair of cherry-red mittens for Freddy and watched fissures of ice etch patterns along the panes of the parlor's windows while listening to the creak of the roof groaning under the heavy layer of snow upon it. Anna had taken the boys to visit Pratt farm for a few weeks, so Orchard House was quiet with only May and her parents tending to it.

Early February brought an unexpected week of thaw, and the Pratts returned. May welcomed the sound of children's giggles, the thud of small bodies landing hard after jumping down the stairs, and even the clatter of knocked over dishes.

"Anna," May called from the kitchen after shoveling a small path to the road. "I just saw Mr. Hosmer—there's a snowman-making party and singing down by Monument Square this afternoon. May I take the boys? It sounds like great fun."

Anna frowned. "I don't know. I cannot bear to have any of us take ill right now. Perhaps we should keep the children out of the cold."

May surveyed her sister's drawn face. She was still exhausted all of the time, but the boys were children; they needed activity. "But fresh air will cure everything. The boys will love it. I promise I'll bundle them up and bring them home well before supper, warm and snug."

Anna sighed. "I suppose getting you to skip a town social event is futile."

"You should come, too. It would be good to get out." May took her sister's hand in her own, but Anna slipped her hand out, shaking her head.

"I really don't feel up to it. You three should go. But please, don't let the boys overdo it."

May didn't wait for her sister to change her mind and dashed off to scour the house's wardrobes and closets for wool socks, long underwear, mufflers, hats, and sweaters. When she finished dressing them, Freddy and Johnny resembled little colorful snowmen.

"Please, don't keep them out late. Come right home," Anna said, waving from the front door.

May nodded, and the trio dashed out of the yard, singing and tossing snowballs at one another. It felt glorious to feel the sun spread across her face. She urged the boys down the road in a boisterous game of follow-the-leader, and they hopped, skipped, and slid the mile into town.

Monument Square spread out before them, transformed into a wonderland of figures carved from snow—a hulking elephant, a circle of dancers—a frozen circus had come to Concord.

"Look, boys," cried May, pointing to a whale tail rising from the field, "there's Captain Ahab's white whale."

The boys darted off into the crowd. Rosy-cheeked revelers drank from steaming mugs of hot cider, catching up on the latest town news, eager to be out of the confines of their homes while children threw snowballs and frolicked. The brilliant sunshine reflected off the snow, leaving May's cheeks sore from smiling and squinting as she caught up with neighbors on the latest town news. Eventually the light weakened, and purple shadows stretched across the square leaving the snow looking bruised, yet everyone lingered, reluctant to return to their chilly kitchens and dark bedrooms.

Johnny appeared at May's side, urging her to come and see

his armory of snowballs, but all she could see were his violet lips. May ran her hand along his cheek and pulled his hat down lower over his sweaty damp hair. "Oh dear, your mother will be sore with me for keeping you out. We better get home."

The sun dropped behind the bare limbs of trees, and the temperature plunged. May and the boys leaned into a lacerating headwind as they trudged along Lexington Street, heavy in wet clothes. May dreaded her sister's chagrin as she dragged them all home.

Anna met them at the door. "My goodness, you were gone longer than expected." She unspooled scarves from the necks of her sons. "May, they're shivering and their teeth are clacking!" She nestled the boys next to the stove to thaw and shot a cross glance at her sister. May's fingers could barely bend, and she could no longer feel her toes, but she hid her own chill.

"Mama, you should have seen the big fat jolly snowman we made! We put a beard of black twigs on his face. He looked fearsome!" Johnny said. His round cheeks glowed, and his small body let off the tinny smell of snow.

"It really was a merry scene. I wish you had come with us," May said, pretending not to notice Anna's frown. Marmee entered the kitchen, and the boys fell over themselves telling her all about the afternoon. The sisters avoided looking at each other and continued to peel sopping layers off the wriggling little pugs.

WITHIN TWO DAYS, the boys were coughing and sniffling. Although Anna did not blame her outright, May could feel recriminations every time Freddy asked for a clean handkerchief. Bitter temperatures returned. The sky darkened, and snow drove sideways into the windowpanes. Johnny's cough dropped into his chest and sounded heavy. His forehead grew warm with fever. May, Anna, and Mrs. Alcott took turns reading and playing endless rounds of gin rummy with the boys to occupy them, all while studying their flushed little faces carefully for signs of worsening illness.

The blizzard ended three days later. They all peered out of the windows marbled with ice. Only occasional glimpses of evergreen boughs and brown tree limbs bobbed in the whiteness surrounding the house—the world outside seemed to be erased. The snow stood three feet deep. Father and May took turns shoveling a path from the kitchen door to the barn, but the wet and heavy snow left them exhausted after only a couple of brief shifts. The quiet was complete, the absence of noise seemed loud.

The boys improved within a few days, but Anna began coughing and looked blanched. One morning, she awoke aching, unable to come downstairs to breakfast. May sat with her sister throughout the day and watched her cheeks bloom red with fever. Her eyes glassed over. Leaning in to dab Anna's forehead, May could feel the heat radiating off her sister, but snowdrifts trapped them in the house, making it impossible to fetch the doctor. May soaked cloths in a bucket of snow and pressed them to Anna's forehead and wrists, cursing her foray out into the village that day of the snow festival.

After several days with no improvement, Father tunneled

a path down to the road to ask a passing neighbor to fetch the doctor. They waited, watching Anna mumble incoherently with fever. Her chest fluttered up and down with labored breathing. May hovered over her, pleading encouragements while desperately trying to cool her burning skin with compresses and urging Anna to recover.

Finally Dr. Hitchens arrived at the door. He listened to her chest and declared the diagnosis they all dreaded to hear: pneumonia. Father took off his spectacles and pinched at the bridge of his nose. May kneaded her fingers into the tight cords of her neck.

She crept downstairs to lean into the doorway of the parlor to check on her nephews. Freddy and Johnny sat on the carpet murmuring to each other with their heads bent over a chessboard. Without saying a word, she returned upstairs to Anna.

Marmee's own fragile health made her an unsuitable nurse, so it fell to Father to help May care for Anna. Though he relieved May for a few hours each night at Anna's bedside, May would fall into bed and sleep fitfully. Sleep did not refresh her. Every time she closed her eyes, nightmares of John and Lizzie imploring her for help set in.

May would awaken rattled and fearful.

Another snowstorm locked Orchard House off from the outside world. Anna's condition worsened. Marmee and Father moved slower and looked grayer. Freddy and Johnny hovered like shadows outside their mother's door. May attempted cheerfulness when she encountered her nephews, but exhaustion and a sense of futility wore at her.

After three more days, Anna's fever still raged.

The doctor risked a return through the snow, but shook his head as he put away his stethoscope. Father stomped along the front yard in snowshoes, heading to the train station to deliver another note they hoped would reach Louisa in Boston.

Trapped inside with too much time to think and fret, May despaired. *If one more snowflake appears in the sky, I will start screaming and not stop.*

Dark thoughts circled around and around in her head like hawks over prey: she should have heeded her sister's concerns and never kept the boys out for so long in the cold; they would never have taken ill; Anna would not be fighting for her life. She knelt next to her sister, who lay flushed and perspiring, and prayed to overcome her selfishness.

Before all of the storms, a letter from Alice had arrived informing May that Miss Knowlton also lost her art studio and all of its contents during Boston's fire, leaving her destitute. Caught up in her own sorrow over classes closing, May had neglected to consider the welfare of her other instructor, and the realization sickened her. All of her careless actions that winter filled her with shame. She had always dismissed Louisa's accusations of selfishness over the years as baseless, but now she wondered—was her sister correct?

Clasping her hands in front of her nose, May whispered, "If Anna is spared, I will give up my art. I promise." The room was dark except for the firelight guttering in the grate. She fell asleep with her face in her hands, leaning against Anna's bed.

The following afternoon, footsteps pounded up the stairs,

and Louisa barged into the sickroom. May leapt up and collapsed into her sister's arms, pressing her face into the shoulder of Louisa's boiled wool coat. It smelled of woodsmoke and felt blessedly cold.

"I'm here. Blast these snowstorms and cursed train delays. I'm finally here." Louisa peeled off her coat and threw it behind her, as she clasped Anna's skeletal hand. "We must feed her some broth. She needs fuel."

Louisa's confidence brought May back into action. It was a relief to relinquish command to Louisa.

May returned with a tray of food, and Louisa spooned some of the broth into Anna's slack mouth. "When I was nursing during the war, we always tried to get something into those soldiers, no matter how much they resisted," Louisa said. "We're not going to lose you, Anna. Do you hear me? Your boys need you. Come on now, eat, and stay with us."

Louisa stopped the spoon midair and smiled at May tenderly. "Dear girl, you look like you've been to battle. Go get some rest. You've earned it."

THE FOLLOWING MORNING, May awoke to the sound of the boys shouting excitedly outside. She unbent herself from her cramped seat next to Anna's bed and limped to the front window. Freddy and Johnny were exchanging a volley of snowballs with a neighbor who had hopped off his wagon and returned fire good-naturedly. The man saw May at the window and waved. She raised her hand in return, tears sliding down her cheeks.

Louisa entered the room carrying a fresh bucket of snow. "What happened? Is she worsening?" She turned to Anna in confusion.

"No, I just saw the boys playing with Captain Clark and felt so overcome to see the kindness of our friends. And I . . . I just . . ." May dropped next to Anna's feet on the bed and sobbed.

"Hold on. Anna's fighting her way out of this. I know you've been working hard. I'm so sorry to have neglected you," Louisa said, putting her arms around May. "Let's put you into bed for a while."

"This is all my fault," May said, strangled by tears as she hung on Louisa's arm.

"Don't be ridiculous. It's not anyone's fault."

"It is. I kept the boys outside in the cold way too long. They got sick, then Anna got sick. What if we lose her? It's *all* my fault."

"Stop it." Louisa held May in front of her by both shoulders. "Stop this now, or you'll get sick next."

May gave a weak nod and let Louisa help her into bed. For the first time in weeks, May rolled over and slept.

MAY AWOKE DISORIENTED by the sunshine scissoring through her window at a low angle. She wrapped herself in a shawl and shuffled next door to find Anna sitting up against some pillows.

"Look who's awake," said Louisa, holding a mug of tea up to Anna's cracked lips.

May dropped onto a stool in relief.

"It's not often we can make May speechless. Well done there, old girl." Louisa beamed down at Anna from her seat next to the bed. "The boys have spoken to their mother. Now they're off with Father, running an errand at the Hosmers' house."

Anna's eyes closed.

Louisa saw May's jaw tighten and said, "She's just sleeping. Her fever has broken. She's weak, but I believe she's turned a corner. We need to continue watching over her, though."

May rubbed her throbbing temples, and twisted from side to side, stretching out the knotted ache in her lower back.

Louisa watched May with concern. "Go back to sleep. You've been under terrible strain. We can't have you falling ill now. Go."

May didn't need further urging.

When she awoke again, it was dark. The click and clack of knitting needles led her to find Louisa next to Anna's bedside. The bedroom had been kept cold for the last couple of weeks due to Anna's fever, but now flames whispered in the fireplace. A warm glow reflected off Anna's sleeping face, making her look healthier, even though her cheekbones protruded sharply now.

"She's been sleeping steadily, and her skin is cool to the touch. She's breathing better," whispered Louisa. May sat down on a chair and watched the rise and fall of the buttons on the neckline of Anna's nightgown. Louisa gestured at the bird May had painted on the mantel above the fireplace. "I love the owl. I've been listening to one outside the window. It's a comforting sound."

May managed a feeble smile. "I know, I've heard it, too. I believe a barn owl has set up a nest nearby."

"I've been thinking—book sales are going exceedingly well, and I've just invested another lump of money with Cousin Sewell. You've been working so hard and have neglected your art. I really didn't realize how bad things were here. I'd like to give you one thousand dollars to return to Europe to work on your art."

May's fogginess lifted. "Really? But what if—" She looked over at Anna.

"Slow down, you won't get on a boat tomorrow. Anna needs to get back to her former glory. Let's plan on a spring departure. This old place can carry on for a while on its own. Or at least, with a little of my supervision here and there."

May's spark of excitement vanished. She had a promise to keep. "I can't go."

"Why not? Of course you can."

"No, I really can't."

"Well, now you're just being contrary. What in the world do you mean?"

May buried her face in her hands. "I made a promise to God that if he spared Anna, I would give up my art."

Louisa fell back into her chair, a look of disbelief on her face. "You did *what*?"

"I was so scared Anna was going to die. It seemed like my fault." Tears ran down May's face.

Louisa sighed and leaned forward to pull May's hands off

her face. "Stop crying. I'm sorry you've been feeling so wretched, but a vow like that makes no sense."

"It does. My art makes me selfish."

"It's selfish to want to express yourself? It's selfish to learn? It's selfish to want to improve yourself?"

"I need to focus on our family and stop chasing this dream. It has always seemed like . . ." May's voice trailed off.

"Like what?"

"It always seemed like I needed to make something of my-self."

"Something other than Amy March?" Louisa rested her forehead in her hands. "Making you little Amy in *Little Women* did you no favors. I'm sorry."

"It's taken me a while, but I no longer worry about little Amy March. I just want to prove that I'm a worthy member of this family."

"Worthy? Worthy of what?"

"Of everyone's respect. Mother and Father always appeared to value you, Anna, and Lizzie because of all of your noble undertakings—Anna and Lizzie's charity, your abolitionism. Once Mother and Lizzie took me to visit a poor family in an appalling tenement building on Lowell Street, and the place terrified me. I never wanted to return. I never wanted to help Mother with her rounds again. Afterward, I felt so inconsequential compared to all of you."

"I remember that. You didn't sleep for weeks. No one thought any less of you for being scared. I remember another time when you almost jumped out of your skin after opening a cupboard in the kitchen in search of the flour and finding a wide-eyed black face peering out at you. You were probably only about five years old, and no one had told you of Father's Underground Railroad work. I fear we all sometimes forgot how much younger you were than the rest of us." Louisa took May's chin in her hand. "Listen, if you want to stop with your art, fine, stop. But don't stop because of some promise you made to God in a moment of self-loathing. I have no doubt God wants us all to find something special inside of ourselves. Your imagined selfishness had nothing to do with Anna's sickness or recovery." Louisa sat back and folded her arms around herself. "But you must pursue your art because you cannot imagine life without it."

"I offered to give up my art because it's the thing I value most, aside from my family," May said tearfully.

"Well then, go after it. You don't need to prove anything to Marmee and Father. And you certainly don't need to prove anything to me. Prove it to yourself."

"Do you feel this way about your writing?"

"Yes. I certainly have a list of people I'm always trying to best, but I write because I must." Louisa bent over to pick up the knitting she had dropped on the floor.

"But you have to do it to make money."

"The money is lovely, but even if no one ever read anything I ever wrote, I would still do it. Even if I couldn't earn a penny from it."

May wrapped herself tightly into her shawl and smiled. After weeks of feeling as though her world was cracking into pieces, she allowed herself to lean into the warmth of the fire and listen to the gentle hooting of the owl outside the window.

Part 3

April 1873–August 1877

London, England

Chapter 22

May sailed for London in late April. Her newfound independence both excited her and frightened her in turns. For seven dollars a week she rented an airy second-floor apartment in a Georgian boardinghouse overlooking leafy Bedford Square in Bloomsbury. She missed the companionship of her sisters, but was determined to revel in being unencumbered by family responsibilities.

At one of her first stops in London, she decided to sketch inside Westminster Abbey. She wandered around the grand cathedral to find a suitable spot to work. Eventually, she settled her camp stool on the black-and-white tiled floor in the grand Henry VII Chapel and brought out her sketchbook. She became mesmerized by the intricate fan patterns in the vaulted ceiling. Colorful pennants rippled over the designs in a draft overhead. With her eyes trained upward, she failed to notice two people approach her.

"Look, that woman has claimed my favorite spot."

May turned to see a woman with her hands on her hips, smiling down at her.

"I'm sorry. I'm sure there's room for more than just me," May said, dragging her satchel closer to her.

"Don't mind me. I'm just teasing. Isn't this just the most beautiful place in London?"

"Yes, it's lovely, but I've just arrived so I'm afraid I can't compare it with much else yet."

The woman clapped her hands together. "You're American! William, come here. There's a new artist, and she's just arrived—from where?"

"Boston."

The woman couldn't have been more than five feet tall, and she clutched a wooden art box. She had violet-colored eyes that glowed like amethysts from under a fringe of long black lashes. Between her size and extraordinary eye color, she looked like a fairy. May eyed the remarkable-looking woman's ears to be sure they weren't pointed. They were not.

A tall dark-haired man came to stand beside the pixie. "What a coincidence. We were just in Boston before arriving here," he said. "Please allow me to introduce us. I'm William Keith. This is my wife, Violet."

May rose to introduce herself with a quizzical look on her face.

"I know, I know—my eyes . . . and my name." The woman laughed. "My parents, well, they kept things simple when they named me Violet." She threw up her hands with a shrug. "It makes it easy to remember me."

Everything about this lively woman was memorable, and May laughed along with her.

"I adored Boston," Violet said. "I grew up in California, and it's amazingly different."

"My goodness—London, Boston, California—you two are so well-traveled. My father has toured the Midwest, but I've never left New England, with the exception of a trip to Europe a couple of years ago."

"Oh, Miss Alcott, you must visit the West Coast someday." Mr. Keith's eyes opened wide. "While Europe's art and architecture is not to be missed, nature's creations in the American West are beyond compare."

A priest rambled by with a dark look to silence them. May tucked her notebook under her arm while Mr. Keith picked up her camp stool, and the three left the chapel and approached the entrance in the nave of the cathedral.

Violet rubbed her white-gloved hands together. "I think we should all forget working and welcome Miss Alcott properly. Let's take her on a little tour of Saint James's Park."

"My dear, we shouldn't bother her."

May couldn't resist the invitation. "Oh, yes, please, I'd love a tour." The tall, rangy man and his tiny, outgoing wife entranced her. The Keiths were the first people in a long time who did not make the connection to her famous sister. Cultivating a friendship with this couple wholly separate from associations with her family marked a milestone for May.

Violet tilted her head at her husband flirtatiously and gave a smug smile. "See? I'm very good at reading people."

He put out his hands palms up in good-natured surrender and laughed.

On their way to the park, William told May he had lost his studio in Boston's fire, and so they relocated to London to work on a commission.

"Mr. Keith, are you English? I've been trying to guess at your accent."

"I was born in Scotland but my father died when I was a lad, and I left for New York City with my mother and sister for a fresh start. I worked for the newspapers for a while, working as an apprentice engraver, but when I was old enough to make my own way, I headed west to San Francisco, looking for work. I thought I'd strike gold somehow, but the California landscape made me realize I didn't want to just engrave anymore. I wanted to paint. So I enrolled in art classes."

"It's how we met," Violet said. "Would you believe I was his teacher?"

"It's true, she was. I met Violet at the Art Academy of San Francisco. She taught me everything I know."

"Oh, you exaggerate." Violet swatted at him. "Yes, I was his first art teacher, but he's caught up and made his own way. You must see some of Mr. Keith's paintings of the Yosemite Valley." Violet smiled almost shyly at her husband. "His command of majestic landscapes leaves me in awe."

They reached the entrance at the southeast corner of the park, and Violet sniffed the air and looked around. "Do you smell peanuts?"

Down the sidewalk, a young boy was selling small brown bags of roasted peanuts that hung from a long stick balanced across his shoulders.

Violet put her hands together and looked up at her husband beseechingly. "Oh, please, buy us a bag? Please?" She turned to May with a mischievous expression. "I know they're vulgar, but will you judge me terribly if I indulge in my craving?"

May laughed and shook her head as William left them to go to the vendor.

"I think we're going to be the loveliest of friends, don't you?" Violet folded her arm under May's and smiled. There was no way May could say no. William rejoined them, and the trio entered the park, cheerfully munching on roasted peanuts. Baby nurses in crisp white aprons marched along pathways pushing prams, while the high-pitched voices of small children playing games trilled along with the sounds of birds. The clanking of the omnibuses rattling along the buzzing hive of Westminster faded away. How quickly the sounds of the city became muffled by the trees and grass. A passel of boys over by the edge of the lake played what appeared to be a lively game of pirates while a governess, tall and rigid, watched them impassively.

May noticed Violet's face fall as she watched the boys. William caught his wife's shift in mood and started discussing the various art collections around the city. "If I may be so bold, I propose we meet tomorrow at the National Gallery. Have you obtained your copyist pass yet?"

"No, how do I do that?"

"We shall be happy to help you." He gave a gentle pat to his wife's hand clasped under his elbow. The Keiths' overt affection for one another reminded May of home. Her parents had their differences over the years, but they always demonstrated tenderness toward one another. May spent enough time in other households to understand this was unusual.

THE NEXT DAY, May awaited the arrival of her new friends next to the lions in front of the National Gallery.

"My, my, you look like a grand adventuress, posed next to those mighty beasts," giggled Violet when they arrived.

"I'm on a grand adventure. This marks the first time I've been on my own." And it was true. In all of her thirty-three years, she had never been so far from home all by herself. London offered complete freedom.

Violet ran a hand along the stone lion's side, as if petting the live beast. "I've never been on my own. It must be exciting for you."

"It is," said May, and she smiled brightly as she watched Violet take her hand off the lion and place it on her husband's forearm. Traveling alone was something she never would have done several years earlier, but more and more women were beginning to undertake tours of Europe on their own, and she loved doing exactly as she pleased. But it would be nice to have a travel partner. She asked Mr. Keith about the logistics of securing her copyist pass, but while he spoke, she watched how her two new friends always remained side by side as if secured by an invisible thread. When they entered the National Gallery, Mr. Keith carefully steered his wife around the uneven cracks in the stone stairs. Violet looked up at him with a grateful smile and leaned into him, brushing some dust off the arm of his jacket.

"What do you paint?" May asked Violet as they wandered through the Dutch room.

"I specialize in watercolors. While my husband seeks out heroic landscapes, I prefer still lifes, the occasional portrait, and smaller landscapes, but I mostly focus on teaching. I'm a private painting tutor for the Earl of Hampton's daughters." Violet paused while she measured her thoughts. "I'm not as ambitious as my husband, but I love to paint. My family came to San Francisco from Philadelphia—my poor mother never recovered from the displacement of being in a chaotic settlement of miners, railroad workers, and financiers. She taught my sisters and me to paint. I think it was her way to reconnect with the culture she felt we lost during our move."

"You've never seen a happier woman than my mother-in-law when I announced Violet and I were going to study art in Europe. She was delighted by the prospect of her daughter going somewhere civilized."

"Oh, I think she was overjoyed before that. She was thrilled when I wanted to marry a man who'd prefer to paint a landscape, rather than blast a railway through it."

Mr. Keith entwined his arm through his wife's. "And Miss Alcott, what kind of art do you create?"

Even after being a student for several years, she seemed to be at a loss for how to explain herself compared to the two bona fide artists in front of her. "I'm here to study J. M. W. Turner," she said. "My instructor in Boston introduced me to his work, and I've been captivated by the English Romanticists' emphasis on light and color. I thought I'd go to Paris to study art, but somehow I landed on London when I planned the trip—it felt a little closer to home."

To her surprise, the Keiths both nodded thoughtfully and accepted her answer. Perhaps she was not the amateur she believed herself to be.

SHE CONTINUED TO see the Keiths and met new friends along the way. There were a few women in her boardinghouse whom she befriended. A watercolor workshop, nearby in Bayswater, introduced her to a couple of other American women studying painting. When she wasn't working, May gathered her newly found companions and shopped along Knightsbridge, ogled at Madame Tussaud's wax figures in Piccadilly, took in the spectacle of panoramic painting in Burford's, and even went farther afield to Windsor and Stratford-upon-Avon—but as summer passed and cooler weather prevailed, she returned to more serious work. Her explorations focused upon studying at the National Gallery where she developed a routine. After walking through the Italian and Dutch rooms to study the masters, she would settle down amidst the extensive J. M. W. Turner collection. There was a small gallery, in particular, in which the paintings hung low enough to comfortably allow her to create detailed copies. The sublime composition of Turner's watercolors and oils appealed to May, and she embarked upon spending the cold months of fall and winter capturing his bold expressive use of color.

Although Louisa's money served May's needs, she longed to produce income from her art, but didn't know where to start. To ask the Keiths for advice was not an option; she couldn't think of a more embarrassing question. Because of her sister's extensive collection of friends and associates in London, she could have written to Louisa for help, but she didn't want to enlist her sister's assistance either. She remembered years earlier when Louisa had sent out story after story to different magazines, looking for someone to accept her work for publication, and although a few acceptances had trickled in, mostly she was told no. But Louisa persevered. Yes, Louisa had crumpled up the rejection notices and thrown them at the wall in a cold fury, but she kept writing, kept submitting, kept going, yet it all was private. No one called her work terrible in print for everyone to read. When May closed her eyes, she could still feel the same paralyzing sense of disappointment that overwhelmed her after her *Little Women* illustrations were panned. She did not want to go through that again. How could she put her work out into the world and risk the pain of having her creations mocked?

She wanted to be independent but feared she did not have the fortitude to withstand denunciation of her talent again. Even after having been in London for nearly a year, she was no closer to selling her work than when she arrived. Every night she took her bank ledger out from where she kept it tucked into her sewing kit. After subtracting her day's expenses, she would carefully pen in a new sum on the balance line. The shrinking number seemed like sand running through an hourglass marking her diminishing time in England.

Chapter 23

On a dreary March day, May took an omnibus to visit the National Gallery. A churlish wind forced itself down the avenues. Rain threatened. Foghorns on the Thames bellowed in the distance. The persistent dampness of the city made her knee joints ache in the morning. Since she arrived, had her boots *ever* been dry? Truly dry? A moldering smell of mildew permeated the museum, sending her spirits even lower. She hoped the Pre-Raphaelites and their rich use of color would distract her from the cold, but instead, the dim light made the paintings look garish.

Disheartened, she dragged herself to the *Liber Studiorum* gallery, filled with hundreds of Turner paintings, and blew on her hands in a futile attempt to warm them as she pulled out a few of her copies to work on. In the outside pocket of her satchel, she found the pair of gray knit fingerless gloves Anna had sent her at Christmastime and put them on. The smell of tobacco made her turn to see a man looking over her shoulder.

"Excuse me, I didn't mean to startle you. I was admiring your work," he said. Steel-rimmed spectacles twinkled under a shag of heavy dark eyebrows. He was reminiscent of a dignified stone statue, chipped away at by rain and splotched with moss, but with a handsome foundation remaining. "I'm John Ruskin." He extended a large hand. May, reluctant to be disturbed, reached out hesitatingly to take it, but then wanted to hold on to it longer for its unexpected warmth. "Your ability to replicate Turner's use of ambient coloring to imply space is impressive. Do you have any other studies with you? I'm the Trustee of J. M. W. Turner's art collection here at the National Gallery."

Good heavens. Now she remembered the significance of John Ruskin. While back in Boston, she had studied both of this man's heavy volumes of *Modern Painters*, in addition to several of his articles and drawing instruction manuals. The man was iconic within the world of art. She introduced herself, telling him she had studied with William Morris Hunt in Boston.

He nodded over the copies she handed to him. "You make Mr. Hunt proud with this work. The attention to detail, paired with the sense of spontaneity, is exquisite. Would you like me to show you how to access the archives for more of Mr. Turner's work?" Still holding on to her papers, he beckoned May to join him.

May grabbed her satchel. He led her down endless flights of stairs into the bowels of the museum. Low fires glowed in the dank storage rooms to ward off mold. Long halls seemed to lead deeper into the center of the earth. Gaping jaws of empty frames leaned up against the walls. Their footsteps echoed along the stone floors of the underground warren.

Finally they reached a room and entered. Mr. Ruskin introduced May to a small man whose bald pate winked in the low light as he led her toward cabinets towering in the shadows, filled with Turner's work. She selected an assortment of watercolors, mezzotints, and lithographs and followed Mr. Ruskin back up to the daylight of the main galleries. Aboveground again, she blinked and wondered if her trip to plumb the depths below the building had all just been a strange dream.

"I feel as though you're a genie." May laughed. "I was having the most horrid morning until you introduced yourself. Our adventure has felt magical, but I must confess that I've been so entranced I'm not sure I'll be able to find my way back there when I'm done with these." She nodded to the prints in her hand.

Mr. Ruskin smiled and pulled a piece of paper from his breast pocket to jot down a small map for her. "I'm always delighted to make the acquaintance of artists who share my appreciation for Mr. Turner. And now I would like to make a request of you. May I borrow these copies for my students to study? I'm unable to take Turner originals from this building, but your reproductions are masterly. My students could learn from these."

May stared at him in surprise. "Of course, I'm delighted by your request. It's an honor." An idea struck her. "Do you know of any dealers here in London who would be interested in selling my work?"

Mr. Ruskin lowered his head in thought, and May was about to apologize for overstepping, but he flipped over the map he sketched her and wrote down a list of names and addresses. "Your reproductions will be sought after. Tell these dealers I sent you. There's definitely a market for your work." He handed her his list and the map. "And these"—he nodded at her prints tucked under his arm—"will benefit my students enormously."

She felt a shot of pride that this serendipitous meeting occurred without any connections from anyone else. Her work spoke for itself. Despite her excitement, she managed to spend several hours working with a newfound energy before emerging from the National Gallery to find low clouds scuttling across the sky under a tentative sun. The cold whipping wind from earlier in the morning vanished, and the day, while breezy, offered spring weather again. A sense of victory made her stand straight and stride home to sort through her Turner work. She would select her best prints and visit the dealers the following day.

LESS THAN TWENTY-FOUR hours later, May's dreams began to pay dividends. The clack of her heels on the sidewalks along Oxford Street seemed to tap out a tune. She marched along, carrying a portfolio noticeably lighter than when she had started out in the morning. Meanwhile, the purse tucked into her satchel jangled with coins. Mr. Ruskin's associates were all too happy to snatch up her work on consignment. Several wasted no time and bought her studies outright with some clients in mind. As an afterthought, May had placed a couple of her painted flower panels into her portfolio the evening before—the dealers took those paintings as well. All of them urged her to return with more.

She hummed, weaving through the throngs of people around Piccadilly Circus, remembering a day the previous summer when she climbed to the top of Saint Paul's Cathedral. Her quadriceps and chest had burned as she slogged her way up the endless narrow dank stairwell, but when she had reached the top, she leaned out from under the rim of the dome and found London stretched out underneath her in a patchwork of streets and rooftops. The height had made her mouth dry and given her vertigo, but a soaring sense of power and possibility had filled her. The same feeling returned to her now. If she kept churning out these copies to sell, she could stretch out her time in Europe well beyond the money Louisa gave her. She could support herself. And maybe go to Paris. The realization left her breathless.

The following morning, as May placed her sketchbook into her satchel to prepare for her walk to the National Gallery, a knock at the door startled her. She opened it to find Alice Bartol jumping up and down, throwing her arms around her. Alice had sent a letter the month before hinting at an upcoming visit, but May did not expect to see her so quickly. The women fell all upon each other, stumbling back into May's room, filling each other in on the latest news from both sides of the Atlantic.

"I'm on my way to Paris. You *must* come with me," Alice said, grabbing May's shoulders. She went on to explain her plan to spend the summer in Villiers-le-Bel, outside of Paris, studying painting with Thomas Couture, the French master painter. May calculated the implications of leaving London. She could continue to send work to her new dealers in London, even if she moved to Paris. The three hundred dollars that remained of Louisa's money could see her through the summer, even if she saw no income from her Turner studies—which seemed unlikely after the enthusiasm of the dealers the day before. Yes, May would go. Why not?

While Alice immersed herself in exploring London, May decided to spend the month of April producing several more Turner studies to leave with dealers. The sales would fatten up her wallet and prepare her for the higher cost of living in Paris. With four days left before her departure, she stood in her room surrounded by piles of clothing, assessing the best way to organize the contents of her steamer trunk, when her landlady knocked on the door to deliver a piece of mail.

March 31, 1874
Boston

Dearest May,

I'm positively tickled to hear about your encounter with Mr. Ruskin. We've all known there's greatness inside of you, so it's wonderful to have it recognized by others.

Freddy and Johnny are thriving in their new school here in Boston, but Marmee is unwell. Our move into the city has left her steeped in melancholy for she says Boston

is too different—it has changed and is no longer recogniz-
able to her. My work demands continue to pile up on me,
making it impossible for me to return to Concord to reopen
Orchard House for the summer.

In short, I'm afraid you must come home. Marmee
needs your companionship and care while I continue to
work. You've had time for adventures. Now it's your turn to
care for the family.

Love,
Louisa

The solid black lines of Louisa's cursive shattered into tiny pieces as May stared at the page, reading her sister's words over and over. Even if Louisa knew May was selling her paintings, her request would not change. May's earnings from her art could not compete with her sister's income. The prospect of leaving all of her progress behind devastated her.

The demanding tone of Louisa's letter also irritated her. She wanted to stomp her feet like a child with the unfairness of it all. But May knew she was abroad because of her sister's money so she must comply with her wishes. Hot tears flowed down her face. Amidst all of her resentment, shame at her own selfishness washed over her. *Marmee needs me. How can I put my own wants ahead of hers?*

Chapter 24

May arrived in Boston Harbor to find the city barely recognizable. The dome of the State House, plain stone a year before, now gleamed with a fresh layer of gilded gold paint. From the edge of the Public Garden, the Back Bay rolled out in flat, even blocks of stylish new homes and shops. Springtime buds punctuated the trees with dots of bright green and added to the sense of newness in the air. Despite the aggravating circumstances of her return, May's frustrations melted when she embraced her diminished mother in the rooms Louisa had rented for the family on Franklin Square. Over the winter, Abigail Alcott had suffered from dropsy of the brain, and the old woman's lack of hearing, which had been worsening for years, added to her confusion. May blinked back her own tears at her Marmee's fragility.

After a long hug from Anna, May pulled back to find Louisa looking at her through narrowed eyes. "You're different."

"I'm another year older."

"No, it's more than that." Louisa cocked her head. "England changed you."

The anger toward her sister that May nursed all the way across the Atlantic now stuttered as she looked into the deep wrinkles furrowed around Louisa's eyes.

"We need to get you a new coiffure." May bit her lip to keep from crying.

"To hide my head of gray hair? Sorry, too late. You can't make a Venus out of an old woman." Louisa swatted May's hip. "Get me a new hat to cover it all up instead."

MAY PAID A visit to the studio near Park Square that Miss Knowlton shared with Ellen Hale, another young woman from the days of Mr. Hunt's class. There she found two large rooms; Miss Knowlton and Ellen shared one for their own work space, while the other served as the classroom. After the fire, Mr. Hunt stopped teaching and gave his classes over to Miss Knowlton. She looked exactly the same except for a couple of deeper crow's-feet beside her eyes and frown lines, no doubt a result of her economic approach to enthusiasm. May paused next to a seascape painting of her former teacher's and admired the vast stormy sky dominating the composition.

"You've been prolific," May said, eyeing the number of canvases leaning against the wall.

Miss Knowlton scratched at some spilled yellow paint on the wooden table with her fingernail. She brushed it away and nodded at the cleanliness of the table before looking at May with her penetrating gaze. "Yes, I have been. The fire was the best thing that could have happened to me." Her tone was matter-of-fact. "Don't get me wrong. It was devastating to lose everything. But it also freed me to start over and forced me to put effort into my own work again."

"Really?"

"Yes. I was Hunt's shadow and depended on him for everything, but he's never really recovered from losing his life's work—he's different now. The entire episode made me realize I needed to live my own life." Miss Knowlton stared at May for an extra moment, before she turned to study her own seascape painting. "Sometimes we can surprise ourselves—I found I could do everything on my own."

Relieved to have Miss Knowlton's eyes off her, May said, "I suppose that makes sense. Still, it must have been—"

"Mr. Hunt took up all the air in my life. I needed to step away." She tapped her fingers on the table. "So, show me what you created in London."

After May spread out her Turner copies, Miss Knowlton studied them carefully, moving from piece to piece, her nose practically touching the art. "With your enthusiasm and all you know about Turner, you would be a fine instructor. If you ever want to teach, I can furnish you with a list of students from my own waiting list. It could be a good way for you to start."

"Thank you, but I don't know if I'm ready to teach anything. I'm still learning so much."

Miss Knowlton frowned and waved May's words away with an impatient toss of her hand. "We're all students. This is one of the beauties of being an artist: there's always more to learn."

May opened her mouth to say something but closed it. "Well, thank you. I need to move my family to Concord for the summer. My mother is sick. But I'll keep your offer in mind. Maybe I could teach in the fall." She placed her sketches and paintings back in her portfolio, but Miss Knowlton put her hand on one.

"The blue in this sky seems endless." Miss Knowlton stared at it. "The vast stretches of deep color are beautiful and imply a real feeling of possibility. This emotional depth to your work represents something worth pursuing. It almost feels like this isn't quite a copy of Turner's, but maybe it reveals something of your own?"

"It's so small, I . . ."

"Paintings don't always have to be big to pack in meaning."

May nodded and thanked her but felt relieved to walk outside and get out from under Miss Knowlton's intensity. The idea of watching everything she owned go up in flames terrified her. She remembered watching the flames dancing down Franklin Street. If anything, she would have bet Mr. Hunt would have been able to right himself quickly, and Miss Knowlton would have been the one left bereft. How did she manage to see the tragedy as an opportunity? She considered her own situation, pondering how she could convert the setback of finding herself back in Boston into a chance to start afresh. She was tired of the power Louisa's money exerted over her. She needed to work on creating a path back to Europe. A path of her own. Louisa's command over May could be reduced if she supported herself by selling her own work. Yes, that was it—by fall, May would return to Boston to begin making some money from her art. The validation of selling her art made her feel as though she was finally an artist, an equal to her sister. Even if the income she made from her paintings was a pittance compared to Louisa's royalty checks, it was a start. Furthermore, it was time for the two sisters to stop passing the responsibility of Marmee and Father back and forth. They could share it.

When she returned back to the family's rooms on Franklin Square, May found Louisa at work in her bedroom. She wasted no time getting to her purpose and said, "In the fall, I've decided to return to Boston and join you at the Bellevue. I'll take the room next door to ours to use as a studio and teach art classes in it, too."

Louisa placed her pen down, looked up from her manuscript of *Eight Cousins*, and rubbed her eyes. "You need to take care of Marmee and Father in Concord."

"I will. I'll get them settled this summer, but I cannot stay away from my work for longer than that. Right before I received your last letter in London, I sold some paintings to dealers. I'm going to arrange to continue working with them, even while I'm here in America. And Helen Knowlton offered to send me some art students. So, you see, I'm making money from my art. After summer, we can share managing affairs in Concord." May tapped her sister's desk as she spoke. Saying the words aloud put her plan into motion.

Louisa folded her arms across her chest and regarded her sister. "Very well, I suppose your proposal sounds fair enough. I'll pay for the extra room at the Bellevue if you want."

"Thank you, but no, I'll do it on my own."

"Will it be loud with students coming and going at all hours?"

"Your work won't be disturbed."

"I suppose some artistic types nearby could be interesting." Louisa picked her pen back up and resumed writing with her head bowed over her manuscript. "And congratulations on the sales of your paintings, although I fear you'll discover income from selling your art and income gained from scrubbing soiled linens all begins to feel the same."

"You don't really mean that."

"What makes you so sure? If money is your objective, selling is selling, no matter what the product. You have to have an objective beyond dollars to make it all mean something more."

"Are you just writing to make money now?"

"I used to think no, but now I'm not always so sure." Louisa lifted her head to stare out the window beside her desk. The incoming light showed the sagging skin beneath her eyes and her thin, gray lips. "Having you nearby may do me some good," she said softly.

Chapter 25

Two years passed. From her room at the Bellevue Hotel, May taught classes and sold her Turner studies while watching Louisa write in the room next door—*Eight Cousins*, *Rose in Bloom*, and *Silver Pitchers* all went to press. May marveled at Louisa's ability to wring as much income as possible from her writing. Louisa would first publish a story as a serial in a magazine and then repackage the same story as a novel and sell it again, essentially doubling her money on each writing project. America and England's appetite for her stories showed no sign of abating.

All kinds of offers poured in for Louisa now. When Mr. Niles came to her with a seven-hundred dollar advance to write a temperance novel, Louisa chuckled and agreed. Though she had never been a teetotaler, Louisa accepted the deal and suddenly took up various compatible causes, becoming anti-tobacco and anti-corset. When she preached about the anti-earring crusade one evening at supper, May decided things had gone too far.

"How is it A. M. Barnard is now against earrings? As I recall, that writer wrote about some fairly scandalous topics: hashish, suicide, obsession . . ."

"A. M. Barnard is completely opposed to any goody-goody causes, but Louisa May Alcott attracts anyone peddling virtue and fully embraces wholesome fare."

"Well, I'm not giving up any of my jewelry for your do-gooder causes. I miss A. M. Barnard."

Louisa looked down at the spread of plates of food in front of them. "So do I."

The two ate the rest of their meal in subdued silence. May reviewed the tasks for the day ahead: paint two Turner cop-ies in the morning, teach a drawing class for beginners at one o'clock, crate and deliver three canvases to be shipped to Lon-don, and then pop over to the art supply shop to refresh her supply of watercolors. She was tempted to squeeze in a lecture titled "Using Photography as a Lens to Understand Anatomy" by a young Philadelphian painter, Mr. Thomas Eakins, but there wouldn't be enough time to arrive at the Athenaeum's art gallery by the appointed hour.

It amazed her to think of how much she could do in one day. Balancing her teaching and her own painting provided just enough tension in her day to keep her productive. And the in-come! She had splurged the previous weekend and taken a trip with her friend Sarah Whitman to Magnolia to visit and paint in another woman's studio overlooking the sea. The trio had eaten lunch in a lovely tearoom near the beach's boardwalk, and May had enjoyed a slice of lemon cake and admired the powdered sugar dusting the top of the dessert like September frost. She'd eaten the entire slice, content in knowing she could afford the trip on her own.

"I've been meaning to tell you, I've been invited to New York," Louisa said, ladling some chocolate pudding into a dessert bowl. "Vassar College asked me to speak at their ten-year anniversary. I'm thinking of spending the winter in New York City for a change of scenery."

May stared at her sister openmouthed as the implications of her sister's remarks sank in.

"You'll be fine holding down the fort in Concord on your own, right?"

May felt as though her chair's legs were folding underneath her. Everything, all of her carefully built plans began to slide away. "But what about our arrangement?" she spluttered. "I can't live here on my own, take care of Marmee and Father in Concord, and work enough to save any money. And I certainly cannot work from Concord."

Louisa's tone became sharp. "Dearest girl, it's not easy—trust me, if there's anyone who knows this, it's me—but you'll figure out a way."

"But this isn't fair at all."

"Fairness is a concept that has always eluded me. It's not fair that when I finally have the means to enjoy life, my health suffers and I'm practically bedridden. It's not fair that I've been working like the devil lately. Now, please, you do not want me to continue with my list of life's injustices. This Dr. Miller in

New York City—his hotel offers treatments that could help with my neuralgia."

May's appetite vanished as the image of how she would have to shift her life sharpened into focus. Louisa continued talking about the logistics of when she planned to leave, and May nodded stiffly, barely able to track her sister's words. May's eyelid began to pulse as she questioned how she could continue to run her classes in Boston from Concord. And then there was Marmee; although she expressed happiness at returning to life in Concord, her capabilities dwindled with every passing month. Gout, deafness, a persistent cough. With fall and winter approaching, the pressures of family responsibilities on May would only increase.

With Louisa finally silent and the last spoonful of pudding in her mouth, May rose and excused herself. It took all of her effort to contain her frustration. She pictured herself sweeping her arms along the table and hurling all of the dishes to the floor. The satisfying smashing of china practically rang in her ears. But instead, she put one foot in front of the other and walked to their bedroom and shut the door behind her gently, before dropping on her bed. She lay on her back, staring at the shadows swimming across the ceiling and tried to think past the anger pooling inside her.

ALTHOUGH IT WAS far from easy, May managed to juggle her affairs from Concord through the fall and winter, helped by the fact that Miss Knowlton decided to take several months off from teaching to write a book about Mr. Hunt and offered May her classes and the use of her studio. It was the perfect opportunity for May to establish herself in the city, and she became a regular on the train, traveling back and forth between Concord and Boston. One warm early June afternoon, May let herself into Helen's teaching studio after taking her class on a trip to the Athenaeum to view a painting exhibit, but she paused in the entrance, sensing something was different. Cigarette smoke curled in the still, stuffy air around her, yet she wasn't expecting anyone.

Through the haze, a vaguely familiar figure became visible. Jane Gardner leaned against the window, looking down onto the street below, but turned at the sound of the door opening.

Jane grinned and held her cigarette out to the side. "Well, Miss Alcott, hello."

"You remember me this time."

"Ha, I try to make it my job to remember every face I meet. You never know when someone will turn out to be useful. I hope I didn't surprise you. I had dinner with Helen last night, and she loaned me a key to get in, so I could get a little work done." Miss Gardner exhaled a long stream of smoke through her nostrils. "So, you're still here in Boston?"

May dropped her paint box on a table and wove her fingers together, stretching them out in front of her. Fatigue rolled down her spine, and she wilted onto a stool behind her. "I went to London to study Turner for a year and have been able to cultivate a brisk business of selling my Turner copies. Now I'm here trying to cobble out a living from teaching and selling my work."

Miss Gardner squinted her eyes through the smoke, sighed, and stubbed out her cigarette in an empty paint can. "So, the copy business keeps you busy?"

The copy business. May swallowed as she noted the fact that Jane pointedly refrained from calling it painting. "It does. I'd like to get back to developing my own original work, but I've been so busy keeping up with business that I can barely find time to think, but really, somehow I'm bored. It makes no sense—how can I be bored when I'm always in motion?" The words surprised her as they poured out of her mouth, but she knew they were true. "I think I need something more."

"Sadly, this is often the price of selling work derived from someone else's." Miss Gardner folded her arms in front of her. "So? What are you doing with the money you're earning?"

"Saving it so I can go back to Europe."

"Do you have enough to get you across the pond? Go. Go to Paris and start working. Get established in a studio for fall. Make money as you go." Miss Gardner smirked. "You'll see enough there to snap you out of your boredom."

"But it's not that simple—" May started to tell her about her mother's health.

"It's *never* that simple, but life never gets easier. We always think it will, but it doesn't. If you want to do something, stop clucking over it. Go. We're not getting any younger." Miss Gardner looked around the studio. "Damn, what time is it? I've got a meeting with an agent."

May fumbled to locate her pocket watch. "Three o'clock."

"Good, the bastard can cool his heels for a few minutes.

God knows, he's going to bleed me dry with his percentage. Bastards, all of 'em." Miss Gardner scooped up her valise and winked at May as she swept by. "Go to Paris. You can thank me when I see you there."

May stood frozen in her place, alone. "Bastards," she said to the empty room, trying out the word. She liked how it felt on her tongue, how it drifted in the air with Miss Gardner's smoke. She smiled and dragged an easel closer to the window to work. This could be the time to go. On her own. The prospect of leaving made her heart beat as though a hummingbird were trapped in her chest. She tapped a paintbrush against the side of the easel and squinted out the window into the brightness. She needed to speak with Marmee. It couldn't wait any longer.

Chapter 26

*W*hen May returned to Orchard House that evening, she found her mother alone at the table surrounded by flannel, broadcloth, and several yards of cotton, cutting trouser legs, waistbands, shirtwaists, cuffs, and collars. At seventy-six years of age, Marmee exhibited a frailness that would have seemed inconceivable to May several years earlier. Now the planes of her skull showed underneath a thin wrinkled layer of skin that looked like crepe after it got wet and dried.

May had to restrain herself from stepping in to help as she watched Marmee struggle to keep the scissors on a straight line as she cut through some yardage of charcoal-colored flannel. "I've decided to make Johnny some new clothes for fall," she said, looking to May with rheumy eyes.

"Doesn't he have plenty of Freddy's old clothes to wear?"

"Freddy's awfully tough on his clothes. Johnny needs some of his own. He shouldn't always be subjected to his older brother's castoffs."

May sat down at the table with Marmee and surveyed the pattern pieces in front of them. Johnny's eleventh birthday approached at the end of the month. He increasingly resembled his father, which was both comforting and heartbreaking. His once-chubby little cheeks were slimmer, leaving him at the sweetly awkward age where his adult teeth were still too large for his young face. May pinned a pattern piece onto some cotton for a waistband, but the fabric puckered under the pattern piece.

Marmee pulled the piece over to her and inspected it close up to her eyes, before giving May a puzzled expression and handing it back to her. "You've gone against the grain."

May rearranged the fabric to get the weave of the fabric lined up correctly with the pattern piece. She looked up to find her mother watching her.

"How was your trip into the city today?"

"Fine," May said, through a mouthful of pins. They continued to pin and cut pieces in silence. Finally, May put down two sleeve pieces and folded her hands in front of her. "I'm thinking about going to Paris."

Marmee placed a leg panel on some yardage of broadcloth without giving any sign she had heard her daughter. May was about to repeat herself, but Marmee asked, "Is Louisa paying for this trip?"

"No, I've been saving all of the money from my print sales and teaching. I'll be going on my own this time."

"Good. I hate to see you leave, but I certainly understand why you must."

"You do?"

"Of course. I've been waiting for you to do something like this for years."

May opened her mouth, yet she did not know what to say.

"May, I admire your discipline, spirit, and creativity, but I've always worried about you. I've never been able to figure out exactly where you were going to land. Anna couldn't wait to start a family on her own; Louisa always wanted to be alone; but you've always seemed to want it all. I'm glad to see you setting off on your own. This adventure could lead you to a path you never expected."

"But I've been so worried about you—"

"Me? Don't worry about me. I'm not going anywhere. I still have my tax petition war to wage against the town's board. I also need to help Anna turn her little beasts into gentlemen. I'm here to stay."

Nothing was holding May back except her own anxieties.

"In fact, Louisa is due to arrive shortly on the train to help me with some letters."

"She's coming here? Tonight? I thought she wasn't leaving New York until next week."

"Well, she came back early. Apparently the heat down there was too much for her, so she returned back to Boston a few days ago and took a room in a boardinghouse somewhere on Beacon Hill. You hadn't heard from her?" When May frowned and shook her head, Marmee shrugged. "Well, with all of your racing back and forth to and from the city, I suppose it's no wonder you missed her letter. She's going to spend the night here and return to Boston tomorrow afternoon. She'll be pleased by the news of your new venture."

May's scissors hovered over the collar piece she needed to cut. She doubted her sister's enthusiasm.

THAT EVENING AFTER Marmee was in bed and Father headed outside to catch the last of the long day's sunshine for his daily constitutional, May found Louisa sitting in the parlor, setting up a round of solitaire.

"Here, deal me in for a game of rummy," May said, sitting down across from her and rearranging the small table to sit between them.

Louisa picked up all of the cards and shuffled before handing the deck out to May to cut it. May picked a spot in the middle of the deck and handed half of the cards back to her sister. Louisa finished her shuffling, dealt the cards, and placed a card—the ten of diamonds—faceup between them. The two sat back to survey their hands, but May's distraction was such that she couldn't focus on her cards.

Louisa frowned as she looked at her hand. "I'll take . . ."

"Louisa, I've saved up enough to return to Europe. I spoke with Marmee about it earlier, and she says I should go," May said in a rush. She watched as her sister's lips vanished into a straight line.

Louisa placed her cards on the table facedown and said coldly, "You can't leave. Can you not see how Marmee's health is suffering?"

May closed her eyes briefly, trying to summon the calm she needed to address her sister. "I'm well aware of Marmee's deteriorating condition. I'm the one who has been here for the last year caring for her. I feel terrible leaving her, but she insists."

"You're doing this to get back at me for going to New York, isn't it?"

May gasped. "No, I'll admit I wasn't pleased when you left, but your absence taught me to be independent. I'm not trying to get back at you at all. This is for me. So I can make something of myself."

Mottled red splotches rose up Louisa's neck and spread across her cheeks. "Of course this is for you. Everything is always for you. Do you realize you may never see Marmee alive again if you leave now?"

May shrank back from her sister. She folded her fan of cards with shaking hands and blinked back tears. "That's a dreadful thing to say."

"Well, it's all true, and you know it. Marmee's hiding her disappointment, but your departure may be the final thing that actually kills her." Louisa's dark eyes flashed in anger, and she stood, pushing at the table in front of them so that the cards spilled over the edge and scattered across the floor. "I've had enough."

In shock, May watched Louisa sweep out of the room. She knelt down, gathered up the cards, and stacked them into one neat pile. At that moment, she hated her sister, partly because she feared Louisa was right. What if this was the last time she saw Marmee?

THE FOLLOWING DAY May knew Louisa was avoiding her. When she entered the dining room from the kitchen, she could see the back of Louisa's brown dress swishing out the doorway ahead of her. The hot, airless rooms of the house did little to assuage the tautness of her nerves. On Louisa's way out of the house to the train station in the afternoon, she brushed past May in the kitchen without saying a word, her knuckles white as seashells as she clasped her valise. Neither sister spoke a word.

May spent the next several weeks in silent agony, watching her mother for any sign of worsening. Each fumbled word, pause, and stumble, each time Marmee struggled to climb the stairs, May held her breath awaiting all of her plans to crumble, but the old woman held steady and continued to talk about the upcoming trip to Europe with enthusiasm. May booked passage on the *China* and considered sending a letter to Louisa before her departure, but abandoned the idea after staring at a blank piece of blue-lined paper for almost an hour without writing a word. Was she supposed to apologize? Thinking about her sister left her innards in knots and her thoughts muddled. She placed the paper back into a drawer and continued packing. Perhaps leaving the bad blood between them to cool was the right tactic.

Three days later, from the deck of the *China*, May searched the crowd looking for Louisa, but her sister never came. She knew Anna had told Louisa of her sailing date. Determined not to let Louisa's absence ruin her excitement, May waved and called to her family with forced merriment. She brushed at her damp eyes and flourished her handkerchief at Father, Marmee, Anna, Freddy, and Johnny. She blew kisses and watched the frothy water churn below as the boat pushed away from the docks. Her family members grew smaller and smaller in the distance. *I'm never returning home at anyone else's behest again. Never again.* She looked up at the gunmetal-gray sky and the gulls circling overhead—they were her witnesses to this vow.

Chapter 27

September 22, 1876
Paris, France

Dear Violet,

I cannot believe I'm finally in Paris! The inside of my poor forearm has a black-and-blue spot because I keep pinching myself to make sure this isn't a dream. You would adore it here. Men and women clad in smart suits and chic gowns spill out of the cafés at all hours of the day and night. The constant parade of people is sublime. I'm living in the ninth arrondissement with Alice Bartol, who has been in France since I left England. She found us a lovely little apartment, and I have a cozy room, complete with a balcony overlooking a small courtyard in which all of the neighborhood cats seem to congregate for daily meetings.

My only complaint about the city is that everything seems to cost three times what I anticipated.

Upon my arrival, Alice insisted we go to the Louvre so I could obtain a copyist pass. We walked along the boulevard des Capucines to take in Monsieur Garnier's newly completed opera house. I cannot even imagine the army of artists needed for such an undertaking—every square inch of the building is covered in statues, medallions, and columns. When we arrived at the Louvre, I could scarcely believe its scale. The National Gallery in London looks positively provincial by comparison.

I've begun to take classes at Monsieur Krug's atelier—one of the few studios in the city open to women. For one hundred francs a month, we can attend up to three sessions with live models and have critique sessions from a number of the city's leading master artists. The cost is a bit more dear than I expected, but there are no other alternatives. Apparently men can pay about half that because the private ateliers are in competition with the free government-run schools—it's all terribly unfair, but I try not to dwell on it.

My daily routine consists of waking in the dark and bolting down a hot mug of chocolate and a delicious flaky butter roll before walking to Monsieur Krug's. At that hour, the streets are full of young men carrying paint cases and sketch pads to their schools and studios, and I cannot help but feel proud to be among the few women who brave this career. There are about thirty other women at

Monsieur Krug's, mostly Americans and Englishwomen. Monsieur Krug is kind enough—I think—he offers up his critiques in a deluge of French, all underneath a shaggy mustache covering his mouth, so I barely understand him. (Fortunately my French is improving daily.) We work until about five o'clock at night, and then Alice and I return to our rooms and have a simple supper, followed by a few rounds of dominoes before bedtime. If I'm lucky, the cats in the courtyard have all gone home, otherwise I'm treated to the sounds of catfights until I fall asleep.

We would have some grand adventures if you were here, but I'm sure you and Mr. Keith are thriving in San Francisco. Please, include some watercolor studies of your new home in your next packet of letters so I can get a taste of your surroundings.

Your loving friend,
May

It was at Monsieur Krug's studio that May first saw the photographic realness some of her classmates were able to achieve with charcoal and pastels. At the end of each afternoon, the women would browse around the studio from one easel to the next—they called this the "walk and gawk" portion of the day. One afternoon, a rough charcoal portrait propped up on an easel stopped May. The face on the paper looked at her with perplexed eyes and an uneasy expression. Charcoal lines bristled at the edge of the subject's head, implying action and immediacy. Frowning, May hurried back to her easel and regarded her work.

"Reveal more personality through your lines," Monsieur Krug said, coming up alongside her, his hand stroking his chin. "Yes, you have a head, but no personality."

"But I don't know anything about the model. How can I do that?"

"You must look at her. Really look. Knowing where to put eyes on a face is not enough. What do those eyes tell us?" Monsieur Krug took a step forward toward May; his black eyes bore down on her. "If you hope to get work onto the wall, you must really look at your subjects."

May glanced at the wall. Each week Monsieur Krug selected several pieces of exceptional art from the class and hung these sketches and paintings on the back wall of the studio. So far, May had yet to have any of her work displayed on it. Cash prizes were awarded to students whose work he selected. The weekly contests motivated the women to try new techniques and produce many studies in the hopes that prolific output would result in more in-depth studies; these final pieces could lead to a piece of work that might be worth entering into Paris's prestigious Salon show. Several weeks earlier, one of Alice's landscapes won twenty francs and the honor of prominent display on the wall. She made a show of spending the prize money on some new shoes with Louis Quinze heels. May wished she had some extra money to spend on supplies at the art supply store on rue du Faubourg Saint-Denis. Spending money on a pair of skimpy shoes made in Paris seemed foolish. Everyone knew shoes made in England lasted twice as long.

Monsieur Krug leaned in closer to May and she could smell

damp leather. "You will have something ready for the Salon's deadline in March, yes?"

"I'll try." She looked down at her knuckle where some black paint clung to her skin and picked at it with her other hand before returning his gaze.

"No, no, no trying. You must do it. Having a piece in the Salon is what launches careers." He narrowed his eyes, as if taking her measure.

May nodded hesitantly. She almost missed Boston, her students, and her comfortable sisterhood of artists.

SINCE ALICE WAS supported by her father and never worried about money, she always had a diversion in mind for them, and May willingly obliged her, while ignoring the persistent voice in her head urging her to work. On weekends, the two women crisscrossed Paris and its environs by train to explore all the charms the area offered. Each of these excursions left May hastily entering expenses into her account ledger, though she tried to keep her eyes from lingering on the shrinking dollar amount she'd pencil in. Jane Gardner's description of her ascetic early days in Paris, working at all hours without taking breaks for amusement, lingered in May's memory and left her with a tightness deep in her belly. She needed to support herself. Asking Louisa for money was no longer an option.

On a cool November morning, Alice suggested taking the train to Longchamp to see the horse races, but May begged off, blaming a headache. She knew she wasn't ill, but she felt heavy and flattened. She decided to walk to the seventh arrondissement where the recently deceased Monsieur Oppenheim's art collection was on view for sale. Though her destination was almost an hour's walk from rue Mansart, she hoped the activity and cold wind, bellowing along the wide boulevards and over the Seine, would revive her.

The previous day she had received a letter from Anna describing a new series of books Mr. Niles planned to publish in the spring called the *No Name Series* in which famous writers could pen anonymous stories. Louisa, taking full advantage of the promise of anonymity, was writing a daring Faustian tale of cruelty, seduction, and betrayal she entitled *A Modern Mephistopheles*. To ensure complete anonymity, Anna explained she would rewrite the story upon its completion so the publishing assistants would not recognize Louisa's handwriting and leak the writer's true identity when it went to press. Marmee added a brief note describing the thrilling wickedness of Louisa's story. The two of them sounded jubilant about the new project. No message from Louisa was included in the envelope. The two sisters had not exchanged a word, written or spoken, since the argument in the parlor and an emptiness hollowed out her chest when May pictured Marmee, Anna, and Louisa all back in Concord, joined in merriment at their daring antics. She shivered. Her fashionable but thin navy blue velvet jacket had been a poor choice for the blustery day.

Relieved to get out of the cold, she entered the building housing the art show. The reflection of her white face in the opulent gilt mirrors lining the walls prompted her to pinch her cheeks as she rode up the elevator. When she entered the Oppenheim family's private apartment, the tightness behind her eyes loosened at the sight of two Meissonier paintings of military scenes immediately in front of the doorway. His richly adorned officers and their beautiful horses were so lifelike the horse flesh practically rippled over the taut muscles of the creatures.

May stepped backward to take it all in and bumped into another woman.

The woman turned to regard May. "You're American." It was a statement, not a question, not an accusation.

"Yes. You are, too?"

"I'm originally from Pennsylvania but have lived here for several years now." The woman, tall and handsome in a decidedly unbeautiful way, introduced herself as Mary Cassatt. Recognition flashed through May for she knew Miss Cassatt was one of a handful of women whose work had been consistently shown in the Salon over the years. Many women at Monsieur Krug's held the Philadelphian in high regard. Unlike the self-taught Jane Gardner, Mary came from a wealthy family, and part of her upbringing consisted of studying at the Academy of Art in her hometown. May introduced herself.

"I'm here on my own. Seeing all of these lovely horses makes me wish for my own back in Concord."

"Where are you living now?"

"In the ninth arrondissement."

Mary smiled. "Are you game for a walk? I'm on my way out and have a little time before I must be somewhere at two o'clock. I'd like to show you something."

Although May had just arrived at the show, she could not

pass on the opportunity to spend time with Mary Cassatt and agreed easily.

A frigid wind whipped their cheeks as they crossed the Seine by the Allée de Castiglione and strolled through the Jardin des Tuileries where May could see the long gray buildings of the Louvre in the distance through the leafless pollarded trees. They crossed the vast square of the Place Vendôme, and May pulled her collar higher in an attempt to stay warm. Where were they going? Mary led her to rue Laffitte in the heart of the ninth arrondissement and stopped to point at some framed pastel sketches in a large window.

"I've become increasingly drawn to these and feel compelled to visit my framed friends several times a week," said Mary.

Reluctantly, May pulled her gaze off the parade of women strutting by in sumptuous furs to study the three drawings in the window. One showed a ballet dancer bending over awkwardly to adjust her slipper, the second showed a row of ballerinas stretching, and the third showed a woman leaning against a table, posed with her hands out and head tilted in mid-conversation.

"These are for sale? They look unfinished."

"They're done and, yes, they're for sale."

May leaned in and looked closer. The women's faces were barely sketched in with features, yet they radiated a sense of boredom and cynicism. How did the artist achieve this? Was it through their slouching postures? No, it was more than that. May leaned in until her nose practically rested against the glass.

Mary laughed. "You're intrigued?"

"Well, yes. I have a distinctly voyeuristic feeling as I look at these, but can't put my finger on why."

"They feel very true, very real, don't you think?"

May tilted her head. "Yes, but they're so unposed. So sketchy."

"They're different." Mary trained her eyes on May, sizing her up.

"They certainly are." May said slowly. "I'm unaccustomed to seeing people posed so informally. These feel spontaneous."

"Yes, exactly. This spontaneity interests me." Mary Cassatt turned back to the glass and continued to stare at the drawings, seemingly forgetting May stood beside her. After a few minutes, she looked around the street and at May as if she had lost track of where she was. "I should go. If you like, please visit me in my studio and we can talk more." Mary pulled a slim silver monogrammed case out of her handbag, flipped it open, and handed May an elegant cream-colored calling card with her name and address printed in a graceful font along the front of it. Holding the card in her hand, May watched the woman glide down the boulevard toward Montmartre and vanish into the crowds.

Chapter 28

Spring approached and the work in Monsieur Krug's studio intensified as the upcoming Salon exhibition deadline neared. While portraiture and heroic historical scenes reigned supreme as the most desirable genres, they were also the hardest to execute. May decided to capitalize on her existing strengths and focus her efforts on a small still life. She assembled an assortment of yellow and green apples on a table in a corner of their drawing room on rue Mansart, adding a jug and bottle of Maraschino wine to the composition as an afterthought. The apples appealed to her New England roots. She spent a little over a week painting every evening after dinner, building up her layers of paint to create rich jewel-tone colors, while Alice attended concerts and shows with other friends.

May arrived at Monsieur Krug's one morning to find Monsieur Muller, one of the other master teachers, in the studio offering critiques. She ran back to the apartment to retrieve her still life and arrived back at the atelier out of breath. These sessions took on the gravity of life and death sentencing with the Salon deadline hanging over them, so no one noticed her dishevelment; everyone's attention centered on the various pieces put forth for critique. Messieurs Krug and Muller stood in front of May's painting and discussed it in rapid French.

"*Très bien, très bien*, Miss Alcott." Monsieur Muller turned to May. "This is a fine demonstration of color. The composition is natural and most becoming."

Monsieur Krug also beamed. "Mademoiselle Alcott, you must submit this to the Salon."

"Please, attach our names to your entry to announce you're our student," Monsieur Muller added.

May's dumbfounded expression prompted all of the other student painters to laugh good-naturedly. All except Alice. Her jaw tightened. She turned away from the group to return to her own easel. At the end of class, Alice scurried out the door.

May plodded back to their apartment, worrying over Alice's reaction to the critique back at the studio. If Alice resented May's success, perhaps she should have been spending less time at the opera and more time working, as May did. After arriving home, May set out a supper of salmon filets and rice and waited. The brightness of the fish's flesh faded by the time Alice pushed the front door open, carrying a bouquet of white roses. Instead of joining May at the table, she turned her back and moved to the far corner of their drawing room to arrange a still life of the white roses.

"Those flowers are lovely, but don't you want to sit down and eat first?"

"I don't have time. I must get to work while there's still some light."

May raised her eyebrows and picked at some rice silently, watching as her friend draped the flowers casually on their sides on a white lace tablecloth. It was a challenging composition, but Alice set to work on capturing the texture and the play of shadows within the white petals without any more mention of eating. May finished her meal and cleaned up the two plates in silence.

Alice skipped going to the studio the next day and stayed behind to work on her still life, and an uneasiness spread through their rooms with the heavy air of a coming rainstorm.

THE DAY OF the Salon's deadline arrived. Alice had stayed up all night finishing her painting. In the morning, her lips looked cracked and painful from being bitten. She pulled the canvas from the easel, gently easing her index finger onto the surface to see if it was still tacky to the touch, but a splotch of dark paint stuck to her fingertip. She picked up some sketch paper and used it to fan her canvas. The messengers were scheduled to pick up May and Alice's submissions later in the morning.

The women waited, largely in silence. May propped up her canvas and made a sketch of it to send to her mother. By noon, there was still no sign of the messengers, so she wrote a letter to Marmee to accompany her sketch. Alice paced the drawing room, stopping every few minutes to check if her painting had dried.

"I feel sick," Alice said, clutching her stomach.

"Don't worry, our paintings will get picked up."

"They're cutting it awfully close."

"They must be overwhelmed with deliveries. They'll come."

Alice chewed at her thumbnail and continued to pace, avoiding the space where May stood looking out the window.

Finally, the messengers arrived in the middle of the afternoon, flustered and distracted by the volume of work they needed to deliver that day. As soon as they left, May and Alice raced ahead to the Palais de l'Industrie to ensure their precious cargo arrived before the magic hour of six o'clock when the doors would shut. A line of wagons lugging sculptures and huge canvases sprawled for blocks. A huge crowd gathered on the stairway to the entrance of the Palais de l'Industrie to preview the work being submitted. As the porters, sweating under the late afternoon sun, carried the artwork into the building, people cheered and booed at the work passing by. The whole scene took on the manic energy of a festival.

At ten minutes of six, there was still no sign that May and Alice's paintings had arrived.

"Could we have missed them somehow?" Alice said, tugging on May's shoulder.

May shaded her eyes against the glare of sunshine and looked down the long line of traffic still waiting to arrive at the Palais de l'Industrie. "I don't think so."

"Maybe the judges will extend the deadline so all of this artwork can get inside."

A snort came from May's side where a fellow stood cracking his knuckles, eyeing the line of frenzied porters trailing down the block. "No chance. They just shut the doors, no matter what," he said in a glum tone. The two women exchanged worried looks. The seconds ticked by. Six o'clock arrived.

"Now what?" May cried.

The man next to them turned and thrust his hands into his pockets. "Go home. If your pieces snuck by in the mess, they're in. If they got backed up and are still out there, they'll deliver 'em back to you this evening."

"And that's it?"

"That's it. Next year, maybe the messengers will pick 'em up earlier." He gave a small shake of his head and disappeared into the dispersing crowd.

May and Alice looked at each other, unable to utter a word. They wandered down the stairs and cut along the grass to avoid the dust kicked up by the wagons and horses. After weeks of working all day and night, May moved as though her buttoned calf leather boots had been dipped in lead. She looked down the line of traffic waiting to exit the front of the Palais and spotted a familiar dark green wagon. One of their deliverymen sat on his bench above the empty cargo bed. He saw May, tipped his cap to her, and gave a wink.

"Look!" May pointed at the wagon. "He's empty. He made it in time!"

Alice pulled May into an embrace, and the women leaned into each other, laughing with relief. May closed her eyes, cherishing her friend's joy after a week of strained silence. Their work had finally made it into the Palais and had a chance to be accepted into the Salon. *But more important*, May thought, *our friendship remains intact.*

Chapter 29

All of Paris obsessed over the upcoming Salon. People everywhere—Monsieur Krug's studio, the hallways of the Louvre, and Montmartre's cafés—spent countless hours debating whose work would get in and whose work would not. When May received a note from Mary inviting her to a different, smaller art show, May readily accepted, eager to be distracted from thinking about the Salon.

Over the winter, Mary Cassatt and May had met several times at the Philadelphian's studio to have tea and discuss the city's art world. Mary told May about a group of artists who were experimenting with composition, style, and technique. After their work was consistently rejected by the Salon for several years, the renegade artists assembled their own independent show. The press dubbed them "Impressionists" and derided the artists as lunatics, yet the group persisted, remaining committed to challenging the boundaries of what was considered art. Their unconventional work and perseverance intrigued May.

On the day she was to meet Mary at the show, May turned onto rue le Peletier and saw her friend wearing a distressed expression as she waited outside the building housing the show.

May hurried toward Mary. "What's the matter?"

Mary tucked her chin down and whispered, "I can't help myself. I'm convinced my entry to the Salon this year will be rejected."

"Goodness, if you're worried, the rest of us don't stand a chance. You've had such successes with the Salon." May thought of the study she had seen of Mary's first entry: a lovely traditionally styled portrait of a young folk girl holding a mandolin. Mary's Salon exposure over the years had led to several of her paintings being sold to dealers in New York City, and she regularly received commissions to create new pieces of work.

Mary shook her head and fidgeted with her gloves. "I just don't feel like I'm painting what I really know. When I was rejected two years ago, my instructor advised me to darken the background, so I did, and it was accepted the following year. It makes no sense. It seems there's no method to the madness, yet our very careers hinge upon these capricious judges."

"I know, but I'm just trying to stay hopeful."

Mary raised a gloved hand to her temple and continued speaking as if she hadn't heard May. "Don't you think it's absurd that all it took was a minor change for my painting to be accepted? I'm convinced it's all very political."

May reached for her friend's gloved hands and looked into Mary's agitated eyes. "We did our best for the Salon, and now we must wait. In the meantime, let's try not to think about it, or I shall get very nervous, too."

"I'm sorry. I've been obsessing over my work and doubting everything recently. But I should remain optimistic like you and not lose my head."

"Well, I'm not exactly optimistic that my painting will be accepted, in fact, I think it's very unlikely." May shrugged and smiled. "But I've nothing to lose by trying."

"True. I admire your fearlessness."

"Some might call it foolishness."

"Well, whatever it is, I like it about you." Mary wrapped an arm around May's shoulders and led her into the exhibit. A huge canvas hung in the entry, showing an intersection of several streets. Paris's hulking new limestone buildings dominated the background.

Mary cocked her head as she studied the painting. "Hmm, isn't that Carrefour de Moscou in North Paris?"

"I feel as though something's wrong with my eyes. It looks fuzzy," May said, blinking furiously as she studied the figures carrying umbrellas in the painting.

"No, I don't think so." Mary took a step closer to the canvas. "Look, the couple right in front of us are slightly out of focus, and it's the people there"—she pointed to the middle of the composition—"who are depicted clearly. Why, it's like a photograph!"

May wrinkled her nose as she tried to make sense of it. "But why is one man cropped halfway out of the painting?"

"I've never seen such a monumental painting that wasn't some sort of Biblical or historic scene."

"I feel as if I've never seen such a monumental-sized painting of anything. It's huge. It must have taken ages." May leaned forward to see the information tag next to it: "*Rue de Paris; Temps de pluie* by Gustave Caillebotte," she read aloud. "Does that mean *Paris Street; time to rain?*"

"It translates roughly to *Paris Street; a rainy day*."

They continued along the wall of canvases. The show was composed of five rooms and a couple of hundred paintings. "Is this much smaller than the Salon?"

"Oh, you have no idea." Mary gave a small laugh. "Just wait."

A tall, gray-haired man with an intense expression passed them and tipped his hat to Mary.

"Who was that?" May whispered.

"A painter named Monsieur Degas. Remember those sketches I showed you when we first met? The pictures of the women hanging in the window of the Durand-Ruel Gallery? He created them."

"The pastels?" May thought back to those ballerinas and watched the man. He looked back at Mary and paused momentarily before exiting the apartment. "Do you know him?"

Mary made a noncommittal sound and continued to study the paintings on the wall.

May was drawn to a series of paintings by a man named Claude Monet set inside a train station. Great swathes of swirling steam hovered in the air, dwarfing the people painted on the bottom portion of the canvas. Looking at the paintings,

May could practically feel the heat rising from the black trains and hear the din of the travelers and shuddering groans of the locomotives. She walked along the series, admiring the man's ability to create atmosphere and lighting. Monsieur Monet's paintings evoked the grand atmospheric landscapes and maritime scenes of J. M. W. Turner, though these had a more modern sensibility with the emphasis on machinery and city dwellers. Upon close inspection, the canvases appeared to be lumpy, as though they had been coated in thick globs of paint; this technique—or lack of technique—would be very different from the thin layers of paint applied with invisible brushstrokes May expected to see at the Salon.

When the women left the show, Mary was quieter than usual as they walked back toward their homes, undoubtedly still worrying over her Salon entry. May allowed herself to imagine how enormous the show at the Palais de l'Industrie would be and her stomach dropped at the thought. Canvases would cover every square inch of wall from the floor to the ceiling while crowds of people covered every square inch of floor. Indeed, the Impressionists' show was small and empty in comparison to what the Salon promised, yet despite this, May couldn't help but marvel at the rebelliousness of their experimentation.

MAY AND ALICE were home from Monsieur Krug's for lunch when a loud rapping at the door startled them. May answered the door, adjusting her eyes to the twilight of the hallway before seeing a messenger slouched against the wall. He thrust two envelopes into her hands and darted away. She shut the door and turned to find Alice watching, her face grave. In silence, she passed Alice her envelope. With sweating hands, May tried to remind herself that entering a painting into the Salon had been merely a lark without any hope of success. Her fingers shook as she pulled off the seal to open the letter.

> *L'Académie des Beaux-Arts est ravie de vous annoncer que votre tableau a été accepté au Salon de 1877.*

May gave a small laugh which came out more as a strangled throat clearing and looked up to find Alice's eyes locked upon her.

"Did you get in?"

May nodded, unable to trust her voice.

Alice stared down at her letter as if the power of concentration alone could somehow alter the wording of the news in her hands. She remained in place, ran a hand through her curls, and looked downward. Her eyes blinked furiously. May's excitement crumpled under the weight of her friend's obvious disappointment.

"Oh, Alice, thousands were turned down."

"But not you."

"I got lucky."

"How are you *always* lucky?" Alice spat out the words and whirled away. Moments later, a door slammed.

Stunned, May left the apartment and went back to the art studio. Why did people always think she was so lucky?

She worked like the devil to make good things happen. She stalked back to Monsieur Krug's, and her classmates were thrilled at her happy news, but the knowledge she must return to face Alice put a knot in the pit of her stomach. After class, her classmates took her to a café in the Place Pigalle to celebrate, but when the group all pushed their spoons toward the plate of chocolate eclairs in the middle of the table, May drew back, a sense of nausea burning at the back of her throat. She swallowed and politely excused herself to walk home alone.

She arrived back at rue Mansart to find Alice sitting on the settee in the drawing room, reading. A stack of addressed envelopes sat on the end table beside her elbow. May hovered, uncertain whether to sit or continue into the next room.

"Claudette made a quiche Lorraine before leaving," Alice said, not looking up from her book. "It's cooling in the larder now."

"I thought I smelled something delicious. I hope she shut the kitchen window or one of those spiteful cats will be in there eating our dinner. I've never seen such fat feral cats before."

Alice did not lift her eyes from her book. In silence, May retrieved cutlery and set the table for two in the drawing room.

"I already ate. I won't be joining you."

May picked up the extra place setting and returned it to the kitchen. When she came back to the drawing room, she sat across from her longtime friend.

"I'm terribly sorry you've been disappointed today."

Alice raised her head from her book and looked at May with a cool expression. "I've decided I'll return to Boston."

"When the studio closes for the summer next month?"

"No, immediately."

"You can't go. We've been on this journey now together for so long. Next year, you're bound to . . ."

Alice closed her book with a decisive snap that made May jump. "I'm leaving. I've been here for a few years now. It's time." She gave an impatient small shake of her head. "I was waiting to see what the Salon would bring, but now I'm just too disappointed to wait any longer. I've been working so hard. I thought I had a chance when Monsieur Krug and Monsieur Muller reviewed your work. It's just . . ."

It's just that you've been studying longer than me? You've opened so many doors for me? You've studied with more illustrious masters? May squeezed the arms of her chair as she imagined all of the things her friend could say. Alice was the one who started May off on this quest when she met her at the Bishops' party, almost seven years ago, and May's heart ached to think of the jealousy now separating them, but at the same time, defensiveness pulsed in her shoulders as if urging her to raise her arms into a fighting stance as she had seen her nephews do. All of her hard work finally yielded some results. All of the times she said no to attending a concert, a race, a dance—all of her sacrifices had finally paid off. She refused to apologize for her success, but she took a deep breath.

"You mustn't take this so hard. Everyone is complaining about the unfairness of the judging. Why, last year Mary submitted a painting they rejected the previous year. All she did was darken the background, submit it a second time, *et voilà*, it was accepted. It's crazy!"

Alice nodded impatiently. "I know, I know, but all of the judging controversies do little to make me feel better. I wanted this so much."

May sighed; she understood. All of them wanted acceptance no matter how much they convinced themselves it was meaningless and unfair. It was absurd that a panel of stodgy old men decided their fates, and even though the Académie had been officially separated from the government's oversight the decade before, everyone knew the judges were conservative and political. Who were they to decide what was beautiful? The old geezers simply continued to reward the male artists who had moved through the system of L'École des Beaux-Arts painting subjects that paid tribute to France's centuries of tradition. May's small still life certainly fit in the vein of acceptable work, but didn't Alice's as well? There was no rhyme or reason to it, May thought crossly.

A memory of receiving the reviews of *Little Women* burned through her mind. She flinched and closed her eyes briefly before looking at her friend. She knew the pain of rejection all too well and uncurled her fingers from the arms of her chair, straightening them to stretch the blood back into each one. "Your painting was beautiful. Those roses, all of the texture, and subtly with shading—it showed great skill. The judges got it wrong. I'm sorry, but please, don't quit Paris, don't leave."

"Thank you, you're kind, but my mind is made up," Alice

said with a taut expression. "Don't worry, I'll pay my part of the rent through June."

"Rent is my last concern. I shall miss you."

After that evening, Alice never confessed to feeling disappointed again, but things shifted, and a distance yawned between the two women. As Alice closed her affairs in Paris, she no longer sought May out for any last shopping trips or excursions. Conversations felt stilted. May missed the easy companionship they once enjoyed. Alice remained true to her word and left Paris for Boston within two weeks.

MARY CASSATT'S PAINTING also suffered disappointment. May dreaded facing her, but nevertheless visited her friend's studio on rue de Laval and found Mary sitting on a couch reading a letter. Every aspect of Mary's studio showed an eye for beauty: the geometric patterned Turkish carpet; the brightly colored Moorish pottery standing on the mantel; the handsome mahogany furniture in the room. Although evening approached, bright light suffused the room, testament to the high rent the space required. Mary's expression looked weary, but she greeted May warmly, congratulating her on the acceptance to the Salon. "You've been working with such dedication. I'm thrilled to see your success," she assured May.

"Thank you. I'd be completely disingenuous if I claimed to not care. My family is going to be so pleased by this."

"They should be. I'm stung by my own rejection, but am beginning to wonder if this is an indication I need to rethink my approach to painting. We'll see." She looked down at a letter dangling loosely in her hand, bit her lip, and attempted to smile.

"What's happened?" May's first thought was that Mary had received news from home about her sister, Lydia, who was beset by chronic health problems.

Mary stood and drifted to the window. "One of my dearest friendships appears to have ended."

May rose to stand by her side.

The blue light of the late afternoon gave Mary's complexion a waxy appearance and made the shadows of her face a dark violet. May followed her friend's gaze out across the street to the view of windows across the way. Lights flickered on, and the outlines of people darted in and out of the windows. Olive greens and indigos appeared in the shadowed stonework of the buildings, and a brilliant flame of orange outlined the mansard rooftops in the distance as the sun began its slow burn downward.

"My friend, Emily Sartain, and I appear to have fallen out of favor with one another. She is closed to any new ideas about painting and thinks I'm crazy to be entertaining the possibility of exhibiting with the Impressionists next year."

A maid entered the studio carrying a tray of hot chocolate and biscuits, distracting May from her surprise at Mary's revelation about joining the Impressionists. The women left the window and took seats to serve themselves from the tea platter. The teacups were so delicate and thin, they let the light through like the pink of a rabbit's ear. Swirls of gold paint and roses decorated the china. May took a sip of her chocolate and admired the array of paintings and lithographs dotting the walls.

Mary pointed to a canvas hanging above them. "I recently purchased this from Berthe Morisot. Do you like it?"

"Her colors are so vivid." Almost lurid, May thought.

"Yes, Madame Morisot is a talent. I envy the way she has boldly created a unique style for herself." Mary's face looked wistful.

"It's easy to be bold when you have resources to fall back upon," May said, knowing of Madame Morisot's wealthy aristocratic Parisian family.

Mary stirred her hot chocolate. The ticking of a clock on the mantel echoed through the studio. "You're always so practical."

"I have to be. I'm trying to support myself."

"Many of the Impressionist painters we saw in that show are also trying to support themselves."

"Yes, and they're making it dreadfully hard to earn a living by distancing themselves from the establishment."

"Well, I'm considering joining this group of painters because I'm tired of the Salon. Its system is too rigid in its values. I've worked too hard to be a victim of the politics of the game any longer. Monsieur Degas has been pressing his case for me to join his band of renegade painters for several months now."

May thought back to the man with the intense expression she had glimpsed at the art show the previous month, and Mary's reticence toward discussing him. Now it seemed the two artists were in regular communication with each other. May put down her teacup, for she didn't want her shaking hands to betray her shock. Since childhood, Mary's art instruction had been exemplary. In America, she'd enrolled at the Pennsylvania Academy of the Fine Arts, and, once abroad, she joined the master studios of Chaplin, Couture, and Gérôme—Mary represented everything May admired and respected. Now Mary stood poised to push her ambitions to a point that appeared inconceivable to May. "So you're really going to do it?"

"Yes. Why should the government tell us what art should look like? Artists should have the freedom to represent the world as they see it without fear they will be ridiculed by a government-sponsored show." Mary placed an uneaten cookie back on her plate. "I apologize for getting my dander up, but I've worked too hard to suffer these indignities any further."

"I admire your daring." May wondered if Mary's emotions would settle as time passed and excitement over the Salon died down. Perhaps this rebellion would be short lived.

"I know, I know, it probably seems crazy, but I just can't pretend to make something that doesn't feel authentic to me."

"You remind me of my sister. She writes all of these books that don't really interest her. She would be happier if she could simply write what she wants."

They both nodded, looking into their teacups. After making plans to meet at the Salon the following week, Mary walked May to the door and took her hand. "Thank you."

"For what? You're the one who served me a delightful tea," May said, laughing as she looked into her friend's dark eyes.

"For understanding me."

"Honestly, I don't understand what you're doing, but I suppose I understand why you're doing it."

"I can always count on you to be opinionated and honest, yet you don't judge. It's a rare combination."

The two women squeezed hands, and May walked out the door.

When Mary had first befriended her, May often wondered what the more accomplished artist saw in her; undoubtedly Mary possessed connections to wealthier society types, and her commissions and fluent French provided her with access into the world of Parisian artists. But over time, May came to see Mary for what she was: a woman caught in between spheres that did not quite fit together. The expatriate American society in Paris bored Mary; the insular male-dominated culture of painters in Paris did not fully accept her. May understood the challenge, for she didn't fit neatly into a category either.

Chapter 30

Varnishing Day was upon them, the day to preview her painting at the Salon, the day to touch up her work and make adjustments before the show's doors opened to the public. May's hands felt clammy just thinking about it all. What if her beloved still life was hanging in some out-of-the-way corner? What if the lighting was too dark?

Rose Peckham, a woman from her class, joined her at the Palais de l'Industrie, and May was thankful she did. Paint boxes littered the floors, and ladders blocked many of the walls. The sheer magnitude of the number of pieces of art took May's breath away.

"How on earth will I find my painting?" May grimaced as she looked at the thickness of the program in her hand.

"It's alphabetical. See?" Rose smiled and pointed to the first page of names and led May forward along the hallway. "Your painting can't be too far in here." Each room looked like a motley collection of assorted genres, colors, and sizes that left May's head spinning.

"I'm just so worried that my little still life is going to be tucked behind a door somewhere."

Rose grabbed her arm. "Here. I've found your painting, and it's right on the sight line. Could you be any luckier?" She tugged May over to a wall. May followed with her heart in her throat and stopped in front of her work. Her humble little still life could have been dwarfed by some of the larger canvases surrounding it, but its vibrant colors made it glow proudly, a nudge over the line that was considered to be the ideal placement. May stopped breathing. It was here, at the Salon. Her painting. Thousands had been turned down, but her work was accepted. Her pulse raced and she inhaled deeply. If only Marmee could see it.

"I don't dare touch it. Am I daft?"

"Your location couldn't be any better." Rose took a step back and squinted. "I'm not sure I'd take the chance either. It looks perfect."

"I'm so dizzy with excitement, I'm worried my hands would shake and splatter paint everywhere."

"Well then, let's not take any chances. Shall we go mingle?"

Rose took her arm and the two women roamed the hallways, previewing the other art. May caught sight of a familiar figure, standing by herself in a black dress, a cigarette held between two fingers.

"Miss Gardner?"

The woman turned. The same narrow pale face from Boston one year earlier gazed back at May. "So, you finally made it to Paris. Do you have some work here?"

"Yes, a small still life."

"Good for you." Miss Gardner's distracted smile became warmer. "Now the hard work really begins—you'll have to capitalize on this victory." She gave a rueful laugh and turned to look at the wall crowded with paintings, all vying for attention.

"Which one is yours?" May asked.

Miss Gardner nodded her head to a large frame of two women standing over the baby Moses in a basket by the water's edge. "This painting has been the death of me. I've been working on it for over a year."

"It's beautiful."

"Thank you. The critics say it resembles my mentor's work too much. I've told those bloody reviewers that if my work looks like his, good—after all, Bouguereau's the best." She dropped the cigarette to the floor and crushed it out with the toe of her boot. "And God knows, this isn't my first show. Maybe his work looks like *mine*, but no, they never say a man's work is derivative."

May and Rose watched the other American chew her lip.

Miss Gardner glanced over at them. "Sorry, you're catching me in a strange mood."

"Well, this is a strange day. We all show up to see our work and size up everyone else's while the anticipation of tomorrow hangs over everyone."

"Yes, tomorrow's the real circus. Normally I enjoy the pageantry of it all, but this year . . ." She sighed and put her hands on her hips while her eyes swept over the room to see if anyone was watching them. She took a step closer to May. "This year has been a tough one for me."

May leaned in closer to hear more.

"I've been studying with Bouguereau, and he's inspired me in so many ways—he's a true kindred spirit to me. But his wife died last week, and it's turned everything to rot."

"I can imagine."

"Actually, I'm not sure you can." She paused and spoke quietly as if speaking to herself. "I can barely understand what's happening myself."

They stood side by side, an island in the midst of surging currents of people surrounding them. Miss Gardner appeared to be in a bad way: chapped lips, shadows under her eyes, and ragged cuticles on her fingers. She fidgeted at her dress's collar below her chin.

"Miss Gardner, it will all be fine. Go home and get some rest for tomorrow."

"Look how the tables have turned; now you're the one propping me up. And honestly, we've known each other for too long for you to still be calling me Miss Gardner. Call me Jane." She rummaged inside the small satchel she was carrying before handing May a card. "Please, call on me. Good luck tomorrow."

May watched as Jane's slender figure cut through the crowds. People recognized her and spread to open a path.

THAT EVENING MAY wrote a letter home to tell her family all about her thrilling day. Nearly eight months had passed since she exchanged letters with Louisa; it was time to extend an olive branch. She ended it with an upbeat boast.

Who would have imagined my good fortune would finally arrive in the form of a painting barely larger than a postage stamp? This is proof that Louisa does not monopolize all of the Alcott talent! Ha! Sister, this is the first feather plucked from your cap, and I shall endeavor to fill mine with so many waving in the breeze that you will be quite ready to lay down your pen and rest on the laurels you've already won.

Love,
May

The thrill of Opening Day filled May with a pride that threatened to make her burst. It all passed by in a crushing swirl of bright colors, cigar smoke, feathers, silk, satin, top hats, and sparkling jewelry. She saw all of her classmates and teachers from Monsieur Krug's and caught glimpses of some of the well-known artists, reporters, and writers working in Paris. Even the famous actress Sarah Bernhardt toured the exhibition.

At the end of the day, May and Rose collapsed in the drawing room of May's apartment after stopping at Tortoni on boulevard des Italiens for ices and sorbet.

"My feet might be permanently stuck in these boots—they feel swollen from walking around so much today," May said. Her cheeks ached from smiling.

"Did you see the man who came through with the parrot perched on his shoulder?"

"Only in Paris."

Over the next few days, her victory at the Salon seemed increasingly hollow. May missed Alice. Her dearest friend had left without a backward glance, and it stung. May tried not to think that their relationship was over. Despite the positive reviews May's painting received in the Salon, no commission inquiries came her way. Without long-standing roots and connections in Paris, she couldn't sell her work. No sales meant no summer classes with master painters out in the country. No sales meant that she couldn't afford the apartment on rue Mansart either. She did not have a plan for what to do when she ran out of money. The only thing she knew was that she couldn't ask Louisa to pay for anything.

The summer closure of Monsieur Krug's studio also meant the disbandment of her circle of fellow artists. During her discussions with her other painters, the town of Grez kept popping up. The village, south of Paris on the outskirts of the Fontaine-bleau Forest, had become an informal artist's colony during the summer, an alternative to better-known Barbizon and Giverny. Grez sounded more and more like the ideal spot for May to shore up her options for fall, but she needed a travel companion and ticked the possibilities off on her fingers—Mary had left for Italy with her family; Alice was gone; Rose Peckham planned to visit Switzerland—but then an idea struck her. May knew exactly who she'd ask.

Chapter 31

July 25, 1877
Grez-sur-Loing, France

Dearest Violet,

I've pulled up stakes from Paris to escape to a quaint artist's retreat south of Paris. This tiny enclave is just the respite I need after all of my hard work in the city last winter. I've brought my friend Jane Gardner with me. When I visited her studio to invite her to join me, she practically had her bag packed before I was done telling her about Grez. You would adore her adventurous spirit and irreverent sense of humor. Now that I think on it, you would adore everything about this getaway.

Grez is so small, there's only room for two modest hotels. It's really more of a jumble of stone buildings with slate *roofs than a village. Jane and I decided to stay at the Pension Laurent, for its quaint stone façade promised to stay cool, no matter how warm the days become. We've been adopted into a motley assortment of writers and painters who have descended upon this little treasure of a spot, ostensibly to hone their craft, but in reality their time is spent drinking red wine, cavorting in the river, playing games, dancing, and carousing late into the early hours of each day. Their prescription for recovery from the highs and lows of artistic life has been just what I needed.*

There's one fellow, a Scotsman, who offered some romance, but he's a poet, and I've no need for more writers in my life. I served as a muse for Louisa once—I have no interest in reprising that role. Though I've always admired your marriage with Mr. Keith, I've begun to think that I've missed my opportunity to find a similar partnership. My thirty-seventh birthday arrives tomorrow, and against all of my expectations, I'm still on my own. I know what you're thinking—I can practically hear you calling out to me to take a chance on love, but I'm just too far down this path and must stay focused on the job at hand: art.

Yours,

May

She put down her pen and leaned back, stretching her arms up overhead, wishing that Violet was not half a world away. Though she kept telling herself that age meant nothing, she knew that wasn't exactly true, time was passing—was it passing her by? Her life did not seem to be unfolding the way she had always pictured, and though she continued to remind herself to enjoy the unexpected delights in her path, a sense of absence lingered.

She let herself think back to when she and Jane had arrived in Grez. Eager to stretch out their legs after the hour-long train ride, the two women had walked away from the village to the river.

They followed a worn path that dipped down into a copse of trees to meet the riverbank, leading them to encounter a group of men and women picnicking beside the water. Abandoned empty wine bottles glittered in the grass and several rowboats appeared to be racing on the river. One veered in toward the shore where May and Jane watched with growing interest.

"Can either of you row?" a man called out in a thick Scottish brogue. "Good lord, my shoulder hasn't recovered from yesterday's swimming races. I hate to admit defeat to my cousin this quickly."

"I can," May said, untying her boots and lifting her skirts to climb through the water and into the boat, as Jane looked on with arched eyebrows.

"Excellent! I'll be your coxswain, although I suppose I'm probably much too heavy for the job." He repositioned himself in the bow of the boat. "Off we go! See you at the finish line," he called out to Jane. She pulled out her handkerchief to wave them off, letting it flutter over her head.

"My manners are abhorrent, I apologize. My name's Bob Adamson. I always admire a lass who will just hop into a boat

with a strange fellow and start rowing." He nodded approvingly
at the smooth motion of May's oars cutting through the water.
"And you know the tricks! What luck!"

"I'm May Alcott. This is my Harvard stroke."

"Aha! An American. Lovely." They both laughed, May luxu-
riating in stretching out the muscles of her back and arms as
she pulled and pushed the oars against the resistance of the
river. They gained on the two other boats ahead. Shouts of
encouragement bounced over the river.

"You're new here?"

"Yes." May gasped in between deep breaths.

"Oh, sorry, I should allow you to focus on the job at hand."
He lifted his head and shouted out at the boat closest to them.
"Ha! I've brought a new recruit aboard. Ahoy there, mates, off
we go."

Their closest rivals groaned, and May sped up her rowing
to pass them. Bob cheered and jeered at their opponents when
May propelled the nose of their boat past a fellow waving a red
scarf along the shore to signify the finish line. May's coxswain
navigated their boat to the riverbank and stood up to announce
to the group, "Ladies and gentlemen, I hereby welcome two
new members into our merry band of misfits!" He turned back
to May and winked. "Bet you didn't know what you were getting into when you stumbled down here—eh?"

That evening, while tucked in the garden courtyard behind
the Hotel Chevillon, May noticed Bob's efforts to keep her glass
of red wine full and the languid way he rested his arm along
the back of her chair. The ease with which he leaned in to tell

a story to the group, the crinkle of lines around his eyes, and the drape of his lanky body as he stretched back confidently on the spindly little wooden chair underneath him—May knew it was all an invitation. They could have sunk into the shadows beyond the candlelight, sunk into each other. Yes, it tempted her, but not enough. She blinked away the dulling torpor of wine seeping through her, brushed her hair out of her face, and excused herself for the night, amidst cries to stay with them *just a bit longer*. She knew where *just a bit longer* would lead. Instead, she wanted to rise in the early morning hours to paint the magic light of dawn on the river. She had a job to do.

A FEW WEEKS later, May found herself lying on her back next to Jane in the shade of the riverbank, watching Bob develop a game that involved swimming and trying to throw a ball at a target—the rules appeared to be evolving in response to the shenanigans ensuing in the water.

"I could stay here forever." May rolled over onto her belly, crossed her arms, and laid her head down upon her hands. She closed her eyes and absorbed the warmth of the sun soaking into the back of her linen dress.

"I probably *should* stay here forever," Jane said, frowning.

May rolled onto her elbows and looked over at Jane expectantly. "Why were you so eager to quit Paris?"

Jane gave a bitter grimace and dodged May's eyes by looking at the sky. "If I told you, you'd think less of me."

"Hardly. Come on, I turned thirty-seven years old last month. Few things surprise me anymore."

"I'm caught up in a romance with my mentor."

"Bouguereau?"

"He's the one." Jane exhaled smoke circles up into the air. "It all started before his wife died. It's a mess."

"Why's it such a mess? Do you love him?"

"Yes, but I swore off ever allowing myself to fall into such a predicament long ago. Now I'm fawning over my teacher like a simpering schoolgirl."

May rolled over and laughed before covering her mouth with a guilty expression. "Sorry, but I think you're being too hard on yourself. Enjoy the romance, consider yourself lucky."

"Well, that's just it. I can't enjoy anything. His mother threatens to disown him if he ever marries me, and his little wench of a daughter says she'll join a convent if he marries again. I say good riddance to both of them, but he doesn't see it that way. I feel like an idiot." Jane groaned and threw her forearm across her face. "I must sort a few things out when I return to Paris. Or maybe I'll simply hide here."

"I'll join you."

The two women stared at the deep blue-domed sky overhead.

Jane propped herself up on one elbow to look over at May. "So, I never realized your sister is the famous Louisa May Alcott."

"Yes." May reached for a wildflower growing beside her and picked off its orange petals one by one. "She's my older sister."

"Well, that can't be easy."

May said nothing and thought of the silence between her

and Louisa. Her sister's cruel words back in Concord haunted her, but really, now it was the silence that left a tightness in May's throat.

"And *Little Women* is based on you and your sisters?" Jane asked, closing her eyes. "It must be complicated to have so much of your life bared out for the world to read. What's it like?"

May stared at Jane. No one ever asked her that. Almost a decade had passed since *Little Women* was published. Everyone loved to nose around what was fiction and what was true, but no one ever asked May how it felt about having a story based upon her. "I . . . we're fortunate Louisa's books have been so successful."

Jane shrugged. "Well, sure. But it doesn't mean you have to *like* it."

May nodded. "It's presented certain challenges along the way."

"Hmm, that's probably an understatement. Is she paying your way here?"

"No, this time I'm on my own." May sighed as the weight of figuring out a way to remain independent in Europe pulled at her again.

"Good for you. Scary, isn't it? But still, there aren't many like us around."

"True, but the bar has been set high in my family for what a woman can achieve. Louisa's earnings support my whole family."

"Now, there's something. How many women can say that?"

"Not many. Now I need to start making some work to sell."

"That makes two of us." Jane rolled over onto her side to look at May. "What's it like for her to be famous?"

"Well, she says she hates it, but I think what she really hates is being famous for creating something she doesn't feel passionate about. She'd rather write different types of books."

"And what about you?"

May closed her eyes for a moment. No one ever asked her about herself. "I've always felt as if the only way to fit into my family was to be ambitious, even though I'm nowhere near as committed to anything as my parents or Louisa."

"You seem committed to your art."

"Oh, I am. But sometimes I think I need more than art."

The two women looked out at the chaotic game in the water for a few minutes. Bob let out a mighty yell as he hurled the ball at some of the fellows deeper into the water. They all laughed.

"Seems like maybe you've found something more there." Jane nodded her head in Bob's direction.

May gave a melancholy smile. "I'm not going to say I wasn't tempted by indulging in a little distraction when we first got here, but I lost my nerve."

"And you're giving me grief for being too hard on myself and not enjoying a little romance?"

"I know, it sounds silly. But I just worry that if I allow myself to fall in love now, I'll lose my way. I've come so far on my own—how would I manage it all if I'm distracted by all that comes along with a romance?"

Jane swiped at some blades of grass on top of her sketchbook. "Well, that's the problem, isn't it? I don't know either, but somehow I lost my ability to make rational choices when I met Bouguereau. Now I'm in it too deep to turn back."

May pondered what it would feel like to lose her ability to make rational choices. It was now late August, she could no longer hide from making choices—rational or irrational. London called with its market for landscape paintings and Turner studies. It wasn't the center of the art world, but at least she could scrape out a living there. London was where things had first fallen into place for her, and it felt like home. She could speak English; it was more affordable; it was a safe choice. She worked so hard for recognition, but to what end? A painting in the Salon was supposed to lead to success, yet it brought her nothing but doubt and cost her a valuable friendship. So much was being sacrificed for this dream of hers, but at what price? She was alone. Was her dream of becoming an artist worth the amount it seemed to be exacting? London offered her the possibility to return to safer ground and start afresh. Its art market embraced her love of Turner and wasn't as exclusive as the one in Paris.

"I'm hungry." Jane rose, brushing off her skirts while looking thoughtful. "So you say your sister supports you all, eh? Maybe I should try my hand at writing."

May glanced up at her to check if her friend was joking, but Jane's face was serious.

Part 4

October 1877–September 1880

London, England

Chapter 32

A dense, noxious fog settled over London that fall. It snaked down the city's streets and alleyways, making daytime dark, cold, and dreary. Nighttime visibility was even worse. Rather than providing comfort, the gas lamps cast clouds of murky green light into the darkness. The *Times* claimed several unwitting men fell into the River Thames and drowned, a pitiful way to go if there ever was one. Stuck inside the dank rooms of the National Gallery, a persistent coldness burrowed deep inside of May.

Letters from home announced Anna's purchase of the old Thoreau house. After all of this time, the family would be leaving Apple Slump. May pictured Anna, entering the small bedroom in the back of Orchard House and throwing out May's collection of seashells resting in the sun on the windowsills, folding up the faded quilt on her narrow bed, and tossing her sketchbooks into a crate. And what of her sketches on the walls? Would the next resident paint over them without a second glance? All signs of her would be removed, and her few possessions would reside in a crate in the attic of Thoreau house. Anna and the boys would finally have their own home, with Marmee and Father established in the best bedroom in the front, overlooking the road. Louisa could return to her beloved Boston. But what of May? Where did May belong now?

The Paris Salon had not provided her with any sales, new contacts, or income of any sort. The memory of those glowing letters she sent home right after her Salon acceptance made her squeeze her eyes shut; her career appeared stalled. Her eyes ached from strain and headaches plagued her. When she visited the doctor, he urged her to rest her eyes, so May refrained from drawing even a line or painting so much as a dab. She had not visited any of her agents since arriving in London, because she did not possess a single painting to be sold. Was it time to return to America? But then what?

The one spot of brightness in her daily existence was the boardinghouse in which she had taken a room, a stately old brick home in her beloved Bloomsbury. The neighbors on her hallway, whom she promptly befriended, were an assortment of appealing people. Across the hallway, twenty-something-year-old Una Hughes hailed from Buffalo and studied painting at a women's art school in nearby Queen's Square. Next door were Phoebe and Walter Pierce, both young schoolteachers from Providence, and farther down the hallway, she found Robert Warner, a newspaperman from New York City, and his wife, Caroline, a poet. May and her new friends avoided going out into the gloomy nights and holed up playing whist, chess, and reading to one another.

One October afternoon as May sat in her room with a compress on her forehead, staring at the stuffed white owl she had purchased in Paris, there was a knock on the door. Alice Bartol greeted her with a jubilant embrace. As May folded into her friend's shoulder, she caught a glimpse of a man standing behind Alice. He was barely taller than Alice and bald, except for a few wisps of hair brushed over his head, the comb lines still visible. He picked at his lapels with soft, white fingers that made May squeamish with the sensation she was viewing a body part better left unexposed.

"I was hoping to catch you for a surprise. I wrote to Anna to find you," exclaimed Alice, pulling the man beside her gleefully. "I know I said I'd never marry, but I've learned to never say never. Meet my husband, Mr. John Meeker. We met on my voyage home from Paris last spring, and it's been a whirlwind since. We're on our honeymoon, can you believe it?"

No, May thought numbly, *I cannot.*

"How do you do?" Mr. Meeker asked, sucking on his thin lips. He appeared to be incapable of producing any sort of excitement, much less a whirlwind. May was left looking back and forth at them, blinking, searching for words. How had her vivacious friend suddenly married this cold fish of a fellow?

Alice insisted on dragging May to a tearoom off Leicester Square, and she gibbered on about the latest news from Boston without ever stopping to breathe. "I share a cunning little studio on Boylston Street with Sarah Whitman who was in Dr. Rimmer's class with us. Remember her? She's barely been there this summer because she goes up to the North Shore. Did you ever see the Whitmans' summer house up in Beverly Farms? It's a splendid spot. I visited with Helen Knowlton the other afternoon. Miss Knowlton's preparing thirty-eight paintings for an exhibition with Ellen Hale at the Boston Art Club this winter." Alice stirred her tea with the energy of a propeller. "Can you believe that number? Thirty-eight! She's awfully busy. Her classes are packed. Her book about Mr. Hunt attracts students, I'm sure." Alice gasped and covered her mouth. "Oh no, I don't suppose you've heard about Mr. Hunt?"

May shook her head.

Alice leaned in and lowered her voice. "He died at the end of summer—the circumstances surrounding his death were a bit mysterious. He was vacationing on the Isle of Shoals and went out for a walk one morning but never returned. A friend discovered the body. Awful." As Alice sat back, her lower lip quivered, and her new husband put out his small hand and rested it atop hers on the tablecloth.

May's stomach turned. Mr. Hunt had always been such a large personality; it seemed impossible he was gone. The three of them sat quietly amidst the churn of conversations surrounding them until Alice's husband cleared his throat, saying he had to see if his new suit was finished at a nearby tailor. Alice nodded at him. May watched the pair exchange private little smiles. Once he left, Alice fidgeted with a silver spoon. "I'm dreadfully sorry about how I left things with you in Paris.

I took the news from the Salon poorly. I apologize for being so upset with you."

"I understand. We've all suffered disappointments. But I've missed you."

Alice stared off toward the door and whispered, "Did you? You never wrote. I was so miserable, yet you never inquired to see how I was faring."

May's surprise brought her up short. "Of course I missed you. I didn't write because . . . because I felt that you were so upset with me."

"Well, I was upset with you. I was upset with everything. But we've been friends for so long, I hated to believe that was the end. I kept waiting to hear from you." She drooped back against the backrest of her chair, her chin trembling.

May leaned toward her. "The Salon didn't work out the way I expected either. I didn't get any commissions from it. I wasn't sure what to do next." She was about to say, *And I've been lonely, so lonely,* but she held back, not wanting to seem desperate, and instead added, "I came here because it felt more . . . familiar."

Alice bit her lip, and her thin, perfectly arched brows rose. For a moment, her eyes seemed to shimmer with tears, but then she blinked, sat up, and smiled quickly, erasing any sign of uncertainty. "Well, I couldn't be happier now that I'm married. Goodness, it's hard to imagine that I ever made that silly vow not to marry. I realize now that my life was a little bleak before. Just painting, painting, painting. Of course, I'm still painting, but I've also realized perhaps my talents could be used to help cultivate more of an art culture in Boston." With each word she spoke, her voice became louder and her face brighter.

"What do you mean?" May's head swam at the rapid torrent of Alice's words.

Alice continued, telling her of how she planned to collect art on this trip to Europe for a new art museum opening in Lowell, Massachusetts. "We're off to Paris next. I wrote to your friend, Miss Cassatt, and she's going to help me obtain some new pieces."

"I . . . I could have written you a letter of introduction to her." May stumbled over her words as she tried to string together what Alice was telling her. Months before, May had introduced her friend to Mary, but after the meeting Alice had been quick to say Mary was too serious, too dour. Back then, May detected Alice's jealousy of her friendship with the Philadelphian, and she avoided getting them all together again. Was Alice trying to punish her by this sudden familiarity with Mary Cassatt? Was she trying to sidestep May's involvement?

"Oh, no need. I managed to reach her. She was very accommodating, very gracious." Alice went on to describe her upcoming itinerary to Italy and Egypt and listed all of the sights they planned to visit. May sat back numbly and watched her friend talk. Alice's mouth opened and closed, she nodded, she shook her curls, but May couldn't hear a thing. It felt as though she was floating outside of her body, drifting toward the ceiling like the vapor rising off the overcoats of freshly arrived patrons. She longed to place her index finger upon the steaming teapot, steaming with scalding tea, to ground herself. Would she feel a burn? Instead, she sat paralyzed in place.

Finally Alice declared it was time to return to her rooms to prepare for a dinner engagement. Unsteadily, May eased out of her chair and unfolded herself over her petite friend. Alice pulled her down into a tight embrace, yet their height difference made Alice's shoulder dig into May's sternum painfully. They promised to keep in touch.

When May shuffled out of the tearoom and into the crowds of theatergoers flowing to Covent Garden, she could not remember how to get home, though she had traveled the street many times before. She turned around and around in circles, looking for a street sign or a familiar landmark to ground her. Dizzy, she staggered under the awning of a flower seller to collect herself. The shop had closed already. She looked down at the crushed petals lying plastered to the cobblestones. If she closed her eyes, she could still detect the faintest scent of wet leaves, but any sweet smell of roses had disappeared long ago. Leaning against a brick wall of the storefront, she struggled to breathe, but her lungs felt collapsed, and she started banging on her chest with her fists as panic began to overtake her.

"May?"

May's hands froze, and she looked up to see her neighbors, Caroline Warner and Phoebe Pierce, materialize out of the fog.

"What are you doing? Are you on your way home?" Phoebe asked, looking at May with concern.

May could not reply but nodded her head. The two women tucked her in between them and walked home to Bloomsbury, their steady hum of quiet conversation soothing May back from the ragged feeling threatening to unravel her moments earlier.

At the boardinghouse, their landlady waylaid the trio as they entered the foyer, and she handed May an envelope with Louisa's writing on the outside. A shiver of anticipation ran down her spine. Finally, a letter from her sister! She hugged her friends and raced up the creaking stairs, tearing the letter open.

November 19, 1877
Concord

Dear May,

    Marmee's health has deteriorated in the extreme. You must come home, for we are in dire need of your assistance. I'm also feeling poorly and am not up to the tasks at hand. I must hand off all responsibilities to you. You've had your fun. Please, book passage on the next available ship. I will pay for your ticket.

May let out a cry after the first paragraph and tossed the letter to the ground. It wavered back and forth as it settled to the floor. Was Marmee as sick as Louisa expressed? Or was this a ploy by her sister to get her home? May clenched her hands at her sides. Louisa still couldn't stand to see May enjoying success; she couldn't bear to see her own position as most talented sister threatened.

It was impossible to gauge the truth of the situation from her sister's letters; Louisa's tendency toward exaggeration muddied everything. May tugged on her earring as she paced around the tiny living room. She undressed for the night, but sleep seemed impossible, so wrapping herself tightly in her shawl, she stared out into the dark night.

The truth appeared indisputable: she was alone and accomplishing nothing, while on the other side of the earth, her mother suffered. May dropped into a chair and buried her face in her hands. She worked so hard, gave up so much, but why? What did she have to show for all of her sacrifice, all of her heartache, all of her efforts? It felt as though her career had stalled, but did she even have any career to speak of? She fooled no one, she was no artist. When she stacked up all of the facts, it seemed obvious she should go home.

Yet her vow to never go home at anyone's behest, especially Louisa's, lodged itself in her heart. She hated to give up. She hated to let her sister rule over her life. Louisa's cruel words before May left for Europe still rang in her ears. Who was really the selfish sister?

Her head throbbed as she remembered the spitefulness of her sister's accusations. Louisa's letter still lay neglected on the floor next to her desk. May walked over to pick it up, plunked herself down in the nearest chair, and commenced writing. Once her hand started moving across the page, she could not stop.

November 29, 1877
London

Louisa,

I was delighted to receive your recent letter, because I desperately hoped to find a thaw in our recent estrangement. It's been over a year since we last spoke, and I have thought of you every single day since I left. I've replayed our confrontation in the parlor many times in my head since leaving for Europe. Each time, I remain convinced your words were unnecessarily cruel and punishing. Yet through all of this, I've hoped for reconciliation.

I can only believe that your demand for me to come home stems from your jealousy of me. I've realized you've always envied me. I believe your unkind portrayal of me in "Little Women" is evidence of it. No matter how much money you make, the truth is that you remain a mean-spirited person at your core. You support me only so you may control me. I refuse to suffer under your dictates for a moment longer.

Before I left, Marmee made me promise to spread my wings and make something of myself, so I'm determined to do just that. Now that you find yourself in the enviable position of producing money, please use it. Hire people to help you with your housekeeping and health. Rather than racing across the Atlantic, my time should be spent improving my artwork. I refuse to come home every time you tire of *tending to our family. Furthermore, I must encourage you to take better care of your own health so you're not constantly beset by misery. Your litany of constant complaints is tiresome. I will return home when I am good and ready and not a moment sooner.*

May

Louisa can stick that in her cap for a few days and see how it feels, May thought while she sealed the envelope. She marched downstairs and stuffed the letter in her landlady's outgoing post basket, expecting to feel satisfaction. Instead, remorse niggled inside her belly.

A week later, May dressed in her favorite navy blue silk dress and prepared to meet Caroline at the Sloane Gallery. As she stood in the front door vestibule of the boardinghouse with her gloved hand on the doorknob, her landlady called to stop her and handed May two letters: Father's graceful handwriting was on one; Louisa's, the other. May's heart plummeted. She turned, willed herself up the stairs, and closed the door behind her.

Father's letter explained Marmee's health had taken a dire turn, but he insisted May remain in London, explaining it was unlikely she would be able to get home in time. May gasped and raked at the envelope to check the postmark. It had been mailed thirteen days earlier. She flipped to Louisa's latest letter and the postmark showed it had been mailed eleven days earlier. A cold, hard pit grew inside May. After she slit open her sister's envelope, a lock of white hair slipped out and fell to the floor. May collapsed. Marmee was dead.

Chapter 33

May lay in bed for several days, allowing the weight of the coverlet to pin her down. She thought about a time when she went swimming in the Concord River with her sisters. She had waded through the water, but a slimy rock made her feet slip out from under her. The unforgiving current pulled her deeper onto the floor of the riverbed, where she lay anchored to the bottom in her heavy woolen swimming costume, looking toward the surface. The distant, garbled sound of her sisters calling her name eddied around her, but May closed her eyes, lulled into the peacefulness of her resting place until a burning in her lungs made her fight her way to the surface, spluttering and coughing. This time, submerged in grief, May did not feel the same burn to rescue herself. Not only had she lost her mother, but she probably lost her sister, too. Somewhere over the Atlantic, in the hold of a ship, a letter lay in wait for her sister. A wounding letter. A letter May regretted writing.

In the distance of her consciousness, someone knocked at

her door. *Go away, leave me alone*, May thought. The knocking persisted and grew to an impatient, constant pounding. Desperate to stop the incessant noise, May crawled out of bed. Her legs buckled as she staggered to the door and opened it.

"Good God, May! Are you ill? Let us in." Una, her neighbor from Buffalo, looked aghast as she took in May's appearance. "The landlady says she hasn't seen you downstairs for meals in three days."

Caroline's face appeared over Una's shoulder. "And you never showed up at the Sloane. What's wrong?"

May stepped back and melted to the floor.

UNA AND CAROLINE fed May, cleaned her, dressed her, and pinned up her hair. They each took one of her arms, and the three women left the boardinghouse. May wanted to huddle down on the gritty sidewalk, in the shadow of a stairwell, and fade away into nothingness. It would be so easy to wander off into the opaque soot-filled clouds enveloping them and disappear. Every winter in New England, stories circulated about people lost in blizzards; these poor souls eventually curled up in the snow and succumbed to a wakeless sleep. May dwelt in a comparable state of surrender, but Una and Caroline maintained firm grips on each arm and propelled her forward.

"Let's go to your beloved Henry VII Chapel. I've seen your beautiful sketches of it, come on," Caroline said.

Her friends led May to Westminster Abbey and slid into one of the pews. The stained-glass windows usually gleamed with rich hues of amethyst, sapphire, and ruby, but now they were dulled from the darkness outside. From somewhere in the distance, the honeyed voices of young choirboys sang hymns.

A commotion disrupted the blankness of May's mind. She looked up to see a woman in rags with ratted hair kneeling in the Innocents Corner. A priest pulled at the old woman's arm, trying to drag her away from the alabaster tomb of a baby in a cradle. The woman sagged in the man's grip. "But this is where I find peace," she moaned.

The priest ignored her and continued to drag her out of the chapel. May's numb chest suddenly seared with anger at the sight of the woman begging for mercy. She jumped to her feet and marched across the chapel to the priest.

"I demand you take your hands off her," May commanded. The priest froze in place, but kept his grip tight on the woman. "If she cannot stay and find some peace, why is this building here?"

The priest's face puckered as if he had swallowed something distasteful.

May did not back down. "I have a letter from the Dean of Westminster granting me permission to paint here. I'll vouch for this woman if you allow her to remain."

The priest gave her a baleful look. "When you leave, so must she."

May rose up to her full height, for even in God's uniform, the priest was still just a man. "As you wish."

The priest grimaced and let go of the woman's scrawny arm. She skittered sideways like a crab back to the Innocents Corner. Without a backward glance, the priest glided away into the gloom.

May went to the tomb of the baby in the cradle and knelt next to the woman. The rancid stench of her unwashed body and God knows what else assaulted May, but she remained.

"My eleventh babe was just carted off to potter's field," the woman mumbled into her hands clasped in prayer. Her voice was so heavily accented, it could barely be understood.

"You have my sympathies," May said.

The woman recoiled in surprise, and May realized, with embarrassment, the woman was not speaking to her. The woman's watery, yellowed eyes took in May's black bombazine dress and bonnet, but she said nothing more and went back to her murmuring. Eventually, she staggered to her feet and hobbled away to the gate. May started to follow her, but the woman vanished like a wraith into the nave of the cathedral.

"It was kind of you to stand up for her," Una whispered.

"My mother would have made that priest weep for his treatment of that woman. She probably would have dragged him over to Parliament straightaway and demanded he be defrocked." May wiped at the tears welling in the corners of her eyes. "She was always trying to help people."

"Well, that poor woman was lucky you were here today."

"I felt my mother in there with me. Do you think I'm crazy?"

Caroline cupped May's chin in her hand and gave her a sympathetic smile. "I think you're grieving. What exactly did you feel?"

"Oh, I don't know. I just miss her." But it was more than

that—May did not hear her mother's voice; May's mother did not appear as an apparition—but May sensed Marmee somewhere inside of her. The location of the feeling was not specific; it was not near her heart, and not necessarily in her head. May never understood where the soul resided, but now she had a sense of it. It was an energy inside her, a burn to move forward, a longing to love.

Chapter 34

May's headaches disappeared, and she began to paint again. The bilious fog outside lifted, making the days brighter and longer. Because of the western-facing windows in May's room, Una set up her easel beside May's. The two would work for hours, rejoicing in the natural light flooding May's room.

An evening in late February brought her neighbors—the Pierces, the Warners, and Una—to her door with a young man in tow. "Goodness, there's not enough room in my cave for everyone!" laughed May, as she waved them all in. "I'm afraid we'll be sitting on each other's laps if we stay here."

"I get May." Robert flashed a wicked grin at Caroline, his wife.

Amid the gaiety, the newcomer stood watching the others, until Walter remembered introductions. "This is Ernest Nieriker. He's taken a room next to Phoebe and me."

"You're a painter?" Ernest asked, nodding at May's jars of

paintbrushes and colored pencils on the windowsill. May detected a faint German accent.

"On a good day," she replied.

Everyone managed to find a spot that evening. Walter amused them with a story of one of his students who had been caught cheating; the boy wrote some formulas for algebraic equations on his hand, and then rested his cheek in the same hand, as he worked on the exam, only to finish with the inked answers stamped across his face. Caroline read some of her poetry, and they finished up the evening singing. Ernest sang in a deep baritone that harmonized effortlessly with the group.

And so a new pattern developed to her days. May would rise, paint in her room, and visit art galleries in the afternoons. She sold two flower panels and a painting of her stuffed white owl to support herself through another month. Evenings often brought her new, young Swiss neighbor to her door. Sometimes he'd come with the Pierces or the Warners, and they would all play whist. Sometimes he'd be alone, and the two of them would talk while playing chess. May tended to play an aggressive game, often leaving her king unguarded to Ernest's attacks.

"You're far more patient than I," she lamented as he announced checkmate. "I always see those decisive combinations too late. You notice everything."

"I think you don't give yourself enough credit. Artists are patient people."

"Perhaps, but my mind tends to wander off the board."

"Well, that is different from patience. You're very curious.

Your questions draw people to you. I admire the ease with which you attract friends."

May could feel herself flushing under his compliments. He spoke quietly as he rearranged the chessboard. She couldn't concentrate on his advice about positioning her pawn structure more strategically, but she watched the seriousness with which he tried to help her. He claimed their evenings together offered him the perfect opportunity to practice English, but his language was already impeccable. His manners were also faultless. Whenever he showed up at her room, he always brought a small cluster of lily of the valley or a sweet treat from her favorite pastry shop in Covent Garden. Though he possessed a solemnity that made him appear to be older, May wondered at his age. His descriptions of his life back in Baden made it clear his employment was relatively new, and she could not glean any further information from him about an earlier occupation.

One evening he arrived carrying a violin case.

"I had no idea you played the violin. Please, play me a song," May urged him. "My eyes are exhausted from a long day of painting."

"Some Viotti will be just the thing." He placed the violin under his chin and closed his eyes as he slid the bow over the strings. The smooth grain of the spruce and the ebony of the fingerboard gleamed. How could a mere four strings bring forth such rich sound?

Ernest moved his body with the music. His brows furrowed during parts of the song, and then his face would relax and assume a dreamy expression, all the while his upper body moved behind the delicate hourglass-shaped instrument. A quick range of emotions played across his face, and she watched the muscles underneath his jaw shift from one expression to the next. His broad shoulders dipped and rose. The rhythm with which his arms struck the bow across the strings was sometimes slow and fluid, sometimes staccato and tense. Uncomfortable with such a private moment—as though she had come upon him sleeping in bed—May turned her head, but found herself pulling her gaze back to him. She could not look away. His light brown hair, pomaded into a perfect part when he started playing, began to loosen, and May had to restrain herself from reaching forward to smooth back some of the stray curls falling across his forehead. At one point, he opened up his eyes and looked directly at her. A shy smile skirted the corners of his mouth.

When he finished playing, May inhaled a sharp breath and then clapped with enthusiasm to cover up the fact that she was trembling. "Beautiful."

Ernest looked steadily at May for a few beats, saying nothing.

"Oh my, it's gotten late," she said, pointing to her clock on the mantel and jumping to her feet to usher him out the door. "I have to visit one of my dealers first thing in the morning."

Ernest stood, tucking his violin under his arm, and bowed his head. "Thank you."

"For what?" May gasped, as though she had just run around the block. "You're the one who entertained me. That was beautiful." She knew she was repeating herself, but couldn't think straight.

"Thank you for being such a gracious host." He spoke quietly, leaning back against the doorjamb, raising his violin from his side to rest on his shoulder. The crook of his arm seemed to fold her closer to him.

May's face flushed under the gaze of his warm brown eyes. "Good night," she breathed.

She closed the door behind him and rested against it before crossing the room to turn off her lamp and pull open the curtains. With the fog gone, stars finally pierced the dark sky like the heads of shiny nails. May placed her forehead against the cool pane of glass. The music from Ernest's violin still seemed to reverberate off the walls of the dark room. She closed her eyes, picturing the suppleness with which he moved with his music.

Later, as she climbed into bed, her eyes rested on a watercolor of Orchard House hanging on the wall over her desk. She had painted it years ago on a hot August afternoon as her nephews ran roughshod around the yard. Marmee brought out a pitcher of apple cider, sat beside May, and read *The Women's Journal* aloud. Her chest did not tighten as painfully as it once had when she thought of Marmee, but her breath shuddered out of her when her thoughts turned toward Louisa. Anna's letters kept May abreast of what was happening at home and provided extensive updates on Louisa, so May suspected she knew of their estrangement. Anna had always played the role of neutral party between Louisa and May ever since they had been younger. Though there had been plenty of occasions of discord, usually arguments lasted a day, maybe several, but never this long, and certainly never with a physical distance like this between them to exacerbate the ill will. May rested the palms of her hands upon the icy glass and then moved her hands to either side of her face. The cold sank into her skin and made her shiver. She wished she could shake off the guilt that had taken root deep inside her core, but it remained, winding itself tighter and tighter around her bones and through her muscles until she felt overwhelmed by how to fix the situation.

Chapter 35

Saturday morning began with a clear dawn so May dressed and placed her sketch pad and colored pencils in her shoulder strap. In the hallway outside their rooms, she encountered Ernest, who appeared to be returning from an errand, and approached her smiling, the damp, mossy smell of spring clinging to his black coat, as he inquired about her plans for the day.

"I'm on my way to Saint James's Park for some sketching," May said, patting her hair into place and hoping her bonnet was on straight.

"It's a lovely day for it. Care for some company?"

A flash of excitement traveled through May. "Yes, I mean, of course. If . . . if you don't have any more pressing engagements, I'd enjoy that."

She worried her stammering made her sound like a dunce, but Ernest seemed not to notice and wrapped his arm around her elbow. They proceeded downstairs and out onto the street. May stole a glance at his profile and admired the confident tilt of his chin. He didn't start any conversation, but simply looked pleased. As they strolled along the street, she admired how their steps and pace matched effortlessly.

"Would you prefer to take an omnibus?"

"No, thank you," she said with a smile. "I try to walk everywhere. I like the exercise."

He paused and tilted his head as he studied her. "We Swiss like to walk everywhere, too."

She hid the flush she knew was rising in her cheeks by turning to watch a grocer place stacks of apples and pears outside his stall while an errand boy swept some dead leaves into the gutter. Ernest pointed out the bakery where he had purchased a lemon pound cake the previous week. She remembered the package wrapped neatly in brown paper and tied with string and how he had carried it carefully alongside his violin when he arrived at her room. The spongey yellow cake's sweetness had been a welcome treat on an otherwise routine day. When she had thanked him, he was gracious without implying any undue heroics, and she noted his humility.

They reached an entrance to the park, and he deferred to her choice of locating a bench with a view of Buckingham Palace in the distance. She could feel him watching her as she settled her sketch pad on her lap and her pencils next to her.

"Why did you pick this spot?"

May lifted her gray pencil and began to sketch light contour lines on her paper. "The last time I was in London, I befriended a lovely couple, both were artists, and we often came here to stretch our legs after sketching in Westminster Abbey."

She smiled to think of how Violet always teased her about her interest in Queen Victoria. The monarchy ran against everything her Californian friend believed, yet the two women always discussed what it would be like to be invited to royal tea at the palace. "Whenever I come here, I always hope to catch a glimpse of the queen. I know it's silly. She's probably not even there." May nodded at Buckingham Palace's gray towers in the distance. "She's probably off at Balmoral, or maybe it's still too cold up there. I suppose it's more likely she's in residence at Windsor, but anyway, I always hope to see her."

He smiled and leaned back, shading his eyes. "She's a rare sight in London, that's for certain."

"I know, she sounds so sad, all locked away in mourning."

"I wouldn't feel too badly for her. She's the most powerful woman in the world. No one has locked her away. Her mourning is her own choice."

"Well, that's just it. It is her choice. To be so powerful and to decide to retreat into her own grief. I think it's remarkable that she was so in love with Prince Albert."

Ernest remained silent and gazed at Buckingham Palace, leaving May to wonder uncomfortably why she had brought up the queen. Why did she have to bring love into the conversation? Her mention of it was too much, too forward. She felt torn between clamping her mouth against any more frivolous talk and wanting to say something more, something that made her sound confident and interesting. "Let's go see the pelicans. Did you know there used to be an elephant here in the park?

"Really?"

"Yes, King James kept a whole menagerie of animals here. Even crocodiles." She closed her sketchbook and dropped her pencils into her bag.

"Wait." Ernest rested his hand her arm. "It's nice here. We've been waiting all winter for this weather. Let's not rush off. Let's stay for a bit. We'll see if Queen Victoria comes out." He folded his hands in his lap and watched a pair of men pass by, both with newspapers tucked under their arms, engrossed in discussing the day's news.

May opened her sketch pad again and smiled at the knowledge he was humoring her, but perhaps he had a romantic streak in him as well, she thought as she sketched the view of the palace.

He watched her for several minutes before asking, "May I try?"

She looked over at him. "Try sketching?"

"Yes."

She giggled and handed him the pad and a couple of pencils. "You're going to pick up a new artistic medium? The violin isn't enough?"

"I want to get a sense of what you do, so I understand you better. Should I begin with a light sketch of what I'm going to draw?"

She nodded, watching his long fingers unselfconsciously grasp her gray pencil. *He wants to understand me better.* She knit her gloved fingers together tightly and forced them to rest on her lap, trying to control the excitement that spread through her like a sip of brandy, the quick burn down her throat and then the warmth seeping through her extremities, loosening her jangle of nerves. She wasn't imagining his interest in her. It was real. Somehow sitting next to him was both the most natural place to be in the world and the most unsettling—the conflicting sensations thrilled her.

"And what about the composition?" he asked. "I shouldn't just copy you. What should I draw?"

"Well . . ." May studied the grassy expanse surrounding them. "Perhaps we should start with something straightforward. If we want to move, we could go see the Boy Statue. I've learned by sketching many statues."

But Ernest's pencil was already moving, sketching the empty bench next to them. "The angle is awkward from this view." He groaned. "I'm already making a mess of it."

Sure enough, the bench looked too long and low to the ground. "You need to enlarge the end that is closer to us and make the back of it smaller. It's called foreshortening. You must imagine a vanishing point and all lines must lead to it. Like this." She began to sketch a more accurate view of the bench with her blue pencil before realizing that she was leaning intimately onto his lap, her balance resting entirely upon him. She froze, feeling his breath against her cheek, and wondered if he could hear the pounding of her heart knocking against her ribs. She slowly pulled back. "Sorry . . ."

"No, I think I see." He looked directly at her without any sign of embarrassment and smiled. "I like trying to see the world as you view it." Even squinting in the daylight, his light blue eyes shone brightly, and she smiled back.

"Let's go see those pelicans." She stood, tossing her art supplies into her shawl strap and slinging it over one arm. He rose next to her and they left the bench and walked past a copse of tall, sinewy plane trees. As they neared the water, a cluster of people came into view, and May and Ernest drifted over to see the attraction. A young man held a bicycle with an enormous wheel in front and a tiny wheel in back. He waved his top hat toward the crowd invitingly.

"Come on, gents, who wants to take a spin on this high wheel? This is the latest development in velocipedes. Be a sport. It's a grand way to experience a bit of speed. Three guineas are all it takes." The man caught a glimpse of Ernest and May, the newest spectators to arrive, and turned his entreaties directly at Ernest. "You, sir. You look like the type of gentleman who's game for adventure."

Ernest laughed and turned toward May with raised eyebrows.

"Go," she urged. She cursed her own layers of skirts, wishing she could be the one to give it a whirl. If riding a bicycle was like riding a horse, she wanted to try it.

"See?" The man gave an impertinent wink and held the bicycle out toward Ernest. "Go ahead. It's a fine way to impress the ladies."

Ernest plunged through the crowd and, upon reaching the fellow, slipped him a couple of coins as he reached for the machine.

"Now, sir, have you ever ridden a velocipede?" When Ernest grinned and shook his head, the man beamed and raised his voice to the crowd. "Ladies and gents, I have a treat for you! We're about to witness a grand spectacle! A *dangerous* spectacle!" The showman slowed his voice and rolled the syllables of the word *dangerous* for dramatic effect. He turned back to Ernest but still spoke loudly enough for everyone to hear. "Sir, are your affairs in order? Does this fine lady"—he nodded toward May—"know your solicitor's name so she may settle your estate if need be?"

The crowd laughed, and May slipped through the crowd, drawing closer to the velocipede. Once next to it, the machine's size gave her pause. The front wheel was high, impossibly high, putting the narrow, tiny leather seat about six feet above the ground. The front wheel, made of metal, could not have been more than the width of two of her fingers placed together. It looked dreadfully unstable, and finally she understood the reason for the crowd's excitement.

A young boy tapped his fingers against the wheel. "It's a real bone crusher," he said with a smug grin at May.

Dubiously, she surveyed the uneven dirt promenade ahead. Why had she encouraged this foolishness? How on earth was Ernest going to ride the contraption? Surely he would break his neck. She tried to move closer to urge him to stop, but the crowd, hungry for something spectacular, pinned her in place. She raised her arm to get his attention, but he was occupied with the man's instructions for mounting the high wheeler. He placed a foot on the peg protruding from the small wheel in back, and the man gave him a nudge to start the thing gliding forward. She inhaled as the crowd parted to make room for him. Silence. Everyone watched in rapt fascination. May's shoulders tensed, and her stomach seized with the pending catastrophe at hand. And suddenly Ernest was atop the high wheeler, rolling away from them.

A handful of small children tore from the crowd and began to chase him, cheering him along. "Don't take a header, mister!" one boy called out as he ran behind him.

May's breath stopped; she stared at his receding figure.

"Turn! Turn! Try a turn," the man beside her cried out.

Amazingly, Ernest turned the high wheeler in a wobbly, wide arc and headed back to the crowd. He searched the crowd in between glances at his handlebars, his lips a thin line of determination, but when he caught sight of May in the crowd, his eyes brightened, and he gingerly raised his arm to tip the brim of his hat at her. The men and women surrounding her burst forth with cheers.

People turned to look at May, nodding their heads approvingly. With her fingers knotted together against her lips, she realized she was still holding her breath and slowly exhaled, dropping her hands limply to rest at her sides. "Keep both hands on those bars," she called weakly but her voice was drowned out in the exuberant commotion of the crowd. How had he managed such a feat?

He rolled up in front of her and somehow hopped to the ground gracefully. Amidst the backslapping, cheers, and women looking sideways at him from under their plumed hats, everything faded away except Ernest. She felt an unfolding of delight inside her chest as he neared her with his hand outstretched.

A cautious smile stretched across his square jaw, and his eyes regarded her carefully as the crowd parted to let him reach her. Relief must have shown on her face because his guarded expression relaxed into one of triumph.

The owner of the high wheeler looked slightly mystified as he took a hold of the velocipede again. "Huh, you've really never tried that before?" He shook Ernest's hand. "Well done, sir."

Ernest took May's arm, and though he nodded distractedly at the volley of congratulatory comments from the surrounding people, he remained focused on her.

"I began to think that was a bad idea," she whispered to him. "Did you?"

"You were appallingly high up there." She shook her head in wonder. "How did you do that?"

He gave her arm a squeeze. "I concentrated with all my might. I really didn't want to fall in front of you."

She leaned into his shoulder, feeling both surprised at her comfort with him and giddy at the delight that he had been trying to impress her.

"But if I had fallen and needed nursing, I hoped you'd be the one to care for me."

She laughed. "Well, aren't you sure of yourself?" She glanced back at the men swarming the high wheel owner as they walked away.

He chuckled. "Honestly, I was just lucky."

She put her hand on his arm that linked them together and squeezed her fingers upon his hand for a moment, feeling as though the happiness filling her was a force that could make her explode. All her cares—money, home, art—reduced to a background hum as she took in the fine form of the man walking alongside of her. She was the lucky one.

A FEW DAYS later, May, Caroline, and Una went shopping near Covent Garden. They wandered through Howell & James on Regent Street admiring jewelry before entering Peter Robinson to look at dresses. While May idled around the department store, she found a collar of cream-colored lace with the delicacy of a spiderweb. She pictured it at the neckline of her pale blue silk gown and imagined Ernest's eyes traveling down from her face, to her neck, and along her exposed collarbone. Her face reddened. She dropped the lace back onto the counter and busied herself with browsing through some racks of bonnets and hats. Before they left the store, May doubled back to the counter, purchased the lace, and tucked it into her basket.

At a tea shop near Covent Garden, Caroline described an amusing correspondence she was exchanging with an editor of a literary magazine. She was signing her name as C. Warner to throw the fellow off the scent that she was a woman. Her ruse worked; he planned to publish some of her poetry in his journal's next volume. They all laughed at her mischief. May smiled to herself, knowing how Ernest would enjoy the story when she repeated it to him that evening. The secret of her attraction for him gave everything extra significance. She saw and listened to everything wondering what he would think of it. How could no one see her distraction? She could barely see straight.

She returned home to find a letter from Princess Louise, the Marchioness of Lorne, congratulating her; two of her paintings were selected for an upcoming exhibition of women painters. Just the thought of the beautiful princess seeing her artwork and deciding it worthy of her show made May want to shout with joy, but instead she read it again and again, marveling that Queen Victoria's daughter, known for her intelligence and artistic talent, had decided May's painting merited exhibition in her show. Her first inclination was to get out some paper to write to Louisa, but she stopped herself. There had been no letters from Louisa since the angry one May had sent. She flinched and closed her eyes for a moment before reaching for her shopping basket to take out the lace purchased earlier. She would not let herself think of Louisa. Not now. Not when everything else was going so well. She slid the thread of the lace through her fingers, imagining how Ernest would smile when she told about the victory of her paintings. She folded up the lace and put it away. *Time to get to work.*

She arranged a handful of bright jonquils from the Covent Garden market into a pewter vase for a still life, flushing to think about the many ways Ernest seeped into her consciousness. This dalliance was merely a bit of fun. She needed a distraction from her worries from home, and he was a fine one, but that's all it was. A small romance. After all, he was much younger . . . there could no future for such a relationship. The whole affair perplexed her. She could not stop thinking of him.

ERNEST ARRIVED ALONE that evening. Her breath caught in her throat as she led him into her small room. He took a seat, and she told him about her acceptance into the Ladies Exhibition.

"How marvelous, congratulations. May I be the lucky gent to escort you to the Opening Day?"

May hid her flushing face by rearranging a chair and tried to keep her tone lighthearted as she agreed. She could feel him watching her, so she composed her face, folded her hands in her lap, and faced him.

"Shall I play you a song I wrote myself?" Ernest fixed his eyes on May's and perched the violin on his thigh, leaning his chest in behind it.

"Of course, yes, please play it."

May loved the first moment when he'd pick up the violin and place it to his cheek to settle his chin against the instrument. He ran the bow down the strings with a long smooth stroke, and the note hovered in the air like a question before the melody started. His eyes closed. His shoulders bobbed and dipped with the song. She leaned back and felt the keening of the song reach inside her and remain there, compressing around her heart. The music buzzed along her nerves, down through her belly, along her thighs and all the way to her toes. She touched the tips of her fingers together gingerly on her lap. All of her senses felt alert, as if she could practically feel the tickle of her stuffed owl's feathers from across the room and the wetness of the raindrops dripping down the outside of the windowpanes. The ropes of his arms and the contours of his shoulders moved gracefully as he worked the bow along the strings, vigorously, then gently. His toes tapped, quadriceps flexed, and torso engaged as he flowed with the music. A glimmer of skin quivered from underneath the cuff of his sleeve, and she could see the delicate flesh on the inside of his pale wrist.

The song ended, and Ernest lifted his chin from the violin to look at her. The final notes still danced in the air around them. There was no longer any questioning in his eye; he did not seek her approval for his song; he looked at her as if he knew everything about her. Without thinking, she rose from her seat and moved across the small space between them. He placed the violin and bow on the table next to them and opened his arms to receive her against his shoulder. She curled into his lap. They said nothing.

Up close, she could see whorls in the blond stubble along his cheek and chin, creating a pattern of trails. A map into the unknown. She traced her fingers along his jawbone. Tiny flecks of gold swam in his light blue eyes, like sunlight reflecting off water. May leaned over, closed her eyes, and kissed him. They pushed together with urgency. Without peeling her lips from his, her fingers unfastened the top button on his shirt and moved along to the next.

IN THE MORNING, she awoke alone, wondering what on earth had possessed her the night before, but her fears over her actions dissipated when she saw Ernest's violin still resting on the table next to her white stuffed owl. Like a spent arrow, the violin's bow lay on the floor. May bent over to pick it up, and the strings glittered next to the clawed foot of the table. The waxed wood of the instrument shone in the knowing light of morning.

She traced her index finger along the swirl of the scrollwork at the end of the violin's neck and then picked it up to hold it as if she were going to play. She pressed her chin against the instrument, the heft of it resting on her shoulder. She dared not ruin the morning's perfect silence, so she placed the bow on the table but rubbed her hand along the violin, feeling the press of the strings dig into the flesh of her palm until it hurt. A red imprint from the four strings glowed on her hand when she lifted it away. Last night was real; there was no mistaking it as a dream. No more worrying about choices, she knew what she wanted. She would never hear the music of a violin again without thinking of this moment.

Chapter 36

*E*rnest arrived at her room again later that evening with a high flush on his face. May prattled on about the rising price of primer she encountered at Brodie & Middleton earlier in the day. The chessboard lay out on a small table between their chairs so the two could play, but he ignored it and paced the room.

"I received a letter today from the company's headquarters in Paris offering me a new post as Inspector General of Trade. It will be in France or Russia and most likely require us to part for a while." He stopped with a desperate look on his face. "You should know that I'm very fond of you."

"But we've only known each other for two months." She held back from giving the exact date they met, though she knew it.

"I've loved you from the first night we met."

May drew in a shaky breath. Love. All this time, she had forbidden herself to think about it, but she felt it, she could no longer deny it. She pictured how his face had glowed when he saw her from the high wheeler and started laughing, collaps-ing onto him, and wrapping her arms around his back as if she could dissolve into him. Every bit of her desired him. She traced his shoulder blades with the tips of her fingers.

"I knew it!" he said. "Does that mean yes?"

Reluctantly, she drew back. "Ernest, how old are you?"

"Twenty-two, but I don't care about age."

May gasped and her hands clutched at her heart. "I do! I'm too old for you." She could barely breathe as she calculated their age difference: almost sixteen years. She was practically old enough to be his mother. And they had only just met. It was insanity. All of it.

"Age means nothing." He took ahold of her waist and rested his forehead against hers, their eyes inches apart. "Admit it. You care for me, too."

She squeezed her eyes shut, she couldn't look at him. "Yes, of course, I do," she said, indignation flooding her as she thought of what she had done the night before. All of the anxiety she held back, sprang forward. "I would never have—"

Ernest grasped May by her shoulders and searched her face. "There's only one thing for us to do. Let's get married. Then you can come with me."

"Married?" she echoed back, weakly. She couldn't bear to think of their age difference, but no one had ever come close to making her feel the way he did. His honesty, confidence, humility—all of these qualities called to her. Shivers ran from the base of her skull down along the back of her arms. She whispered, "Where will we go?"

"I don't know yet. Does it matter?"

Her legs felt liquid. They stared at each other.

"You're right. None of those details matter. Yes . . . yes . . ." May said as the idea picked up momentum. In the brief time they had spent together so far, she didn't dare allow herself to picture a future with him, but now a sense of absolute certainty gripped her. No matter the obstacles, she wanted a life with this man whom she loved. Her face burned with intensity. "I need fresh air."

In their haste, they left their overcoats behind as they raced down the three flights of stairs to the outside door, but it was no matter. The evening's rain had stopped, leaving the sidewalks glistening like a sheet of glass. Except for the occasional sound of raindrops filtering through the trees, Bedford Square stood still. The world looked brand-new. A full moon hung overhead. In the houses surrounding them, she could see people behind the windows: a serving girl checked her reflection in a silver spoon as she cleared a dining room table of dishes; a woman yawned while reading a novel in her bedroom; a man in a tweed vest blew lazy cigar smoke circles while he sat in his library. The normalcy of the night soothed the tumult inside of her.

"I plan to keep painting."

"Of course. Why would you stop?" He looked at May and tucked some loose hair behind her ear. His closeness made her dizzy. "I'd never ask you to give up painting. You're an artist—I understand that. But you should also understand I'm still making my way in the world. I may not have all of the comforts you're used to, but I'm a hard worker and will get us there in time."

She let out a half-gasp, half-laugh. "Oh, I care nothing for that."

"All I care about is you."

May could feel goose bumps rising on her arms. He pulled her to him in the gloaming of a street lamp. She never wanted him to let go of her. After all of this time, she had finally met someone who understood, respected, and admired her. Here was a man committed to earning his way. All of the years of frustration with her father's instability wafted away in the darkness. Here was a man who honored her work as an artist. This relationship would be a meeting of two minds, two souls. She closed her eyes tightly and surrendered her head onto his shoulder. Finally, a man who cherished her. She felt it in the way he ran a tender hand down her cheek and grasped her tighter.

Alone in her room later, May wrote to Anna telling of her engagement, glad for the two weeks she would have before the letter arrived at Orchard House to be read. Anna would be overjoyed for her. Her father would be nonplussed and distracted by his own concerns. Louisa's reaction was tougher to imagine, but enthusiasm seemed unlikely. May wanted to protect and treasure her new joy before opening it up to the scrutiny of others, because it felt fragile but full of possibility.

WHEN THE LADIES Exhibition opened the following day, Ernest arrived at May's room in a state of agitation. "Paris. I've been posted to Paris. We must be there within two weeks."

He grinned at May's befuddlement. "I realize this doesn't offer much time for planning a wedding but—"

May's life's accumulation consisted of the possessions jammed in around them, and she waved her hands at all of it. "I don't care about a fancy wedding."

Ernest smiled with relief. "We can be married within the week and honeymoon in France while I work out the details of my new post there."

"Yes, perfect." May glanced at the clock. "Now we must go to my show. Let's keep this news to ourselves and announce it to our friends afterward."

The exhibition consisted of a flurry of greetings and conversations May would later forget. The thrill of her secret with Ernest consumed her. Throughout the event, the couple looked at each other with a giddiness that felt impossible to hide. May spoke too fast and laughed more often than decorum called for, but she could barely contain herself. Afterward, they went out to a nearby tearoom with the Warners, the Pierces, and Una.

When they all sat down to lunch, Ernest interrupted the chatter about the show and cleared his throat. "Friends, congratulations to our dear May for her work in today's show." There was an echo of good wishes and clapping that Ernest acknowledged by raising his glass before continuing. "And now, there's more good news to celebrate. May and I are to be married by the end of the week."

May beamed. Everyone else looked stunned. Her heart sank. She knew it. No doubt they all thought he was entirely too young for her and the courtship too hasty. Walter recovered first. He stood to bow to May and to shake Ernest's hand. "By Jove, you two have caught us all speechless! What's brought about this excitement?"

"Goodness, congratulations," Una murmured, wide-eyed.

"I know, it's a surprise to all of us." May looked across the table to see Ernest watching her with a tender smile that made her heart ache. "But I've learned not to waste any time when you've discovered someone precious."

"Hurrah!" Robert said. "Let's get some bubbly to toast the happy couple." A bottle was brought forth, glasses clinked, and conversation zigzagged around the table. All the while, May watched Ernest. He showed no sign of anxiety or doubt as he discussed his new position in Paris with Robert and Walter.

"May, I must ask you something." Caroline pulled May aside as they all spilled out of the restaurant after lunch. Her clear round face fixed upon May in seriousness. "Is it possible you're somewhat rushing into this marriage?"

"Oh, I'm rushing in wholeheartedly." May smiled and looked at the concerned faces of her friends gathered around her. "I'm thirty-seven years old and always hoped to find love. Recently I'd begun to believe this would never happen—yet it has, at a time when I least expected it. Really, Ernest is all I've ever hoped for."

"Well then, I'm very happy for you." Caroline hugged May, while the other women nodded their approval. "Truly. You deserve love. And I have something to share with you. I'm to become a mother." The poet rested a hand on her belly, making May see a faint swell through the folds of her friend's gown.

"Congratulations. What a thrill," said May with a squeal as she embraced her friend. "Oh, goodness, I'm so happy for you." She tenderly kept an arm around Caroline. "We should hail you a hackney and give you a rest."

"I'm not made of fine china. I can make it home on my own two feet," she answered, laughing.

As they walked home, the women all discussed possible baby names, but May drifted to the back of the group, deep in thought. Questions about her age difference with Ernest would not go away. She had to stop dwelling upon what people thought of her. She remembered what Marmee used to say: *It's none of your business what other people think of you.* Looking ahead at Caroline happily arguing over the merit of spelling the name Catherine with a C or a K, she smiled wistfully, thinking of her own mother. Wherever she was, Marmee would be so happy knowing May had found love.

THE FRIDAY OF the wedding brought rain, the type of gusty rain that blew sideways and rendered umbrellas useless. When she stepped outside, May's fawn-brown silk dress speckled with dark water stains, and the festive ostrich feather adorning her hat drooped in soggy defeat, but her spirits brightened as she climbed into the hansom cab with the Warners. They would all meet Ernest at the Office of the Registry for the brief ceremony. Later, she would barely recall the details, but somehow a gold band landed on her finger under the narrow nose of the weedy officiant who married them. The bride and groom whisked themselves to Waterloo Station and boarded a train for

Southampton with the final destination of Le Havre stamped on their travel itineraries. After a week of honeymooning on the coast of France, the couple landed in Meudon, a village fifteen minutes outside of Paris by train, and rented a small apartment with a view of the Seine River valley.

When they arrived in Meudon, a backlog of mail awaited her. May sat on a crate in her new empty drawing room to read the first letter she had received from Louisa since her mother's death.

March 3, 1878
Concord

Dearest May,

    I have just received your letter about your engagement to Mr. Nieriker and must confess to being astonished this is all happening so quickly. You seem adrift in England. This young man has come along and given you some romance when you were in dire need of cheering up. You're moving too quickly and acting foolishly. Furthermore, Anna tells me your Swiss suitor is considerably younger than you. At your age, why bother marrying? Be brave enough to lead a life of independence. It seems you have selfishly forgotten all of the time, effort—and dare I point out expense?—that has been put forth toward your artistic training?

    I have recently read "The Story of Avis" by Elizabeth Stuart Phelps Ward, which has been released to great de-

bate here at home about the role career ambition should play in a woman's life. Avis is a painter, who in many ways reminds me of you. She marries a "modern man" who promises she shall carry on with her art. Must I tell you the outcome? Lest you think I am overly obstructive of your wishes, I must inform you the inevitable interruptions that beset the life of a wife interfere with her art. Squalling children, unruly servants, an unaccommodating husband, and the demands of running a household all leave Avis depleted and unable to continue with her painting.

I only share this story with you in an attempt to give you pause in your race toward marriage. Come home.

Yours,
Louisa

Too late, thought May as she tossed the letter aside. What did Louisa know of love? The rest of the letters from her family expressed congratulatory wishes, but Louisa's overshadowed them all. May did not need her sister's help. Not anymore. The accusation of foolishness burned with a particular intensity inside of her. Ernest placed another crate on the floor next to May and wiped a handkerchief across his brow.

"So, what does your family have to say?"

May got to her feet and unpacked some of her artwork from a crate. "They're delighted. My eldest sister, Anna, thinks our elopement sounds like something straight out of *Little Women*—Amy March marries suddenly while studying art in Europe."

"I still regret there was no time to secure your father's permission before our marriage."

May shook her head. "He probably read my letter and went straight back to analyzing Plato." She rubbed the feathers down on her stuffed white owl, before setting him gingerly upon a shelf.

"And what of your sister, the writer?"

May's hands dropped from the owl and hung empty as she stared into the blankness of the creature's glass eyes. "She's very happy for me." She stood with her back to Ernest for a moment and then turned to continue unpacking. She pulled out a rectangular box and opened it to see the small red leather diary Ernest gave her as a wedding present in Le Havre. When she had first opened it, she feigned delight, but in truth, she detested journaling. Why dwell on the past when you can look ahead? Without saying a word, she placed the journal underneath some sketchbooks. After several minutes, though, she slid the diary back out, walked over to a spot by the window, and began to write.

Chapter 37

June 19, 1878
Meudon, France

Dearest Violet,

First of all, thank you for the lovely painting of the San Francisco Bay you sent to Ernest and me for a wedding present. I've hung the painting in our new bedroom and look at it every evening as I go to sleep in hopes I will enjoy lovely dreams of you. My sweet, thoughtful friend, I long to see you. It's a shame we are so far away, for I know you would adore Ernest. Ever since I met you and Mr. Keith, you've both shown me a harmonious marriage based on love and mutual respect, and now I'm blessed with a partnership that promises the same values.

In your last letter, you asked if I miss Paris. Surprisingly, I don't. I love our quiet country life. We're renting a small stone house, fifteen minutes by train outside of Paris. Ernest's superiors could announce a move to a new locale at any moment, but I don't mind these vagaries for I'm used to a life of moving around. As long as Ernest and I are together, I shall be content. Here in Europe, I feel free to make a life of my own design. Europeans seem far more forgiving of the unconventional lives of artists than Americans do, but the amusing aspect of my life is its very conventionality at the moment. Every morning when Ernest leaves for the train station, I walk down into the village center to visit the boulangerie and the butcher shop. Bundled with brown-papered packages and breathing in the loamy smell of overturned soil from the nearby farmlands, I walk home and relish the smell of fresh air. The days here always begin cool, no matter the brightness of the sun overhead. By midday I'm home and usually painting or sketching in the garden behind our rooms—I'm still in touch with my dealers in London and have added a couple of new ones here in France. After dinner, I usually sew while Ernest plays his violin.

Last week we took the train out to Gare du Champ de Mars to attend Paris's Exposition Universelle. Although the day was full of wonders, the best part came in the evening when we followed the crowds to the Place de l'Opéra, and suddenly streetlamps flickered to life brilliantly all around us. The whole crowd sighed with awe and then applauded wildly. The pavilion had been wired to show off Mr. Edison's newest developments in electricity, and Ernest and

I danced cheek to cheek under the lights as an orchestra played—you would have loved the romance of it all.

May smiled to herself and paused in her writing, thinking about when twilight had fallen at the Exposition Universelle, and shadows purpled the dusty streets while the smell of buttery popped corn blew in the air. The warble of laughter, a trumpet's call, and the swishing of bustled skirts had faded into a distant hum as May delighted in the space in between the tilt of her husband's cheek and the curve into his neck, the solidity of his shoulders and back, the warmth of his chest pressed up against hers, and the slow steps they took together in the mass of dancing couples. A trace of his shaving soap from the morning had still clung to his collar, and the musky smell of sweat at his temples had made her lean in deeper. Her own head had fit perfectly in the negative space of his body. *Oh, this world*, she thought as she nuzzled up against him. It amazed her to live in a time where people could light the night and build replicas of whole countries and continents within the space of a few city blocks. She smiled and returned to finishing her letter.

That evening Ernest came home with a stack of mail, including a letter from Massachusetts. She opened it to find an update on Concord happenings from Anna, but another piece of paper lay behind the letter. It was a bank check for one thousand dollars with a small piece of paper wrapped around it that said: *a wedding present for you*. Louisa's spidery scrawl sent prickles up the flesh of May's arms. Was this an apology? A dare? A test? May's hands shook as she placed it back into the envelope. Ernest had gone outside into the back garden. She quickly took her watercolor painting of Orchard House down from the wall, tucked the edge of the envelope into the back of the frame, and placed the painting back on the wall. By the time Ernest entered the drawing room with the newspaper under his arm, she had resumed painting.

LATER IN THE week, May ventured into the city to meet Mary Cassatt at her studio to view her most recent paintings. Mary had included cryptic remarks in her letters warning May to expect some major departures from earlier work, so May was eager, and even a little anxious, to see the newest paintings. From her window aboard the train, she studied the pale blue sky marbled with veins of wispy clouds. As the train rolled toward Paris, the landscape changed sharply from farmland to low-lying buildings to tall dense city blocks. When the maid let her in to 19 rue de Laval, she found Mary setting white sheets over seven canvases leaning against the walls of the room.

"You're going to make me wait to see your newest work?" May said, from the embrace of her friend.

Mary held May out in front of her. "Yes, but first, I want to hear all about your new life, Madame Nieriker."

May feigned a puzzled expression and looked around the room. "Who's she?" Both women laughed and sat down to a spread of peach slices, strawberries, a wedge of Gervais cheese, and a *pâté douceurs*.

Mary said, "Tell me what you've been doing to occupy yourself."

May watched as the *femme de ménage* served her some fruits and cheese. "I'm painting and settling into our new little home. I'm enjoying freedom such as I've never had before."

"How so?"

"Since I'm not running back and forth to a studio all day long and filling my evenings with social events, I'm much more focused and productive about my art. Our tiny corner of France is quiet but nice."

"And Ernest is every bit the husband you expected?"

May blushed. "Yes, when we visited the ruins of Château du Diable on the coast, he held an umbrella over me while I painted. You'll like him."

"So, he admires your work?"

"Yes, he's a trained classical violinist—all art seems to interest him." May smiled. "Have you gone to the Exposition Universelle yet? We went last week and it was full of wonders. That personal printing machine! I tried to imagine my sister writing her stories on it, but I can't imagine people will ever use such a cumbersome impersonal thing when we can simply write with our hands. The machine made a terrible clanging noise every time a letter was struck. They call it typing." She shook off the memory, imagining the terrible headache all of the noise would cause. "Oh, and you know how I love Meissonier's horses—there's a whole room dedicated to his paintings."

"Did you see Cabanel's work?"

"I did. His *Death of Francesco da Ramini and Paolo Mala-testa* gave me the shivers."

Mary raised her eyebrows. "It's that same cursed Exposition that's causing me great distress."

"Oh? Why?"

Mary swept her hand around at the canvases propped up around the room, a ruby ring on her index finger shining scarlet like a drop of blood. "I prepared all of this for a show with the Impressionists, but it was canceled. Mr. Degas said it would be too hard to compete with the Exposition."

"But you've been preparing for this show since—"

"Since you left for London? Yes." Mary sat back in her chair, crossed her arms, and her brow crinkled in consternation.

May knew her friend felt acute pressure to produce new work. The distraction of family loomed over Mary, for her parents planned to move from Philadelphia to Paris in the fall. Any time Mary could take away from working in her studio was spent house-hunting and preparing for the arrival of her convalescent sister, Lydia. "Well, I'm eager to see your newest work."

Mary rose, extending her hand out for May to take. "Yes, come, let's see what I've been doing since you left."

When Mary pulled the sheets off the canvases, May sucked in her breath with surprise, struck by her friend's unapologetic use of vibrant unmixed colors. The vividness of crimsons, blues, and yellows did not have the luminosity of color achieved by the Dutch masters and their endless, painstaking thin layers of color, but the brightness dazzled nevertheless. Shouts of color splashed along the canvases in loose brushstrokes to create the implication of action and light.

The first canvas showed a young girl slouched on a riotously patterned upholstered turquoise chair, her plaid skirt wrinkled up around her waist with layers of lacy white underskirts revealing splayed legs. More of the dreadful-looking chairs could be seen behind her, and the ground was tilted unnaturally toward the viewer to create odd shapes of negative space on the floor of the scene. The bored-looking little girl did not resemble the neatly posed figures normally displayed in portraiture, yet the child's sentiments were clear. Once May got over the shock of the horrid print on the chairs, she felt some sympathy for the girl. Despite the distractions of the composition and colors, May could see there was an understanding between painter and sitter—she felt it, thanks to the dreamy expression on the child's face and her informal positioning.

"She reminds me of my nephew Freddy. This is exactly how he would probably look if I asked him to pose for me. Minus the skirts, of course. He'd forget I was even painting him and simply start telling himself a story or singing to himself in an entirely unselfconscious way."

"So it feels real?" Mary twirled the ruby ring on her finger.

"Oh, yes, although the interior space looks so strange that it shouldn't. I'm hoping those hideous chairs aren't real."

"Do you see them?" Mary laughed, gesturing around the sunny room.

"Thankfully, no, so at least I know you haven't fully taken leave of your senses."

May walked to the next canvas of a woman clad in black sitting in an opera loge studying something outside of the frame. The background of the opera was bright with sketchy brush lines, but a figure lurked in a loge across the way with his opera glasses trained upon the woman in the foreground. May realized the man in the picture was unabashedly ignoring the stage and focusing on the woman instead.

"I like your sense of humor here, but don't you feel uncomfortable leaving the background so unfinished? It goes against everything we've been taught."

"I'm experimenting. You may think I'm crazy, but I've been completely invigorated working on these. It's liberating to move beyond what I see and to incorporate what I feel."

"But aren't you worried about what your viewer may feel? What they'll think about you?"

"All I can do is put out my own expression."

May raised a knuckle to her lips and moved along to a canvas showing a woman in a morning dress sitting in the privacy of her own small garden. Rather than following the formal portrait convention of having the woman with a book in her hand seated in a space fit for public scrutiny, this painting felt very voyeuristic, as if the woman did not know she was sitting for a painting. May stepped back as she took in the chaos of flowers framing the woman's head; roses, peonies, and geraniums were worked onto the canvas with sweeping circles and daubs of paint that reflected flowers while not giving any of the particulars. Colors used for shadowing were audacious and looked unnatural yet somehow the cerulean blue visible in the woman's hair, along her cheekbones, and in the folds of her dress and the newspaper felt beautiful. How did Mary accomplish this? May glanced at the other canvases and could see more of the same style.

"It's very spontaneous. Mr. Hunt used to talk about the importance of color value and light and dark . . . you're really experimenting with this concept. Are you mixing your colors at all?"

"Often they're just coming straight out of the tube." Mary pointed to the woman in the garden. "This has sold and is traveling to Boston tomorrow."

"These are selling?"

"Don't sound so shocked. I felt confident about exhibiting these until the cursed show was canceled."

"They're just so unexpected. So different from what you've always done."

"But that's the point. And I would argue they're not entirely unexpected. You, of all people—with your love of Turner—*you* should appreciate these."

May recognized a pleading tone within the bravado and knew what this critique cost her proud friend. Turner also used sketchy atmospheric effects in his paintings and placed an emphasis on values over detail—Mary had a point. And yet, in Turner's seascapes, his loose paint strokes and big splashes of color felt truer and evocative of the natural elements, whereas Mary was playing with these ideas within small interior spaces, personal moments. As she considered the changes in her friend's work, the floor seemed to be tilting underneath

May, almost like the painting of the dreadful chairs. All that May thought she knew was shifting. The whole world was shifting—all of the innovations on display at the Exposition Universelle certainly proved that. Or did they? At the root of Mary's painting talent lay a well-honed sensibility and skill set achieved through years of study.

"My father told me I must finally make my artwork support my studio."

May looked at her friend in amazement. "And you're still taking these chances?"

"I have to. Otherwise what's the point? It would be inauthentic to myself to do anything else."

May thought of Louisa, hiding the writing she loved under the name A. M. Barnard, and could have cried. She thought of her own Turner copies and her still life from the Salon. When she tried to push her life drawing into something more complex back at Monsieur Krug's studio, she had been all too quick to give up. A little criticism left her scrambling back to familiar territory. Since then, she had played it safe and striven to create sellable work, telling herself it was out of necessity, she needed to support herself. The colors on the canvas in front of her blurred, as if she had looked directly at the sun.

"You're terribly brave," May said, but Mary no longer faced her.

The other artist stood with her back to May, looking out of the window. May joined her to watch a farmer's wagon trundle down the street below. It was loaded with crates filled with squawking chickens. The wagon seemed lost, an interloper here in the artists' district near Place Pigalle, perhaps off course from its route to the market at rue Cler. White feathers trailed the wagon, gracefully floating through the air in meandering curlicued paths that defied gravity. The women watched the cloud of feathers hover behind the wagon as it reached an intersection and paused before turning and vanishing out of sight.

Chapter 38

May arrived back in Meudon to find Ernest not yet home. Without noticing what she was doing, she unpacked the ingredients for supper she had purchased in Paris and spread the contents out on the table. She wandered out the kitchen door to stand in the back garden. Shadows consumed the space, yet heat still radiated off the bricks of the courtyard. Warmth worked its way upward through the soles of her boots. The skin of her face felt grimy from the city. If she clenched her teeth together, the grit she'd inhaled all day ground against her teeth, as if she had a mouthful of sand. She longed to change out of her dress but could not leave the sweet air of the valley, so she remained in her spot, gulping in the refreshing feeling of twilight as if it were pink lemonade. From inside the house, the front door squeaked open and banged shut. She could hear footsteps, and then Ernest stood behind her, wrapping his arms around her while he rested his chin against her shoulder.

"How was Miss Cassatt?"

May squeezed her eyes shut against the unexpected arrival of tears and felt her husband's arms tighten against her.

"What happened?"

She didn't know how to answer and gave a shake of her head. How could she explain Mary's newest work both intrigued and repelled her? How could she describe the feeling of competitiveness and envy that pulsed through her when she heard Mary describe her exhilaration over her new style? As she had walked along Montmartre, she had felt conflicted between the pleasure of being removed from the tumult of city living while missing the excitement and grandeur of Paris.

"Maybe I should return to studying art in Paris."

"Do you miss the city?" Ernest's voice was low and steady in her ear. May opened her eyes and could see the circling trail of a bat flapping up in the sky above her.

"I don't know. Apparently the Académie Julian has a class for women now." She ran the tips of her fingers through the hair at her scalp. How could she explain her mess of feelings over Mary's new body of work? It all served as a suggestion—or was it a challenge?—for her to return to studying art in Paris. There was no way to deny the lure of the city and all of the benefits it offered to an artist, but May was afraid to upend the joy she had been feeling since she and Ernest moved to Meudon. A return to an atelier could threaten the security and comfort she felt now. Joining a studio was a surefire way to welcome petty jealousies and self-doubt back into her life. On the other hand, she worried she could not stay content painting Turner copies in her little garden forever.

Ernest moved to stand beside her, his arm slipping down to wrap around her waist.

"When the Salon accepted my still life, it felt as though everything fell apart, even though it should have been one of the most marvelous moments in my life. It made me question if all of my hard work really resulted in anything good. I lost a good friend, and no commissions came my way."

"Well, did anything good come from it?"

"Not at first. I moved to London, became terribly homesick, and lost my mother. Eventually I recovered, but—" She trailed off.

"So you found you were stronger than you expected, correct?"

May nodded. Yes, she had discovered a newfound confidence in the wake of crushing disappointment. Just like when her *Little Women* illustrations were ridiculed, she had risen up from that humiliation and worked on improving herself. She couldn't stop now. To stay in place, to not push for more— she realized these were no longer acceptable options. The fear she felt after leaving Mary's studio receded, and she folded her arms against her chest. "You're right, now I don't want to settle on being an artist creating predictable work because I'm afraid to try for more. I should go to Monsieur Julian's studio in Paris."

Ernest looked at the ground as he gently kicked at a loose stone in the wall edging their garden. "But your work is beautiful now. And it sells. Couldn't you create new work from here? How much will it cost to take lessons at the Académie Julian?"

May's fervor was brought up short by the shift toward caution in Ernest's tone. His job as Inspector General at a mercantile was far from lucrative. The flame of ambition that had reignited in her again, suddenly guttered with an apparent lack of oxygen that accompanied the realization there could be a price beyond the tuition money if she started to work in Paris.

"Four hundred francs a month. The prices have gone up since I left." She held her breath as her words hung between them.

Ernest let go of May's waist, but he remained standing next to her.

She thought about the envelope containing the check hidden behind the painting in her studio. If she fetched it now and presented it to Ernest, the check would solve everything. Yet it was Louisa's money. Once again, she would be indebted to her sister. Her hair rose on the back of her neck. She could not be reduced to that position again. They both looked out onto the dusky valley below, saying nothing before turning back to go into the kitchen. After a quiet supper, Ernest retired upstairs, complaining of a wearisome day with several of the agents with whom he worked.

May settled into her studio. She sifted through her receipts from her dealers and scratched out some numbers onto a scrap of paper. She glanced up at her watercolor of Orchard House, but left it untouched and went upstairs. When she entered the bedroom, she found Ernest resting his elbows on the windowsill and looking out at the dark sky. The smell of the honeysuckle bush below their window drifted through the open shutters. May changed into her nightgown and brushed out her hair before moving to stand behind her husband at the window.

"I just looked at my bills of sale. I can pay for classes at Monsieur Julian's while also bringing in some extra money through my work with the galleries."

Ernest continued to stare out the window. "How will you find the time to do all of this?"

"I will paint on the weekends. We may not always have time to loll around on Sunday afternoons anymore, but there will still be time for us." May reached out to lay a hand on Ernest's shoulder, and he rose from stooping at the window. She stepped next to him, feeling the warmth of his body against the cool air drifting in from the window, and wrapped her arms around him while stepping backward to lead him toward bed.

Afterward, they lay on their backs in the dark with their eyes open. Ernest rolled onto his side and stroked May's bare shoulder. "I said I would never ask you to give up your painting."

May said nothing and felt his hand as it moved down and brushed along her breasts. Sharp callouses on his fingertips gave her a jolt of wakefulness, and she turned her head to look at him.

He gave a tired smile. "I meant what I said. I would never ask you to give up your art, but we will barely be able to afford your new studio time."

"I know." May looked away and closed her eyes. If she simply walked downstairs and removed the check from the back of the watercolor of Orchard House, she could alleviate Ernest's concerns about money. But there would be a cost to that decision she was unwilling to pay. She remained in bed.

Chapter 39

On a cloudy day in September, under a low ceiling of clouds, May took the train into Paris and walked to the Passage des Panoramas for her first day at the Académie Julian. A damp breeze nipped at her skirts as she strode down the sidewalk, making her wonder if the weather would improve or if rain was on the way.

When she arrived in the airy studio, her feet froze in the doorway. She almost turned and walked back out. Instead, she was greeted by the studio's assistant and completed the terms of joining the class. There was no acceptance process here in Paris. If an art student had the money, she could join a teaching studio. If she was bad, she would be ridiculed and told to leave and find a new profession. Paris had no room for niceties.

She found an open easel and placed her paint box down, watching a model move into her first pose at the front of the room. The woman stood with her head tilted away from

May. Loosely draped gauzy fabric revealed the fullness of her breasts, the taper of her hips, and the roundness of her back-side. She stood proudly with her long arms resting gracefully along her sides and curly hair loosely gathered atop her head. Her weight rested to one side to form a long sinuous line. Forty other women stood at their easels, focused on their work. May turned toward her paint box and pulled out tubes of paint and some brushes, hoping if she looked confident, perhaps she would feel it.

Two years had passed since she had worked from a live model. Closing her eyes, May reduced the figure in her mind's eye to its most basic lines and shapes. After opening her eyes and assessing the model, May decided the figure would stand at about seven heads tall, so she drew a vertical line down the paper before creating a slightly curved streak like a single pa-renthesis on top of the vertical line to represent the woman's off-center positioning. Next, she divided up the model's propor-tions. She found the shoulder and hip marks on the arcing line and blocked in the rib cage and pelvic areas. The process was returning to her, and her arm moved in familiar motions. She sketched in a race against the clock before the model shifted to a new pose. May wanted to get far enough in her sketch to put in tonal variations. She resisted the temptation to look around at the surrounding easels to view the work of her classmates and instead rounded in the shoulders, back, breasts, hips, but-tocks, thighs, and calves. A quick rendering of the elbow and knee joints came next, followed by the small lines of fingers and toes. Shading the planes of the body brought out the dimensions of the woman, and May settled into a rhythm. The morning flashed by in a series of poses and a quick refreshing of new paper on her easel. She forgot the fidgeting of classmates around her, the movement of daylight across the floor of the studio, and her body's own needs as she lost herself in feeling her years of training coming back to her as she created sketch after sketch.

Monsieur Robert-Fleury, the master painter who ran the atelier, stopped by her easel. "You understand this is life painting, yes?"

May nodded. She stared at the unsmiling man's long slope-nosed face.

"But I see no life here. Just lines and shapes."

May was about to explain she was out of practice, but he continued.

"You must bring something unique to your figure. Clients want to see something of themselves in anything you create."

May felt a sting of unfairness. She was simply trying to get a feel for the human figure again, but she said nothing and got out a new sheet of paper. When the class took a break for lunch, May stayed in the studio and looked at the art pinned on the walls. Like Monsieur Krug's, the studio ran a series of weekly contests to encourage student improvement, but the quality of drawing and painting vastly exceeded the work at her old studio. A line of cartoons ran down the side of a different wall, and she could see several unflattering pictures of Monsieur Robert-Fleury amongst the collection.

"You'll want to avoid finding a picture of yourself on this

part of the wall," said a woman's voice behind her. May turned to see one of her classmates from Monsieur Krug's studio, standing behind her.

"Miss Klumpke, I didn't know you were studying here, too." The young American's familiar face was a relief. "Doesn't Monsieur get mad about these cartoons?"

"No, some of the women sell them in the newspapers and magazines. Any art form that produces recognition—and better yet, money—is encouraged. It's much different here than it was at Monsieur Krug's."

"I can tell."

Miss Klumpke chuckled. "And just wait until the Russian arrives."

"There's a Russian instructor as well?"

"No, Monsieur Julian and Monsieur Robert-Fleury are the only regular teachers. But we do have a classmate who fancies herself above the rest of us." Miss Klumpke gave May a conspiratorial smile. "She's some sort of Russian nobility, and it's a one-woman show whenever she's around. She hasn't arrived yet. Probably sleeping off too much champagne from last night's opera."

Within minutes the rest of the class returned, and women clustered together talking quietly and reviewing each other's work in a murmuring of English, German, French, and Italian. A loud commotion at the door and a staccato rapping of heels called everyone's attention to the back of the room. A young woman, about twenty years old, stomped into the room, a small Roman wolf dog cradled in her arms. She gazed around for an open easel. May realized with dismay that the only one sat next to her. The woman spotted it and elbowed her way through the room, knocking other people's materials askew as she passed.

When she arrived at the open easel, she wrinkled her nose in disdain. "This is a dreadful place. I can't see a thing." The Russian glared at everyone, and Monsieur Robert-Fleury picked his way through the room toward her. The woman noticed May. "You're new." It was a complaint.

"Mademoiselle Bashkirtseff, this is Madame Nieriker." Monsieur Robert-Fleury now stood next to the Russian and gestured at May. His earlier abrasiveness vanished, and he appeared to be slinking around the Russian, trying to appease her. "She exhibited a painting in the Salon of '77."

The Russian's eyes narrowed, and she took a closer look at May, studying her up and down, before turning to a maid following behind her. "Take Pincio out for a walk but make sure he doesn't get wet. Use an umbrella." She held up the little black-and-white furry face and kissed its nose before handing it off to the swaddling arms of the maid. She gave a dismissive wave at Monsieur Robert-Fleury before unfastening her gray silk mantle, letting it drop to the floor in a pile. She kicked it aside to reach her art box and tugged out a handful of paintbrushes.

Once everyone resumed painting, May discovered her momentum from the morning had vanished. She struggled to try to create something acceptable. The only good thing about standing next to the Russian appeared to be that Monsieur Robert-Fleury avoided her area of the studio, so at least May did not worry he was going to come back to review her work. She returned to working on basic figure sketches. She caught Miss Bashkirtseff looking at her easel with contempt. May looked over at the Russian's easel, expecting to be mutually unimpressed, but she was amazed to see a graceful rendering of the model in oils.

At the end of the day, May left the studio wondering if she had made a terrible mistake by returning to the city. She overtook Miss Klumpke in the dank stairwell that reeked of spoiled fruits and vegetables from the market below. The younger woman moved slowly because she walked with a limp; one leg was slightly longer than the other.

"I fear I shouldn't have joined this class. I feel so out of practice."

"Don't worry, every day we're expected to sit somewhere new in the room, so tomorrow let's sit together."

"I could kiss you right now for your generous offer. Thank you." May shifted her paint box to her other arm. "I recall you being a talented portraitist. Do you think you could help me?"

"Of course." They walked a block together discussing basic portraiture strategies. After they separated, May walked alone to the train station, relieved to have found an ally in the new studio. The competition at the Académie Julian appeared to be fiercer than anything she had encountered before.

May regaled Ernest with all of the details of her new studio at dinner that evening. After they finished their meal and moved into the parlor, their house girl, Sabine, interrupted them with a letter she had forgotten to deliver earlier.

May recognized the handwriting of Una Hughes and tore the envelope eagerly. "Oh, this is just what I needed after a long day—some happy news from London. I'll need to write to Una and tell her all about Académie Julian. It's so different from London."

Ernest tuned his violin while May leaned back in the love seat across from him and read her letter. She let out a small cry, causing Ernest to look up from his instrument.

"What does she say?"

"It's Caroline." May rested her hand at her chest. "She died."

Ernest stared at her.

"Dear God, it says she died after giving birth to a son." May dropped the letter to her lap and stared at Ernest. "The baby survived."

"When did all of this happen?"

May swallowed back tears, looked back to the letter, and raised it up again to continue reading. "A month ago, apparently. Una reports she's been caring for the baby to help Robert." May scanned the letter. "Oh my, she and Robert plan to marry within the next few months."

"That's rather sudden, but I suppose there's the baby to care for." At the sight of May's distraught expression, Ernest propped his violin and bow against the chair and moved to sit next to May on the love seat.

May was not naïve enough to believe that a widower with a small infant would remain unmarried for long, but she could not help but be a little shocked by the suddenness of it all. "I always admired Caroline. She was so passionate about her poetry." She leaned into Ernest, remembering Caroline's talent to affect voices as she read aloud. He took her hands into his.

"It's a shame. She was a good friend to you. But at least this way, Una can honor Caroline's memory by raising her son. It's better than Robert marrying a stranger."

May buried her face into his shoulder and let the wool of Ernest's jacket scratch her forehead. His Swiss pragmatism was admirable, but her chest ached and her eyes burned. She knew his own mother survived all nine of her pregnancies—a feat that defied all explanation. May understood the dangers of childbirth, but this knowledge did not make the grief any easier to bear.

"I'm just so tired of losing people. First Lizzie, then John and Marmee, and now Caroline."

Ernest nodded his chin against her head. "We will all miss Caroline. What bad luck."

May closed her eyes against her husband's words, thinking about how she had lost Louisa, too.

MAY BURIED HER sorrow by working and attending the daily sessions at the Académie Julian. Through Monsieur Robert-Fleury's scalding comments and Miss Klumpke's more constructive suggestions, May could see improvement in her painting. She had always avoided portraiture in the past, but now she welcomed any opportunity to experiment and try it.

At the end of one of the afternoon sessions, Mademoiselle Bashkirtseff came by May's easel. "I hear your older sister is a famous writer in America. I just read her book *Little Women*. You're Amy?"

May nodded as she bent toward her canvas to add more shading to a section.

"Interesting. I didn't think it was you, since she is described as beautiful." The Russian shrugged, a small smile playing at the corner of her mouth. "Did you really try sleeping with a clothespin on your nose to make it smaller?"

May stared at her canvas for a moment to settle her composure before arranging a smile onto her face. "It's a shame you've never met my sister. You're exactly the type of woman who would be in one of her books."

A surprised smile lit the Russian's face. "Yes, I've always thought a book should be written about me."

"Absolutely." It was all May could do to contain her laughter. Louisa would consider the woman a treasure trove of absurdities for a character.

Mademoiselle Bashkirtseff nodded and swept off, but not before calling out over her shoulder, "It's good to know the clothespin trick doesn't work."

May shook her head at the woman's nerve, but as she packed up her materials for the day, she sighed. She missed Louisa terribly.

ON THE TRAIN home, May extended her stiff legs in front of her. All of the other women in the studio were so much younger. They relished the competition of the class, but May felt weary of it all. Once home, she sat with Ernest in the drawing room after a quiet dinner. May halfheartedly sketched her Venus de Milo statue resting on the mantel before switching to sewing a button back on one of Ernest's shirts. He folded up a letter and leaned back in his chair.

"My mother wants to come and visit."

May's needle slipped and stabbed her index finger. She watched a tiny bead of blood appear there. "When?"

"Perhaps next month. She's not sure yet."

"Would they stay here?"

"There's room in there." Ernest pointed to the small room off the drawing room that May used as a studio. "It would only be for a couple of days. My parents are looking forward to meeting you. It's been six months since we married, and they're eager to meet you."

"What have you told them about me? What do they think of our age difference?"

Ernest stacked the letter on top of his newspaper. "Our ages are not a topic that will concern them."

May dropped her sewing into her lap and stared at her husband. "Have you not written anything about my age?"

"No." He shrugged. "They're Swiss; they're simply pleased I'm married and settled. Remember, my mother has eight other children; she does not dwell on my decisions. She doesn't have the time."

Her heart stopped. Ernest was putting too much faith in European pragmatism. Her age was probably closer to Ernest's mother's than it was to Ernest's. She placed her needle in a pincushion and felt her shoulders tighten as she imagined how Frau Nieriker would react when she met her. She doubted Ernest's understanding of his mother; men could be immune to the machinations of women. She feared she would have more in common with Ernest's mother than she cared to admit.

Chapter 40

Three days. That was the promised length of their visit. When Herr and Frau Nieriker disembarked from the train on Saturday morning, they made a distinctive couple. She possessed the stout figure of a pickling jar whereas he resembled a fork, long and thin with a thatch of white hair that stuck straight upward in tines. Each carried a small valise. As her in-laws approached from the train, May tried for a surreptitious glimpse of her reflection in the glass window of the station, but other travelers blocked her view. Before leaving the house, she had arranged her hair into a coil of braids, hoping the hairdo gave her a more youthful appearance. When the older couple reached May and Ernest, Frau Nieriker took May's face in her hands. She inspected her new daughter-in-law for a moment, nodded, and leaned in to kiss May on both cheeks.

At the house, May watched Frau Nieriker circle the drawing room and realized there was no clearer way to see the shortcomings in one's own home than to look at it alongside a stranger. The room was small and the furniture showed signs of its previous owners, but May took pride in the way she positioned the gilt mirror across from the biggest window to reflect the natural light. Her strategic arrangement of chairs in the center of the room made the space seem larger and covered up a few rents laddering the Turkish carpet. She had done the best she could with limited resources. Frau Nieriker stopped to inspect two of May's watercolors: one of Westminster Abbey and one from Dinan.

"These are yours?"

"Yes."

"You're good." Her pronunciation of "good" was clipped with her German accent. "Ernest says you have studied art for the last decade. It shows." She sat down on one of the chairs and accepted a glass of lemonade from Sabine. "I'm relieved. This visit would have been awkward otherwise."

"I appreciate that, thank you." May stretched a smile across to her mother-in-law.

"Mother never minces words," Ernest said to May, chuckling.

"Ernest wrote that you studied French all summer."

"I did. I can no longer get by on English alone. I'm always impressed by how many languages Europeans speak."

Frau Nieriker gave a dismissive shrug. "When you live in a country as large as America where everyone speaks the same language, why bother to waste time learning anything else? Here, we're all together in a small space. We speak each other's languages only out of necessity."

Herr Nieriker had been outside studying the plants in the garden before joining them in the drawing room. "It's a lovely afternoon. We should go for a walk."

Frau Nieriker stood. "I agree. We've been sitting since we left Baden this morning."

"Good idea, there are some lovely paths here in the village's park." May rose to walk into the kitchen to give directions for dinner to Sabine.

As the foursome left the house to walk the paths around Saint Cloud, Ernest pulled May behind. "See? They tell you exactly what is on their minds."

May smiled, but was not sure she wanted to know exactly what was on their minds.

THAT EVENING, THE foursome settled into the drawing room. Frau Nieriker concentrated on her needlework while May knit. Herr Nieriker paced around the room; he had not remained still all day. On their earlier afternoon walk, he had blasted ahead of them. Impatience? A search for solitude? A simple desire to stretch out one's legs? May couldn't tell. He stopped in front of the mantel to inspect the small collection of flowers that surrounded a small photograph of her mother.

"What's this?"

"Oh, that's my shrine to my dear mother. I miss her dreadfully."

May was surprised to find Frau Nieriker reach forward and pet her arm in sympathy. May's eyes misted with unexpected tears, and she looked down at the muffler she was knitting. Keen for a distraction, she said, "Ernest, how about you give us a little concert?"

Frau Nieriker's right arm froze as she had stopped her needle. She lifted her gaze quickly from her embroidery hoop. "Yes, we would love that."

Herr Nieriker stopped moving and stared at the rug.

Ernest did not look up from his newspaper, but his nostrils flared and he clenched his jaw. "No."

"Son, please."

He peeled his gaze from the newspaper and looked back at his mother. "No."

May had never heard her husband speak so sharply. She looked back and forth from Ernest and his mother. Frau Nieriker slowly balled up her stitching before standing.

"It is time for me to say good night." She spoke with formal precision, pronouncing each English word carefully. "Thank you for welcoming us into your home."

"Good night," May called back as she watched Frau Nieriker retreat to the art studio, repurposed into a guest room for the weekend. "I shall follow suit and head upstairs. Good night."

Once in bed, May waited for Ernest to join her, but he remained downstairs. Eventually she fell asleep alone, Ernest's terse refusal echoing in her head.

THE NEXT DAY, the group decided to go into Paris to explore the city. On the train, May watched her husband and his parents for any sign of uneasiness; yet unperturbed, they all read through sections of the newspaper. The four arrived in the Left Bank and strolled down rue de Sèvres, along the long front of Au Bon Marché. Frau Nieriker reached for May's arm and nodded up at the department store's domed entrance on the corner.

"Let's go in and browse."

The two men decided to visit the store's reading room, while the women entered the main shopping gallery. May wandered the aisles of umbrellas and shoes and came upon Frau Nieriker at a counter fingering some silk scarves. The contrast between seeing the woman clad in black from head to toe admiring a dainty silk scarf the color of red geraniums made May smile.

"Are you looking for a gift?"

"No," her mother-in-law answered without lifting her eyes from the scarf. Letting it slide through her fingers and fall back onto the counter, she looked at May with a sheepish expression. "I've always wanted to wear something like this."

May reached for the scarf and sighed at the softness of its texture. "It's a wonderful color. You should buy it for yourself."

"No, I would never wear it. My whole life, I have looked like this." She gestured at her squat shape. Her gray eyes ran across the silk scarves below the glass with longing. "I'm too old. But on you . . . I will get it for you."

"That's kind, but I don't need it." May placed it back on the counter in a careful rectangle, Frau Nieriker's large hand closed on top of hers, holding it in place. May found herself looking down into her mother-in-law's square face.

"I am so happy to hear Ernest plays the violin for you. You saw how he refuses to play for us anymore."

"Yes, but why?"

Frau Nieriker removed her hand from May's and smoothed down the front of her dress before speaking. "For years we encouraged him to play the violin, we paid for his classes, we sent him to the finest instructors. Everything was for his music. And then my husband lost our family's savings in a failed investment. He told Ernest art was no way to make a living and demanded that he go into business to help support the family, even though Ernest was offered a position in a symphony in Dresden. Ernest followed his father's wishes, but he has never played for us again."

The two women stood in the swirl of shoppers, looking away from each other. Tears pricked at May's eyes as she considered her husband's sacrifice. No wonder he insisted May travel into the city daily to study at the Académie Julian.

"I'm sorry," said Frau Nieriker.

May shook her head and tried to clear her eyes by blinking.

"I'm sorry I asked you to play for us on Saturday night. I didn't realize why you stopped playing until your mother told me."

May and Ernest were lying in bed later that evening, both on their backs, facing up at the ceiling.

He was quiet, and she wondered if he had fallen asleep. He had the enviable ability to drop off at a moment's notice.

"Why didn't you tell me what happened?"

"I didn't want you to dislike my parents from the outset."

"And you didn't tell them about my age, because you didn't want them to dislike me?"

"I never worried about them loving you. Your age means nothing to any of us. I knew your charm would help to bridge the gap between my parents and me. But still, I'll never forgive them for making me give up my music."

May closed her eyes and conjured a memory of her laughing with Louisa over cups of rich hot chocolate in Dinan. She missed her sister with an intensity that made her unable to breathe. She tried to loosen her jaw and sighed past the burn in her lungs. "You might. Someday."

FALL AND WINTER passed by May in a blur, as if she were watching her life from the window of a fast-moving train. She spent every waking minute painting, shipping artwork to her galleries, or traveling back and forth to Paris; the harried routine was wearying her, and now the mid-March deadline to the Salon show hovered in her mind. Almost every woman in the Académie Julian had a painting to submit to the show, except May. She sat at the desk in her studio and glanced at a group of canvases leaning against the wall—she could enter one or two of those into the show, but none of them represented what she was capable of, and this frustrated her. Her thoughts were interrupted by the front door banging open. Ernest leaned inside, grasping the doorway as he stomped mud off his boots before entering.

"This is a treat—you're home early." May smiled as she looked up from an invoice she was creating for a package of paintings that would soon be on its way to an art dealer in Lille. She rubbed her eyes. "I could use a break. Shall we go for a walk?"

Ernest tramped across the drawing room, threw his hat to the ground, and kicked it. He raked his hands through his hair before meeting May's gaze. "I have bad news."

She looked at Ernest's dented hat on the floor in surprise and then up at her husband. "What in the world happened?"

"I've been taken in by scoundrels." Ernest rubbed his hands over his face. "A team of rogues out of Brussels have robbed me. Robbed me blind. The deal they promised me on a shipment of tobacco was too good to be true, I should have known, but I fell for it." Ernest collapsed into a chair.

Fear descended upon her, and she dropped the pen from her shaking hands to the table. "What do you mean?"

"I mean I lost almost a thousand francs today." Ernest's breathing came in ragged bursts. "I sent money for the tobacco in advance of receiving it, and the shipment arrived today and is basically a crate of sawdust. Normally I would never send payment in advance, but their references seemed in order and the deal they offered was so good, I couldn't resist."

"Well . . ." May shook her head, struggling to comprehend the enormity of the loss. "Where are they now?"

"Who knows? Gone." He shook his head angrily. "They're long gone by now."

May dropped from her chair to kneel in front of him, and although the uneven floorboards cut into her knees, the solidity of the ground gave her comfort. She took his hands into hers speechlessly.

"I wanted so desperately to make this money. I thought it could help us to settle in and be the foundation of our savings." Ernest's face flushed as looked down at her. "But now I don't think we can spare the money for next month's studio fee. I need it. I must cover this loss somehow, and it's the only way." His eyes looked red and frantic. "I've been trying to come up with an alternative the whole way home, but I simply can't. I'm sorry; it's no better than what my father did to me." He choked on the last few words.

"Don't say that. This is a small setback. We'll figure something out."

"Small? It's a thousand francs!"

The gears of May's mind slowed as she absorbed his words. At first, the idea of stopping the demanding daily schedule of going back and forth to Paris appealed to her. She could say good-bye to the dreadful hectoring of Mademoiselle Bash-kirtseff and Monsieur Robert-Fleury's ill-tempered sneering. Here was an excuse to give up under the guise of sacrifice and selflessness. She felt tempted to acquiesce, but then her eyes fell onto a streak of red paint on the sleeve of her gray silk dress. It looked like blood. Indeed recently it felt like she was working herself into a bloody pulp, yet her work was improving. In fact, her work was good. Her gaze lifted in the direction of her art studio, landing on the painting of Orchard House. She could simply hand Ernest the check from Louisa and resolve everything. She could.

"I can't," she whispered.

"What?"

"I can't stop now. I'm too close. The deadline for the Salon is in two weeks. I know I can get a painting into it."

Ernest shook his head in disbelief. "I thought the Salon was a disappointment to you last time."

"Yes, but this time it will be different."

"Different?" Ernest dropped her hands and rose to stalk around the room, his fists bunched at his sides. "How can it be different?"

"Because this time I'm making something that really shows how far I've come."

"You're working on it now? The painting is already under way?"

"Well . . . no," May admitted, still kneeling, but she raised her chin. "I'm about to start working on it. Take the thousand francs for your business. I will pay my own studio fees."

Ernest let out a frustrated chuff of air. "How?"

"I'll get it." The painting of Orchard House called to her, but she stayed put.

"What are you going to do?"

"I'll earn it." May stood. Her bare feet padded across the room to her studio. She took out a sheet of watercolor paper, willed herself not to look up at the painting of Orchard House, and dipped her brush into a jar of clean water. Even after creating hundreds of watercolors, the startling tingle of awakening that accompanied beginning a new piece ran up her arm as she began to paint.

WHEN SHE ARRIVED back at the Académie Julian the following morning, a new girl took her place on the model's dais. Her dark skin was the color of strong Roman coffee, and the white-ness of her chemise reflected off her arms, chest, and face, making her entire body shine. An orange scarf tied around her head gave her a youthful appearance. May guessed the woman to be around twenty years of age. The short chemise hung at an angle to expose long, lithe, toned legs. Her hands wrung together for a brief moment before she let them fall to her sides. The girl shifted her weight from one leg to the other, letting her pensive gaze sweep above the faces looking up at her.

May studied the downward tilt of the model's face, how her eyes glanced away from the painters, and the way she chewed the inside of her cheek. Monsieur Robert-Fleury approached the model, and the two conferred in low voices about her posi-tioning. One strap from the model's white muslin chemise fell from her right shoulder, leaving the shoulder completely bare and the upper swell of her breast revealed. She moved to cover herself, but it was not the exposed skin that caught May's eye. It was the model's left hand. The girl's left index finger and her middle finger were gone. They were cleanly severed and pink scar tissue peeked out from the place where the finger should have been, like the inner green of an emerging plant visible right before it blooms from its casing.

A few years ago, May would have painted the woman as a study and focused on the long lines of her lean body and avoided any details. She would have sidestepped anything that felt too personal, but now May felt inexplicably drawn to the woman's face. Later, she would see how her classmates all cap-tured the exquisite lines of the exotic model's entire body and posed her in historical and biblical settings—this was the expected, predictable course of action. After all, historical scene paintings were what launched careers. But May wanted an intimacy she had never attempted before in her compositions.

She covered her canvas with a gesso mixture and watched the chalky primer harden into place before sanding it slightly. She then took a charcoal pencil and lightly sketched the understudy onto the canvas to get the basic shape of the skull, neck, shoulders, and chest in front of her. Before she could even begin to consider the model's features, she needed to see the basic shape of the head. Starting with the skull, she sketched a cube with a slightly rounded top, almost like a loaf of bread, with the smaller wedge of the jaw underneath. After the overall shape of the head took form, she shadowed in its planes. The model was facing her in a three-quarter view, making the depth of the skull easier to represent. When the overall shape satisfied her, she divided up the skull to locate the features: first, there was the halfway point to mark the eye sockets and then she divided the face into thirds. May sketched a dividing line at her hairline, and then one-third of the way down the face to indicate the woman's brow, and then the brow to the base of the nose. By this point, her canvas resembled a series of etched lines, some rounded but mostly long, straight, dark lines. Dr. Rimmer would have been proud at the precision with which she envisioned the skull below the surface of her model's face before tackling the features.

"Use straight lines here. The ramus should be almost vertical in this view." Monsieur Robert-Fleury stuck out a bony finger and traced the far side of the face's upper jaw. "The bottom of the body of the jaw should only turn in slightly."

May nodded and followed his suggestion, continuing to sketch in charcoal lines until she created a convincing shape of the woman's portrait. Only when she finished this outline did she start to work on features. She could not see the details of the girl's eyes from her vantage point, so she relied on what she already knew. Several times she stopped her sketching and felt the circular indentation of her own eye socket to help feel the shape under her own fingers. As the day neared evening, the model finished her posing and disappeared behind the curtain at the back of the room to change. Miss Klumpke appeared next to May, studying her canvas.

"A close-up portrait? In oils? This is new for you."

"I know, but I think I like it."

"You have the beginnings of her tentative expression."

Mademoiselle Bashkirtseff stood back in a corner, but her voice carried. "We've had some ugly models before—some of those old people, ugh—but we've never used someone maimed before. Poor thing. One look at her hand and she's ruined. What good is a woman if she's not beautiful?"

Miss Klumpke remained unexpressive as she faced the canvas, but May balled her hands against her hips and scowled. Along with everyone else in the room, she knew the young American was the real target of Mademoiselle Bashkirtseff's cruel words. Everyone knew the Russian envied Miss Klumpke's exceptional talent, but May would not tolerate her young friend's lameness to be ridiculed. She spun to face the wretched Russian. "There are many ways to be beautiful. And ugly, too, for that matter."

Mademoiselle Bashkirtseff looked back at May with surprise and then scoffed. "I feel as though I am being scolded by my mother. My poor *old* mother," she said, addressing the crowd around them with a triumphant expression. No one met the woman's eyes, and the Russian, for once, sensed the room's coldness toward her. She bent over to scoop up her little dog and swept out of the room, leaving the maid to scurry after her.

"Thank you," Miss Klumpke whispered.

May collapsed in fatigue on a nearby stool. Maybe this whole thing was a younger woman's pursuit after all. But no. She must work. This portrait would earn her a spot in the upcoming Salon, even if it killed her. For the following week, Ernest said nothing when May picked at her food and gazed out the window distractedly. She painted her Turner copies to sell while he played the violin for her in the evenings.

On the final day the model was in the studio, May put finishing touches on the painting. The canvas was small, but she felt pleased by its intimacy. *La Négresse* gazed out from the canvas with a wide-eyed pensive look, and May knew she had never achieved such a sense of emotion in her work before. Monsieur Julian approached her easel on one of his stops through the Passage des Panoramas atelier. He rolled back and forth on his feet, looking at the portrait, pushing out his stomach and exhaling loudly, as he rested his thumbs behind his suspenders. Despite his pompous mannerisms, May liked the short, rotund man with his dark, pointed mustache and long, sharp nose. He had no formal art training; in fact, rumors circulated that he had spent his youth training as a gymnast. Nevertheless, he had a good eye for what could sell.

"You'll submit this to the Salon, *oui*?"

"Yes, I'll purchase a frame for it when I leave today."

"*C'est bon*. Please, attach my name and Monsieur Robert-Fleury's. I think this stands a good chance, Madame."

She nodded gratefully and stepped back to look into the eyes of the girl. She could picture the slow smile that would ripple across Ernest's face when he saw this painting. But with a fervor that surprised her, she wished she could show the portrait to Louisa. Her sister would remember the rough sketches of May's youth, the cumbersome attempts at paintings; she would be able to see the distance May had traveled, and only she would understand May's slogging through those years of uncertainty and self-doubt. She would know because she had traveled the same path. May understood that now. Louisa's journey had been fraught with similar fears, magnified by the responsibility of being the sole provider for the entire family. May realized she had doubted herself for far too long and relied upon her sister. Even when she committed to supporting herself through her paintings, she had been blind to the worries and concerns threatening to overwhelm Louisa. She allowed her sister's resentment at her departure for Europe to leave her riddled with guilt and anger instead of recognizing it for what it was: a call for help. They had all taken Louisa for granted,

May thought as she ran a rag over the bristles of her brushes and pulled it away to see the muddy blend of ocher, cadmium yellow, and burnt sienna bleeding across the white cloth. Although she did not know exactly how to clean up the mess with her sister, she knew she needed to. Louisa needed her.

Chapter 41

A battered envelope with a Parisian postmark arrived in Meudon in late April. May opened it to find an official notice that *La Négresse* had been accepted into the Salon of 1879. She tacked the letter below her watercolor of Orchard House in her little studio and stood back to look at them both. Somehow she had known her painting would be accepted—it represented everything she had been working toward. She rubbed at her two fingers, both missing fingernails as a result of carelessly hammering crates to pack up artwork for her dealers. This was the type of accident that happened after spending too many long nights painting her work to sell, but it was all worth it— she had managed to scrape together the money to pay for her studio fees.

She attended Salon Opening Day in May with Ernest, wearing a pale blue spring suit of woven jacquard silk restyled from one of her older dresses. As she attended to her toilette in the morning, queasiness made her drop her hands from arranging her hair. She sat down on the side of the bed, inhaling and exhaling deeply, waiting for the waves of nervousness to pass. After a few minutes, she was able to resume her preparations.

The sun was shining, though a cool wind whipped at women's hat ribbons and their new Worth gowns as they paraded along the gardens in front of the Palais. Opening Day at the Salon coincided with the first day of the social season, prompting all of Paris to turn out for the grand show in haute couture. The couple forged their way through the masses swarming the front steps. A dull headache pounded at the back of May's skull, but the sight of Mary Cassatt in the entrance distracted her. The two women embraced. May introduced Ernest.

"You must be terribly proud of your bride," Mary said, holding May's hand tightly within her own.

May laughed, as she held the hands of both Ernest on one side and Mary's on her other. "We've been married for over a year now. I don't think we can call me his bride forever. Now I'm just his wife."

"The glow will never vanish; you'll always be my bride." Ernest grinned at May. "Miss Cassatt, I hear your show is going well."

"It is, much to my relief," Mary said. "Leaving the Salon exhibitions to show my work with the Impressionists has certainly not been any less stressful. I've traded worrying about getting into the Salon for worrying about the public coming to see us. But this year, people are finally beginning to accept our work. When I stopped in yesterday, the gallery was actually crowded."

"And the critics are catching up. *Le Figaro* wrote a positive review." May beamed at her friend, knowing how Mary suffered from critics' barbs, despite her insistence on aligning herself with the controversial Impressionists.

"Oh, May, what would I do without your optimism?" Mary squeezed May's arm and smiled shyly. "The review wasn't exactly positive, but it wasn't murderous either. So, that's an improvement."

The trio followed the throngs of people along the corridors of the Salon. Again, May's painting enjoyed a prime spot on the eye line, and they parked themselves by her work. May enjoyed the deluge of congratulations from all of her friends and acquaintances who were in attendance. Miss Klumpke, Monsieur Krug, Monsieur Robert-Fleury, Monsieur Julian—all made their way to May and complimented her on the strength of her portrait.

Even Mademoiselle Bashkirtseff came through the show with a retinue of society types following in her wake. "Here. This is the American I was speaking of." Half a dozen women, all in colorful silk dresses, swarmed in front of May like butterflies. "This artist creates work that will brighten your walls. Madame Nieriker, hand them your cards." May smiled and chatted briefly with the potential clients, for once, happy to comply with an order from the woman.

"May, you look peaked," said Mary. "Are you all right?"

"I think so. My head hurts, but I think it's because I've overtaxed myself dreadfully in the last few weeks."

Mary squeezed her hand and smiled, but continued to look

over at her friend with concern until the two women spotted Jane Gardner, dressed in crimson, jostling her way through the crowd toward them.

Bright-eyed and breathless, Jane said, "I've been looking all over for you two. I'm going to start a women's cooperative art studio over in Montparnasse. Want to join me? There are so many American women here to study art now, I think there are enough of us that it could work."

May nodded. "Why, that's a brilliant idea—Julian's is packed to the gills. I'll spread the word."

"Perfect." Jane clapped her hands together. "These newly arrived doe-eyed girls need all the help they can get. There are too many thieving studio owners all too eager to bilk them at every turn."

May took in Jane's sparkling eyes and gave a knowing smile. "Your spirits have improved since I last saw you."

"Work is going well. I have a painting here, too."

May cocked her head. "Anything else?"

"Well, I suppose it's because I have happy news. I'm engaged." Jane spoke quickly with a sheepish expression.

"You are? Who's the lucky fellow?" May asked.

"Bouguereau," Jane said, pausing for a moment to enjoy the surprise registering on both women's faces. Seeing Mary's confusion, she added. "Monsieur Bouguereau, the master painter." Satisfaction bloomed across her narrow face.

"I'm aware of who Bouguereau is," Mary replied coldly, but her piqued countenance gave way to bewilderment. "But I didn't realize . . ."

"I thought his mother had forbidden him from marrying you," May asked.

"She did. But"—Jane fanned a show program in front of her face and gave May a wink—"we're merely engaged, not married. He's a grown man, for God's sake, he doesn't need to do everything the spiteful witch says. The ol' harridan will die off soon anyway."

May giggled. "You take the cake."

"Thank you, I'll accept that as a compliment. Now I've got to go visit with clients, but I'll send you a note with more on this co-op idea." Jane smiled before allowing herself to be swept away by the crowds.

"I confess, I didn't see that coming. Did you?" Mary wore a perplexed expression and studied the ground before looking at May. Her eyes widened. "We need to get you outside. You look like you've seen a ghost."

Small black flecks had appeared in May's vision; she furiously tried to blink them away as Mary steered May toward Ernest. The sweet smell of cigars wafting through the air made May's stomach flip. Ernest took one look at his wife, grabbed her other arm, and pushed a path through the crush of bodies until they were outside. Slumped on a park bench, May inhaled the cool breeze in an attempt to settle her stomach. She was aware of Ernest and Mary talking, but closed her eyes to focus on breathing through the nausea burning in her throat. She swallowed. Their voices rumbled quietly above her.

"May, I'm sorry, but we're going home," Ernest said. May

opened her eyes to find him crouched down, looking at her in concern. "Can you walk?"

With each forced nod of her head, her world spun.

Ernest helped to lift her to her feet, and the two of them followed Mary, who ran ahead to hail a carriage. Though it took only a quarter of an hour, the train ride home was lost in a fog for May.

THE NEXT MORNING, she awoke to find Ernest sitting beside her, reading the paper. The shutters were open and sunlight poured in, striping the planked floors. Her stomach felt tight and empty.

"Good morning. Don't get up." Ernest shut the paper and snapped it into its folds. "Sabine will bring up something to eat. How do you feel?"

"I'm not sure." May wriggled herself into sitting higher in the bed. "What happened?"

"You fainted yesterday, remember? When we got home, you went straight to sleep, but I had Dr. Cotnoir come over to check on you. He's due back today and wondered . . ." Ernest stopped and flushed. "The doctor wondered if you could be . . . expecting." He leaned forward and took her hand in his.

"Expecting?" May's brain labored to string together the meaning of Ernest's words. Expecting what? But then she realized the reason for Ernest's pink cheeks. She thought back. Consumed with preparing for the Salon, she could not remember her monthly courses since . . . since when? She held her breath.

Excitement fluttered around her chest just as someone knocked at the door. Sabine ushered in Dr. Cotnoir.

Ernest kissed her on the forehead. "I'll be outside." He left her with the fatigued-looking elderly doctor, shutting the door behind him. May could only imagine that the half-stunned, half-thrilled look on Ernest's face mirrored her own.

The doctor came to May's bedside and looked down at her. He gestured at her to raise her wrist, so he could take her pulse. In heavily accented English, he said, "So I am correct? You are expecting?"

May nodded, not trusting herself to speak.

He sighed. "This is your first?"

"Yes."

"You are . . . how would you say . . . aged?"

"I am older."

"Old. Yes."

May closed her eyes for a moment. *Older. Not old.* She wanted to correct him, but lacked the energy.

"You must be careful. No more Paris. Rest at home." He nodded at her sternly to ensure she understood.

"*Oui.*"

"*Bien.*" He paused for a moment to look at her one more time before tipping the brim of his hat and making his way out of the room. When she was alone, May picked at the fold of the chenille coverlet in front of her, hoping the unease inside her would dissipate. She wished for her family, but most of all, she missed Louisa. She rubbed her hand in circles over her belly.

This baby offered a fresh start, an opportunity to mend the rift between them.

When Ernest came back into the bedroom to check on her, she asked for some paper and a pen. "I need to write a few letters. Violet won't believe the coincidence in all of this. I told you that she's expecting a baby at the end of summer?"

"You did. It all seems preordained—two babies at the same time, but on opposite sides of the world." He reached down to cup May's cheek in his palm.

"I know, perhaps someday they will be best friends, too. Or maybe if one of us has a girl and the other a boy, they'll marry. Wouldn't that be something?"

"Indeed, my dear. Rest a bit. I'll bring you some paper and a pen."

"Thank you," May said as Ernest turned to walk out the door. "Ernest?" He stopped and looked back at her. "I love you."

His eyes crinkled over his smile and returned to her side to kiss her tenderly. "I'll be back."

MAY MANAGED TO get down a small breakfast and found herself alone again. She sat up and started writing. Outside, carriage wheels clattered along the ruts of the road in front of the house and the bleating of a herd of sheep from the neighboring field echoed off the plaster walls of her bedroom. None of this disturbed May from her task, and the words came easily. She hadn't been aware of it, but now she realized her mind had been composing this letter for over a year. Perhaps even longer. Her hand moved in steady precision across the page without faltering. She finished, put the letter aside, and closed her eyes.

She fell asleep and dreamt of floating, soaring through the air, looking down on the landscape below, with a sense of freedom and lightness that amazed her. She bobbed above the trees, and their rustling leaves whispered back the words from her letter to Louisa.

> *Over the years, you've shown endless generosity and devotion to all of us. It shames me that I've allowed my own concerns to obscure the many sacrifices you've made. As unromantic as this is to admit, your money has done what affection alone could never do. You've delighted in making us all happy in your own way although much of your own life and health has been given in exchange. Thank you.*

The *thank you* repeated itself like sighs. She finally felt the deadening weight of regret lifted and could not remember feeling so unencumbered. Through forgiveness, she was free.

Chapter 42

The pungent smell of the turpentine nauseated May. Varnish. Clean paper. Colored pencil shavings. All of the scents that once welcomed her to work now made her stomach turn. Despite landing several commissions since the Salon, she was unable to paint, or even sketch, yet Jane Gardner's cooperative studio idea lodged itself in her mind. The thought of American girls looking for assistance had sparked an idea. She pondered creating a guidebook for women who were interested in studying art in Europe. Over the years, she had often lamented that no such resource existed. Why not write it herself?

July 11, 1879
Concord

Dearest May,

    Poor girl, I'm sorry to hear you've been under the weather. You've always been the most stalwart Alcott sis-

ter, so I cannot even imagine you incapacitated. But I must confess to being a bit pleased by your current state if it leads us back into a creative collaboration. It won't be the same as us working side by side at the Bellevue Hotel, but it shall have to suffice. Send me a draft of your book, and I'll be happy to send back any comments.

Mr. Niles agrees there is definitely a market for your idea with so many swarms of women descending upon Europe in hopes of becoming the next Tintoretto or Rembrandt. He will be all too happy to publish it for you and suggested we consider serializing it as a newspaper column first. I'll continue to make inquiries.

You've always been a person who looks for opportunity. This is a fine project.

Yours,
Louisa

Encouraged by her sister's letter, May pushed a wrought-iron table and chair into the shady nook of their garden and started scratching out ideas onto paper. She could write about England, France, and Italy and her focus would be on telling women how to live and study art abroad. When Sabine left for the day and Ernest returned home late in the evening, May still sat in the waning summer light amid scattered white papers, absorbed in her project.

Ernest leaned over her shoulder and chuckled. "What are you working on?"

"I can't just sit here staring at the wallpaper all day long until this baby is born. I've decided to try my hand at writing a guide for women on how to go about studying art in Europe." May held up a handful of completed pages. "My goodness, it's rather hard, but it feels wonderful to be so consumed in a project again."

Ernest reached over, took her right hand in his, and rubbed at her palm and fingers. "Sometimes I would need this after playing the violin for too long. It's good to see you feeling energized." He bent over to kiss the top of her head. "Let's go inside."

May giggled as she let him pull her to her feet, and they both bent over to gather all of her papers. "Louisa writes only one draft when she works." May shook her head. "I'm afraid I shall have to write a few versions of everything. But I don't mind; it's fun. It's just like talking to a group of friends."

Summer progressed, and May could track the days passing by both her growing manuscript and the increasing roundness of her belly. Often as she sat in the cool shade of the stone wall and listened to Sabine cooking in the kitchen, she would rest her hands on the swell of the baby and feel the fluttering of life inside of her. Cataloging and reviewing all of her stops and adventures of the last ten years left her swimming in fond memories. She remembered climbing the round tower at the ruined English castle of Kenilworth, shopping for oil paints in the dusty cabinets of No. 4 quai des Oeuvres in Paris, and admiring the picturesque shepherds following their herds amongst the high slopes of Albano. May smiled as she wrote the chapters of her book. The brisk exchange of letters back and forth with her sister also helped to keep her spirits up.

August 18, 1879
Concord

Dearest May,

Your chapters make for a fine stroll down memory lane. What larks we enjoyed together. Your chapters about France and Italy bring it all back to me. I particularly enjoyed that you wrote: "the indiscreet, husband-hunting, title-seeking butterfly is not the typical American girl abroad"—bravo, your readers will applaud the fact that you champion their noble intentions! Reading your draft makes me long to return to our former stomping grounds.

I'd been planning to work on a memoir about Marmee, but stopped. I'm simply too sad for such a project. After casting about earlier this year with his anchor gone, Father is now a model of industry with his School of Philosophy. Thanks to a generous donation by one of his followers, his vision of creating this school is finally happening. Last spring he built a modest building out behind Orchard House that he calls Hillside Chapel, and he's using it for his classes. I envy his unflagging energy. Yet can you guess where I have found solace and a newfound spark to inspire me? Your letters. I enjoy our daily missives in a way I can-

not even describe. Yes, it's true—I'm at a loss to explain how happy our correspondence makes me.

In other news, I swear Freddy and Johnny grow inches overnight. Anna and the boys escorted me into Boston last week to meet with Mr. Niles about your book. Afterward, we rode on these marvelous little pontoons called Swan Boats in the Public Garden. An inventive fellow has capitalized on the bicycle craze and created a paddle-wheel boat in which the driver propels the boat by peddling—all while the driver's presence is covered up by the statue of an enormous swan. Apparently, he was inspired by the German opera "Lohengrin" in which a knight of the Grail must cross the river in a boat disguised as a swan to rescue his princess. And you've said Boston has no culture! You would love the romance of these beautiful boats. Sadly, the man who invented the fanciful little fleet perished unexpectedly, yet his wife wants to keep the operation afloat. The city has demanded she drum up letters from locals testifying to her ability to run a business on her own. Of course you can imagine who's first in line to write a letter for her—me. It's appalling that women be put through such absurd paces to prove their worthiness.

Although our writing is one of my few delights, I long to see you. Would Ernest tolerate a visit from an old spinster after the baby is born? I promise to be a charming guest. Or perhaps you would consider coming home next spring for a visit?

Yours,

Louisa

ONE AFTERNOON IN late September, May sat in the garden stitching a tiny nightgown, enjoying a quiet afternoon. Her finished manuscript sat on the dining room table ready to be mailed in the following day's post to her sister. A knock at the front door interrupted her musings. There was no sound of Sabine in the kitchen, so May heaved herself out of her chair and ambled through the house to the front door to find her friend from London, William Keith, standing on the front steps.

"Mr. Keith, my goodness, what a happy surprise! Where's Violet?"

Upon seeing May, his face drained of color, and he staggered backward on his feet.

"Mr. Keith, *where's* Violet?"

He gasped, shaking his head. "I shouldn't have shown up unannounced. I should have written first."

With shaking hands, May reached out to take hold of his forearm and led him into the parlor. He collapsed into a seat and buried his head in his hands.

"She's gone."

A cold dread settled over May. "Gone where?"

"Five weeks ago, she and our baby passed away. Neither survived the birth."

May's knees buckled, and he jumped to his feet to help her to a chair. Sabine stood in the doorway to the kitchen, looking back and forth between them with a frown.

"I'm sorry to have just shown up on your doorstep with this news. I should have written first. I couldn't stay in California.

Not without her. I've come here to get away from all of my memories of her. I'm going to work here."

"Until when?"

"I don't know." He looked around the room with an overwhelmed expression. "Until I can bear to return."

"Of course. Please, rest." May looked down upon her friend's stricken husband helplessly and rested her hands on her stomach to feel her own baby. Her mouth felt dry, her face stiff. What could she say? It was impossible to imagine a world in which Violet did not exist. They sat in the parlor, staring off into the distance until Sabine waved him to the table where she gave him a plate of cold chicken, gravy, and brown bread. Mr. Keith picked at the food listlessly. His skin had the grayish tinge of soggy paper, and swathes of black whisker stubble streaked his neck and cheeks where he had missed spots shaving, doubtlessly distracted by his sudden emptiness.

"She was so happy," Mr. Keith muttered, shaking his head with disbelief. Next to his elbow, balancing on the edge of the table, stood a small stemless glass of red wine. May wanted to warn him to watch out, to move it, but before she could get the words out, his arm knocked it off the table. The glass crashed to the ground. Shards of glass glittered on the dark floorboards, while a blotch of red wine pooled like a bloodstain. Everyone froze, watching the liquid spread, before Sabine sprang forward and began scrubbing at it.

Mr. Keith lowered his head in apology and gathered his hat to take his leave. He handed May a slip of paper with his address in Paris on it. They did not make plans to meet again.

From her front door, she watched him wander down the street, immune to the low rosy afternoon light over the golden hills rolling down to the Seine. May tried to take a deep breath, but could not get the air far down enough into her chest. She was that glass, balancing at the edge of the table; one accidental movement, and she would be broken into a million pieces. What would happen to this baby if something were to happen to her?

ERNEST ARRIVED HOME several hours later to find May, pale-faced, waiting for him in the parlor. "We must speak about what will happen in the event of my death," she said quietly.

Ernest's hand lowered slowly from hanging his hat on a hook next to the door. "What's this?"

She told Ernest about the death of Violet and her child.

"May, you're a portrait of good health. All is well. Let's not worry about this now."

"Let's not worry about this now? A woman who does not consider her child's welfare upon her death is a fool!"

Ernest slumped into one of their parlor chairs and rested his elbows on his knees as he stared at the floor. The youthful glow on his face suddenly seemed like a recrimination. May felt every single day of the sixteen years that separated their ages.

"I *must* think about this."

"Now?"

"Yes. If I wait too long, it could be too late. If I die, you must send our baby to Louisa."

"To America?" Ernest looked at May as though she had begun to speak in Chinese. "To Louisa? Why?"

She ran her trembling hand across her face.

"And what if I want to keep this baby with me? I'm its father. I don't want to send our baby anywhere." Ernest stood and tried to put his arms around May, but she shook him off.

"You know your life wouldn't accommodate caring for a baby. And I barely know your family. My family should do it."

"Your family? I've never met anyone from your family. You were estranged from Louisa." By now, he was yelling. "You thought I didn't notice, but I figured it out: Louisa didn't approve of our marriage, did she?"

May's head throbbed at the prospect of trying to explain it all to him, her mind felt stretched taut. She wasn't even sure she could explain her feelings. "It wasn't our marriage, not really. She didn't want me to leave home in the first place. My family is all I've ever really had." Tears spilled down her face.

Ernest's face softened. He spoke quietly. "What about me? You've had me."

May wept. She hated measuring her marriage against her family back in Massachusetts, for the two were incomparable; her marriage with Ernest seemed too new and raw to compete with the bonds of her family. All she could see was his unlined face and the firm posture of his shoulders. How could she tell Ernest he was young and would marry again and raise another family? May would be reduced to an early chapter in the story of his life, their child a footnote in his story. She had seen it happen many times, and she couldn't blame him. Wives died, husbands remarried, children fended for their positions in their new households. It was how the world worked.

"Violet's death is a sign I cannot ignore. Louisa will be able to raise our child with the help of Anna. They will *need* this baby if something happens to me."

"Louisa's an unmarried spinster. She knows nothing about raising a baby. My mother raised nine of us; she can do it."

"Louisa will do it. She loves me." May sobbed.

"And I don't?" Incredulous, Ernest turned and looked out the window, his back rigid.

"Ernest. Please. In Louisa's care, this beloved baby will have everything it needs. She has money, all the resources a child could need. How will you care for a baby? And work? And do everything that a young man must do to get ahead in life?"

"My mother will help me."

"Your work could involve travel, you may be sent away." May pictured her baby being added to the large Nieriker brood back in Baden. Probably one of Ernest's sisters would be charged with the infant's care. She resisted shaking her head and spoke slowly to remain calm. "I have no doubt your mother would help, but I want *my* sister to do it."

"So she can provide in ways I cannot," he said in a defeated tone.

May closed her eyes. Ernest's words stung to her core.

"You have given me more joy than I ever dreamed of experiencing, but I think our baby will need a reliable home. My sister loves me. She will love our baby. She will give our baby a home." The neglected homes of her childhood came to her:

the leaky roof at Hosmer House; the low, cracked ceiling of the attic room the sisters shared at Fruitlands; the cracked parlor windowpanes at Wayside that left them all shivering. Despite her past painful moments with her sister, May understood Louisa could provide the constancy May craved for her baby. She had known this truth with a painful clarity in the moments following the doctor's warnings about her age. "This child will have everything I never had."

Ernest took May's hands to his lips and closed his eyes. "Except for parents."

"Please. You *must* promise me."

He lowered the knot of their hands and sighed with his eyes closed. "I promise. I know you'll be fine, but I promise anyway." Resignation pulled the two together, and they stood immobilized, slumped against each other. Outside the birds seemed silent; the street was empty.

"But why?" Ernest whispered. "Why are we even arguing about this?"

"Because women die having babies, women die every day."

"But you won't. You'll be fine. We'll be fine." His voice was soft. She felt the ticklish warmth of his breath on her ear. May closed her eyes, the solidity of the baby between them, and surrendered her qualms to the calming caresses of his hands upon her back.

Chapter 43

May awaited the mail every day. As soon as Ernest entered the house, she would pounce on him looking for a letter. He'd reveal empty hands but waste no time reaching for her and pulling her close. Wrapped in his arms, she could not stay disappointed with no word from her sister. But one evening he surprised her by marching into the house with an envelope held high overhead.

"Oh, you devil, please, give it to me."

"And what do I receive in exchange? I had to carry this all the way from the center of town." Smiling, Ernest brought the envelope up to his shoulder, and it disappeared into his vest.

May pressed in to kiss him while her hand searched for the crackle of paper. "Ha, got it." She yanked the envelope out from the silk lining of his vest.

He laughed. "You're cruel to use me like this."

"You'll survive. Now let's see what Louisa has to say about my book."

October 18, 1879
Boston

Dearest May,

Well, now you've outdone me. You will soon be a published author and a famous painter. Mr. Niles has offered you a contract. I've reviewed it, and all appears to be above-board with the terms of the sale of your book. His paperwork is included in this envelope. After all of my years publishing with Roberts Brothers, we can count on them to offer a square deal. Congratulations. "Studying Art Abroad and How to Do It Cheaply" by May Alcott Nieriker is slotted to be published at the start of the new year.

But now how am I to keep up with you? Based on your reports of those rogue Impressionists, perhaps they would allow me to exhibit some canvases strewn with paint? Fortunately for the art world, I shall refrain from picking up a new creative medium. If you were here, I'd simply give you a gruff pat on the back and perhaps permit you a few extra lumps of sugar in your tea, but since the Atlantic separates us, and I can only write (my preferred mode of communication anyway), please indulge me some lines of praise . . . all joking aside, I'm very proud of you. You've managed to create a career for yourself with grace and tenacity. Your practical and entertaining book will help other aspiring women to follow your lead and improve themselves—that is a great service. Soon you will have a new baby and a pub-

lished book to show off to all of the denizens of Meudon. You should be proud.

Do you remember that old mood pillow you sewed for me almost ten years ago? Its color has faded—Anna was kind enough to mend a split seam on it a few months ago—but I can see it from where I sit now in the parlor. It rests in a place of honor on the horsehair love seat underneath the portrait that Rose Peckham painted of you in Paris. You'll be happy to know it's indicating I'm in a fine mood.

Anna would like to remind you not to forget us small-timers back at home when you're having tea with the kings and queens of Europe. We all miss you.

Yours,

Louisa

When May finished reading the letter aloud, tears coursed down her cheeks.

"Come now," said Ernest, kissing her on the forehead, "let's go for a stroll through the village to celebrate." May nodded through her tears.

HOURS LATER, MAY lay awake in bed, unable to get comfortable. Beside her, Ernest snored. She rolled to her side and forced herself up to sitting. Silver moonlight slipped through the spaces of the window shutters. Despite her enormity, she heaved to her feet, wrapped herself in a housecoat, and tottered downstairs, rubbing her aching lower back. She crossed the parlor to locate Louisa's letter lying on the mantel, propped up against a photo of Marmee. May's fingers followed the lines of her sister's handwriting as she read. Out of the corner of her eye, she caught a flash of white, but when she looked up, she realized the nearby mirror was simply showing her own reflection.

She stepped closer to the mirror. Even in the low light of the moon, wrinkles cut across her forehead. Her once pale creamy skin now showed faint spots resembling tea stains. Wiry silver hairs sprang from her scalp. In July, she had turned thirty-nine years of age. Thirty-nine. She had once been a girl who dreamt of wardrobes full of gauzy gowns, of nights at the opera, of houses full of marble floors and matching brocaded furniture. Now the only luxuries she longed for consisted of listening to Ernest play his violin, laughing over a letter from home, and lulling her new baby to sleep—these new aspirations were not a reduction of her dreams, but simply a reorienting, a refocusing. It was as if she had stumbled off a listing ship in a storm and realized that the solid ground beneath her boots was the only blessing that mattered.

LESS THAN A month later, on a cold November night, the pains started at night after Ernest climbed into bed beside May. While his breathing slowed into a steady rhythm, her insides clenched, mildly at first but then more insistently, slow aches like the gradual tightening of a vise; these pangs of discomfort grew until her bones began to grind against each other. Her awareness of her surroundings receded, and she focused only on trying to survive one wave of pain after another. She stumbled out of bed and paced the bedroom, the floorboards squeaking nervously underneath. Soon her nightclothes were drenched, but she did not pause to investigate the cause, she simply tried to breathe through the pain hammering inside her. When her legs tired, she dropped to her knees and rested her forehead on her arms, eyes screwed shut, inhaling and exhaling.

By this point, Ernest roused and stumbled into clothes. He might have told her he was leaving to bring back the midwife, but she couldn't be certain. She only knew her body strained to turn itself inside out; she could only be aware of the throbbing inside of her as she rested her head against the edge of the bed while her hands tore at the sheets, searching for something to hold on to, something to anchor her against the pain hitting her in waves without respite. Eventually hands guided her up off the floor. A soothing voice murmured encouragement in her ear, but May could only hear turbulence sweeping through her.

The midwife materialized in front of her, folding strips of white linen. May experienced a moment of wanting to grab one of those white pieces of fabric and wave it overhead, while calling, *I surrender.* She wanted to laugh at this vision in her head but was too tired. And humbled. *This pain is the great leveler,* she thought, curling in on herself, *in the end we are all reduced to fighting the forces inside of own bodies and minds to survive.*

May would never know how much time passed. In the end, a cry mewled out—not hers—and the midwife lifted up a red, wrinkled infant in triumph. Hot tears streamed down May's face as she took the baby in her arms. A daughter. Dark, knowing, ancient eyes looked up at May. She studied the exquisite hand grasping her index finger, the pink leg curled up along her own chest, the rosebud of puckered little lips. "I created you," May whispered. She closed her eyes, treasuring the heft of the body resting on her chest. *Oh, this world.*

Chapter 44

Despite the warm breezes wending their way through Boston's wharves, Louisa shivered. She and Anna were clad in black, although both decided their attire seemed morbid, given the occasion.

"We look like a pair of old crows," Louisa announced the day before as the two sisters caught glimpses of themselves in the plate glass windows along Beacon Street.

"Well, we can't have that. I shall trim our hats tonight with some colorful ribbon," Anna said. "We must look welcoming when we meet the ship tomorrow."

One of the new yellow ribbons on Louisa's bonnet flapped against her forehead, and she brushed it back to see a dark speck appearing on the horizon grow larger and assume the shape of a steamship. She rested a hand on her breast as if she could massage away the pounding of her heart. So many things can go wrong on an ocean journey, and every single heart-wrenching possibility had plagued her in the months leading up to the ship's arrival. She took Anna's hand. They propped up against each other, waiting for the ship to reach the inner harbor.

Almost ten months had passed since Mr. Emerson had found Louisa at home alone. Before he held up the telegram, Louisa knew the message. She wanted to turn to flee and run through the back door out onto the trails into the woods where she could pretend she was thirteen again, merely escaping the noise of her three sisters and the endless list of chores awaiting her. But now she was almost forty-eight years old, and her days of effortless running were long behind her.

"She's gone." Mr. Emerson's craggy face had looked stricken, and he put out his palm onto the wall to steady his gangly frame. Louisa turned and stared at the portrait of May hanging in a place of honor over the piano. *How could May die?* It was the cruelest injustice that the healthiest, strongest, and most energetic Alcott was taken long before her time should have been due. Louisa blamed herself. She should have gotten on a ship at the first news of May's illness. Hell, she should have gotten on a ship during their rift after Marmee's death; Louisa hated to think she had lost three precious years of her sister's life, thanks to a stubborn grudge between them. What foolishness. Louisa would have brought the finest doctors in France—in all of Europe—to her sister's bedside. But instead she had assured herself May would battle and outlive them all, happy in France with the sweet family she had built for herself. Instead, after six weeks in a coma, May had succumbed to the fever that reared up and devoured her immediately after the baby's birth. And so Louisa's golden sister, the sister who held so much promise, the sister balanced on the cusp of reaping all of the rewards for her relentless work—this sister was gone after fighting desperately to save herself. Louisa would regret her decision not to go to France for the rest of her life.

Of all of the losses Louisa experienced in her life, May's death struck her with the hardest punch. The only saving grace was that she would raise her infant niece, May's daughter. The memories of all the folly caused by May's thoughtless, young husband still made her neck ache from the tension she had carried for the last ten months. He had been so difficult about bringing her the baby. She had been willing to concede that winter wasn't the best time to send a baby across the Atlantic, but then more waiting ensued with Mr. Nieriker's claims of teething, fevers—the entire lot of every excuse he could dream up. All of his delays and silences; she was sure he conspired to wrest money out of her. That's what everyone wanted from her these days—money. When he sent the telegram from Le Havre announcing his last-minute decision not to accompany the baby to Boston and send his sister instead, Louisa felt only relief. The thought of seeing the man who stole her sister and then let her perish turned her stomach.

A clatter of church bells rang out from a steeple peering down on the wharf and made Louisa jump. Men and women awaiting the steamship pressed closer to the dock, and the sisters were left like two pebbles stranded on wet sand when a wave pulls back to the ocean.

The steamship lumbered in front of them, blocking out the sun's light. Anna and Louisa huddled closer to the crowd and watched preparations for docking. Stevedores barked to each other in unrecognizable languages, and the crowd shouted greetings, but the sisters remained silent. A stream of passengers trickled down the ship's ramp. Louisa searched the faces parading by. She realized she was no longer breathing. At last, the tiny round face of a baby held in the protective arms of the captain appeared. The baby's wide eyes gleamed more brightly than the brass buttons on the captain's uniform. An attractive woman with chestnut-colored curls followed the man. Louisa guessed her to be young Sophie Nieriker.

Louisa reached for Anna's hand, and they surged toward the captain and Sophie, eager to claim their cargo. Louisa knew Anna was talking, but she could not hear her voice over the din of the crowd and the thrumming in her own head. When they reached the captain, she leaned in and somehow clearly heard the baby say, "Marmar?" The baby reached to her with a wistful expression, leaving Louisa devastated by the realization of what this baby represented: on the other side of the world, surrounded by people who barely knew her, May had died. This motherless scrap now belonged to Louisa. Motherhood managed to find her, even after all of these years. Although tears made her vision swim and her chest ache, Louisa held out her arms and smiled into the bottomless blue eyes reflecting the Atlantic. Of all the packages and paintings to arrive, this baby was the one remaining piece of May that Louisa most craved.

IN THE EVENING after Louisa rocked her namesake, little Lulu, to sleep, she placed the baby on the bed and peered into May's steamer trunk. There, amidst tiny embroidered bibs and knit caps, she found the parcel Ernest promised to send. She carefully lifted the package and undid the string to open up a stack of letters. The sight of her sister's cursive left Louisa's knees weak and brought a knot to her throat. She opened the top letter.

November 20, 1879
Meudon, France

Dearest Louisa,

If you are reading this, the worst has happened. By now you have my baby. After many long months of waiting, she arrived quickly on November 8th yet I still do not feel like myself. An insufferable headache punishes me relentlessly, but despite my discomfort, my elation over the miracle of this sweet baby knows no bounds. We named her Louisa May Nieriker though we've taken to calling her Lulu. I wanted to honor you, but this little rosy, golden-haired cherub doesn't resemble your dark, brooding nature in the slightest, so it seemed only appropriate to call her by a shortened name with a certain amount of playfulness and style.

Perhaps it's ironic I'm handing my precious girl to a woman who renounced motherhood in her youth, yet I know of no finer person to watch over this child. Despite our differences, you have always been my true north and have set the course of my life. A sister's influence is not as obvious as a parent's, but your influence over me has been indelible in the choices I've made and the goals I've toiled toward. Because of the love and sacrifice you bestowed upon each member of our family, I can think of no fiercer guardian than you to care for this baby.

The last two years have been the happiest of my life, and I do not regret any of my choices, with the exception of excluding you from my joy. I know you have your own struggles and hope you can find your own fulfillment as I found mine.

Always yours,
May

Louisa studied Lulu's face in the glow of the candlelight and could see a hint of May in the curve of the baby's nose. Louisa took the passel of letters and found the papers dated from around the time Marmee died. Bitter words had been exchanged that never needed repeating. She lit a match from the fireplace mantel and let the flame catch the corner of the paper before dropping the burning letters down onto the grate of the room's fireplace. They curled and blackened while the flame pirouetted above the pile of papers. When the letters smoldered into charred chunks, Louisa rose and walked back to the trunk to continue her search through its contents.

She lifted out a small red leather book. A diary. Louisa laughed quietly, for May had never embraced the daily journaling Father encouraged over the years. She opened it and found entry after entry, all written as letters to her. A sob escaped from her as she flipped through the pages. Even though the sisters had been at odds, May hadn't fully relinquished her sister during all that time. She put the diary aside and reached into the trunk to take out several framed paintings.

The rich colors in the small still life from the Salon of 1877 blazed in her hands. But where was the portrait? The painting from last spring's Salon? She rifled through the trunk, but *La Négresse* was not in it. She had asked for it in her list of items she wanted sent home, but it appeared May's husband had ignored the request. With her palm atop May's red leather diary, she let out a windy exhalation. Fine, if he wanted to keep that painting, so be it. She turned to a watercolor of Orchard House and traced the lines of the house with her finger before grasping both sides of the frame to hold it up to the light for closer inspection. A splinter on the rim of the frame caught at her thumb. As she jerked her hand away from the spot, she felt a lump of paper alongside the back side of the painting. She turned it over to see an envelope tucked into the frame up against the painting. Louisa peeled it off and realized it was the uncashed wedding check she had written out to May almost two years ago. *That headstrong girl!*

The check trembled in her hands as she studied it. May's determination to find her own way had been relentless. In her letters, she had put up a cheerful front, but Louisa could tell they were scraping by on Mr. Nieriker's small salary. All along, she suspected the young man's interest in May hinged upon access to Louisa's wealth. But now, with this check in her hands, she questioned everything. Had her imagination led her to dream up a nefarious scheme where there was none? She reread her sister's letter. Yes, May's words all indicated true happiness; there had been no front, no scheming upstart of a fiancé, no conspiracy to bilk Louisa of her earnings. Her shoulders slumped forward, and she lowered the check, placing it on the ground next to the watercolor.

Across the room, Lulu lay upon the coverlet with her arms flung up over her head and her chubby legs sprawled out in a position of complete surrender. Louisa climbed onto the bed. She lay down next to her niece, and the baby stirred, rolling closer to her. All this time, she had assumed the worst about Mr. Nieriker and his intentions, but maybe it took ten months for him to let go of this last piece of May. Could she blame him for wanting to keep the baby close? It would be impossible for a young man to raise a daughter on his own, and yet, what had it cost May to deprive her beloved husband of their only daughter? And what did it cost him to respect his wife's wishes and permit the baby to travel to a distant, foreign country? The depth of the couple's love and the power of their sacrifice made Louisa bite her lip to keep from crying out.

The baby rolled and nestled her back and buttocks against Louisa's stomach. Little Lulu's skin radiated warmth and her velvet skin glistened. The perfection of the little body brought tears to Louisa's eyes. It amazed her to feel this tiny life, this piece of her sister, lie so intimately next to her as if they were one body. Louisa felt the baby inhale and exhale beside her. Here lay a chance to create something real. A new start. She made a wish and exhaled, watching the baby's wisps of blond hair tremble like the top of a dandelion in the breeze of Louisa's own breath.

Afterword

This novel began the day my younger daughter began kindergarten, and I returned to my empty home to face a stack of books about the Alcotts from the Seattle Public Library. With both my girls in elementary school full-time, I could begin a project that had been calling to me for months, or years, depending on how far you want to go back into my fascination with the quirky Alcott family. I grew up near Orchard House, the Alcott family home-turned-museum in Concord, Massachusetts, and along with consuming all of Louisa May Alcott's books as a girl, I visited the museum regularly with school trips, for drama camp, and to see the house decorated for Christmas. Although Louisa was the focus of these activities, it was always May Alcott's little bedroom in the back of the house that spoke to me. I found myself drawn to the youngest sister, the one with graceful pencil sketches on her walls, the one who had been known for dreaming of travel and romance.

Because of the fame Louisa May Alcott achieved within

her own lifetime, her years are well-documented for posterity. Her diaries, letters, essays, and novels have all been trawled through by scholars to create a complete portrait of this intriguing, complex woman. May, on the other hand, seemed to have been overlooked because of the public's longtime interest in her older sister, and her life contained enough blank space for me to begin imagining a rich emotional journey. As my research took me deeper into her life, I also found a group of women artists languishing in the margins of the historical record. Boston was filled with women, such as Helen Knowlton, Sarah Whitman Wyman, and Anne Whitney, forging their own artistic careers, despite the limited opportunities at the time. Art schools offering instruction to women could be found in New York City, San Francisco, and Philadelphia, but Boston, otherwise a city known for its progressiveness, was still catching up. As a result, most Bostonians, and arguably most Americans no matter where they lived, traveled to Paris to advance their artistic careers. The capital of France reigned supreme for its role as center of the art world and drew ambitious women, such as May Alcott, Mary Cassatt, Elizabeth Jane Gardner, Anna Klumpke, and Maria Bashkirtseff.

While this book remains true to the major contour lines of May's life, I allowed myself some leeway to create a story befitting a novel. When I was researching the Alcotts and piecing the facts of May's life together, I encountered a brief line in a biography on Louisa stating that when *Little Women* reviews were released, Louisa's story garnered great critical praise, but May's illustrations were panned. I read the line again. And again. *Ouch*, what must that moment have been like for May? This question sparked my imagination to create a complicated emotional life between the two close, ambitious sisters. Although May and Louisa never went through a long period of estrangement like what occurs in this novel, shadows of envy and competition can be detected throughout Louisa's letters and journals. The fact that Louisa was known for regularly burning letters and rewriting portions of her journals gave me the opening I needed to imagine the inner lives of these two women and the difficulties that can accompany sisterhood. All of the letters in this novel are largely my own creation, although I've melded real lines from May's letters into them in places.

Although May did study art prior to 1868 when her illustrations in *Little Women* were published, her artwork improved dramatically in the 1870s, so I focused on her instruction during this period of her life. In London during 1873, she experienced a chance encounter with the art critic John Ruskin, who admired her Turner copies and took some of her paintings for his students to study.

May's time in Paris coincided with a momentous period in art history, because the 1870s mark the beginning of Impressionism, an artistic movement that challenged France's rigid conventions surrounding acceptable art. Every year the Académie des Beaux-Arts held a juried show in Paris, the Salon, which was intended to exhibit the best artwork. Selected art represented the classical style that French authorities believed best exemplified France's cultural traditions. Religious and historical scenes and portraiture were esteemed. Landscapes and scenes of everyday life were not. In 1863, Emperor Napoleon III permitted a new show to open, the Salon des Refusés, so the public could see examples of rejected artwork and laugh, and yes, people visited and laughed, but the new show gave some artists, such as Claude Monet, Berthe Morisot, Edgar Degas, and others who experimented with loose brushstrokes and informal compositions, the idea to form the Société Anonyme Coopérative des Artistes Peintres, Sculpteurs, et Graveurs. Despite endless mockery in the press, this group challenged the establishment and exhibited work together annually and eventually became known as Impressionists. May's friend Mary Cassatt joined this band of renegades, but May persevered with the establishment, and her paintings were exhibited in the Paris Salons of 1877 and 1879, major accomplishments for an artist of the era.

After her mother died in November of 1877, May went through a period of deep grief alone in London. Her whirlwind meeting, engagement, and marriage to young Ernest Nieriker all followed within the brief space of a couple of months. And sadly, it's true that seven weeks after giving birth to her daughter, May Alcott died of cerebral spinal meningitis, and her baby was sent to Boston to live with Louisa May Alcott ten months later. By all accounts, Lulu Nieriker led a pampered existence with her two aunts, Louisa May Alcott and Anna Alcott Pratt. At this point in her life, Louisa's health was suffering badly, and she hired a retinue of nannies to care for Lulu, but she continued writing and published several books that she dedicated to her niece. Louisa May Alcott died on March 6, 1888, a mere two days after her father passed away. Anna Alcott Pratt and her son traveled with ten-year-old Lulu to Germany to return her to live with her father. Lulu Nieriker went on to marry and live in Germany until 1975 and died at the age of ninety-six.

Ernest Nieriker never remarried, an unusual thing for a young widower. *La Négresse* remained in his possession and remains in Europe with his descendants.

With the exception of the Bishop family, all of the characters in this book are inspired by real people. So, what became of them?

Alice Bartol is a composite character based on two of May's friends: Alice Bartlett and Lizzie Bartol. Alice Bartlett (1844–1912) accompanied May and Louisa to France in 1870–1871 and had her own account of their trip to Europe published as *Our Apartment: A Practical Guide to Those Intending to Spend a Winter in Rome*. She went on to marry her first cousin and travel several more times to Europe. It is said she gave Henry James the idea for his novella *Daisy Miller*. Lizzie Bartol (1842–1927) was the only child of Cyrus Bartol, the Unitarian minister of West Church in Boston and fellow transcendentalist with Bronson Alcott. She studied art with May in Boston, both with Dr. Rimmer and William Morris Hunt, and went on to paint and exhibit her artwork until 1899. She never married. She was one of a community of women who furthered the development of Boston's artistic world through writing, shows, and the creation of the Society of Arts and Crafts. I found *A Studio of Her Own: Women Artists in Boston 1870–1940* by Erica E. Hirshler and the article "Women Artists in Boston,

1870–1900: The Pupils of William Morris Hunt" by Martha J. Hoppin in *The American Art Journal* (Winter 1981) to be critical sources for learning more about this group of women.

Helen Knowlton (1832–1918) studied under William Morris Hunt and took over his classes from 1871 to 1875 after he decided to focus his attention on developing his portrait business. She published both *Talks on Art: Hints for Pupils in Drawing and Painting* and *The Art Life of William Morris Hunt*. This last book helped me to better understand Hunt's theories on art instruction. Miss Knowlton traveled to Europe several times and exhibited her work with fellow friend and artist Ellen Day Hale through the 1890s.

Anne Whitney (1821–1915) enjoyed a long, prolific career as a sculptor, creating work reflecting her abolitionist and suffragist views. She spent four years in Rome with her lifelong partner, Adeline Manning. It's true that she won a blind competition to have her sculpture of abolitionist Charles Sumner exhibited in Boston Public Garden in the mid-1870s, but her entry was cast aside when her identity was revealed, because the Boston Arts Committee believed it to be indecent for a woman to sculpt a man's legs (even in pants). Her sculpture now stands in Harvard Square.

Elizabeth Jane Gardner (1837–1922) never had a documented encounter with May Alcott, but their New England roots and years in Paris coincided, so I couldn't resist joining the two women artists in fiction. Miss Gardner won a gold medal at the Salon, and her paintings were exhibited in the Salon more than those of any other woman. Her engagement to fellow painter William-Adolphe Bouguereau stretched out to seventeen years because of his mother's opposition to their relationship. The two finally married in 1896 after years of openly living together.

Anna Klumpke (1856–1942), an American artist hailing from San Francisco, studied in the Académie Julian. She led a long, successful career as a landscape painter and portraitist and became the lifelong partner of the great French artist Rosa Bonheur. *Overcoming All Obstacles: The Women of the Académie Julian*, edited by Gabriel P. Weisberg and Jane R. Becker, was an invaluable source for learning about the women studying painting in Paris during the late 1800s.

Marie Bashkirtseff (1858–1884), a Ukrainian painter, also studied at the Académie Julian. Her confidence and competitive spirit is best demonstrated by the title of her diary: *I Am the Most Interesting Book of All*. This colorful figure died at the early age of 25 from tuberculosis.

Mary Cassatt (1844–1926), the well-known American Impressionist, befriended May Alcott in Paris during the period when she joined the group of artists called Impressionists who were confounding the Parisian art world with their new style and beliefs. *Cassatt and Her Circle: Selected Letters*, edited by Nancy Mowll Mathews, was a wonderful source to learn more about this talented yet very private artist.

While in Rome, May studied art with Frederic Crowninshield, but I changed his name to Frederic Crownover in this novel, because I dramatically altered the details of his life for my story. In real life, there is no evidence that Frederic Crowninshield and May had anything but a positive, professional relationship.

William Keith also existed and worked out of a studio in Boston briefly before the fire of 1872 destroyed it. He was friends with John Muir, founder of the Sierra Club, and is best known for his grand landscapes of the American West. When I read that Keith's first painting instructor in San Francisco went on to become his wife, I imagined him to be the type of character who could fit into my story line. Although Violet is a figure of my own creation, his real first wife died young, and his second wife was a suffragist in California.

All of the artwork referenced in this novel is real, but sometimes I changed the timeline of when and where certain works were exhibited to better serve my story.

I visited Orchard House several times during the creation of this novel, and a rich sense of history still permeates every room of this wonderfully preserved house. Tourists from all over the world still line up daily to view the Alcott's home, and the staff is incredibly knowledgeable about all things Alcott.

Aside from the books previously mentioned, I relied on the following books for my research:

Alcott in Her Own Time, ed. Daniel Shealy

Eden's Outcasts: The Story of Louisa May Alcott and Her Father, by John Matteson

Little Women Abroad: The Alcott Sisters' Letters from Europe, 1870–1871, ed. Daniel Shealy

Louisa May Alcott: A Biography, by Madeleine B. Stern

Louisa May Alcott: The Woman Behind Little Women, by Harriet Reisen

Marmee & Louisa: The Untold Story of Louisa May Alcott and Her Mother, by Eve LaPlante

May Alcott: A Memoir, by Caroline Ticknor

Studying Art Abroad, and How to Do It Cheaply, by Abigail May Alcott Nieriker

The Journals of Louisa May Alcott, ed. Joel Myerson and Daniel Shealy

The Selected Letters of Louisa May Alcott, ed. Joel Myerson and Daniel Shealy

Acknowledgments

My love for the Alcotts would have remained a quirky obsession if not for the support and encouragement of many people who helped bring this novel into the world.

I traveled to Louisa May Alcott's Orchard House in Concord, Massachusetts, several times during the creation of this novel, and Lis Adams and Jan Turnquist, both experts on all things Alcott, always answered my questions and provided me with access to the museum's archives, including May's unpublished diary from her final years. Mary Smoyer of the Boston Women's Heritage Trail took me on a fascinating tour around the Back Bay to view sites important to the history of the city's women artists.

I cannot thank my agent Barbara Braun enough for being my champion and counsel. My editor, Lucia Macro, has shown boundless enthusiasm for this story, and her kind guidance and expertise has been invaluable—Lucia, thank you. To the wonderful team at William Morrow and HarperCollins, I'm forever appreciative for your hard work on behalf of this novel.

I've been fortunate to be surrounded by friends and family who've encouraged every step of this journey by offering tennis breaks and glasses of wine, and most importantly, by taking my children so I could write. Diane Hooper, John Hooper, Gretchen Moores-Hooper, Stacy Burns, and Kelly Larson, I couldn't have done this without you. Nat and Sarah Worden, I'm grateful for your love and reading notes. Thank you to my early readers: Kristin Beck, Kristie Berg, Ellen Dorr, Felicia Hyllested, Toby Miller, Rachel Pelander, Alana Scott, Shannon Smith, and Kat Yun. Thanks also to my supportive colleagues and students at The Bush School. To Waverly Fitzgerald and Joan Leegant and my friends at Hugo House, your feedback and advice were invaluable. Carrie Kwiakowski, my writing buddy, thanks for all of your comments in the margins of the countless drafts you read.

This book would never have taken shape without my parents, Kathy and Doug Worden, who've nurtured my love of reading and writing from the beginning. To Kate and Caroline, you're my favorite little women and provide me with endless inspiration and joy. And finally, Dave, thank you for always saying *yes* when I need to hear it. You're everything to me.

About the author

About the book

Insights,
Interviews
& More . . .

Meet Elise Hooper

Linda Terry Hickam

Although a New Englander by birth (and at heart), ELISE lives with her husband and two young daughters in Seattle, where she teaches history and literature. *The Other Alcott* is her first novel. ∾

A Conversation with Elise Hooper

Q: *Why did you feel compelled to write about May Alcott?*

A: I grew up in Massachusetts near Concord and attended drama camp at Orchard House. In addition to my visits to the Alcott family home, I read many of Louisa's novels, but it was really *Little Women* that gave shape to my desire to be a writer at a young age, so for my first novel, I wanted to revisit the historical figures who played such a formative role in my own interests.

Many writers have already covered interesting aspects of the Alcotts' lives so I felt pressure to find a unique path. I researched and researched and experienced a few false starts, but found May's story largely untold—which is amazing because it's so compelling! She was such an optimistic figure, despite the many challenges that faced her, and she's always been overshadowed by her infinitely more famous older sister, making me feel that her story needed to be told. Furthermore, I thought many modern readers would relate to May's struggle to balance her desire for a career with her search to find love. ▶

3

A Conversation with Elise Hooper *(continued)*

Q: *Upon reading* The Other Alcott, Little Women *fans may be surprised at Louisa's conflicting feelings about the beloved classic. How much of the portrayal of Louisa is true and how much did you fictionalize?*

A: To understand Louisa, readers must understand the real circumstances of the Alcotts prior to *Little Women* being published. Unlike *Little Women*'s March family who live in a state of genteel poverty, the Alcotts were flat-out impoverished. May's father, Bronson, refused to accept monetary reward for work, so they relied on the generosity of family members and a small inheritance May's mother, Abigail, received upon the death of her father. While struggling to stay afloat financially, the Alcotts moved more than twenty-two times in almost thirty years before eventually settling in Concord, Massachusetts, after Ralph Waldo Emerson offered to support them. Although all of the Alcott sisters grappled with poverty's challenges, Louisa, in particular, vowed that one day she'd be "rich and famous," yet for years her various writing endeavors didn't lead to riches. It wasn't until Louisa's longtime publisher, Mr. Thomas Niles, saw the success of William Taylor Adams's novels for boys that he proposed a "domestic story" for girls to Louisa. Initially she dismissed the idea, feeling the book would be dull, but eventually Niles wore her down.

Q: *Did Louisa really resent the success of* Little Women *the way she does in* The Other Alcott?

A: Louisa had a complicated relationship with *Little Women* from the start, and I wanted to explore this complexity in my novel. She often called her writing for the juvenile market "rubbish" and declared she only produced it for the money. She became annoyed with the fan mail that focused on marriage and felt "afflicted" by the pressure her publisher placed upon her to marry all of her characters in a "wholesome manner."

I think most artists can identify with the tension Louisa faced between creating work that satisfied her own need for self-expression and producing work that held the market's interest.

4

Because the Alcotts depended upon her income, Louisa chose to answer to the market, but I believe she remained uncomfortable with that decision for the rest of her life. All of her journals and letters make her insecurities clear; she is forever tallying up her income in her journal and lamenting writing the juvenile content her audience demanded. Fame and fortune did not live up to her expectations.

But despite her uneasiness with writing for children, it must be noted that she took her young audience seriously and never condescended to her readers. In fact, many of Louisa's stories tackled fairly adult themes, such as injustice, duty, and self-reliance.

Q: *Did Louisa really teach herself to write with both hands?*

A: Yes, she did! She wanted to be able to write for long stretches of time without stopping, so she simply switched back and forth between her right and left hands while she worked.

Q: *In* The Other Alcott, *Louisa always seems ill. Was her health really that bad?*

A: Unfortunately, Louisa was bedeviled by a variety of ailments throughout adulthood. During the American Civil War, she served as a nurse for the Union Army in Washington, D.C., and caught typhoid fever while working at Bellevue Hospital. Although she eventually recovered, doctors used a compound to treat her illness that she later believed gave her mercury poisoning. Today, doctors suspect Louisa suffered from lupus. But her health woes may have been even more complicated than physical ailments alone. In her documentary *Louisa May Alcott: The Woman Behind* Little Women, Harriet Reisen speculates that Louisa may have suffered from manic-depressive disorder based on her tendency to immerse herself so completely in her writing that she would neglect to eat and sleep for days at a time. Louisa referred to these manic periods as "falling into a vortex" and would emerge from them depleted and in poor health. ▶

A Conversation with Elise Hooper *(continued)*

Q: *It seems like Bronson Alcott, Louisa and May's father, could be considered radical for his era. What contributed to his unusual views?*

A: Bronson was a unique individual, even by today's standards. Among other things, he was a philosopher, abolitionist, vegetarian, suffragist, and progressive educator. In fact, today's kids who love recess can thank Bronson Alcott because he introduced the idea of "physical activity breaks" during the school day well before this was the norm. When May was a toddler in the early 1840s, he even started a small utopian community in Harvard, Massachusetts, called Fruitlands and moved his family there. Daily life at Fruitlands was a challenge— its residents ate no animal products, bathed in cold water every morning, wore plain tunics and slippers made of linen (to avoid wearing slave-picked cotton), and refused to use any livestock for farming. Hungry and cold, the community's residents chafed at the group's stated goal of being self-reliant. When Bronson started discussing celibacy, Abigail Alcott announced she was leaving and taking Anna, Louisa, Lizzie, and May. The whole Fruitlands experiment fell apart after only seven months, but Bronson stuck with his transcendental philosophy for the rest of his life.

Q: *What was transcendentalism and how did this philosophy impact May?*

A: Transcendentalism was a philosophical movement of the early nineteenth century rooted in the belief that human nature was inherently good but could be corrupted by society's institutions, such as organized religion and political parties. Transcendentalists believed self-reliance and independence to be the ideal state of man. Because of his transcendental philosophy, Bronson Alcott didn't want to participate in economic systems and refused to receive money in exchange for work. Luckily for the Alcotts, Mr. Emerson believed Bronson to be a great philosopher and helped the Alcotts in many ways over the years. While May didn't identify herself as a transcendentalist explicitly, the movement's beliefs undoubtedly influenced her desire to forge her own path that differed from mainstream society.

Q: *Of all of the women artists in* The Other Alcott, *only Mary Cassatt is a name that most people today recognize. If women began studying art in larger numbers during the late 1800s, why are there not more well-known women artists?*

A: While studying art became more accessible to women during the late 1800s, the commercial arena of artistic success still remained mostly closed to women for many reasons. For one, it took years to hone the skills and business connections needed to become a successful painter or sculptor. Most women did not have decades to develop their talents and build connections with art dealers because they often needed to marry to ensure their own financial well-being. In addition, women lacked access to birth control, and their long-term careers as artists were compromised since marriage ensured periods of creative unproductivity due to childbearing and child-rearing.

The best-known American women artists of the late 1800s—Mary Cassatt and Cecilia Beaux, to name a couple—remained unmarried because they were from wealthy families and possessed the means to be independent. Several of the women in *The Other Alcott,* including Rosa Bonheur, Anna Klumpke, Anne Whitney, and Adeline Manning, lived in "Boston Marriages" a term used to describe two women living together in a long-term relationship, but these women had the means to eschew traditional marriages and focus on their careers unimpeded by familial responsibilities.

One of the few women who juggled motherhood with her professional career as an artist was Berthe Morisot, a wealthy member of the French aristocracy. She continued to work as an Impressionist painter after the birth of her daughter, Julie, because she could hire help and her husband, also a painter, supported her endeavors. This was unusual. Overall, most women painters found it challenging to maintain professional artistic lives once they married and started families of their own. ▶

A Conversation with Elise Hooper *(continued)*

Photo credit: Frances Benjamin Johnston, "Académie Julian, Paris, group of art students" ca. 1885 (source: http://www.loc.gov/pictures/item/2001697170/)

Q: *What kind of research helped you better understand this family and the era?*

A: I started by learning as much about May Alcott and her family as possible. Biographies of the Alcotts are plentiful, especially about Louisa and Bronson, so I immersed myself in secondary sources to get a broad sense of the major milestones in their lives and formative experiences before turning to primary sources. The Alcotts were a family of prolific letter writers and journal keepers, so there was a wide selection of material from which I could experience their individual personalities. Rereading some of Louisa's novels, especially *Little Women* and *An Old-Fashioned Girl* educated me on Victorian life, from big topics to small details, ranging from Victorian recreational activities to the types of flowers an upper-class family would have on their dining room table.

 As I delved deeper into creating my story, I discovered I needed more information on Victorian life, such as steamship and rail travel, so I studied everything from ship menus to railroad timetables. The Seattle Public Library provided countless books about the Impressionists and the Salon, art exhibition catalogs, and out-of-print books about various women artists from the era. I scoured antique maps of Concord, Boston, Rome, London, and Paris and used Google Maps to virtually "walk" some of the neighborhoods that May trod, all while sitting at my computer. Honestly, writing historical fiction must have been very, very, very time consuming before the Internet came along. Sometimes I stretched the truth, such as when May tries to reach Hunt's studio during the Great Boston Fire of 1872. In fact, I don't know where May was during the fire, but Louisa writes about her own experiences watching the conflagration, so I decided to put May in Boston too because the fire significantly impacted her art studies. ▶

Photo Credit: author's photo of her bulletin board with Beacon Hill houses and Josiah Johnson Hawes's photo, *Snow Scene on the Northeast Corner of the Boston Common*

A Conversation with Elise Hooper (*continued*)

Q: *Describe how you wove fictional elements into a real story.*

A: When I needed an activity to engage characters, I turned to artifacts and some quintessential Victorian activities and let my imagination loose. For example, how would I set up the moment when May begins to doubt a future with Joshua Bishop? An old photograph by Josiah Johnson Hawes titled *Snow Scene on the Northeast Corner of the Boston Common* made me realize I could literally put my two characters on a collision course with a sleigh. When I needed to make May realize how much she cares for Ernest Nieriker, I capitalized on the Victorian bicycle craze and stuck the poor fellow atop a big wheeler, sending him on a bumpy ride. Perhaps one of my favorite historical details came to me as I was researching the Boston Public Gardens and learned the history behind the city's beloved Swan Boats. Although to the best of my knowledge Louisa never wrote a letter endorsing the widow who wanted to run the family's Swan Boat business after the death of her husband, it seemed like a cause Louisa would have wholeheartedly embraced, so I worked it into one of her letters to May. ❧

Photo Credit: author's photo of Swan Boats in 2016

Reading Group Discussion Questions

1. At the end of Part 1, when Alice tells May that "a thinking woman . . . sounds dangerous," what does she mean? What made a "thinking woman" dangerous in the late 1800s?

2. How does May change over the course of the story? What moments mark critical turning points in her journey?

3. What is your perception of the relationship between Louisa and May? How did Louisa's financial support of May affect their feelings toward each other?

4. What were the challenges that women faced while studying art? How were these challenges different in Boston than in Europe?

5. When May marries Ernest suddenly, do you think it's because, as Louisa says, "she's unmoored?" What do you think contributed to May's quick decision to marry?

6. Louisa appears to send conflicting messages about May's marriage to Ernest—she discourages May from doing it, but then sends a substantial check as a wedding present—how do you think she felt about May's decision to marry?

7. Between their beliefs on education, abolitionism, women's suffrage, and other causes (Bronson was also vegetarian), the Alcotts were viewed as radicals and seen as unconventional. What do you think it was like to grow up as part of this family? As the youngest family member, how difficult do you think it was for May to grow up in this family? In what ways does she seem to forge her own identity, separate from that of her family?

8. What do you think it would be like to have a family member write a thinly-veiled account of your life? Since May doesn't think *Little Women* was a favorable portrayal of her, how would that shape her relationship with her family? ▸

9. Louisa struggles with the tension that exists between the success of *Little Women* and feeling trapped by being famous for something that she didn't really want to write. Did you empathize with her feelings? What would it be like to become famous for something you resented?

10. At the end of the novel, the author provides a postscript with more information about all of the characters. Was there anything in there that surprised you?

11. Of the two sisters, Louisa is infinitely more famous. Were you surprised by anything you learned about her in this novel? Were any of your previous impressions of her challenged by this new information?

12. Louisa remains dutiful to her family to the end and continues to write stories that the market welcomes so that she earns money to support her family, while Mary Cassatt breaks from the establishment and creates work that satisfies her. Which character can you relate to more? Do you understand the motivations behind both women? ᢒ

Alcott Trivia

1. May Alcott gave Daniel Chester French his first art supplies and encouraged him to try his hand at sculpture. French went on to become known for creating the statue of Abraham Lincoln at the Lincoln Memorial, Washington, D.C., and always credited May with starting his career.

2. May Alcott taught an early form of art therapy at Dr. Wilbur's Asylum in Syracuse, New York, in December of 1860.

3. Louisa May Alcott, an ardent suffragist, was the first woman ever to vote in Concord, Massachusetts. She voted for a school board position.

4. Following her illustrations in *Little Women*, May published a series of landscapes in the book *Concord Sketches*, in 1869. In the preface to accompany May's artwork, Louisa wrote:

   These sketches, from a student's portfolio, claim no merit as works of art, but are only valuable as souvenirs, which owe their chief charm to the associations that surround them, rather than to any success in the execution of a labor of love, prompted by the natural desire to do honor to one's birthplace. ▶

This unflattering description of her sister's work prompted me to explore the tension that might have existed between these two ambitious women.

5. Louisa served as a Civil War nurse in Union Hotel Hospital during 1862 but resigned in early 1863 due to contracting typhoid fever. She wrote about this experience in *Hospital Sketches*.

6. Using the pseudonym Tribulation Periwinkle, Louisa authored a letter to *The Springfield Republican* newspaper in which she contemplated using a garden engine (the Victorian version of a garden hose) to spray her fans who dared to visit uninvited.

7. Bronson and Abigail Alcott were firm believers in the importance of physical exercise for young women, so they encouraged their daughters to learn to swim and run around Concord. Now every September, Louisa May Alcott's Orchard House in Concord, Massachusetts, hosts an annual road race to celebrate Louisa's love of running.

8. The well-known essayist Henry David Thoreau served as a private academic tutor to the Alcott sisters.

9. In the late 1980s or early 1990s, two professors discovered *The Inheritance,* a novel written by Louisa when she was 18 years old. This manuscript, now believed to be Louisa's first novel, had been miscataloged within the Alcott collection of family documents at Harvard University's Houghton Library and remained unknown to scholars for over 150 years.

10. May's remains are somewhere in a common grave in Montrouge Cemetery on the outskirts of Paris, France. Back in 1879, graves were secured for only 10 years unless a family member paid an additional amount, and although Louisa always intended to bring May's remains to America, Louisa was unable to accomplish this before her own death in 1888; however, she did erect a headstone in Sleepy Hollow Cemetery in Concord, Massachusetts, to memorialize her sister. ∽

Photo Credit: author's photo of Louisa May Alcott's Orchard House in Concord, Massachusetts

May Alcott's Illustrations

These images can be found online
at Harvard University's Houghton Library. ❧